Catherine Fox was educated at Durham and London Universities. She is the author of three adult novels: *Angels and Men*, *The Benefits of Passion* and *Love for the Lost*; a Young Adult fantasy novel, *Wolf Tide*; and a memoir, *Fight the Good Fight: From vicar's wife to killing machine*, which relates her quest to achieve a black belt in judo. She lives in Liverpool, where her husband is dean of the cathedral.

'A delightful portrait of the follies and foibles in a contemporary Anglican diocese, written with wit, wisdom and impeccable liberal sympathies.'

Michael Arditti, author and critic

'Clear-eyed, moving and mischievously funny, *Acts and Omissions* is at one with the deep linguistic and human resources that make the modern Church of England what it is. The novel brims with wit and heart, acknowledging the awkwardness and consolations of Anglicanism in the twenty-first century. Hugely entertaining and highly recommended.'

Richard Beard, author of *Lazarus is Dead*

'Catherine Fox writes so well about the Church of England that she can make sense of a world in which the salacious and the sacred are intimately entwined. This is a novelist who is never frightened to enter ecclesiastical territory where bishops fear to tread. She writes not merely with affection but with love for an institution that is creaking under the weight of its own contradictions.

'*Acts and Omissions* will help people in the Church who already pray for one another daily to like one another a little more. It is also a great collection of intertwining stories that throw a welcome ray of light for those who find it hard to understand why an institution made up of good, caring people has become better known for hypocrisy than for happiness.

'The Diocese of Lindchester is full of people who bless one another, sometimes without realizing it. They blessed me.'

The Very Revd Kelvin Holdsworth, Provost,
St Mary's Cathedral, Glasgow

'This is a delicious novel: clever, witty and subtle – and as good a rendering of the Church of England as you could wish to read. I want to live in Lindchester. I want to visit the cathedral, drink prosecco with Fr Dominic, become friends with the Dean and marry the Archdeacon. Most of all, I want Catherine Fox to hurry up and write the sequel.'

The Baroness Sherlock

'*Acts and Omissions* is brave and beautiful, devastatingly honest, mercilessly funny, fundamentally kind. It will make you think, laugh – possibly even cry. It's one of those hugely enjoyable novels which has you racing on to find out what happens, but that you never really want to come to an end.'

Dr Margaret Masson, Vice-Principal,
St Chad's College, Durham

ACTS AND OMISSIONS

Catherine Fox

First published in Great Britain in 2014

Marylebone House
36 Causton Street
London SW1P 4ST
www.marylebonehousebooks.co.uk

British Library Cataloguing-in-Publication Data
A catalogue record for this book is available from the British Library

ISBN 978–1–910674–28–4
eBook ISBN 978–1–910674–29–1

Typeset by Graphicraft Limited, Hong Kong
First printed in Great Britain by Ashford Colour Press
Subsequently digitally printed in Great Britain

eBook by Graphicraft Limited, Hong Kong

Produced on paper from sustainable forests

For
John and Molly with love, and in grateful memory of Kate Jones

Acknowledgements

I would like to thank my original readers, who followed *Acts and Omissions* faithfully as I blogged it week by week. I'm also grateful to my Twitter followers for their suggestions, corrections and encouragement.

Dramatis personae

Bishops

Paul Henderson	Bishop of Lindchester
Bob Hooty	Suffragan Bishop of Barcup

Priests and deacons

Dominic Todd	Parish priest
Marion Randall	Dean of Lindchester
Mark Lawson	Cathedral canon chancellor, 'Mr Happy'
Giles Littlechild	Cathedral canon precentor
Matt Tyler	Archdeacon of Lindchester
Martin Rogers	Bishop Paul's chaplain
Philip Voysey-Scott	Cathedral canon treasurer
Virginia Coleman	Deacon, curate to Wendy Styles
Wendy Styles	Parish priest, 'Father Wendy'

People

Andrew Jacks	Director of the Dorian Singers
Miss Barbara Blatherwick	Cathedral Close resident, former school matron
Becky Rogers	Estranged wife of bishop's chaplain, mother of Leah and Jessica
Danny Rossiter	Jane's son
Freddie May	Bishop Paul's driver, former chorister
Gene	Husband of the dean
Helene Carter	Diocesan safeguarding officer
Dr Jane Rossiter	Lecturer at Linden University
Janet Hooty	Wife of suffragan bishop
Jessica Rogers	Younger daughter of bishop's chaplain
Leah Rogers	Older daughter of bishop's chaplain
Mickey Martin	Danny's New Zealander father

Penelope	Bishop Paul's PA
Simeon E. Dacre	Poet, colleague of Jane's, 'Spider'
Susanna Henderson	Bishop of Lindchester's wife
Timothy Gladwin	Cathedral director of music
Ulrika Littlechild	Precentor's wife, voice coach

JANUARY

Chapter 1

When the Linden bursts its banks, the ancient city of Lindchester is safe. It rises from the sky-filled fields like an English Mont St Michel. Even when the river keeps to its meanders the place has an island feel to it. It is landlocked, though, as far from any coast as it is possible to be in Britain. There are no motorways near. Tourists never Visit Historic Lindchester because they are passing; they have to go there on purpose. Once upon a time the city lay on a busy coaching route, as the Georgian inns of the Lower Town attest. But when the stagecoach was superseded, it was twenty years before the railway came to Lindchester, and the city has never shaken off that backwater heritage.

But backwaters escape the attentions of town planners, who focus their ruinous zeal on more important places. Places like Lindford, county town and seat of local government, its once-beating heart now concretized by 1960s improvement. Lindford still has its attractions. People must head there if they are looking for nightlife and shopping malls, for the Crown Court and council offices and someone to lambast about wheelie bins. Lindford is where you will find A&E and multi-screen cinemas, trains to London and signs saying The North, The South.

What does Lindchester have to offer? It is the sort of place where you take your American visitors and bored grandchildren to mess about on the river and get punt poles tangled in the willows. You can visit the History of Lindchester Museum, with its 1970s model Vikings and merchants in dusty periwigs. You can explore the cobbled streets, or climb the very steps John Wesley was tumbled down by a mob when he tried to preach here. This is where you finally find a present for someone impossible to please – in the specialist coffee merchant's, or the antiquarian book dealer's. Afterwards you can treat yourself to Earl Grey and homemade scones in a tea shop with beaded doilies over the milk jugs, just like Grandma used to have.

But above all, on the summit of the island, Lindchester boasts a medieval cathedral. It is so perfect it looks like a film set; a toy Cathedral Close. You expect giant hands to reach down and move the canons in and out of their houses, lift off the cathedral roof and post the choristers into their stalls, then shake the spire to make the matins bell tinkle.

It is New Year's Eve. Light is fading. Before long the residents of the Close will be partying. Not the bishop and his wife: they are away in their little bolt-hole in the Peak District. He is a lovely, lovely man, but we can have a naughtier time without him, because he is an Evangelical. We can drink more than we ought, tell cruder jokes, be cattier about our colleagues when Mary Poppins isn't at the party. At midnight we will reel out into the Close and assemble in front of the cathedral's west doors around the giant Christmas tree, and wait for Great William to tremble the air as he tolls out twelve ponderous strokes. Rockets from the Lower Town will streak the sky. We will cheer and champagne corks will fly – or rather, the corks of special-offer cava, because these days canons aren't made of money – and we will busk our way through 'Auld Lang Syne', not quite knowing the words.

But that is still hours off. Let's while away the time somewhere else in the region. The diocese of Lindchester is not large, squashed as it is between Lichfield to the south and Chester to the north; so don't worry, we will not be travelling far. Tonight I want to take you to an ordinary parish and introduce you to its priest, someone who toils away fairly unglamorously on the coalface of the C of E, and seldom breathes the rarefied air of the Close, except when he's buying books or candles in the cathedral bookshop, or attending an ordination service.

Come with me. We will launch ourselves on the wings of imagination from the cathedral's spire, swoop down over the city to where the Lower Town peters out into water meadows. Do admire the river below, if you can still glimpse it in the dusk. There's the lake – an oxbow lake! that one feature of second-form geography we have retained, when everything useful has long since vanished – where herons stalk and shopping trolleys languish. We are heading south-east, towards Lindford, over fields striped with ancient ridge and furrow; cows and pigs, rape and wheat; this is gentle midlands countryside, with hedges not drystone walls, punctuated by mature trees. Soon these hedges will look like smiles with the teeth punched out. We don't need to weep for the ash trees quite yet, but they are going the way England's elms went forty years earlier. Our children's children will never see their like.

Look down again: that's the dreary politeness of 1930s suburbia, the dormitory village of Renfold. This is where I am taking you. You will notice that they like their Christmas lights in Renfold. Twinkling Santas clamber over roofs like burglars. Blue icicles dangle from eaves. In every garden the magnolias and cherry trees are festooned with lights. We are coming in to land now. We circle a brick church, make a pass over the detached house next door just to be sure: yes, this is the one. St John's Vicarage.

Inside is Dominic Todd. He is seeing the New Year in with an old friend, Dr Jane Rossiter. I hope you will suspend judgement on Father Dominic. I am very fond of him, but I'm aware you will not be meeting him at his best. Go on in. That's his cassock hanging on a peg, and that pompom hat there is called a biretta. (Insiders will know from this that Dominic is no Evangelical.) Go straight past the study and the downstairs loo (which every vicarage must have). You will find them in his sitting room.

'Oh, rubbish! He is not gay.' Jane put her hand over her glass. 'I've had enough. You can always put a spoon in the neck.'

'Put a spoon in my *arse*!' Dominic cried in horror. 'You do not spoon 1989 Veuve Clicquot!'

Jane gave in. 'Paul Henderson is not gay,' she repeated.

'Yes, he is.'

'Oh, you think everyone is gay.'

'Do not. I so don't.'

Jane recited a list of those prominent churchmen and politicians who, from time to time, had strayed into the cross-hairs of Dominic's gaydar. One by one Dominic re-certified them gay. A couple of them he had no recollection of ever identifying before. Perhaps Jane was testing him? That would be like her, the cow.

'Anyway, everyone knows Paul Henderson is gay.'

'Of course they do!' said Jane. 'Except *his wife*.'

'Even back in Cambridge we all knew,' said Dominic. 'In Lightfoot we kept a list of closet queers and Paul Henderson was right at the top.'

'You're making that up.'

Possibly Dominic was. He couldn't remember. But Jane was annoying him. 'Poor, poor Paul! He is so far back in the closet he's in Narnia! Always winter and never Christmas,' he mourned. 'I actually pity him, you know. No, really.'

'I preferred Narnia before Aslan came and melted the snow.'

'*Oh!*' shrieked Dominic. He was a great shrieker. He sounded like a duchess with mice in her pantry. 'You can't say that, Jane! Aslan is Jesus! Every time you say that, an innocent Evangelical dies!'

'Anyway,' Jane said, 'you're only saying it because you hate him.'

'I do not hate him.' Dominic took a prim sip of champagne. 'One does not hate one's bishop. He is my Father in God. And anyway,' – yes, they had reached the 'and anyway' stage of drunkenness, I'm afraid – 'you only think he's not gay because you're still in love with him.'

Jane sat back and tilted her head, giving this accusation proper academic scrutiny, for she was a university lecturer. Was Dominic right? Was she still in love with Paul Henderson? Or not? She turned the notion this way and that.

While Jane is pondering, I will provide a bit of helpful background information. Many years before, when she was an earnest young woman in her mid-twenties and God still seemed like a viable proposition, Jane Rossiter began training for the Anglican ministry. She spent two whole years at Latimer Hall Theological College in Cambridge. Paul Henderson was also there, with his young wife Susanna, being great with child. The Hendersons lived out, but Paul had a study next door to Jane's college room on G Staircase. They prayed together in Staircase Prayers, they attended lectures together. Together they waded through Wenham's *Elements of New Testament Greek*, in which blaspheming lepers threw stones into the temple. And yes, back then Jane was more than half in love with Paul Henderson. But as belief gave way to doubt, she needed ever more urgently to escape from the clean-limbed heartiness of Latimer to the loucheness of Lightfoot House, where the liberal catholics trained for ordination. The Lightfoot students rather pitied the boorish Evangelicals, metaphorically tapping fag ash on them from their far greater aesthetic and cultural height. This was where Jane got to know Dominic.

But that will have to do for now. Jane has reached her considered conclusion: 'Bollocks I am.'

'Are.'

'Am bloody not.'

I think we'd better leave them to it. They are not far from shouting aggressively how much they really, really fucking love one another, and conking out, so we may as well speed on fiction's wings back to Lindchester Cathedral Close.

An almost full moon hangs picturesquely in the sky above the spire. Wind stirs the branches of the Christmas tree, making the lights dance. The lights are white. They are tasteful, because this is the Close, not Renfold. All around in the historic houses we can see windows – round ones, arched ones, tall, narrow ones – with pretty trees glowing. It is like a huge Advent calendar.

Down in the Lower Town there is some vulgar roistering. You can probably hear the shouts. Sirens tear the night. A rocket goes off prematurely. It is five to midnight. And now the big door of the canon precentor's house opens and people spill out. Next comes a troupe of lay clerks from Vicars' Hall. Stragglers from other houses join the throng and stand shivering on the west front. The precentor carries a jingling box of champagne flutes, his wife and sons have the cava. Here comes the canon chancellor, Mr Happy, and here's the dean, Marion Randall – yes, a woman dean! In deepest Lindfordshire! – with her supercilious wine merchant husband.

Someone asks, 'Where's Freddie?' Where's Freddie, where's Freddie, goes up the cry. Yoo hoo, Freddieeee!

Freddie woke with a lurch. What the fuck? He was up on the palace roof still. Ah, nuts. What time was it? The first boom of Great William rocked the air. He scrambled to his feet. Naw. He'd been so-o-oo going to enjoy this New Year, and he'd now fucking missed it?

Should auld acquaintance be forgot?

But just then: how silently, how silently! A flock of red Chinese lanterns floated up from some hidden garden and over the cathedral. Freddie watched them in wonder. They trailed wishes behind them. Prayers. Resolutions. This year everything will be different. I will be a better person. Let it be all right. Off and away they sailed into the night, carried by the wind.

And the days of Auld Lang Syne.

Then, sure-footed as Amadeus, the cathedral cat, Freddie made his way back over the bishop's roof to the window he'd left open.

At the last second a slate slipped under him.

He clawed at air. And fell.

Chapter 2

New Year's Day dawns meek and mild over the diocese of Lindchester. The dog-walkers are out in municipal parks and suburban streets, or squelching along the Linden's banks, armed with biodegradable scented dog-poop bags and tennis balls. Here and there we spot hungover parents trying not to vomit as they bend wincingly to push small people along on their Christmas scooters and tractors and bikes. It gets better, we want to tell them. Your babies will learn to sleep through, they'll grow up and leave home, and one day you will understand what all those kind old women meant when they admonished you to 'enjoy them while they're little'.

Father Dominic is awake. It's such a nice morning that he's taken his coffee and croissant out on to his rubbly patio – with 300 vicarages devouring money, the diocesan housing officer is not going to stump up for something as frivolous as a patio, unless Dominic makes a total nuisance of himself, and he won't, because he is cursed with empathy and can imagine how horrible it must be to be a diocesan housing officer – and after he's smoked a cheeky cigar, he will get out his iPhone and say the Morning Office, using the Common Prayer app.

The New Year is smiling upon him. Look at the sunshine on the birch twigs! And there's a little chaffinch! Well, considering how much he drank last night, he's got off rather lightly, he thinks; because he is still pished. He casts his mind back. Probably oughtn't to have slagged off Paul Henderson like that. Dominic holds the office of bishop in high regard, even when he does not entirely like or esteem the individual holders of that office. He does not for one minute believe Paul is a closet queen. Oh Lord, by the age of fifty-three he really ought to have grown out of promulgating that kind of mischief. I'm afraid my readers are not impressed: a parish priest quite seriously having to make a New Year's resolution not to tell whoppers in the coming year! We leave him with his cigar and his conscience, and see what's been happening in Lindchester.

As dawn breaks, a little red car rumbles its way up the cobbled street and in through the gatehouse of the Close. It is driven cautiously, but well, by Miss Barbara Blatherwick – yes, that is genuinely her name – and she parks it in her designated parking space. She is seventy-eight and, *pace* the lusty chorus of seamen in *South Pacific*, she is remarkably like a dame, although in fact she only has an MBE. She reaches over to the passenger's seat to gather up her handbag, and tuts. There is blood on the headrest. Now she will have to postpone her cup of tea and tackle the stain with upholstery cleaner straight away, or it'll never come out. What a dratted nuisance.

Come, come, Miss Blatherwick! Don't you know this is AB rhesus negative, very rare? The people at the donor clinic get very excited about this blood you are tutting over. Until the would-be donor starts populating the questionnaire with rather too many 'yes's, that is. It belongs to Freddie May.

There, you see? You take fright far too easily. A novelist does not kill off her characters before the reader has had a chance to start caring about them. Freddie did not fall very far when the slate slipped under his foot up on the palace roof, because there was another roof ten feet below. He did knock himself out and split his head open, however. You missed the heart-stopping sight of him climbing from that lower roof on to the wrought-iron fire escape. Looking at the back of the house in daylight, I honestly don't know how he managed it. But he did: he has nine lives, that boy. Nine? He has forty-five! He is quintessence of cat! He then staggered, clutching his poor head, from the bishop's garden across the Close to the precentor's house, and hammered on the door.

The precentor, Giles Littlechild, was wrenched from cava-sodden sleep by the row. He wrangled a dressing gown on and cantered his long legs wildly down the stairs like a giraffe encouraged by a cattle prod.

'Argh! What bloody man is that?' he cried. (This is the Close. People quote under pressure.) 'What have you done to yourself this time, May? Oh, dear Lord! Come in! Are you all right?'

And Freddie, being English, replied, 'I'm fine,' and threw up in the precentor's lavender bush.

He was not fine; that much was obvious. It was also obvious that Giles was in no legal state to drive. Nor was his wife. Nor was anyone else Giles could think of. Getting hold of a taxi would be a nightmare. He ran his hands through his mad scientist hair. There was nobody.

Except Miss Blatherwick.

It was 2 a.m. Unthinkable to disturb her! But disturb her he did, knowing that Miss Blatherwick would shake off sempiternal rest and get up out of her grave if one of her boys needed her.

That's how Miss Blatherwick came to spend a jolly night at Lindford General Hospital A&E, sitting straight-backed in tweed and frank astonishment among the caterwauling drunks and silly girls who had fallen off their stilettos. It was hours before Freddie was seen to and had his head glued up, and then they kept him in for observation because he'd been concussed.

I had better explain why Miss Blatherwick demonstrated such heroism last night. For three and a half decades she mothered the generations of boys who passed through Lindchester Cathedral Choristers' School. She comforted the homesick ones, sat beside the bad ones in the naughty pew in evensong, accompanied them to the secret lavatory that the public did not know about when they were caught short during a service. She dished out plasters and cod liver oil and common sense, found lost socks, did battle with verrucae (this is the Close, we are pedantic here), combed out nits and straightened caps. She stood by them when the choirmaster was a brute. She was their rock, their fortress and their might; and they were her life. Freddie was in the last cohort before her retirement and she would have driven that boy to Timbuktu.

I call him a boy. He is not a boy, he's twenty-two. But oh, he's a Lost Boy, up on the roof with Peter Pan, stranded in Neverland. People despair of him. He has so much going for him, why is he such a disaster area? How can someone that good-looking and talented be so wilfully self-destructive? And he is good-looking and talented, believe me. Five foot eleven inches of such astounding golden beauty that your gaze flinches away embarrassed, the way it would from a disfiguring birthmark. And his voice! People who know about such things tell me he has the potential to be one of the finest tenors of his generation. He was certainly well on the way to becoming a famous boy soprano, when his voice broke catastrophically early at the age of not quite twelve. You can still buy a CD in the cathedral shop, with Freddie in his ruff on the front, looking as adorable as a blond baby duckling. His friends here are all hoping and praying that he has steadied down now; that if he cannot stay out of trouble completely, he can at least stay out of custody. Don't ever lend him your credit card, by the way, or let him look over your shoulder when you type your computer password. He will tell you this himself. But his candour is so disarming that you will probably not heed the warning.

What more do you need to know about Freddie May? Since his release, he has lived with the Hendersons – Paul and Susanna take in waifs and strays now their girls have grown up and left home – and Freddie has an attic room with (if you are fearless) access to the roof. He likes to lie under the stars and smoke weed. This is something the bishop chooses to know nothing about. The bishop's chaplain, whom we shall meet later, is barred from driving for twelve months (a suspected epileptic seizure, not a drunk driving charge), so Freddie makes himself useful by acting as the bishop's driver when required. He also helps out in the bishop's office. Penelope, the bishop's PA, doesn't let him anywhere near the PC unsupervised. Freddie does not know her password. Thinks Penelope.

What else? In common with most people his age, Freddie's conversation is composed almost entirely of like, questions? He uses the word 'literally' metaphorically. He adores children and mountains. He prefers *presto* to *largo*. He is incapable of refusing a dare. He does not have Common Prayer on his iPhone. He has Grindr. But provided Freddie does not twoc the episcopal car for his jollies, this is something else the bishop (hating the sin, loving the sinner) chooses to know nothing about.

By now Miss Blatherwick has done battle with the bloodstains, so we will administer a well-earned cup of English Breakfast and a bowl of porridge. I expect she will have a nap, while keeping an ear open in case Freddie texts to say he needs picking up. A text? On a mobile phone? I thought you said she was seventy-eight? Oh, ageist reader! Miss Blatherwick is perfectly up to speed with modern gadgetry. Does it matter that her text messages are infested with rogue cedillas and umlauts? They are perfectly cogent. We will repose her on the sofa, set aside her glasses, and spread a plaid blanket over her legs. Sweet dreams, Miss Blatherwick! You are a good woman and Freddie is lucky to have you in his life.

The year is off to a faltering start. New Year's Day is Tuesday. Everyone's asking if it's worth going back to work for three days. Normal life won't really be resumed until next Monday. We are left inhabiting a rather listless Saturnalia, restrained from excess by resolution, yet assailed by all the tempting leftover food and drink. Many clergy people, whose work/rest boundaries are at best porous, are sort of taking holiday, not exactly working, just catching up on emails and filing, and preparing for Sunday, which is Epiphany, of course. The four-by-fours are converging on the Close as parents return their children to the Choristers' School. Curates all over the diocese are racking their brains for myrrh-based all-age worship or Messy Church activities (flash paper? Any way I can use flash paper?); while in Quires and Places where they sing, they are rehearsing 'Three Kings from Persian lands afar', or perhaps 'Lo, star-led chiefs!', music by Crotch. Smirk. (Will we ever grow up on the Close?)

Epiphany: time for the wise to come seeking. If you are a stickler, only now will the magi make their way into your crib scene (which may remain on display until Candlemas). But it's the twelfth day of Christmas, so take down your decorations, please. Put your tree out by the bins and rediscover the universal law that there will always be one decoration left on it that you've missed. Have you remembered the wreath on the front door?

There. Christmas is back in the loft. We can now raise our eyes and look out across the vistas of the coming year. What does it hold for my characters, I wonder? Before long there will be an archiepiscopal vacancy in York. If you are bishop of the historic See of Lindchester, well, who knows what dizzy elevation this year might bring?

Chapter 3

Even the most unchurched of my readers will be aware that we have a new archbishop elect, the Most Revd Dr Michael Palgrove. His translation from York is what will create the vacancy I mentioned. He is not that far off retirement age, and the papers have dubbed him a 'nightwatchman' archbishop; little more than a safe pair of hands while the rising generation of more stylish bishops gain enough experience to take over the helm. Whether this is fair, I leave for others to decide. My concern in this tale is with bishops, not archbishops.

Let me introduce you to the bishop of Lindchester. At this moment he's at Lindford station boarding the London train. He's heading for the House of Lords, where he will do what bishops do; thwarting this, defending that: being a force for good or a bunch of barking bigots, depending on which paper you read. Bishops sit in the Lords for historic constitutional reasons. But do we want unelected clerics in government, a constitutional idiosyncrasy we share solely with Iran? Oh dear, perhaps we ought to clamour for an elected Upper House and sever at last the ties between church and state? Yet to what impoverishment of our national life will that lead? Our towering elms, never truly valued till they are gone, all gone!

Anyway, for now Bishop Paul is going to London. He is situated towards the rear of the train in standard class accommodation. He only travels first class when Penelope, his PA, books him a first class ticket because it is cheaper than standard class – and even then he does so unostentatiously, not in a parade of prelatical entitlement. To the untrained eye he does not even look like a bishop. Where are his gaiters? (Do they still wear them, come to think of it? I have never seen gaiters adorning an episcopal calf – and I always check.) Why is he wearing a black shirt? Because he detests the symbolism of purple, with its connotations of imperial Rome. Insiders will infer the struggle entailed here: Paul is an Evangelical. Black is for Catholics. (Or funerals.) He has solved this to some extent by the type of dog collar he wears. Slip-in ('tunnel style') collars tend to be evangelical; full collars ('neckband style') are favoured by the catholic wing. I refer you to the website of J. Wippell & Co. Ltd, Clerical Outfitters & Church Furnishings since 1789. What Wippell's will not tell you, however, is that slip-in collars have one huge advantage: they may be improvised at short notice from strips of postcard or folded copier paper.

So there sits Paul, in the quiet coach. The only thing that betrays his status is the silver chain round his neck. Look closely and you'll see that it disappears into the breast pocket of his shirt. That's where his plain silver pectoral cross is stowed. Are you still wondering how to picture him? He is tall, dark, and (racy thought!) if we were to peer at the label in the episcopal trousers we would see that he wears 34 long. This, perhaps, is the only thing that lends credence to Dominic's mischievous claim – for how many straight men of fifty-eight can boast a flat stomach? We are, of course, not shallow enough to hold a 'hottest bishop' contest; but if we did, I think Paul might well win. You might object that the bar is set very low, but I'd retort that in any walk of life Paul would count as quite a nice-looking man – so much so, I sometimes think he looks like an actor playing a bishop. He ought to trim his eyebrows, mind you; their raffish upward quirk suggests they are plotting a career of their own as a roué.

Before long the train will cross the border into the Lichfield diocese, so we must bid him farewell. He is slogging through a tedious report of some kind, poor man. Occasionally his thoughts stray to York, but he calls them to heel. He is not personally ambitious, but like his fellow senior diocesan bishops, he cannot help wondering what the will of the Lord might be. Safe journey, Paul. Mind the gap between your hopes and the treacherous platform of church politics.

Freddie has just returned from dropping the bishop off at the station. He swings far too fast into the palace drive and parks in a shower of gravel. Boom! Look at *me* parking the bishop's car. This is aimed at the bishop's chaplain, the Revd Martin Rogers, who has made the mistake of glancing through the office window. One time, just one time, let him misjudge it and hit the wall, begs the chaplain (hating the sin, hating the sinner even more). He stabs the photocopier buttons.

I'm afraid you will write Martin off as a homophobe; but he is genuinely doing his best. He has already repented of his malediction and is shooting prayers at the implacable ceiling of heaven. Give me grace, Lord! Freddie comes crunching over the drive and presses his face against the window. Martin refuses to look. Freddie's tongue stud rattles against the glass as he snogs the pane. The sound might be Martin's prayer arrows clattering back to the floor unanswered.

We, too, are going to ignore Freddie, in the vain hope that he will stop doing it, and head to the palace kitchen. Here we will find the bishop's wife, Susanna, having coffee with a dear, dear friend, Jane Rossiter.

Jane gazed round while Susanna made the Fair Trade coffee and got out the Cath Kidston china mugs. As usual the Aga-warmed kitchen looked as though it had just been styled for a *Palace Beautiful* photo shoot. Today a bone-coloured cachepot of paperwhites stood on the scrubbed farmhouse table. *Sucre*, *Farine*, said the antique French storage jars on the dresser. Everywhere Jane saw polite suggestions of colour that never quite came out with a positive statement: washed-out raspberry gingham curtains, faded pistachio stripes on the linen chair cushions. Susanna put out a plate of homemade cookies, which Jane would eat and she would not.

I had better take a moment to describe the two women. Susanna, at fifty-six, is five years older than Jane, but looks ten years younger. She has the caramel-coloured hair you would expect from a well-groomed woman of her age. She watches her weight, dresses well, and loves her Pilates class. Her large blue eyes brim with empathy. She is very lovely. Jane, on the other hand, is not. Her face in repose says, 'Yeah, right'. If she makes the effort she still has it in her to be, as Dominic puts it, a good-looking broad. But why bother? Her frizzy dark hair currently sports a badger stripe down the parting. She has rolls round her middle. Pilates, schmilates. Jane played rugby in her youth. She's wearing black. You don't have to think about what goes with what if you always wear black. Her black boots need reheeling. Her black jumper is bobbly. Her black leggings are laundered to grey.

Of all this Jane was well aware as she watched Susanna potter prettily in her perfect kitchen. She felt frowzy, misplaced, and bloated with malevolence, like Shelob squeezed into a knicker shop. That morning she had roused herself to add a clutter of chunky silver jewellery, but it hadn't really helped. So she consoled herself with the thought that she could sit on Susanna and squash her. Squash her till she heard all her tiny bird-like bones crunch.

The coffee was poured. The plate of biscuits was nudged towards Jane, who took one.

'So!' said Susanna, head tilted pastorally, as if Jane's dog had just been run over, 'how was Christmas? How's Danny getting on? Have you heard from him?'

'Oh, we Skype, so I know he's still got all his limbs. He says everything is sweet. Or awesome,' Jane emended, bringing her customary academic rigour to bear. 'How was your Christmas?'

'We had a lovely time!' Susanna listed the family frisks and jollities the palace had resounded to. But the head was still tilted: Jane knew she would circle back shortly to dump more pastoral concern. Jane did not want to talk about Danny. She did not want consolation from someone who knew all about the empty nest syndrome.

She headed her off: 'What does Paul think of the latest on gay bishops, then? Looks like the C of E has shot itself in the foot with its usual aplomb.'

'Oh, I know!' wailed Susanna. 'It's all so sad. I do wish—'

Freddie padded in.

An interesting little pause followed.

'Ssh! Fag in room!' he whispered.

'Morning, Frederick,' said Jane.

'Hey, Janey.'

He gave her that smile, the one that either enslaved people or made them want to slap him. Jane felt both impulses. He looked as though he might start winding himself round ankles and table legs any moment, purring.

'Jesus! – Sorry, Suze. Is that a black eye?' she asked. 'Whatever happened to you?'

'Oh-h-h. I like fell over? Hit my head?'

'Omigod, you look terrible?'

'Nah, I'm good?'

'I'm relieved to hear it?' Jane sometimes played this game of escalating uncertainty with her students as well. She watched Freddie lean over to get a cereal bowl out of a cupboard. 'I see Santa didn't bring you a belt, then.'

'Checking my ass out again, Dr R?'

'Freddie!' chided Susanna.

'Looking pert,' said Jane.

'Jane!'

I think we'll leave them at this point. Take it from me, there is seldom much serious conversation once Freddie appears. Instead, let's follow Jane along the steep cobbled street that winds down to the Lower Town. She plans to spend the morning mooching about, soaking up the atmosphere, and trying to recreate in her imagination the cholera-infested riverside slums of the mid-nineteenth century, and work out where the tanneries once stood. This is where her current subject of historical research, Josephine Luscombe, lived and worked.

A great Victorian activist, was Josephine: improving the lot of the poor (Lindchester leather workers), confronting the indifference of the rich (Lindchester Cathedral Dean and Chapter). Josephine was the kind of woman Jane very much enjoyed researching, but would avoid if she saw her coming in the supermarket.

I ought to mention that Jane is employed by Linden University in Lindford. That is its name. It is not called Poundstretcher University. I'm afraid Jane isn't popular. She forgets departmental meetings. She has migraines on peer appraisal days. She is so cunningly thick about IT innovations and anything on a spreadsheet that people have stopped expecting her to engage with them. Overworked colleagues complain to the head of department, but what is Professor Bleakley to do? Yes, Dr Rossiter weasels out of administrative roles; but she does fulfil her teaching commitments, and she does get published.

But as Jane walks along the muddy riverbank past Gresham's Boats, swiping the willow fronds aside, she is not thinking of Josephine Luscombe. Her thoughts speed all the way round the globe to New Zealand. She sniffs back her tears. Dammit. He's fine. He's having the time of his life. But she'd had Danny with her all his eighteen years till Boxing Day. Brought him up single-handed from day one. This feels like amputation.

We won't risk giving Jane a big hug and telling her it will pass. We would only get an earful. She carries on walking till the Lower Town gives way to countryside. Behind her the cathedral on its mount is erased by fog. Mist lies low on the fields, bounded by the hedges, like cream poured into square dishes. The cows all stand motionless. Here and there white stripes of water lie along the old ridge and furrowed earth. A crow caws from an empty poplar. I am every dead thing, thinks Jane.

Then she calls herself a silly mare, turns, and walks briskly back towards Lindchester.

Up on the misty mount, in the palace office, Penelope is panicking over the bishop's electronic diary. Tomorrow 8 p.m.: Argentine Tango? Argentine Tango?! What on earth? Some fundraising event for their partner diocese? Paul won't even be here, he'll still be in London. She must be going mad! She had no recollection of booking that in whatsoever.

Chapter 4

Snow! Look, look! Snow, everybody! Snow over the entire UK! Schools are closed, meetings cancelled, planes grounded. Visitors from North America look on in astonishment and make the mistake of belittling our snow. We are extremely offended by this, for obscure reasons locked up deep in the English psyche.

Let us rise up on wings like eagles until we can survey the whole diocese of Lindchester beneath us, tucked up under a white blanket. Then off, off forth on a swing! And down into Renfold, where the good people of the borough have been hanging up fat balls and replenishing their feeders because they worry for the garden birds. More for the birds than for the homeless, but that is the way of things: they can see the robins, they cannot see the homeless. (And the robins are not smelly and weird and doing drugs.)

And look – even the brick church of St John the Evangelist looks pretty in the snow. Already we can see footprints leading to the door where the faithful few fought their way bravely to Morning Prayer. It has finished, and Father Dominic is on his drive now, trying to scrape the snow off his car with the Methodist church magazine someone has kindly popped through his letter box. He swears as snow goes up his sleeve. Suddenly he laughs at himself. Why is he even trying to take the car?

Five minutes later we see him come out in his thick socks and wellingtons, and set off on foot to his meeting. He's wearing a nice knitted hat with Nordic snowflakes on and little plaits dangling from the earflaps. His mum gave it to him for Christmas. He'll be late, but his frazzled soul will be restored by the grace of snow. It renders all gardens lovely, both the kempt and the unkempt, blessing wheelie bin and wisteria alike. He cuts through Prince Albert Park on his way to meet with his fellow Renfold ministers. Together they are setting up a food bank. A food bank in Renfold? Lindford, maybe; but Renfold? When, Lord? When did I see you hungry and naked and homeless and not come to your aid? Keep your eyes peeled. You will shortly be seeing a lot more of the Lord. The north wind of austerity doth blow and we shall have snow. Dominic will be handing out more sleeping bags and mugs of tea. He'll be spending longer on the phone checking out sob stories and trying to find hostel spaces. He'll end up paying for more and more emergency overnight B&Bs. Yes, sometimes he'll be taken for a ride; but on the Last Day he won't end up on the side of the astounded goats.

But Dominic is not contemplating the beauty of Big Society as his wellies creak through the silent park. He's not even stressing about his church electoral roll renewal. He's wondering whether to give old Janey a ring and drag her out – snow permitting – to the cinema tonight, to watch *Les Mis*. He's a bit worried about her. He stops under a beech tree. A squirrel curses him roundly from a branch in gruff little quacks. 'And also with you,' says Dominic.

We'll leave him standing in the snowy park making his call, and mount up again on our biblical wings and speed to Lindchester and circle the Close. See that old-fashioned lamppost under the trees? We might be in Narnia. Any minute now Mr Tumnus will come trotting by with his parcels. Aw, there on the cathedral lawn – a crocodile of snow choristers processing to evensong! And high up on the cathedral roof, another snowman in a pointy hat gazes pontifically down. Who on earth has climbed all the way up here with a purloined crosier? Down below, the vergers are busy strewing grit on the steps and across the paving, melting safe pathways for the faithful and the litigious; while over on the south side of the Close a wretched penitent shovels snow. He's been instructed to get out of the bishop's sight. It's Freddie May. Not happy. Seriously not happy. Right now he's like totally starving? Literally? And he's right by Miss Blatherwick's door. She'll have cake. Cake! No, I'd keep shovelling if I were you, Freddie. The bishop has not yet spotted that his spare crook is missing from the umbrella stand, and right now he will not be amused.

Round we wheel to the north side. Look down again: that grand Georgian house there is the deanery. It's very big, you say? Indeed yes, so big it generates its own microclimate: permafrost. It is not as big as the palace, naturally; but it is bigger than the precentor's house, which in turn is bigger than the houses of both the canon chancellor and the canon treasurer, because the canon precentor is the first canon. (We like everything done decently and in order here in the Close.) The deanery is where Mrs Dean, the Very Revd Marion

Randall, lives. Come with me. We are going to be cheeky and have a nose around.

You will notice straight away that it is not as perfect as the palace. It is, however, effortlessly posher. Those are real Eric Gills on the walls. I am strongly tempted to pinch that William de Morgan lustreware bowl on my way back out. Did you hear a gale of laughter coming from the dean's study? The canons are assembled there for their weekly canons' coffee. I dare say that in a more gracious era they would have been having canons' breakfast in the huge dining room, with kedgeree and kidneys in silver chafing dishes. But this is the twenty-first century, and they are having coffee. The dean's husband is about to carry in a second cafetière. Let's follow him. There's a fire in the hearth, but the canons are sensibly still wearing their coats. I apologize in advance for the language.

'Is this Fair Trade, Gene?' asked the precentor.

'Certainly not.' Gene had the fabulously snooty accent of someone who grew up in South Africa. He crossed to the fire and placed another chunk of last year's cathedral Christmas tree on it. There was a brief roaring crackle. 'It's Monsooned Malabar.'

'Oh good,' said the canon chancellor. 'Because I really hate that un-monsooned crap.'

The canon treasurer laid a hand on the chancellor's arm, tilted his head and made big melting eyes like the bishop's wife. 'Oh dear! Another bad night, Mark? I'm so, so sorry!'

'Put it this way: I've started googling adoption services.'

'Come, come, Mr Chancellor!' said the precentor. 'Like as arrows in the hand of the giant, even so are the young children!'

'Fuck off,' said the chancellor.

'Right, people,' said Marion. 'Let's make a start, shall we?'

They are about to get down to business. A sneaky glance at Marion's list shows that they will be discussing such things as the Choristers' School, FAC, Safeguarding, HLF, Food Bank (yes, even here in Lindchester), Employment Tribunal – Lord have mercy! We will leave them to their acronyms and hot potatoes, follow Gene out and shut the study door. There is another gale of laughter. The precentor has just stated that he sees no liturgical objection to holding an Argentine Tango Mass and calling it a Fresh Expression. Yes, news of the bishop's diary malfunction has whipped round the Close. Keep shovelling that snow, Freddie.

It occurs to me that you are frustrated by that closed study door. You may be wondering what the canons are like, what they do? Very well. I will introduce the Dean and Chapter clergy in turn.

The most important person in any cathedral is the dean. The cathedral may be the bishop's seat, but the dean is the boss. The Very Revd Marion Randall is fifty-four, and I find her rather dashing: tall, with a strong jaw, direct gaze and cropped hair. She reminds me of a 1920s aviatrix. She ought to have a biplane parked on the lawn. Actually, I think I may have a crush on her. There were flutterings in the theological dovecot when she was appointed, as you can imagine. I'm told that the school chaplain snatched up his biretta and left for another job, lamenting 'the creeping protestantization of the Church of England'. Ah yes! Creeping relentlessly up on us since the Act of Supremacy in 1534.

Next comes the canon precentor, the Revd Canon Giles Littlechild, whom we have met. He is in charge of worship and music. Traditionally, cathedral canons come in two styles: tall and cadaverously thin, or robin redbreast. You may categorize them as they pass you in procession on Sunday mornings. Giles conforms to the former type. His mad hair suggests he forks his toast out of the toaster without unplugging it first. Precentors need to be full-time professional pedants and control freaks. It's in the job description. They are born and bred in the briar-patch of the English cathedral choral tradition. Giles ticks those boxes, but he is blessed with a sunny disposition and a puerile sense of humour.

The charism of grumpiness has been bestowed instead upon the canon chancellor, the Revd Canon Dr Mark Lawson. He is the scholar priest of the outfit. Education and outreach are in his portfolio. He tends, I fear, towards the robin redbreast physique. By the time he's fifty he will need a 'front measurement' taken when he has a new cassock fitted. You can see him in his stall at evensong with his Greek and Hebrew Testaments, like a mage scowling at ancient runes. Systematics is his thing. I was once told the title of his DPhil, but I'm afraid it sounded like white noise to me. Bear with him: his six-week-old son and heir is colicky. Mark paces his study for hours every night, jiggling the screaming scrap, while poor Miriam sleeps upstairs. Up and down, up and down: he croons Latin irregular verbs and observes how ably his son declines to sleep.

Lastly we have the canon treasurer, the Revd Canon Philip Voysey-Scott. Before entering the Church Philip was a city banker, a full-blown 1980s coke-snorting, red braces yuppie. Give him numbers, he'll crunch them for you. He has the carrying voice of one born to halloo above the yammering of hounds, receding fair hair combed back in the Dracula manner, and a jumble of Scrabble tile teeth. I'm told he skis like a James Bond stunt double. Talk to him for more than five minutes and he'll be able to impersonate you mercilessly.

So there we are: Maid Marion and her Merry Men. We will be seeing more of them, never fear.

Dusk falls. The bishop's wife is baking a carrot cake. *The Archers* is on. Susanna is making cake because she cannot put the world to rights. Cake is her default mode. It was just a naughty prank, not hacking as such. Paul's being too strict. No, no, don't be silly, Paul's right. Freddie needs boundaries and accountability. Oh, if only he'd sort himself out and apply for uni, or something! Whatever will happen to him? No, she mustn't feel bad. It's not as though they're heartlessly chucking him out with no warning! He's known from the word go it was only ever for one year. He's still got three months to sort something out. They'll just have to be firm with him. She renders the top layer with a coat of cream cheese icing, plastering over the cracks.

A dark, deep winter's night in the diocese of Lindchester. More snow is forecast. The gritters are out. Cold has settled like a grey lid over the country. How long, O Lord? When, when will the winter be over and past and the time of singing come again? Jane is crying at her computer. New Zealand is a long, long way away. There will be no singing any time soon.

Chapter 5

And still it snows. It snows, it thaws a little, it freezes. The pavements are treacherous. Shops and restaurants are quiet as art galleries. This is the glummest week of the glummest month, enlivened only by the peaty glow of Burns' Night and the approach of February. February is a short month. And then it's March. Amen, even so, come quickly, Spring.

In the village of Cardingforth (that is its name, it is not called Lardingforth) dawn breaks pink behind the power station. In Sunningdale Drive (that is its name, it is not called Cooling Tower View) Jane stares at her coffee. Outside, the shouts of children sliding to school. Inside, silence. The radio is off because the *Today* programme got too strident. Upstairs nobody is taking their customary forty-five-minute shower, or wallowing under their duvet because they've got a late shift today. Then again, nor have they joined up, gone to Afghanistan and got shot in the head. She has not seen their naked body tossed into a gutter. Nice. Thanks for that one, Dreams R Us. Jane stares at her coffee and thinks: Half the time he's living a day ahead of me. I'm living in his yesterday. Ha. Stuck in yesterday. The plan had been not to end up like this: not to be one of those mothers so over-invested in her child that life feels pointless once he's gone. But then, the plan had been not to have children. Furthermore, it would pass. Jane slaps her thighs. Up, and be doing, gal. But she continues to sit, staring at her cold coffee, and watching Danny, in an endlessly replaying loop, walk away from her under the big sign: 'All Departures'.

Reader, I have been remiss. I have taken you up onto rooftops and into kitchens but not into the cathedral. Come with me to Lindchester, and I will put that right immediately. We will fly there, rather than toiling like medieval pilgrims over landscape plotted and pieced and up the cobbled streets. A biting wind blows today. The snow choristers are two rows of sorry stumps on the lawn. The bell chimes for Morning Prayer.

One by one the retired priests totter up to the cathedral door, eyes watering, noses pink with cold. The day will come when their old bodies can no longer get them to church, but their souls will attend until their *Nunc Dimittis* on life's last evening. The habit of faith has worn a groove in their lives. Where else would they go? I have been young and now am old; and yet saw I never the righteous forsaken. Yet never. Yet never. They lean on the heavy door – dear me, this implausible frailty, this affront of elderliness that has come upon them! – and stagger into the warmth and shelter, where the memory of myriad candles lingers in the air. They pull off their furry Russian hats, their leather gloves, and wipe their noses on pocket handkerchiefs. Then begin the long walk up the south aisle to the chapel of St Michael and All Angels.

You will like this chapel, I think. Take a seat and admire the Burne-Jones stained glass: angels and archangels and all the company of heaven. On summer days the flagstones are puddled with colour. A macho bronze of St Michael (school of Epstein) offsets the androgynous languishing in the windows; while above the altar hangs a vast abstract, brooding, shot through with wild joy (or quite possibly terror). If you like your Annunciations with lilies, this will not be to your taste. The Chapter clergy are all waiting prayerfully, apart from Mr Happy, who will rush in with sick on his shoulder as the late bell starts chiding. Miss Blatherwick is here, of course, along with a handful of other stalwarts; and so, today, is the bishop. Beside him sits his chaplain, a tightly wound coil of Evangelical passive-aggression. Quite a gathering for eight o'clock on a January morning.

Freddie is here too. Does that surprise you? Perhaps he has struck you so far as utterly irreligious. By no means. He was a chorister, remember: cut them and they bleed Psalms. He is staring up at the altarpiece the way he stared at another by the same artist, in a different chapel, in unhappier times. He's remembering how he vowed that when he got out he would do two things: go up onto the moors, lie on his back and see nothing, nothing but sky, literally, and hear the larks? And second, he'd find the guy (he wrongly assumes) who painted this and thank him. He has done the first, borrowing the car without permission, and earning himself a right reverend bollocking when he got back (Paul rather leapt to conclusions, I'm afraid: Lindford Common, police car on the drive). Freddie has not yet fulfilled his second vow. This is what he is thinking about as he stares up at the canvas. He should totally do it? Yeah, he should really get on to that? But this triggers a cascade of dread: so much he should do! He should get his act together, look for work, apply for stuff? He shoves his hands up his hoodie sleeves. His fingers play the guitar fret scars on his upper arms. Time is running out. Should have applied for the Winchester job. Shit, why does he keep missing the closing dates? He's got to check out the *Church Times* ads again, bound to be something somewhere. Please let there be. But what if there's not? Oh, shit. Oh, Jesus. Help me? He hugs himself and shivers under the glass gaze of Burne-Jones's angels, looking, with his ragged hair and fading black eyes, not unlike a trashy angel himself.

I don't want my readers to think that the bishop is unaware of Freddie's distress. He is not a brute. Even now as the matins bell picks up speed and Mr Chancellor comes clattering in, Paul is praying for Freddie. How to handle this? He knows from experience that any attempt to force Freddie to face reality will provoke panic and a knee-jerk barrage of bad behaviour, which must then be confronted, punished and forgiven. And frankly, he just does not have the time for another spin on that pointless merry-go-round. Yet having agreed to this arrangement, he is in some sense responsible. So he prays. For wisdom, and for Freddie, who he can see on the other side of the chapel there, shivering. The way he had that first evening. Standing in the palace hallway, ashen-faced, shaking with misery. Paul had known at a glance he was trouble, yet he couldn't find it in his heart to turn him away.

O Lord, open our lips.
And our mouth shall proclaim your praise.

We will tiptoe out now and leave them to their prayers, while I take you to the shrine. As you may know, Lindchester has its very own saint, William of Lindchester. He was demoted at the Reformation when his shrine was broken up, but I believe we are still entitled to think of him as a good and godly bishop, even if we no longer look to him to cure us of scrofula. His cult rested on a miracle: he waded, crosier in hand, into the Linden, and by prayer alone diverted the course of the river, thereby saving the Lower Town from catastrophic flood. Here's the shrine, in this space behind the High Altar, right under the famous rose window. Look down. Just a simple grey stone with his name and dates; and a place where you may light a candle and leave a prayer request.

If you are feeling nosy you can step closer and read some of the prayer cards pinned to the board. *Please help my Nan. Be with those serving overseas. Pray for baby Josh, desperately ill in Special Care.* Already a little group of candles flickers in the gloom. The organ begins to play. Some twentieth-century French voluntary? I see why you think that, but no, merely the organ tuner. At the top of the prayer board is a verse from the hymn often associated with William of Lindchester:

> Lord Jesus, think on me,
> That, when the flood is past,
> I may the eternal brightness see
> And share thy joy at last.

Oh, that January were over. The first snowdrops tremble under trees, and look! – the daffodils are up. Not long, not long now. I dream of crocuses, their Cadbury's Creme Egg hues rioting on every municipal roundabout! Sunday will be Septuagesima, three Sundays before Lent. It is also Holocaust Memorial Sunday. (The precentor fires off an email to the director of music: 'Abbot's Leigh not Austria!', to head off any risk of singing 'Glorious things of thee are spoken' to *Deutschland über Alles*.)

But today is Friday. Generally speaking, Friday is clergy Day Off. It is certainly Dominic's day off. He has succeeded in impressing this upon his congregation. They now preface their requests with the formula, 'I know Friday's your day off, but . . .' Tonight he has finally managed to drag Jane out to see *Les Mis*. They are in the posh bit of the Odeon in Lindford, sitting in a little booth before the showing, drinking prosecco and absorbing popcorn by osmosis. Let's edge close and eavesdrop.

'Come along, Janey. You have to eat your body weight in nachos. It's the rule.'

Dominic was at the thin phase of his three-year dieting cycle, and looking rather trim. In fact, right now he probably weighed less than Jane. Not a quality she'd ever admired in a man.

'Yeah, right. I don't see *you* eating nachos.'

'Pig out as a tribute to Danny, then. How's he getting on, by the way?'

'Fine.'

'And how are you getting on?'

'Fine.' There was that loop again: All Departures. 'I hope this film has a happy ending.'

Dominic did his dowager's shriek. '*What?!* I can't believe you've never seen the musical.'

'I vaguely read the book for A-level,' she lied.

'Well, then. You know what happens.'

'She sells her teeth. That's all I remember. Is this going to depress me? I need a happy ending.'

Dominic hesitated. 'We-e-ll, let's just say the eschatological hope remains.'

'Pah!' said Jane.

Well, you've seen the film, surely? Then you can imagine Jane watching the young men mown down, their blood running along the gutters. Empty chairs at empty tables. Dominic flipped up the armrest and said, 'Come here, darling.' He held her while she bawled and cursed herself for being a silly cow. He agreed, yes, she was a silly, silly cow, and stroked her hair. And as for that final scene— Lord have mercy on us all.

They walk through the streets of Lindford back to Dominic's car. It is snowing again now. Dominic links his arm through Jane's. Why was she still hoping this? That somewhere on the far side there might yet be – against all logic, against all the evidence – an Arrivals Gate, with someone there looking out for her?

Chapter 6

Jane is out running. Running? Towing a dead elephant out of the swamp with a tractor, more like. But at least she is out there. Oh, that it has come to this, the consoling mantra of the middle-aged jogger. Time was when she could crank out six, eight, even ten miles without thinking about it. It's muddy on the river bank. Jane is not going far. Just a mile-and-a-half loop to ease herself back into it. The cooling towers rear up to her right, vast cathedrals of climate change. Yeah. Like she doesn't use electricity. In the distance now is the old bridge, lovely as a Cotman painting. The halfway point. She will cross it and plough home along the opposite bank. Come on, old girl, old carcass, you can do it. Blue sky today. Mild. Black hedges, blond fields. Rushes sshh gently beside her and the sheep as they graze are all haloed with light. Somewhere nearby a thrush dusts off his spring repertoire. *Toodle-oo, toodle-oo!* he carols. *Chewie-chewie-chewie! Chewie-chewie-chewie! Free kick, free kick!* (Jane is fluent in *turdus*.) The Linden races by, full and joyous. Spring. It will come. No woe of hers can hold it back.

There's a pounding behind her on the opposite bank. Another runner, gaining fast. They will reach the bridge at the same time. She flicks a glance. Young man. Black running skins, green beanie. Jane knows she's invisible to young men (unless she falls and breaks a hip), but pride forces her to pick up her feet and power jauntily towards the bridge. They'll cross in the middle. Here he comes, mirror shades, white iPod wires trailing. Tssh! Tssh! Tshh! of his music.

'Morning!'

'Hey, Janey!'

'Freddie!'

They swap a couple more nothings over their shoulders, then return to their private running worlds. The moment it's safe, Jane stops and leans on the parapet. Beetroot-faced, lungs exploding. Stitch. Freddie dwindles rapidly along the opposite bank. They are nine miles from Lindchester. One of those insane punishing runs of his. Freddie, Freddie. What will become of him? Not her worry, however. She can't fret over all the feckless young men on the face of the earth. Freddie has a mother of his own, presumably, somewhere. And he certainly has Susanna, fretting away like a busy bee. Jane peels herself off the bridge. There's a slagheap of marking waiting for her back at home. On with life!

The Most Revd Dr Michael Palgrove has preached his farewell sermon in York. I presume his goods and chattels have been swaddled in purple lambswool and suavely conveyed to Lambeth or Canterbury. Early next week an arcane ritual will be enacted in St Paul's Cathedral, after which we will have a legally constituted new archbishop of Canterbury. We wish you luck in the name of the Lord, Dr Palgrove! And in His hands we must leave you, obeying our self-imposed unity of place by not venturing beyond the boundaries of the diocese of Lindchester.

Candlemas approaches: the Presentation of Christ in the Temple. Here we turn our backs on Christmas and set our faces towards Jerusalem. On Sunday the crib figures must go back into bubble-wrapped hibernation till December. It all feels a long time ago now: the parties, the carol services, that last-minute supermarket dash for goose fat. Here and there evicted Christmas trees still lie beside wheelie bins. MORE FURTHER REDUCTION'S says a sign in the Lower Town.

I'm about to take you on a short cut through the Luscombe Centre, Lindchester's 1960s shopping precinct. I will require you to gaze upon vistas of bleak concrete where neat Victorian terraces once stood (themselves replacing medieval squalor). Who can say now what was in the town planners' minds? I expect someone somewhere was making a mint. Lindford fared worse, of course, yet the blight seems more appalling here, here in Historic Lindchester, where the cathedral spire is visible over the brutal multi-storey car park; aloof, in a different world. A gull circles in the blue. Down here we must hurry past betting shops, charity shops, pound shops, amusements, a mad person muttering on a mobility scooter, a clipboarded bouncy person: 'Can I borrow you for a minute? No? Have a nice day!' Oh dear, vomit – don't slip! Chip wrappings blown into corners; the massively fat, the huddled homeless; a *Big Issue* seller. Remember to make eye contact and smile kindly as you say, 'No thanks.' At least you haven't pretended she doesn't exist.

What a godforsaken spot this is – assuming God forsakes the poor and hopeless – but we're out now. And here's the river, just a few yards away, down these steps. It's looking pretty turbulent right now. All that snow and rain, I suppose. (William of Lindchester, pray for us!) This is Gresham's Boats we are passing. In the summer you can hire a little rowing boat or a punt and tack with hilarious incompetence from bank to bank up and down the Linden, and then picnic under the venerable willows. In a moment – if we have timed this right – Freddie will appear, mud-spattered, sweat-slicked, at the end of his eighteen-mile run. He will force himself to run up that steep flight of steps you can see on your left. Three precipitous zigzags up the wooded bank to a narrow passage: a secret back way on to the Close when the main gatehouse doors are closed and locked at 10.30 p.m.

Here he comes now. Ah, it would console Jane to see this, to hear him whooping for breath. She'd be able to keep pace with him easily now as he stumbles up the steps. He gets two-thirds of the way before he collapses. Sits, head between juddering knees. Oh, shit. Man. Like, total running whitey? He retches. Lies down. Dark closes in. Stars. Then it clears. He's on his back looking up at trees, sky. Except he's not looking up, he's looking down. Stuck like a fly to the world's ceiling, looking down on the abyss of space. Whoa, paradigm shift? *What is man, that thou art mindful of him?* Then it flips back to normal. That was mental! Totally – fucking – *mental*. He lies there a few minutes longer, laughing, then hauls himself to his feet. Slowly, slowly, fumbling the handrail, he climbs the last flight to the narrow gate at the top.

5.29 p.m. The late bell chimes. Here comes the chancellor, sprinting in a magpie flurry of cassock and surplice towards the west door. It is the last day of January and look! Are we right to say it is not wholly dark at the beginning of evensong? From inside the cathedral the windows are grey, not black, surely? Yes, the year's corner has been turned and before long we will be cantering towards light evenings again. The choir is already assembled in the vestibule. Mr Happy pants in, just as Giles is testily consulting his watch. The lay clerks exchange smirks; the director of music presses the magic button. Upstairs in the loft the sub-organist wends her improvisation to a seemly close. The precentor says a prayer. A lay clerk strikes himself on the head with a tuning fork, listens, then begins to sing. The room fills with music. It radiates out, like the glow of a fire, until it fills the whole cathedral. The small congregation waits in the quire. Candles burn in their glass columns. Yes, the old familiar service, like sleep, always knits up the ravelled sleeve of care.

Marion the dean draws a deep breath and exhales. At last the employment tribunal is over. A whole year it's been hanging over her: endlessly deferred, adjourned, rescheduled. It has meandered through so many baroque twists that her clergy colleagues call it Jarndyce versus Jarndyce. Despite her best prayerful efforts it blighted Advent and Christmas for her. And today it ended. She's been fully vindicated in court. But already the next most menacing card has risen to the top of the deck: the cathedral budget deficit. Under that lies the south side restoration appeal, and the Choristers' School ... She shakes her head at herself. Sufficient unto this day is the tribunal thereof. The antiphon ends, the procession begins to move. She drops into place behind the head verger and brings up the rear. This is the kingdom: the first shall be last and the last first.

Over in the deanery Gene is putting out champagne flutes. There are six bottles of something rather special in the fridge, along with something *divine* from his favourite smokery. Sound the trumpet: John the Bastard has been vanquished! Marion will not crow; she is far too decent a human being. By tacit agreement she outsources her venom to Gene, who is more than happy with the arrangement. John the Bastard has wasted a year of Gene's life by proxy; so a select little surprise gathering of a celebratory nature has been convened. Mr Happy has undertaken to detain Marion with some interminable rant about the medieval library, while the others scurry on ahead to the deanery. Mary Poppins and Pollyanna have not been invited. Gene cannot abide the Hendersons. For Marion's sake he is prepared to be courteous. His courtesy does not, however, extend to wasting his 1996 Dom Ruinart Blanc de Blancs on Evangelicals.

'I took some flowers and a card round to Marion,' Susanna told Paul that evening. 'I hope that's all right.' It was unfair of Jane to describe Susanna as fretting like a busy bee. Susanna had a whole busy hive of bees fretting away. 'It's not too, too, oh, triumphalist, is it?'

'Of course it's not,' said Paul. 'We're all relieved for her. I'm glad the cathedral was so fully exonerated.' He did not add that he hoped he'd be as lucky when a serially litigious priest in the diocese finally got his day in court. Paul could do without being branded the Bullying Bishop of Lindchester, frankly. 'So how was your day?' (This, before Susanna's bees scented the pollen of dread and became agitated.)

It is not the business of this novel to intrude into clerical bedrooms and delineate marital relations; but I should probably mention that the Hendersons were tucked up in bed. It was gone ten, after all. Susanna told the bishop about her day. He listened to the sleepy murmur of the hive while he processed his own day's business and then moved on to speculate about England's chances against Scotland on Saturday. (Women are wrong when they say men can't multi-task.)

'Paul? Um—'

Um! The very word was like a bell, to toll him back from line-outs to his sole self!

'No. Absolutely not!' Then he smiled. 'I'm teasing. What is it? Go on, darling.'

'Well. Um—'

'Unless it's something about Freddie May, and can we let him stay a bit longer until he's got himself sorted out.'

'Well—'

'Look, I'm very happy to have a conversation about this, Susanna, but not now. I've had a long day, tomorrow's my day off, and I don't want to fall asleep thinking about work.'

'Sorry. Of course.' She kissed his forehead. The Hendersons had a pact not to talk about nasty worrying things after ten at night. Uneasy lies the head that wears the mitre.

I'm sorry to tell you that the bishop was woken at one in the morning by a group of revellers weaving home past the palace and caterwauling, 'It's a jolly holiday with Mary!' The poor man then lay awake for over an hour, wondering how the game of musical bishoprics – triggered by the empty chair at York – would play out. In the end, to put a stop to this vanity of vanities, he went downstairs to make a cup of tea.

We will leave him there in his dressing gown in the perfect kitchen: a mug of tea, a book of verses (Shakespeare's Sonnets – his New Year's resolution was to read more poetry). His Thou is not beside him singing in the wilderness, admittedly. But it is paradise enow. Life is good. He is thankful.

FEBRUARY

Chapter 7

Jane gets in from work and turns on her radio. Whoopee-doo. Access to an institution that has been oppressing women for centuries!

It's true: despite the leftie liberal blood pumping through her veins, Jane is thoroughly pissed off by the whole equal marriage thing. You may have spotted by now that she's a bit counter-suggestible? The hashtagification of the debate has pushed her 'don't fucking tell *me* what I've got to believe!' button. How many #equalmarriage campaigners does it take to change a light bulb? Homophobe! She contemplates ringing Dominic to share this thought. But then she chickens out. She doesn't feel up to being shouted at right now. And neither, when it comes down to it, does she want to be mean. Why rain on his parade? She has no theological axe to grind, after all; so surely she could find it in her heart to be glad the bill has made it through the Commons? She gets out her phone and sends him a nice text: 'Two bearded men snogging AT THE ALTAR! Yay!'

I should probably explain that this is an old joke. It dates back to the Federation of Theological Colleges Summer Ball of 1985, when Jenny 'That's Not Funny' Bannister – in a burgundy taffeta bridesmaid's dress – turned her shiny face to Jane in the marquee and shouted above the music, 'I really don't see why we should have to look at *that*!'

'At what?' Jane shouted back.

'Two bearded men snogging!'

Jane scanned the theological throng as it bopped, in a miasma of trampled grass and Opium, to 'You Can't Hurry Love'. Later it emerged that Dominic had been one of the bearded men; completely, *shamefully* pissed, and indulging in a bit of naughty Lightfoot Evangelical-baiting on the hallowed lawns of Latimer. A minute later she saw Paul Henderson leave the ball early, shepherding Susanna away from all that, face rigid with disgust. She never did admit to Dominic how shocked she was herself, even though she hadn't seen anything.

Her text prompts a phone call. Shall we be nosy and listen in? Go on then.

'*Oh!*' (shrieked the dowager) 'Two *bearded* men *snogging*! God, I haven't snogged a bearded man in *years*.'

'Sail on, Silver Boy!' yodelled Jane.

'My t-i-i-me will c-o-o-me toooo shiiiine!'

Jane held the phone away from her ear. 'I've got a confession: I never did tell you this, but I was actually a bit shocked.'

'I know you were, darling.'

'In fairness, it *was* pretty shocking back then.'

'Well, we've all come on a journey.'

'Yes, haven't we,' agreed Jane. 'I remember the days when marriage was a heterosexual construct that shouldn't be imposed on gay men, not a human right.'

Pause. 'And?'

Don't even *think* of parking here, read the sign. Jane wisely pulled away from the metaphorical kerb again, without enquiring what equality *she* had a right to, or observing that single people were being pushed even further to the margins. 'So. Are you free for a drink later? Or are you off celebrating with your fellow beardies?'

'I wish. PCC subcommittee, followed by funeral sermon. Friday?'

They fix a time and hang up. Dominic rubs his beard. Yes, he still wears a beard: a vestigial much-sculpted affair these days. To his horror the 1970s full beard is making a comeback. If he goes down that route now he'll look like a hobo! A homo hobo! People will start giving him their spare change in the street! No, he prefers to cut a suave Renaissance gentleman sort of dash. Funny old world. Here he is at fifty-three, chastely abiding by the current Statement of the House of Bishops. More by accident than design. Equal marriage? *Of course* equal marriage, you grumpy old hag! (Sometimes he hates Jane.) But not, in all probability, for him.

This is big news, as my reader is doubtless aware. Right now equal marriage is being discussed throughout the whole diocese of Lindchester, in homes and churches, in the street, in the pub.

Everyone has an opinion. Or at any rate, a gut reaction. How many Anglicans does it take to change a light bulb? Ah, if only it were that simple! What sort of bulb are you talking about? Furthermore, we need to discuss the whole concept of bulbhood – is it timeless, or can it be contextualized? Who decides, and on what basis? After decades of anguished debate the C of E is more or less OK with screw-in as well as bayonet fittings – for table lamps, that is. When it comes to overhead lights, bayonet remains less controversial; but so long as it's shining, most good-hearted folk won't insist on scrutinizing the packet it came in. In theory we can even use screw-in bulbs in chandeliers – provided the screw-in bulbs aren't ever actually screwed in. You're asking me how many Anglicans it takes to change a light bulb? Thousands. Hundreds and hundreds of thousands. Millions, maybe. And how long does it take? God only knows. In the meantime, it's night; and from the outside it seems for all the world as though the Church is dark and closed.

Come with me and we'll take a closer look. The recycling box outside the deanery is full of empty champagne bottles again. I believe there was another little celebration there yesterday. Discreet, in deference to the views held at the palace; but gleeful all the same. We will turn a blind eye and pop in on Miss Blatherwick instead. I wonder what she thinks about all this? This morning Miss Blatherwick is hanging up her bird feeder which she's just refilled with niger seed to attract the goldfinches. Unfortunately, in doing so she has also attracted Amadeus the cathedral cat. Bad puss! She claps her hands at him and shoos him away; but of course, Amadeus will just bide his time and slink back when she's not there. Nothing in this life is ever simple, that is what Miss Blatherwick thinks on the subject. One acts with the best of intentions, but there are always unforeseen repercussions. Casualties. Tears and regrets and recriminations. Doesn't she know it. However, Miss Blatherwick is of the firm opinion that this ought not to deter one from doing all the good one can. Careful on that stool, Miss Blatherwick: we need you! You're no use to the birds or anybody if you fall and break your neck!

In the perfect kitchen of the palace Susanna is baking again. The passing of this bill means that Paul is in for another round of flak. Later this morning he's giving his reactions on local radio. He will reiterate his support for the Statement of the House of Bishops, and then everyone will brand him a homophobe, just like they did poor old Michael Palgrove yesterday. Honestly! What do they expect him to say? What a way for him to start his new ministry as archbishop of Canterbury! She pauses her electric mixer – dear Lord, please be with Rosemary and the children in all this – then resumes beating the dough.

They are probably going to quiz her this afternoon at work, too. Susanna volunteers for a charity that supports young offenders on their release. This is how her path crossed with Freddie's and why she feels so responsible for the situation. (She has successfully lobbied for a three-month extension to his stay with them, by the way.)

'What do *you* think, Susanna?' they will ask in the office. What does Susanna think? She doesn't know, she just doesn't *know*! She doesn't want anyone to be hurt and left out, so her instinct is to support gay marriage. (*Equal* marriage, Susanna!) But then there's the Bible and the worldwide Anglican Communion to think about. Oh dear, oh dear! She tips three packets of chocolate chips into the mixture. As soon as they're baked she's going to take a plate of warm cookies through to the office to cheer everyone up. Susanna is not so naive as to think that home-baking has a genuine soteriological function. She knows she cannot solve the gay issue in the C of E with her triple choc chip cookies. But she can make the world a little bit nicer, a little bit kinder. And who are we to denigrate small acts of kindness? Those who perform them will surely not go without their reward.

A bit of kindness will not go amiss in the bishop's office this morning. The diocesan communications officer is busy briefing the bishop in his study. Penelope, the bishop's PA, is fielding emails. She now has a new and closely guarded password which Freddie does not know. Thinks Penelope.

The bishop's chaplain is at his desk scowling at some paperwork. The Revd Martin Rogers is in his mid-thirties and looks like an Action Priest™ fresh out of the box: buzz-cut hair, be-zipped and multi-pocketed navy blue trousers, all-terrain hybrid trainer-shoes and a navy blue fleece over his navy clerical shirt. Armed with Bible and Swiss army knife at all times, he looks poised to mountain bike over the peaks and take the gospel to Hull. He is not actually reading his paperwork through his flexible titanium-rimmed glasses, because that little *git* Freddie May is in the room.

The little git is waiting to drive the bishop to his radio interview. He lolls in a swivel chair, with last night still gleaming over him like a smutty halo. He yawns, stretches vastly, rumples his hair, sorts the nads out, checks his phone, smirks, swivels the chair back and forth. He looks as though he might slide off at any moment. His clothes look as though they might slide off at any moment. Skin-tight, or falling off: that would just about sum up the clothes of Freddie May. He starts humming 'I Believe in Miracles', and working his tongue stud into the gap between his front teeth. Martin can hear it.

'Would you *stop* doing that, Freddie?' says Penelope. 'You'll hurt yourself.'

Freddie rears up without warning: 'Maggie-eee Thatche-e-er! Po-o-ope Benedict! Uganda-a-a! Westboro fucking Baptist Church! Martin Rogers! Can you hear me? Your boys took one hell of a beating yesterday! Your boys took one hell of a—'

Martin snatches up the staple gun on his desk and fires off a volley of staples in Freddie's direction. They fall harmlessly onto the carpet. Martin goes back to his paperwork.

'Oooh!' Freddie pours himself out of his chair and slinks over to Martin's desk.

But here's Susanna with her plate of cookies, thank goodness. Martin will not get a tongue in his ear this morning. He will not be squeezed or tweaked or cupped. He's had to endure all these things over the past nine months. I don't want you to imagine that he makes a note of each separate incident. He is not logging a record for HR. There's no way he's going to make himself ridiculous by lodging a complaint about sexual harassment in the workplace. But that's what it is, though, isn't it? It's bullying. Martin is powerless to cope with it. Sometimes it reduces him to tears, almost. Aha, because he is seething with repressed homosexual lust! the reader concludes. Wrong: because it catapults him straight back to the misery of school – the other boys hiding his underpants after swimming, flicking him with towels in the changing room, humping him in the lunch queue, calling him a fag. I wish Martin could tell Freddie this. Freddie would be *distraught*. He would cry with remorse! He has no idea: he just plays with Martin the way Amadeus plays with a baby bird. Because he's bored and thoughtless and destructive.

I wavered there for a moment. It would be so easy for me to sit Martin and Freddie down and make them open their hearts to one another. I know this would head off a whole world of trouble later on in my tale. I'm like Susanna: I want to rustle up a batch of narrative cookies and make everything lovely for everyone. No. I must resist. Life is not a vicarage tea party. It's a pilgrimage up a steep and rugged pathway. There may be cookies along the way, but they are only food for the journey.

Chapter 8

Shrove Tuesday. Already the shock of the pope's resignation has receded. Across the diocese of Lindchester, clergy (or their spouses) are buying in eggs and flour and lemons for the parish pancake party. By now – unless they are very low church – they will have rounded up last year's palm crosses ready to burn for Ash Wednesday. Getting the proper consistency for liturgical ashing is not as easy as you might think. Dominic has been known to cheat and grind up charcoal in his pestle and mortar. This year he's going to follow a colleague's advice and microwave the palms first.

The colleague is Father Wendy. Yes, I know, but that's what they call her. She's given up trying to stop them. Mother Wendy would be worse – flying round in a nightie tending the Lost Boys! I think the Revd Wendy Styles will cheer you up, because like most parish priests, she's just faithfully getting on with it. Her patch is four small villages where Renfold straggles out into almost-countryside. These villages include Cardingforth, so technically Wendy is Jane's vicar. Wendy is how Jane might have ended up, had she pursued her theological training, got ordained, and been given a niceness implant.

Come, let us stretch those eagle wings and shake Lindchester out of our feathers. It's good to cleanse our palate with the sorbet of normality, after the rich fare of the Close. Follow the river out over mournful industrial estates and retail parks until we reach fields ashed with snow, a shriven landscape. Willows burn bronze and copper in the sunshine. We'll keep the Linden below us, ignoring the Cardingforth cooling towers as they plume out their cumulonimbus warnings. There, look: beyond the tin-roofed tyre place and the allotments, can you see a little square-towered church in a huddle of yews? That's All Saints, Carding-le-Willow.

Here comes Father Wendy, in floral wellies and a pink puffy gilet, her cheeks red, robes bag over her shoulder. She pauses to wait for Lulu, her chocolate Labrador, who is now a waddling arthritic. They pass under the lichgate, dedicated to the boys of the village who never came back from the war. Thomas, Walter, John, John, William. Seventeen of them. All the boys of Carding-le-Willow. 'Come along, old girl,' says Wendy. 'Good girl.' We'll follow them through the churchyard and go inside and wait for the midday Holy Communion to start. Lulu's claws click on the tiles. Breathe in the scent of lilies and old stone. Keep your coat on.

Wendy, as she stands behind the altar and looks out, knows she's in the right place. This is what she was made for. Behind her the low winter sunshine slants through the window. As the service progresses it angles slowly round her flock like a patient searchlight, illuminating each bowed head as it passes. All they need to do is sit there and they will be touched. That's all we have to do, thinks Wendy. Turn up, put ourselves in its path. Sometimes faith is that simple. What she can't know, of course, is that from where we are sitting, she is transfigured too. Her grey hair and oatmeal cassock alb are edged with glory; light streams from her upraised hands. Let all mortal flesh keep silence.

Afterwards Wendy boosts Lulu into the back seat then gets into her car. She's off to Cardingforth now – to Sunningdale Drive, funnily enough, though not to see Jane. She's calling on a pastoral case, at the request of the archdeacon. It is, as they say, complicated. A priest in the diocese has fallen in love – plunged disastrously through the floorboards of life and into love – with someone else's wife. The wife of the bishop's chaplain. Poor Martin, yes. It was a mutual falling. Becky Rogers moved out before Christmas, taking their two little girls. She rents a house on Sunningdale Drive, because she cannot, cannot be with Martin any more! The priest is still in his rectory; he has not moved in with them, may never do so. He too is married and has three teenage children. The situation is not good. Good may yet come out of it, but right now it's hell. Becky, when she opens the door, looks as though one of Emily Dickinson's imperial thunderbolts has scalped her naked soul.

We will not intrude. I will just tell you that all Wendy does today is listen. Lulu listens as well, and every time Becky cries – in fact, in the split second before she does – Lulu senses it, raises her old head and cries too, because she cannot bear the pain.

I'm afraid that won't have cheered you up as much as I'd hoped. We'd better head to Lindchester for a bit of light relief. We will fast-forward to evening, and gatecrash yet another party in the deanery.

Yay! The choristers were in the kitchen experimenting to see if pancakes will stick to the ceiling. Simmer down, simmer down! Sixteen prepubescent boys, all hyper, all with well-trained vocal cords, some painfully virtuosic in the whistle register. The approach to total meltdown was being accelerated by that catalyst of naughtiness, Freddie May. Marion had already been forced to confiscate the Jif lemons.

Gene glided suavely round the adults, like the serpent before he was condemned to go on his belly, taking the edge off things with a last-chance-before-Lent Pouilly-Fumé. Present in the kitchen were: Giles the precentor and his German wife Ulrika; Timothy, the director of music; Iona, the sub-organist with the dragon tattoo; the inevitable group of liggers (three lay vicars, four choral scholars); and Miss Blatherwick's successor, June, who right now could cheerfully have strangled Freddie for winding her charges up to fever pitch right before bed. Not present was the cathedral organist, Laurence, on the grounds that kitchens typically only have four corners, and there was no guaranteeing one would be available for him to hide in if he came tonight. He was practising alone in the dark cave of the cathedral instead.

'Mr May! Sir! Mr May!' piped the choristers (we like a spot of 1950s formality here in the Close). 'Mr May, will you do your thing for us?'

'Do my thing? You want me to do my thing?'

'*No!*' shouted Timothy, Giles and Ulrika together. (Ulrika is a singing coach.)

'Dudes, the grown-ups say no.'

'Oh, ple-e-ease, Mr May!'

So Mr May took a deep breath – the adults clapped hands to ears – and gradually a noise emerged from his mouth. Oh, horrible! What on earth? A human didgeridoo, a concrete mixer full of lost souls!

Let me explain. In his schooldays, Freddie – beguiling the hours spent in corridors after being ejected from lessons – somehow taught himself to split his voice in the manner of a Tibetan Buddhist monk. Don't ask me how – vocal resonators? Harmonics? Ulrika could probably explain. Anyway, this transgressive noise thrills the choristers to their core and they are always begging for another demonstration.

'Stop it, Freddie!' ordered Ulrika. 'Boys, *don't* try to copy him! THOMAS GREATRIX!'

Thomas froze. Head chorister. Ought to know better. Tomorrow at evensong he was due to sing that soaring treble line in Allegri's *Miserere*. Silence. No boy moved a muscle as the juggernaut of Mrs Littlechild's wrath swept past them, stirring their hair.

'FREDERICK MAY' (beautifully, from the diaphragm), 'I'll deal with you later!'

A grown-up! Being shouted at! The choristers quivered in terror and glee.

'So yeah, don't ever do that?' agreed Freddie. 'It like totally trashes your voice?' He shone his radiant 'if I only had a brain' smile in Ulrika's direction. If she'd been standing any closer, I believe she might have cracked him round the head with her fearsome assortment of dress rings.

'Well! Who'd like the last pancake?' said the dean, as the lay clerks smirked into their Pouilly-Fumé.

Allegri's *Miserere*! Music so beautiful that once upon a time the pope kept it to himself, fencing its secret about with threats of excommunication. For over a century it was performed only in the Sistine Chapel, on the Wednesday and Friday of Holy Week. Then one year the fourteen-year-old Mozart heard it, wrote it down from memory and debased its spiritual currency for ever. Ah, if only we could hear it again for the very first time! Even now, domesticated though it is by overuse, it makes the hair on the back of the neck stir when you hear it echo round a medieval cathedral.

Later, as he walks back to the palace, Freddie hums that treble line. It's a ghost of his performance eleven years ago, when he stood where Thomas Greatrix will stand tomorrow, way up in the triforium looking down the nave of Lindchester Cathedral. Totally nailing those high Cs. *Et a peccato meo munda me*. Cleanse me, cleanse me from my sin. He will never sing like that again. He knows he will never outdo his eleven-year-old self.

You may be wondering why he believes this. Ulrika, driven to distraction, took Freddie by the shoulders tonight and tried to shake some sense into him: 'Idiot! Why do you waste this incredible talent?' But he just gave her another vacuous stoner smile. Nobody has any idea that when Freddie was fifteen, someone very important whispered in his ear – like a wicked fairy godmother leaning over a cradle at a christening – that while his adult voice was pleasant, it was nothing special. Warned him, kindly, that he would probably never equal, let alone surpass, his early achievements. Freddie internalized that prophecy and then blanked out the incident because it hurt too much. This why he believes that there's no real point either hoping or trying.

Smoke alarms go off in vicarages across the diocese. Dominic shrieks as he nearly takes his eyebrows off. In the cathedral vestry the vergers are doing it properly. They are old hands at this, with their big stainless steel bowl and blowtorch. It is, perhaps, Gavin's favourite moment of the church year, if you don't count the Easter fire. (How lovely that there should be a niche for the high-functioning pyromaniac in our cathedrals.)

So Lent begins. No flowers or alleluias till Easter. By some piece of bungling mismanagement, Valentine's Day falls on the second day of the fasting season. Who's going to eat all those heart-shaped chocolates and drink the pink cava now? – the giving up of booze and confectionery being, of course, the traditional way of keeping Lent these days; a kick-starting of those stalled New Year's resolutions in the spiritual spa. Evangelicals, for whom Lenten discipline still smacks faintly of popery, prefer to *take something up* for Lent. More Bible and prayer, usually, or a worthy Christian paperback of some kind.

Ironically, this is what Dominic will be doing. He will be reading the bishop's Lent book! He wanted the book to be crass so he could despise it with a clear conscience, but no such luck. It's actually rather good, despite being written by an Evangelical and recommended by Paul Henderson. Dammit. Unlike his happy-clappy brethren (who seem to natter with the Lord all day long), Dominic seldom thinks he's heard God address him directly in actual words. He could count those occasions on the fingers of one hand. All the same, last Sunday – as he leafed snippily through *The Desires of the Heart* – he very nearly heard a voice say: Get over yourself, queen.

The words come back to him during the imposition of ashes. 'Remember you are dust and to dust you shall return,' he says to each person as he marks them with the cross. 'Turn away from sin and be faithful to Christ.' On his own forehead he can still feel the cold smears of ash. Remember you are dust. Get over yourself. Remember.

Jane has neither given nor taken up anything for Lent. Yeah, like the knowledge we are dust is ever far from her thoughts! On Thursday morning Danny Skypes. Danny's father wanders past in the background. 'Hey, babe. Happy Valentine's Day.' He blows her a kiss and ambles out of the screen. Jane drives to Poundstretcher University. It could have been different. She could have dropped everything nineteen years ago. Gone to New Zealand.

Oh well.

She parks and gets out. Another grey day. Someone has lost a balloon. Jane watches as the red foil heart sails off over Lindford. Smaller, smaller. Gone.

Chapter 9

Monday. Jane wakes. 8.20 a.m. and Sunningdale Drive is spookily quiet. No cars. No oafs surging past in a fug of Lynx and hormones. No screams or 'omigod!'s. Unless the Rapture has occurred and Jane's been left behind, it's half term. At Linden University, half term is called Blended Learning Week. Because it is a week for blended learning, that's why. Not because Poundstretcher has totally given up on expecting seven days of reading from their students. It's a week without teaching, at any rate. There's a peer appraisal day on Thursday, but unfortunately, Jane has a migraine then.

She should get up. Her 'To Do' list hasn't changed since she finally forced herself to shovel handfuls of paperwork into a big envelope for her accountant, so she could cross off 'Tax'. Which means the rest of the list has started to accuse her. Bloody car needs servicing. Dentist check-up long overdue.

Interesting: the thought of visiting the dentist appears to be the only thing capable of generating an urge to tackle Danny's room. It's been untouched since he left, and is acquiring a Miss Havisham aspect – had Miss Havisham been a stinky great crap-eating rugby slob. Half the crockery in the house is probably lurking in there somewhere, under rancid duvet covers, pizza boxes and busted lever-arch files spewing semi-literate A-level work. There's still a note from last July stuck to his door: TIDY YOUR ROOM, PIG! Underneath, in tiny, tiny letters, the reply: *You do it, bitch!*

Ah, dammit, now she's crying again. Jane gets up and stomps to the shower. Danny's so like his father. What was she nineteen years ago? Apart from an idiot, obviously. Just an incubator for a blunderbuss-load of mongrel genes, that's what. Scots, Irish, Spanish, Maori, Samoan? God knows what's there in the Mickey mix, but he discharged it with a will, ba-boom, and now there's Danny, apparently undiluted by Rossiter DNA.

The hot water widdles down onto her head. Why is her shower so crap? Why is her life so crap? And how come her boy has turned out to be one giant lump of contentment? A seal basking on a rock. He simply lets the waves of maternal stroppiness wash over him, then says, 'Yeah, so anyway, Mum, can I have five quid for the train?' Big grin? Please?

She gets out and dries herself, towels her hair, blots her tears. The mirror is not her friend. God, look at yourself. Make an appointment, Badger-Woman! Alternatively, she could hack it all off with a Stanley knife. Maybe she'll look like Anne Hathaway in *Les Mis*. Only grey. *Les Gris*. She gets dressed and goes downstairs to make coffee.

It's quiet in Lindchester too. The Close is not clogged with the black four-by-fours of yummy mummies dropping off Jack and Daisy. There is no choral evensong this week, it's evensaid. The Mass setting yesterday (Byrd, for Four Voices) was sung exquisitely by an ad hoc quartet, including Freddie May; now why can't he always be like that?

A taxi pulls up outside the precentor's house. The front door opens. Out come Giles and Ulrika; Ulrika, glorious in ankle-length fake fur and Valkyric jewellery. Both of them put a little suitcase in the taxi boot. The suitcases are so very little they *must* comply with the hand luggage restrictions, surely, unless Giles has cocked it up. If he has, oh Lord! His life won't be worth living. He pats himself down. Online check-in, tickets printed on the back of a recycled music list. Passport. Wallet. Phone. He returns to the house for a last scan round.

'Oh, for God's sake, Giles, come on!'

They are off to Germany on a recce for this summer's choir tour. They will also visit the in-laws, but that is not why Ulrika is accompanying him. She's there to keep Giles on the straight and narrow, because once, many years ago when he was but a callow young man on a similar recce, Giles very nearly disgraced himself. There was a hotel. A massage. I would love to tell you more, but I'm not supposed to know about this. Anyhow, by sheer incompetence, he remained faithful to Ulli. (Giles is pretty useless at being wicked. There was also that time when he went out to buy cannabis and came back with the most expensive Oxo cube in London.) Ulli is entirely safe, but twenty-five years on she still does not trust him in hotels on his own. When he confessed his almost-infidelity, she chased him through the parish with her Swabian spätzle-maker, a fearsome piece of culinary hardware like a large potato ricer.

I should not have told you any of that.

'Bye, boys!' calls Giles. There's no answer. Their sons are fifteen and seventeen. Of course they aren't awake at 8.30 a.m. (Ulrika's instructions are stuck to the fridge: *Do your homework. Don't live off junk. Put the brown bin out. No parties. DON'T smoke weed on the palace roof with Freddie May.*) Tickets-passport-wallet-phone. Giles pulls the front door to. He goes and folds himself into the back of the taxi. Ulrika, all fur and Fracas. Five days. He smiles.

Mr Happy, the canon chancellor, is in residence this week. This means that he leads Morning and Evening Prayer, and is custodian of the residency mobile phone, which the vergers ring when there's a crank in the cathedral demanding to see a priest. To be 'canon in residence' these days means, essentially, to be on the duty rota. Victorian canons had to interrupt their butterfly hunting in Italy to come back and be in residence for a few months each year, while in the glory days of sinecures, the canon chancellor of Lindchester was probably simultaneously dean of Ely and bishop of Ravenna, and could scarcely be expected to locate Lindchester on a map, let alone reside here. Today, even when not in residence, the canons residentiary reside permanently on the Close in their gorgeous National Trust-style properties, but without the private income or the staff to make that any kind of fun. Especially in the winter.

Mr Happy emerges from the cathedral. Morning Prayer has finished and he's heading back to his house, via the builders' skip outside the school, to see if there's any firewood in it. He meets the canon treasurer coming the other way, carrying a pallet.

'Bastard!' says the chancellor.

'Excuse *me*, father,' replies the treasurer. 'But you had the cathedral Christmas tree.'

'Yes, but it hasn't fucking dried out yet, father, has it? Fucking thing won't burn properly.'

The treasurer perceives that this is not about firewood, it's about lack of sleep, and recalcitrant volunteers sending snotty emails saying they are 'saddened and disappointed', about how the hell that book was ever going to get written, and whether coming to Lindchester from Oxford last summer was a ghastly mistake.

'You're right,' says the treasurer. 'That's fucking terrible. Have my pallet.' He carries it to the chancellor's house for him. 'Look, Mark, I'm around this week – want me to cover your residency for a couple of days, so you and Miriam and the babe can get away? Have a think, let me know.'

Sudden tears threaten. 'Thanks.'

The treasurer props the pallet against the gate and dusts his hands. 'I'd offer to lend you my chainsaw, but I'm scared you'll run amok. Not that you could run far, come to think of it: it's electric.'

'I can always borrow an extension lead,' says the chancellor.

The Revd Canon Philip Voysey-Scott walks to his house, singing a hymn in a warbling nasal tenor. 'When the woes of life o'ertake me, hopes deceive and fears annoy.' (His Giles Littlechild impersonation.) He's remembering when the sprogs were tiny. They have four. Admittedly, he and Pippa (yes, they really are Philip and Philippa, I'm afraid) had a string of nannies and au pairs, but all the same, it could all get pretty torrid. Each individual day seeming never-ending, but the months – and then the years – zooming past. Can't quite believe he's been here for four years now. Four years! Not the new boy any more. He lets fly his trademark laugh, the single bark guffaw: Hah! Pigeons scatter.

Given the state of the cathedral's budget and the number of listed buildings round the Close he's responsible for – to say nothing of the crumbling gothic sandcastle that is Lindchester Cathedral – a lot of people think Philip has no right to be this cheerful. His predecessor was a right Eeyore. But Philip was a 1980s red-braces yuppie – so maybe cathedral finances are a bit of a breeze after the trading floor? Or maybe his faith sustains him: he knows that here we have no abiding city. Whatever the reason, the microclimate of the Close has been sunnier since he arrived. He's frictionless. Other people's angst and hostility gain no purchase on his soul. May the Church be granted more like Philip Voysey-Scott. He lets himself into the chapter office. A warble trails after him: 'Lo! it glows with peace and joy.'

Half term goes by. The days are stealthily lengthening. Daffodils are up and poised to bloom in clusters on the cathedral lawns. At night half a moon sails above the spire. The cathedral clock chimes midnight, and up on the palace roof Lukas and Felix Littlechild smoke weed with Freddie May.

Like the bishop, we will pretend we know nothing about this, and instead fly off across the city towards Renfold, and call in on Father Dominic. It's rather late, but he's still up, I think. The lights are on in the vicarage. And there's Dominic on his drive. Oh dear. A patrol car. Dominic is waving his arms and shouting at two police officers.

Right. Let's do a tactful lap of the parish until they've got this sorted out. Along Church Street, quickly, towards Prince Albert Park, which we last saw clad in the wonder of freshly fallen snow. Below us now lies the lake with sleeping swans, white on black. Grey moonlit paths wind through formal gardens. A little bandstand. Vast poplars sigh. Children's play area. A car park, where cars jiggle and we will not linger. Let's wheel round, following the long curve of Renfold High Street, with its boring little crescent of shops, and then back to St John's Church.

The patrol car pulls away. Dominic goes back into the vicarage, straight to the kitchen and pours himself a whisky. It's Lent, but fuck it. His hand shakes with rage. If he were a medieval bishop, he would anathematize them all. He would curse their going out and their coming in, their downsitting and their uprising. Their eyes, their noses, their teeth, the legs they ran away on. He would smite their geese and their swine and all their cattle.

What can it be that has reduced our poor friend to this state? That's right: lead thieves. Tonight he interrupted them in their evil trade (curse them cock and balls!). He managed to get a photo of the truck they fled in, which PC Plod has failed to act upon, because the number plate is illegible. Hence the shouting and arm-waving earlier. The lead was only replaced a month ago. The arseholes just wait, then they come back for the new lot! The insurance premiums are now – ha ha – through the roof. But the little shits left their ladder this time. Dominic is going to chop it up to smithereens and burn it on his Easter fire.

He takes a deep breath, and pours another slosh of whisky. He looks at his watch. He'd sound off to Jane, only he knows that if he rings at this hour, she'll only freak out, think something's happened to Danny.

At the precise moment he is thinking this, Jane's mobile rings. She lurches awake. Snatches the phone. Sees it's Mickey. Oh, God. Something's happened!

'Yes?'

'Jane, it's me, Mickey, eh. Listen. I'm really sorry. It's Danny.'

Chapter 10

Danny's dead. Jane is at his funeral. They bring in the coffin. All this takes place in the nanosecond before Mickey (who'd forgotten the time difference) adds, 'He's fine.'

He's fine. Oh, dear God.

Actually, Danny is not really fine, but a busted collar bone will mend. Come off a quad bike, that's all. Was he wearing a helmet at the time? Yeah, course he was, no worries.

'You are so full of shit, Mickey Martin! You just make him wear a helmet from now on, you hear me? You go out and *buy* him a helmet, or I will fucking get on a plane and come and tear you limb from limb!' And more of the same, until finally all pride crumples and she's sobbing, 'He's my boy, Mickey, he's all I've got!'

'Yeah, I know, babe. Sorry I scared you. He's my boy too, eh. He's a great kid, you've done a great job. I'm proud of you.'

'I don't need you to be proud of me. I need you to buy him a fucking helmet!'

'I'm on it.'

'And make him wear it.'

'You bet. Want me to make him wear a frenchie too? For his mum's sake?'

'Piss off.' Like I've forgotten your track record with condoms, Mickey Martin. 'And another time, what's the first thing you say? You say "Danny's fine". That's the first thing you say when you ring at one in the morning!'

'Got that.'

'Don't humour me. I'm still mad.'

'Aw. Be nice. Danny's fine.'

By Wednesday Jane has more or less stopped jumping each time her phone rings. Danny has Skyped her most days. Wearing a motorbike helmet. Mickey has dug one out from somewhere. This is clearly going to be a running gag.

She's out for a jog now, a brief lollop along the Linden before she heads to Poundstretcher where non-blended learning has resumed. *Mummy's doing her best! Mummy's doing her best!* The words keep going round her head. 'I hate you, Mummy, I want Daddy!' Charming. Jane just heard some little madam scream that on Sunningdale Drive. They'd moved in right before Christmas; mum and two little girls, refugees from a marriage that had just imploded, Jane was guessing. And that's what the poor woman had just shouted on the drive: 'Mummy's doing her best!' The timeless maternal *cri de coeur*. Neanderthal women probably shouted it.

Catkins! And the first clump of primroses in the hedge, nearly out. Soon there will be baby lambs in the fields. It will be all right, Jane. Your boy is fine. You have done your best.

I expect you've worked out that the poor mummy doing her best is Becky Rogers, wife of Martin, the bishop's chaplain. The two girls spent half term with their dad, who took them to stay with Granny and Grandpa by the seaside. They've been having all kinds of treats. Of course they prefer Daddy! Mummy has turned into a wicked shouting witch.

The little girls are six and eight. They know it's their fault for being naughty. That's why Mummy and Daddy have split up. So they try harder. They try to be so bad that they are really, really shouted at. Then they can sob and sob and say sorry and then they'll be forgiven and cuddled, and at last everything will be all right again. That's why they say and do the worst things they can think of. The little one wets her bed and cuts Barbie's hair off. The older one says, 'I hate you, I hate you, I hate you.'

Becky is at her wits' end. She must learn not to think about him, must close the door on the thought of him, over and over. Because he's not coming to her; he's staying with his wife. He has chosen the better part, like Mary. He has chosen to sit at the Lord's feet and listen to him. To be faithful. And here's Becky, like Martha, at her wits' end with nobody to help her. She should go back to her husband. For her daughters' sake. But that Dickinsonian lightning bolt has reconfigured her brain and she can't bear Martin. She's allergic to him. To his presence in the room, and his bitten nails. To his rearranging of her recycling. She hates his voice, his skin, his letter knife, his shoes, his logic, the trousers that cling to him, the hair on the back of his fingers, his Swiss Army knife, his Swiss Railway watch, his being the wronged one.

If she had to share a bed with him again she'd probably go into anaphylactic shock.

Father Wendy calls and Becky tells her some of this. 'I know I shouldn't feel these things,' she weeps.

'Why shouldn't you?' asks Wendy.

This Sunday is the Third Sunday in Lent. How is everyone doing? Some of those who have given up alcohol have discovered that they took up grumpiness at the same time. Father Dominic is one of these. It is Saturday night and he's just looked in his diary at the week ahead and shouted, 'Oh, *God*!' and kicked his filing cabinet.

He'd completely forgotten that this Thursday he is due at the palace for an informal fork supper with the Hendersons. What possessed him to accept? He knows it will be dire. Nobody likes these get-togethers. Probably not even Susanna Henderson, with her signature chicken and broccoli bake. Paul should just divvy up his entertainment budget and send his clergy an M&S voucher each. And because it's Lent, Dominic can't even anaesthetize himself with alcohol. This is all the Hendersons' wine has to commend it: its concussive properties. Marginally nicer than a blow to the head with a pulpit Bible. Informal fork supper! God! He gives the cabinet another kick. Who else was going to be there? Clergy and spouses. Clergy spice (how droll!). Maybe he should swing by Lindford Common on the way there and pick up the most disgraceful little tramp he could find. Bishop, I'd like you to meet my friend. My *spice*.

You will notice that in all this ranting, the thought of simply not going hasn't crossed Dominic's mind. This is because he is basically a good egg. He's a turner-upper. If Dominic promises to do something, he does not consider he has the option of not doing it, simply because he doesn't feel like it. He will go. He will take Susanna a nice bunch of flowers and be the life and soul of the party. By the end of the evening he will have identified the naughtiest clergy wife and they will retire to a corner and be as outrageous as it is possible to be in an Evangelical palace with no wine.

Tonight the Close is busy. You can hear the clopping of court shoes on the cobbles as smartly dressed middle-aged, middle-class white people flock to the cathedral. They are here to attend a performance of Bach's *St Matthew Passion*, performed by the Lindchester Cathedral Community Choir. The Community Choir comprises about ninety keen amateurs who can hold a tune and read music. Or at any rate, can follow the contours of the musical landscape with a finger, provided they are standing next to someone confident. The proper placing of individual choir members falls to the conductor, Timothy. If you, Brenda, could stand next to Emma on the third row. And Roger, if you could go and stand in Lindford, or better still, Birmingham.

So far you have only glimpsed Timothy Gladwin (the cathedral director of music) in the distance. I will now introduce him properly. He has not been in post very long, a mere four years. He took over from an illustrious predecessor. The illustrious predecessor was in post for twenty-one years, and still bobs up from time to time like Banquo's ghost. The Illustrious One is Gregory Laird – I'm sorry, *Sir* Gregory Laird – who, as you probably know, set up the North-West Three Choirs Festival (Chester, Lindchester and Lichfield). Laird is that much-loved thing in church and Oxbridge circles: a character. He still haunts Lindchester Cathedral Close in his swirling cape and broad-brimmed fedora, booming fruitily through his Pavarotti beard like an RSC *ac-torrr*, either because he is actually making one of his visits, or more often because the canon treasurer is impersonating him. Laird was an old-style cathedral organist and master of choristers. When the music department was restructured on his retirement and Timothy took over, the choristers scented a weakness and ran him ragged. But Timothy's in control now, ruling with kindness rather than whimsical tyranny.

There, you see? I've done it myself: I've talked more about Gregory Laird than poor old Timothy. Briefly, then: Timothy is almost as tall and thin as Giles Littlechild. He is thirty-nine, and has short red hair that curls when it gets damp. It will curl tonight. Conducting is warm work, but he has a white silk handkerchief with musical staves printed on which he will use.

Let's sneak into the cathedral now and see what's going on. You'll see at once that it's packed. The front row is reserved for the chain gang (the civic bigwigs, Mayor This, Lady Mayoress That), the Lord Lieutenant, the high sheriff, the chapter clergy and spouses – spice! how droll! – and the bishop and his wife. They are seated right in front of the stage block where the row of soloists' chairs is waiting, empty. They are close enough to be spat on, close enough to see the tonsillectomy scars. Some of the gentlemen have consulted their programme, and are rather looking forward to glimpsing the lissom and glamorous soprano. This is because, in their innocence, they are unaware of the convention that soloists' publicity photos are always fifteen years out of date.

Here come the orchestra. The cathedral organist, Laurence, is playing continuo on the chamber organ. Tuning-up commences. Mr Happy, the canon chancellor, comes in apologizing. He takes his place on the front row, where he will sit reading a theological journal throughout, hiding it inside his programme. If we glance up we will see the ripieno choir of choristers already stationed high in the triforium. And now the Community Choir file in, dressed in black. Tenors and basses, first sopranos, second sopranos, altos, each to their allotted seat in the raked rows that the vergers have erected. A lot of extra work for the vergers, these concerts. Let's hope the dean remembers to thank them when she comes to the microphone to welcome the audience, and apologize that the nearest loos are approximately a hundred miles away. Yes, she remembers. Well done, Marion.

When the dean is seated, the principal first violinist enters. Applause. Then the soloists are applauded on to their stage block. The gentlemen check their programme in surprise. Swizz!

There's Freddie May. He's been selling programmes. Timothy begged him – *begged* him! – to sing tonight, because they are woefully short of decent tenors. But Freddie suffers from perfect pitch, and sorry, dude, he'd rather piss on an electric fence than stand within ten feet of Roger. Freddie is lounging against a pillar where he can command a good view of the hot principal first violinist. He looks like Amadeus the cat contemplating goldfinches.

The bishop on the front row commands a good view of Freddie May. He looks like Miss Blatherwick when she spots Amadeus loitering by her birdfeeder.

Another burst of applause propels Timothy up the clanking steps on to his podium. Look, his socks have musical staves on, too! He bows to the audience with a shy smile. Then turns. He gestures the choir to its feet. Light spangles off many a sequinned bosom. Timothy raises his baton. The two buttons on the back of his tailcoat glint.

Silence settles. The silence of eight hundred souls. It has a velvety texture, night-time in a giant roost, tiny shiftings, folding of wings. There will be another silence later tonight, a moment of cosmic desolation. It will come after the Evangelist sings the words, 'But Jesus, having cried again aloud, yielded up the ghost.'

But for now, the passion lies in the future, and the silence is charged with expectation.

MARCH

Chapter 11

The Supreme Governor of the Church of England is taken into hospital. Does the Most Revd Dr Michael Palgrove quake? Is he wondering whether his first major state occasion as archbishop of Canterbury will be the Queen's funeral? We will not presume to guess. But happily for us all, Her Majesty recovers. Meanwhile, the cardinals gather in Rome to select a new pope. The conclave will take place behind closed doors in the Sistine Chapel, as it has done for centuries. By contrast, the process for choosing a new archbishop of Canterbury is – shall we say – still evolving. It lurches from transparency on the one hand (nominations are welcomed, bishops are invited to toss their mitre into the ring, the names of those on the selection panel are published), to paranoid cloak-and-dagger secrecy on the other (dark-windowed taxis whisking candidates to undisclosed destinations); before finally being announced on Twitter. The C of E: a work in progress. As are we all, as are we all.

This week marks the midpoint of Lent. The Sunday coming is variously called Laetare Sunday, Refreshment Sunday or Rose Sunday. If you are spiky high, you may wear pink vestments to celebrate the Mass. For the more ordinary Anglican, this is the moment when Lenten discipline is relaxed somewhat. A glass of wine with lunch, perhaps. But for the general population next Sunday is simply Mothers' Day. Or Mother's Day? Oh dear. Where should that apostrophe go? Purists brush this dilemma testily aside because it's *Mothering Sunday*. They would no more say Mother's Day than they would split an infinitive or drop litter. Such people make up ninety-eight per cent of the population of the UK's Cathedral Closes.

Lindchester Cathedral's flower guild is all set. The daffodils have been ordered, and will be made up into hundreds of little bunches for distribution – a welcome burst of industry in the floristry lay-off of Lent. Across the diocese similar posy-making arrangements are in place. In one of Father Wendy's villages they will be giving out heart-shaped gingerbread cookies as well. The local Fair Trade café has volunteered to bake them. Isn't that a lovely idea? It will be controversial, though. Some members of the congregation will shake their heads and say, 'We've never done that before, father.' But if Wendy grits her teeth and weathers the storm for three more years, gingerbread hearts will become traditional, and the same people will say, 'We've always had gingerbread hearts, father.' Bless them.

Wendy is out walking Lulu on the banks of the Linden. They don't go far these days, just to the first bench, where they have a little sit down before plodding home. One of these morning walks will be their last. Not quite yet, but soon. Wendy is feeling a bit weepy today. Mothering Sunday is always hard. She has two sons who will remember to send a card and ring for a chat. She has a ten-month-old granddaughter, Poppy, who will come to the phone and gurgle to Granny. But there will always be a Laura-shaped hole. Wendy will never be mother-of-the-bride, never see Doug walk their daughter down the aisle, never hear her daughter's daughter gurgle on the phone.

Here's the bench. Lulu lowers herself down with a sigh. Wendy sits and watches the Linden. Oh, how full the churches will be of absent children on Sunday. The ones who have died, the ones who never managed to be born, the far away, the out of touch. And absent mothers, too. The ones now over on the far shore, the ones who failed, who abandoned and ran. Wind hisses in the old bulrushes. Thirteen years since the police arrived on Wendy's doorstep. Will it never pass? Lulu raises her poor old head and cries.

On the opposite bank a woman jogs slowly by. Wendy knows who she is, knows that her son has gone off to New Zealand. Be with her, dear Lord, comfort her. She watches until Jane is out of sight.

But it's cold for sitting. 'Come on, old girl. Up you get.' Lulu hauls herself to her feet, and they set off back the way they came. 'Well done. Home we go. Good girl. Not long now. Not long now.'

Mothering Sunday costs the dean a pang, too. Marion has no children of her own. Last year after the Eucharist she looked out over the congregation and thought: your mum died last week; and your mother is wandering in the wastes of dementia; and you, and you, have lost babies; your son is in prison; your daughter is anorexic; you are unhappily single; you are dealing with infertility. And there's my Gene, whose first wife died, leaving him to mother three little boys as best he could. You should all be given daffodils today.

That's why this year is going to be different. Everyone will be able to collect a posy when they come up for communion, for whatever private reason they might have.

'Ooh, you'll get pissy emails!' Gene says. '"I was saddened and disappointed to learn of the totally unnecessary changes you have seen fit to make to the daffodil distribution."'

Marion tries to look stern.

'"I always say, if it's not broke, don't fix it. Yours, more in sorrow than in anger."'

'Well, it is broke,' replies Marion. 'And I'm fixing it.'

'Shall I compose your reply? "I am The Dean, so swivel on it, little people."'

'You're a bad man.'

He smiles. 'That's how you like me.'

They have been married for twelve years now, and Marion still needs reminding that Gene doesn't care if he makes enemies. Genuinely does not care. He makes them by accident, he makes them on purpose. It's rather exhilarating.

Freddie is washing Miss Blatherwick's car for her when he remembers.

Gah! Mothers' Day. Fuck. He's missed the last posting date. He'll have to email, and he's still not replied to her last email inviting him for Easter, offering to buy his ticket. Shit. Two weeks on the ranch? Of course he'd love to go! But his passport needs renewing and he's left it too late probably. Plus there's his record: I mean, does it impact on the Argentine visa situation?

His hands are shaking now as he wrings out the chamois.

Yeah, she'd pay the passport fee too, but that would mean admitting he's got no money. None. He gets paid whenever he deps for one of the tenor lay clerks, he gets board-and-lodging and pocket money from the Hendersons, who think his dad pays something into his account each month, which is kind of not true, he just cleared his credit cards that time. Man, he hates asking Dad for help? He's twenty-two, he can't keep leeching off people the whole time. He should get a part-time job, except they'd be all, 'Any criminal convictions? Ri-i-ight, we'll get back to you.'

That's the car done. He stands back, checks himself out in the driver's window. Hey. Looking hench.

Don't think it.

But he's thought it. He's thought, aw c'mon, it's like busking, no? Like getting paid for your hobby? Just to tide you over, for the passport? No. *No!* He is *so* not getting into all that again. Plus Paul would go mental if he found out. Literally? Freddie's not forgotten the Lindford Common thing, when he hadn't even done anything, it's just the police insisted on following him back to check his story? He hates when Paul's mad at him.

Freddie, Freddie, Freddie. What *are* we going to do with you? I'm so glad you have Miss Blatherwick in your life. When you've finished polishing her car, she's going to feed you homemade cake, quash your protests and pay you £20. Then she's going to get out her *Church Times* and sit you down till she's satisfied that you've looked directly at the choral scholar and lay clerk ads she's circled, and made a sensible decision about whether to apply for anything. You will probably cry and feel horrible, but never mind. Miss Blatherwick loves you. She has a long memory. She remembers how acrimoniously your parents fought over you when they split up, and how neither of them ever bothered to pay you any real attention.

It's Thursday evening. The palace smells of good things. Susanna was up at the crack of dawn making chicken and broccoli bake for thirty (aubergine for the vegetarians), before setting off for work. Choice of puddings: apple crumble, chocolate truffle torte (Delia's recipe) and fruit salad. Oh dear, were there any vegans? Coeliac sufferers? People with lactose intolerance, nut allergies? Paul's PA has enquired of all the guests, but still Susanna frets. The chicken was cooked right through, wasn't it? Yes, of course it was. She has never yet given her guests salmonella, she's just being silly. When she gets in from work, will there be enough time to get changed, pop things in the oven, set the chairs out, glasses, forks, napkins? Fret, fret, fret. The anxious hive is a-hum all day long.

She's back now. Everything's under control, naturally. She bustles happily. Freddie slinks into the kitchen, purrs his way round her – ooh, she looks stunning, anything he can do to help? – and filches some garlic bread.

'Oh, that's very sweet of you. Are you sure?' (head tilt) 'Well, maybe you could look after the drinks?'

Paul has just come in, and hears this. Oh dear, is that all right? He's frowning.

Freddie sucks the grease off his thumb and gives the bishop a big slutty smile. 'Hey. Promise I won't get shit-faced.'

'Much appreciated, Frederick. I thought I'd given you the evening off.'

'Oh, but darling,' says Susanna, 'he's just offered to help me!'

Paul is outmanoeuvred. 'Fine. Could you change into something smarter, please.'

Freddie spreads his hands, all innocence. His pink T-shirt says *What Wouldn't Jesus Do?*

Father Dominic is late, but he's on his way. On the passenger's seat is a lovely bunch of blue hyacinths for Susanna. Remembering his Lenten discipline, Dominic has got over himself. Paul is, after all, his father in God, and however tedious the evening proves to be, crucifixion was doubtless more tedious still.

Aha! You see what I am about? You think I'm steering Dominic in the direction of Freddie May? Well, let me tell you that Dominic has more sense than to allow some pretty boy to wander into his life, wipe his feet on his heart, and wander out again. I'm almost certain about that. We'll follow him in to the palace and see what happens, shall we?

The big drawing room was full when Dominic arrived. He smiled, shook hands, and air-kissed his way round the throng. 'Meet my wife.' 'Hi!' 'Have you met my husband?' 'Hi!' It was all sugar and *spice* and all things nice. Lord, how he needed a drink. But no. Forty days and forty nights. Mingle, mingle. Lovely, lovely. He headed to the drinks table, resolute.

Oh. My. *God!* 'Um. Hello!'

The vision smiled at him. 'Hey. What can I get you?'

'Something soft?' Argh. The conversation was being dubbed into innuendo. 'Ha ha! Yes, well, this looks like elderflower.'

'Seriously? Du-u-ude, I can totally get something hard for you?' Sly flash of tongue stud.

'What, supermarket Shiraz?' (You little tramp!) 'I think not.'

Mercifully, Susanna appeared and asked Freddie to help carry things through to the dining room.

Dominic watched him go. My. Oh. My.

Then he recollected himself and (tempted and yet undefiled), picked up a glass of sparkling elderflower. When he turned the bishop was at his elbow.

'I'm very much appreciating your recommended Lent book, father.'

There. See? We will leave them now to their chicken and broccoli bake. But the bishop is not pleased. I fear his earlier sartorial intervention misfired. Freddie is no longer in trackies and flip-flops. His black trousers are smart, if a little snug. But he's wearing a tight black ultra-low V-neck T-shirt and sporting more cleavage than any clergy wife present.

Has he overstepped the mark? Not quite. But he is deliberately standing right *on* the mark, defying the bishop. And the bishop is deliberately ignoring him.

For now.

Chapter 12

The cardinals are in conclave. Tempting though it is, we mustn't loiter with the crowds in the piazza, nor yearn with them for a glimpse of white smoke. Our business lies with the diocese of Lindchester. We are on the brink of Passiontide. On Sunday our focus will shift from the Wilderness to Jerusalem. But today is Tuesday. At 9.17 a.m. a little local train (this train is made up of two carriages) rattles out of Cardingforth towards Lindford. Let's follow it.

The Linden flows beside the track among rush and willow. To our left the cooling towers serenely manufacture clouds. Look away. A solitary crow lollops over a field greened with winter wheat, and here and there along the hedges we can make out a sly haze of hawthorn leaf, a frosting of blackthorn blossom. The train clatters on, *knackerty-tack, knackerty-tack*. Allotments, houses, a square-towered church in a huddle of yews. We will shortly be arriving into Carding-le-Willow. If you are leaving the train, please ensure you have all your luggage and personal belongings with you. Carding-le-Willow, our next station stop.

Personal belongings? As opposed to what? Impersonal belongings? Arriving *into*? Station *stop*? What, to distinguish it from the other places where we stop for no apparent reason, which are not stations?

That is correct: Dr Jane Rossiter is on this train. Her car is being serviced, and she is on her way to work. Today she's wearing a black beret because she still hasn't been to the hairdresser. It looks rather good on her. When Danny was growing up, public hat-wearing was among her most heinous maternal crimes. Nowadays she could sport a ten-gallon diamanté-studded Stetson with impunity. Nobody cares. Was Jane remembered on Mothering Sunday? She was. Danny and Mickey Skyped her and performed the haka. Thanks, boys.

Before long Jane is looking down on back gardens. White conservatories, blue-edged trampolines. A Union Jack. Two swans on a canal. The sports stadium over the rooftops. Lindford, our next station stop. Jane takes care when alighting, and walks to the campus.

There it is: the Fergus Abernathy building, with all the glamour of a multi-storey car park. Doors closing. Sixth floor. Ding! At least her office (sweet FA 609) has a nice view. In that it's physically impossible to see the Fergus Abernathy building from its own windows. Jane dumps her bag, sits at her desk and turns on her computer, resolving to delete unread any email with an acronym in its title.

There's a little tap at the door. It's Dr Elspeth Quilter. That is her name. She is not called Dr Elspeth Quisling.

'Hi, Jane. Hope you've recovered. Sorry you had another migraine so soon after the last one.'

Jane bares her fangs in a smile. 'I'm much better now, thanks.'

'As you weren't at the departmental meeting, can I trouble you for your—'

Jane's mobile rings. She checks who's calling. 'Sorry, Elspeth, do you mind? It's my agent. New book contract.'

Elspeth retreats and closes the door.

'I dined at the palace last week,' says Jane's agent (who is called Dominic and is not in fact Jane's agent at all; and while we're at it, nor does Jane have a new book contract). 'You knew, and yet you didn't warn me!'

Jane laughs. She has a filthy laugh. People turn and stare when Jane Rossiter laughs.

'Well?' prompts Dominic. 'Yonder trollop, who is he, where and what his dwelling?'

Jane tells him all about Freddie. She fingers her chin as she talks. One of those annoying bristles, too short to tweeze out.

'So he's another Henderson rescue dog,' says Dominic. 'Well, that's very commendable, I suppose.'

'Yeah, right,' says Jane. 'Or very strategic. *Vis-à-vis* "the gay issue". Paul can't be written off as a frothing homophobe if he takes queers in and employs them, can he?'

'Ooh, cynical!'

'Meanwhile, Freddie's on the lookout for a silver fox with a convertible, to take care of him for ever. He told me.'

'My car has a sunroof. Does that count?'

Jane laughs again. Filthily. 'Your car's a Honda! Buy an Audi. But you are very, very foxy, my darling. And getting quite silvery too.'

'Meow.'

I don't want you to get the wrong impression here. Dominic did not ring to gossip. He was checking up on his good friend Jane. Well, all right then; maybe he was a *tiny* bit curious about that incarnation of sluttiness made manifest in the episcopal drawing room. However, his main object was to see how Jane was doing. He's reassured. She's laughing again. Goody-good.

Dominic swigs his last mouthful of coffee. Holy Week services all planned. Daphne stroked back into contentment about the Easter lilies. Fair Trade mini eggs sourced for the children's Easter egg hunt. Kindling for the Easter fire. Mustn't forget kindling. The lead thieves' ladder is still in his garden, but he's calmed down, and is no longer vowing to chop it up for firewood.

Right. Off to Lindford General Hospital. It's outside official visiting hours, but a dog collar opens many doors. One of his churchwardens has just had a chap's plumbing op. Dominic is very much hoping not to be told the details. Or shown any tubing, catheters, stitches, cannulas, dressings, mesh, needles, wounds, seepage, or anything latex. There can be a parent–child dynamic to bedside visits. Forty-nine stitches, father, look! Look, father, it's still oozing! Look, Dad, watch me, Dad! Even after a quarter of a century in Holy Orders poor Dominic remains squeamish. Dead bodies: not a problem. Suppurating ulcers: good Lord, deliver us. He gets into his trusty Honda and sets off.

Audi, Schmaudi.

Wednesday. White smoke! A new pope, and we Anglicans are still waiting to enthrone the next archbishop of Canterbury. The mills of Anglicanism grind slower than those of Rome.

Thursday, late afternoon. Dean Marion looks at her watch. Just time for a quick cup of tea before evensong. She's been in a senior staff meeting. As usual, she feels like Switzerland. (Hmm. Come to think of it, I will not pursue that metaphor any further. I foresee a risk of characterizing the bishop as a Nazi.) As usual, Marion feels like an embodiment of Anglicanism: a *via media* between the warring forces of change and conservatism.

The bishop has a Growth Strategy. (Lindchester: A Missionary Diocese!) Everything must be strategically lined up behind mission: all the systems, the finances, the processes, every parish, every appointment.

And the cathedral must become a missionary cathedral. I will now permit you a fastidious shudder, followed by a short interlude of hand-wringing. Ready? Off you go:

Ew! Oh, my dear, how crass! How vulgarly McDonaldizingly Evangelical! As if the mission of the Church can be reduced to evangelism, and success to numbers, and the priesthood to *doing*, not being! Anyway, we tried a Decade of Evangelism and it didn't work.

And . . . stop.

The bishop has powerful allies in his corner. The Church Commissioners have sunk a not inconsiderable sum into promoting this shift towards missional thinking. But cathedrals are bastions of conservatism. Hence Marion's dilemma. She has been won over by the bishop's proposals (while remaining temperamentally allergic to them); but she knows many of her flock – to say nothing of colleagues and staff – will fight them tooth and nail. She must bring folk to look at tables and figures, at incontrovertible evidence demonstrating that growth is possible, that the relentless decline in numbers can be reversed. She must commend strategies that have already been proven effective elsewhere in the Anglican Communion. And folk will dig their heels in.

Meanwhile, the safeguarding issue at the Choristers' School rumbles on. And Linda, Marion's high-maintenance PA (inherited from the previous dean), is off with stress again. Stress (with a whiff of litigation) is Linda's default mode when asked to change her working methods. Does Marion have the heart for another employment tribunal? John the Bastard was vanquished before Christmas, and since then – coincidentally? – someone has been sending Marion little turd offerings in padded envelopes. The police are involved. There is talk of CCTV for the deanery porch.

Oh, and the south side of the cathedral is falling down. They've just finished propping up the north side, and the laws of stonemasonry – nay, of physics itself! – dictate that the pressure now exerted by the restored side must push the crumbly side over, unless 4.6 million pounds' worth of work is undertaken, let's say, now-ish.

Marion has not given anything up for Lent. She doesn't need to.

She lets herself in. A pile of post waits for her in the deanery hallway on the round mahogany table. Gene appears. He sees her poor weary face. 'Would like me to cook Coquilles St Jacques for you, in the nude with a red rose clamped between my teeth?'

'You know what, Gene? Just a cup of Earl Grey. That would be lovely. But thank you for the offer.'

'It's because you're worth it,' he says.

Saturday. Tomorrow is Passion Sunday. It is also St Patrick's Day. This will be celebrated in Lindford the age-old way, by Englishmen who cannot confidently tell you the date of St George's Day getting bladdered on Guinness. The origins of this custom are lost in the mists of the late 1990s.

Susanna is out. The bishop is off duty. He's watching the rugby in the family sitting room on the palace's first floor, all alone. It's half time. Wales are winning, but he's not despondent. So far it's been pretty close. We just need to run the ball a bit more, get a couple of tries. It's only half time, and it could still go either way.

But then, just to complicate things, Freddie appears, bearing four bottles of Peroni.

'Hey. What's the score?'

'Nine three to Wales.'

'Sh-i-i-t.' Freddie came in and leant over the sofa. 'You doing OK? Want some company?'

There was a short pause. 'Yes, why not?'

'Cool.' Freddie sat. 'Wanna beer?'

Again, why not? 'Well, thanks.' Paul took one. 'Bottle opener?'

'Ah, crap.'

'*No!*' Paul stuck out a hand. 'You'll crack your teeth, darling. Go and get an opener.'

Freddie blinked. Scrambled to his feet. 'Yep. Sure. An opener. I'm on it.'

'Second drawer down,' Paul called after him.

Gah! Freddie stood in the kitchen. His heart thumped. He stared at the kitchen drawers, began opening and shutting them at random. His mind was all, What the—? He—? Say *what*? Darling? *Darling?!* Aw, c'mon, what's *with* you? Some guy who you *know* totally judges your whole lifestyle . . . And what? What kind of weird fucked-up shit *is* this? You need him to, like, *validate* you? *Love* you?

Meanwhile, upstairs on the sofa, the bishop was also processing the data. Oh dear. Was this a problem? Normally a term he reserved for close family, distressed children, and babies who cried when he was baptizing them. Home/work boundaries. Blurred. Perhaps he'd better—

No, he was refining on it too much.

But Paul's multi-processer insisted on crunching the emotional numbers. His feelings for Freddie: seventy per cent affection, fifteen per cent concern and ten per cent exasperation. That didn't add up, did it? His feelings for Freddie May didn't add up. What was the other five per cent? He really didn't want it to be . . . revulsion?

Homophobia? But it probably was. And now he'd have to sit through the whole second half with Freddie beside him on the sofa.

Reader, we must leave them now. Paul is still discombobulated by his slip. (Yes, but suppose it were a twenty-two-year-old blonde *woman* lolling on his sofa beside him, rattling tongue stud on bottle neck, clogging the air with pheromones, flashing an acre of knicker elastic whenever she leant forward? Would that not make him equally uncomfortable? Of course it would!)

(Then again, Paul would know never to allow that situation to arise.)

The second half kicks off.

It's going to be a rout.

Chapter 13

Monday smiles, mild and sunny, over the diocese of Lindchester. Everywhere you look, your eye is gladdened by the jocund company of daffodils. Bend down and sniff. Isn't that the quintessential smell of childhood Easters? All Peter and Jane and new Clark's sandals, and cards made from sugar paper and Gloy gum!

At Easter time the lilies fair
And lovely flowers bloom everywhere.
At Easter time, at Easter time!
How glad the world at Easter time!

You half-remember that song from Infants?

But enough of this cosiness. Cast off your (retro crocheted) comfort blanket and venture with me into the hurly-burly of a modern primary school. Shall I take you into St John's C of E in Renfold to watch Dominic take an assembly? No, he sets a very bad example, I'm afraid. The head is forever having to stand up at the end and say, 'Now, boys and girls, I know we just saw Father Dominic sticking pencils in his ears/playing a recorder with his nose, but I don't want to see any of *you* trying it.' We'd better make for Cardingforth instead, where Father Wendy is doing an assembly at the village primary.

'Gooood *mooo*rning, Mis-ter Crow-ther. Gooood *mooo*rning, teach-uz. Gooood *mooo*rning, Revrun-Dwendy.' (Oh. Looks like nothing has changed after all.)

Wendy smiles at the children sitting cross-legged on the hall floor in their red sweatshirts. The teachers are in a row at the back, on chairs, keeping a beady eye out for mobile phones and farters. Wendy has something to show them. Does anyone know what it is? That's right, it's a daffodil bulb. And what's this? A daffodil. You'd never guess, would you children, looking at this bulb . . .

Death, new life, et cetera. You can imagine the kind of thing Wendy says. Wendy is never going to set the Linden on fire. Mr Crowther will not have to say, 'Boys and girls, I know we just saw Reverend Wendy eating a daffodil . . .' All the same, there's something so, well, just plain *good*, so kind, in the way Wendy says these rather trite things. It bypasses the cerebral cortex to land, thud! on target, right in your yearning heart. The way the smell of daffodils dumps you straight into your childhood garden.

On the back row Mrs Fry is in difficulty. Her mum died last month. But Wendy's little talk is over now, and she's inviting the whole school to Cardingforth parish church on Sunday, because there will be an extra special guest coming! Does anyone know who will be coming? Yes?

'*Jeeesus* is coming on a *donkey* coz it's Palm *Sunday*.'

The voice drips such sarcasm that this can only possibly be a child of the vicarage speaking. Yes, it's little Leah Rogers, elder daughter of the bishop's chaplain. She eyeballs Wendy, a look of withering scorn on her face. Dominic would probably reply, 'Ha! that's exactly where you're wrong, young lady! Bananaman is coming on his Banana-scooter because it's National Banana Day. What? It isn't? Curses!' But Wendy recognizes Leah. She understands where this hatred is coming from.

'Yes, well done,' she says. 'It's Palm Sunday. And everyone is welcome.'

Mr Crowther activates the data projector, Mrs Fry goes to the electronic keyboard, and the school scrambles to its feet. They sing '1 2 3 it's good to be me'. The 288 young voices of Cardingforth Primary stoutly declare: 'I'm a special person and there's only one of me, and no one else is prouder of the person that is me.' Or rather, 287 young voices declare it. Leah Rogers has her arms folded, her eyes narrowed and her mouth clamped firmly shut. She's making a wish that on Palm Sunday the stupid donkey will do A GREAT BIG GIANT POO right in the middle of CHURCH.

Meanwhile, special person Freddie May (there's only one of him!) was in the bishop's office, helping PA Penelope stuff envelopes. This time it was a lovely, lovely letter and a leaflet from Susanna, inviting clergy spice to a quiet day with aromatherapy at the Diocesan Retreat House.

I regret to tell you that Freddie was – how to phrase this? – dealing with some surfeit-related low self-esteem issues. He was not proud of the person that was him. He was currently in possession of a wodge of cash liberated from drunken wallets, and a hangover the size of Wales. Everything that could hurt was hurting. If only he knew the '1 2 3' song! But the '1 2 3' song would not begin to scratch where Freddie May was itching that Monday morning. Hard-core stuff, that's what he needed. The bad boys. The Psalms. Behold, I was shapen in wickedness! Against thee only have I sinned, and done this evil in thy sight. Turn thy face from my sins! Cast me not away, cast me not away!

O-o-oh God. Oh God, oh God.

'Are you feeling all right, Freddie?' asked Penelope.

'Yep, I'm— No.' He bolted out.

The bishop and his chaplain were next door in the bishop's study, looking ahead in the diary at Holy Week.

They paused. Glanced out of the window.

'Ah!' said the bishop. 'My driver, "emptying himself of all but love" again.' He noticed Martin's teeth clench. 'What is it, Martin?'

'Forgive me, Paul, but is this really a joking matter?' Even Martin's nostrils were rigid. 'He behaves like a spoilt brat and everyone always indulges him! What's he *paid* for? I mean, how can he be your driver when he's never in a fit state to drive? With all due respect, you sometimes appear to have a blind spot where he's concerned.'

The bishop deployed his formidable eyebrows. 'You can leave *me* to deal with this, brother.'

'I beg your pardon.' Martin coloured, dog collar to buzz-cut, and returned to the diary. 'Maundy Thursday, Chrism Eucharist. You're preaching, the dean's presiding.'

'Excellent! I'll use Freddie as a sermon illustration of kenosis.'

He shouldn't have said that.

But honestly, could Martin really not hear how he came across? Like the prodigal's older brother! It was beyond Paul how anyone could have been in ordained ministry this long without developing some mechanism for dealing with personality clashes. It was basic stuff! Why should Paul be called upon to umpire the whole time?

Nor did the bishop take kindly to being told he had a blind spot by a man completely oblivious to his own foibles, thank you very much!

But of course, Martin was not in a good place right now. After a brief inward tussle, Paul apologized to the Lord and got back down off his high horse.

'Well, hang on in there,' he said. 'He'll be gone in a few months.'

'He was supposed to be gone by Easter!' Martin burst out. Then bit his lip.

The bishop sat back. Ah. Right. 'Um, Martin, is this more complicated than I've realized? Do you want to put me in the picture?'

Tell him, Martin! Tell him the little shite makes your life a misery with his hot breath in your ear, his smut, his blatant pocket billiards when the bishop's not looking.

'It's just—' Martin took off his glasses and breathed on them as though he intended to gnash a lens. He polished them savagely with his fleece. 'He gets away with murder, Paul. And he's taking advantage of your generosity, in my humble opinion.'

'Well, that's Susanna's and my worry, I think,' said Paul. He waited. But Martin had the lid clamped back on the crucible. 'So. Where had we got to?'

Martin put his glasses on and looked at the computer screen. 'The Triduum. I assume you're going to that?'

'Of course.'

'I can't believe chapter still haven't invited you to lead it. You've been here seven years!'

'I wouldn't do it properly,' said Paul. 'I'm an ignorant Evangelical bumpkin.'

'You're the diocesan bishop! It's your cathedral!'

Paul will never have to stand on his dignity. He has a man to do that for him.

Outside, the sun still smiles mildly, and crocuses bejewel the palace lawn: purple, mauve, gold, white. There is even a charm of goldfinches tinkling in the silver birch, but the little shite is still in a far country, feeding swine. There he is, bent over, hands on knees, shivering on the drive.

Gah! It's no good, he's going to have to stick the lot in the collection plate.

Why? Jesus, *why*? Why's he like, 'Hey guys, I don't even *like* you, but I'm all yours, do whatever the fuck you want, seriously, I don't care, be my guest?' Why can't he find some nice guy for a change? Who actually maybe *cares* about him?

But Freddie knows he can't be trusted with the nice ones who care. He has to trash their niceness, he *wants* to, he *has* to fuck stuff up, so that the outside matches the inside in his fucked-up miserable life.

He dry-retches till his eyeballs nearly drop out of their sockets onto the gravel.

No, right now it's not good to be Freddie May. Not one little bit.

Thursday. At last! The Most Revd Dr Michael Palgrove is enthroned as archbishop of Canterbury. The thoughts of many a senior bishop quietly stray to York, and the vacancy there. Even the good bishop of Lindchester cannot entirely keep his imagination reined in. The sun goes down red. An angry smear hovers above one of the cooling towers in Cardingforth, as though it's belching fire. Shepherd's delight. But when Friday comes, what is this? Blossom from the ornamental plums, wafting on the zephyrs of spring? Sorry. The shepherds were lying. We're dreaming of a white Easter.

Oh, what's happening to our English weather? We don't like it. It never used to be like this, did it? Why's everything so muddled? Why can't it be like the good old days, when we had proper seasons, and Peter helped Daddy with the car, while Mummy cooked with Jane? Please don't worry. It's not happening, and if it is, it's just part of the normal cycle of variation. It's only a blip. An atypically large blip. The largest blip ever. Anyway, we aren't responsible. Well, maybe we are, but it doesn't matter, the implications are always wildly overestimated by scaremongering killjoys with wind farm shares. It'll be fine. Keep calm and carry on shopping. (New word: la la la!)

Palm Sunday. The farmer has brought Nigel the donkey to Cardingforth parish church in a horsebox, which we trust is not too confusing for Nigel. She leads Nigel down the ramp and through the snow to the lichgate. The disciples and the crowd line the church path. Our Lord mounts, and the strains of 'Ride on, ride on in majesty' come from within the building. An awkward English 'Hosanna!' goes up. Nobody is keen to take off their cloak and throw it down in this weather, but they do it anyway. Nigel clops his way towards the church porch over stripy bedsheets and curtains. He's an old hand, is Nigel. Been doing this for years. In he goes. Clop, clop on the old stone, crunch, crunch on the palms. Oops! Messy Church. Little Leah's prayer is answered. Nigel brings his peculiar donkey honour to the king. But Wendy, unsurprised, is ready with a shovel.

And what of the rest of Lindchester diocese this snowy Palm Sunday? There are all-age activities: paper palm fronds are waved to 'We have a King who rides a donkey!' (tune: The Drunken Sailor). There are palm crosses, which small boys use as swords to stab one another at the communion rails. There are processions both short and long. There are Gospel readings both short and long, too. Very long, in the case of Lindchester Cathedral, where great swathes of the Passion narrative are intoned, and people are kept standing for an unconscionably long time; though admittedly, nowhere near as long as Jesus was inconvenienced upon the cross.

The clergy of the diocese gird up their loins. The last and fiercest strife is nigh. We draw a deep breath and prepare to enter the carpenter's shop once again, and put our souls to the lathe.

Chapter 14

Jane's boiler is kaput. She is sitting in her kitchen in a fetching beret and sleeping bag combo with the gas oven on, swearing and googling plumbers. Should have gone to New Zealand for Easter, silly cow. Both Danny and Mickey begged her to. Why didn't she? Because she doesn't want to stomp all over Danny's Big Adventure, that's why. A gap year is not a gap year if your mum comes too. Well done, Jane. That's very selfless of you.

And now the real reason: she doesn't trust herself not to end up in bed with Mickey. Which is stupid. Mickey is married(ish) to Sal, and Sal will be there too. But Sal is worryingly laid back and unpossessive; might simply say, 'No worries, hose him down when you're done.' Hell, Jane is more possessive about Mickey than Sal seems to be. And all Jane can lay claim to is a fling with a horny young Kiwi barman back in 1993. (And oops, there was Danny.) Given that Jane does not believe in marriage, what is her problem? Why is Sal's putative broad-mindedness a reason not to go? A proper grown-up civilized open relationship where everyone is cool about everything – what's not to like?

Here's what's not to like: Dr Jane Rossiter is what not to like. Jane knows all about the ogress dozing in a chair. It wouldn't take much to wake her, and then it would be all, 'Fee fi fo fum, he's fucking mine, take your fucking hands off my man.' Et cetera. No, Dr Jane Rossiter cannot do proper grown-up civilized relationships. She wants exclusive shagging rights to her bloke. That, or nothing at all. Which is what she's got. Good. So stop grumbling, you silly mare. She dials a plumber. She's betting it won't turn out like it does in porn films. Unless the plumber brings a sleeping bag of his own and they zip them together.

Happy Holy Week, Jane.

Freddie May is also cursing himself. He's left it too late to get his passport renewed, like he knew he would, so he's not going away over Easter either, not going to be riding his stepfather's horses on the *estancia*, not singing his heart out under vast skies. There will be no Andes on the edge of his vision, no smell of leather, no rude gaucho sex in tack rooms, no forgetting himself, losing himself, blanking all this shit out.

Happy Holy Week, Freddie.

Susanna is not swearing at herself, of course, because she is an Evangelical; but she does say 'Oh, rats!' rather crossly when she realizes she forgot to buy marzipan for the simnel cake. Now she'll have to make another trip, because Easter wouldn't be Easter if the simnel cake did not have a layer of marzipan and eleven marzipan balls on, one for each apostle minus Judas.

Susanna and Paul are going away after Easter. They are going to their cottage in the Peak District, along with two of their daughters and their families. It will be a squeeze! So no, they really can't take Freddie, she can see that. Even though he's clearly in a bad way at the moment and in need of a holiday and she hates to abandon him all by himself in this big house. In the past the Hendersons have gladly scooped up any waifs and strays and included them in their holidays, but '*No!* Sorry, I'm in need of a holiday, too – from Freddie May,' is what Paul had said. So that was that. Oh dear, who'd be around on the Close next week? Miss Blatherwick is going to Jersey, unfortunately. Will Giles and Ulrika be here? She'd never forgive herself if... No, that's silly. The self-harming was in his early teens. Done with. She's being very silly. But perhaps she could ask Jane to keep an eye on him? Or Marion? The dean has told Susanna she's not going on holiday next week. Fret fret. Buzz buzz.

Happy Holy Week, Susanna.

The dean did indeed tell Susanna she is not going on holiday, but the dean is wrong about that. She will be whisked away to Prague by Gene for five days, business class, and screw you, environment. He's been planning this surprise for weeks now. If he thought he could get away with it, he'd drape her in sable and conflict diamonds as well, and feed her veal stuffed with foie gras and powdered rhino horn. Off an ivory spoon. While castrati serenaded them. Why are people so pissy and judgemental about harmless fun these days, he'd like to know?

Happy Holy Week, Gene.

Timothy, the director of music, is not cursing himself. He is not even cursing the choristers. Or not out loud, anyway. The sixteen boys are working hard on their Holy Week and Easter repertoire, but concentration is an issue; and Thomas Greatrix, the head chorister, is struggling with the tail end of a cold. O Lord, let it only be that. But that very richness developing in his voice (which they've all been relishing) probably signals the lengthening of his vocal cords and the beginning of the end. Who else have they got capable of the treble solo in the *Sparrow Mass*? Josh Wilder, solid workhorse, nothing special? Or Harry Bianchi, tendency to sing sharp under pressure? Let Thomas last another week, just one more week. The Freddie May voice-breaking catastrophe of eleven years ago still hasn't faded from Lindchester choral memory, when an adult soprano had to be parachuted in at the last minute to sing his part in the new, specially commissioned *Lindchester Mass*. (And great was the *Schadenfreude* in other cathedrals.)

You'd better believe Timothy is going away after Easter. Straight after choral evensong. The car will be packed and ready. He's going to his parents, where he'll sleep for five days solid.

Happy Holy Week, Timothy.

Oh, it's cold, it's so cold! There is snow again on Wednesday. But Maundy Thursday dawns sunny. All over the diocese of Lindchester, clergy scrape their windscreens, get in their cars and head to the cathedral. Bishop Paul has issued a three-line whip: be at the Chrism Eucharist, or feel the full force of my wrath – that is, he will be Very Disappointed. Being Very Disappointed is about as wrathful as Anglican bishops are allowed to get nowadays, anathematization and thumbscrews being frowned upon. But most of the clergy will be there, apart from the ones unable to accept the authority of a woman dean, for gynophobic reasons. I'm sorry – theological reasons. The rest come, the bishop preaches, the oils are blessed – for baptism, for confirmation, for anointing the sick – the dean celebrates, then they go. Tonight some will hold Christianized Seder meals, others will have Lord's Suppers and foot-washings.

Foot-washing! Seriously? Ew. Corns, bunions, rough skin, chipped nail polish, hairy toes – who wants to handle cheesy, pongy, sweaty feet? Or worse: let someone else handle your cheesy, pongy, hideously embarrassing feet! This ritual belongs in a hot country, where dusty roads and sandals and reclining at table make it a routine necessity, not in wintry England in the twenty-first century! Yet Christians feel obliged to give it a go, because Jesus washed his disciples' feet. It's a symbol of leadership through service. The first shall be last; the greatest, least. That's why it's the clergy, the bishops, deans and popes who do the washing. Generally, in Anglican cathedrals only one foot per person is washed. (The *via media*, let's not get carried away, please.) The symbolic twelve sit, a trouser leg rolled up, a foot bared, waiting, while the choir sings Duruflé's *Ubi Caritas*. Some foot-washees will have cheated and had a sneaky pedicure. I hope the water's warm. I hope nobody's wearing tights. I hope nobody's ticklish. Or a fetishist. An air of awkward silliness hangs over everything, as if some ceremony of Masonic toe-curling is under way.

Odd, then, that it should still be so moving.

Let's go to Lindchester Cathedral and snoop. Marion the dean has instigated another of her changes: instead of a representative twelve, anyone who wants to can have a foot washed. Giles the precentor is not keen on this innovation (it is, after all, an innovation), but Marion is the dean. She wants to try it. If there is no take-up, they can go back to the old way next year. There are four foot-washing chairs waiting empty. There are four foot-washers: Marion, Paul Henderson, Giles, and the leader of the Triduum, Charles De la Haye, a retired bishop who cuts rather a saintly monkish figure, and is not in the least an Evangelical bumpkin. All four have stripped off their outer vestments and are waiting on their knees with white towels. Water is poured into four basins.

The choir begins to sing. *Ubi caritas et amor, Deus ibi est*. Ah, that haunting alto line, those unsettling harmonies. The sound rises to the great vaulted ceiling, fills the whole dark cavern of Lindchester Cathedral. Where charity and love are, God is there. And one by one, people come forward. They actually do! They dump their pride, they fling away the embarrassment, they sit and peel off a sock, and get a foot washed. *Deus ibi est. Deus ibi est.*

Freddie May holds it together until the moment when the treble line comes in. *Exsultemus, et in ipso jucundemur*. Ah, cock. He remembers this, maybe the last thing he sang as a treble. Struggling to hit the notes. Not high, even. Let us rejoice and be pleased in him. He's crying. Can't stop himself. Shit. There's no holding it back. So he kicks off his flip-flops and pads barefoot to the front, to the only empty chair: Marion's. He sits and sobs. He's like the apostle Peter: not my feet only, but also my hands and my head. Wash me, wash me, and I shall be whiter than snow. So Marion, kneeling, washes his feet and dries them with the white towel. But he's still sobbing, face hidden in his hands. She takes him in her arms and holds him. Just holds him.

From where he is kneeling washing another foot, Paul sees. Ah, Marion's got him safe. She can do what Paul longs to, but can't, because it's too complicated.

The altar is stripped. The clergy and people depart in silence. On the hillsides under the snow, ewes lie frozen with their newborn lambs dead beside them.

Good Friday. *Is it nothing to you, all ye that pass by?* Tesco's in Lindford is heaving. Great mountains of three-for-a-tenner Easter eggs are tumbled into bins. The air is full of the spice of hot cross buns. Frazzled mums shout, 'Right! That's *it*! You're getting *nothing*!'

Holy Saturday. In Lindchester Cathedral the flower guild are surrounded by boxes of white carnations, yellow tulips, lilies. Gavin the deputy verger is constructing the Easter bonfire in the brazier. He smiles. Tomorrow at 5 a.m. this thing'll go off like an incendiary device. Tinder-dry twigs and kindling from the 2011 Christmas tree. Shredded paper. He shakes his bottle of lighter fluid, shoosh-shoosh. Yeah!

In his mind's eye he sees the flames streaming in the wind, the Paschal candle lit, and carried into the dark cathedral. One tiny point of light. And the dawn coming.

APRIL

Chapter 15

The cherries are not wearing white for Eastertide. Father Wendy reflects on this as she and Lulu plod along beside the Linden. It's Easter Monday, a bank holiday, but she's on her own. Her husband Doug is off on the NUT conference, which was scheduled for Easter weekend. It's the first of April already, and the hawthorn leaves are barely out in the hedges. There's dog's mercury in the undergrowth, though. And the first feathers of cow parsley are coming up. Dandelions, coltsfoot, a clump of primroses. And 'the stars of lesser celandine'. Wendy knows her wild flowers pretty well, mostly from Cicely Mary Barker's *Flower Fairies* books, which she used to read to Laura at bedtime. To this day she cannot see a daisy without hearing Barker's little rhyme jingling about 'closing my petals tight, you know, sleeping till the daytime'.

This morning it's all right, surprisingly. You can never tell in advance. You can never spot the wonky paving slab that will cast you headlong again. Wendy, who can't sing for toffee, hums an Easter hymn as she plods: 'My flesh in hope shall rest, and for a season slumber. Till trump from east to west shall wake the dead in number.' Sleep tight, my darling girl. Close your petals. See you on that morning. As ever, she prays for Lucy too, the harassed mother who thirteen years ago turned to yell at her squabbling children in the back seat and ploughed into Laura on the zebra crossing.

Here's their bench. On the opposite bank the young man in black running skins passes. Wendy has seen him several times before. Maybe he's training for a marathon? She calls down blessings on his blond head as he dwindles towards the distant bridge. Behind her, a lark begins to climb. Up, up, above the cooling towers, bubbling down his beads of bright music on the righteous and the unrighteous.

I need to reassure you about Jane, I think. The ease with which plumbers can be summoned by bored housewives has been exaggerated, but never fear, she has not perished from hypothermia. She is snug and warm in the palace. That's right: Susanna, hearing of Jane's boiler problems, immediately offered the use of one of the many episcopal guest rooms until she gets it fixed. As we have just seen, Freddie is off on one of his insane long runs. We will find Jane sitting by herself in Susanna's lovely kitchen, ranting at Susanna's floral Cath Kidston Roberts radio. If you are a Conservative voter, or easily offended, look away now:

Shut up, shut up, shut up, you vile Tory twats. I was at college with wankers like you. You know nothing, *nothing* about poverty. The taste of it in your mouth, the feel of it on your skin, in your hair. Culture of dependency, my arse. Struggling to make ends meet does not mean forgoing the skiing trip so you can pay your kids' school fees. No, tosser, you could *not* live on that much a week. You could probably lose that much down the back of your fucking antique French sofa and not notice! Fuck you and your fucking bedroom tax. God, let this be your poll tax, the thing that brings you down, you Boden arseholes. If only this were an April Fool. Ho ho ho, had me going for a minute there: but thank God, we actually all voted for Gordon and none of this ever happened.

My apologies. We will tiptoe away now. Ironically, Jane has managed to turn the air blue. Tsk. Not really in keeping with Susanna's ivory and pastel colour scheme.

Who else is around on the Close this week? Rather a lot of people, as it happens. Gene, true to his promise, has whisked the dean away to Prague, but Mr Happy the canon chancellor is still here. Mr Happy Junior, who was baptized on Easter morning at the vigil, has just got the hang of sleeping for four entire hours at a stretch – ssh, ssh, don't say that out loud, you'll break the spell! – and neither Mark nor his wife Miriam dare jeopardize this by disrupting his routine. Perhaps, just perhaps, they are through the worst? Perhaps the chancellor will no longer want to kill the nice old ladies who say, 'Enjoy him while he's little!' (Could you enjoy him for me? For half an hour, maybe? While I sleep?) Nor will he want to kill any parent of a contented little baby who offers smug advice. Best of all, he won't want to kill Mr Happy Junior. He won't catch himself thinking at 3 a.m., I'll just smother him now, and we'll deal with it in the morning.

Because Daddy would never do that really. Would he? Would he? Woody-woody-woody? No, he wouldn't, he would not do that, because Daddy loves his little boy. Yes, he does. Oh yes, he does. Mr

Happy Junior braces his little arms and legs and goes rigid with bliss. He gives Daddy a great gurgling grin and latches optimistically onto Daddy's nose. Milk? Milk?

On the opposite side of the Close the Littlechild family are all home, too. As we know, Giles and Ulli had a short half-term break in Germany on a choir tour recce, so they are staying put this week. They are taking it in turns to sit on Lukas and Felix, and force them to revise for their GCSEs and A-levels, impressing upon them that this activity is best undertaken with books and notes sitting at a desk, rather than in bed with YouTube, or up on the palace roof with Freddie May.

Philip Voysey-Scott, the canon treasurer, has gone away. He and Pippa have popped across to their house in Norfolk for a few days. Timothy, the director of music, is flat out on his parents' sofa recovering from Holy Week and Easter. I'm sorry to say that Laurence, the cathedral organist, has snuck off to be unfaithful to his lawful wedded wife, and fumble some younger floozie in Liverpool with more pipes and manuals.

A word is in order here about organists. Better still, a joke. Question: what's the difference between an organist and a terrorist? Answer: you can negotiate with a terrorist. This is unfair. It ought to be viewed as a spectrum, rather than a simple disorder, and Laurence is very high-functioning. He is another tall, gangly man. If you lined him up with Giles and Timothy I'd defy you not to laugh. Laurence is tall, but Iona (the sub-organist with the dragon tattoo) is tiny. Oh, the battles over organ bench height up in the loft! On Easter morning Laurence was a happy bunny. During Lent we have restrained use of the organ. (Smirk.) But along with flowers and alleluias, unrestrained use of the organ greets our Lord's resurrection. In the case of Lindchester Cathedral – hold on to your biretta, father! – it was a stonking great Niagara Falls of a Vierne voluntary, the kind that makes you long for a cigarette afterwards, even if you don't smoke. Not everyone is a fan of Vierne, mind you. Laurence, when he emerged from his loft, was greeted by a wild-eyed lady who accused him of being the organist. Laurence admitted it. 'Well, fuck off. That was horrible.' Laurence, being English, merely ducked his head shyly as if receiving a compliment and said, 'Oh, thank you very much!'

It would have played out differently had the wild-eyed lady accosted Iona. Iona is further out along the organist spectrum. She plays beautifully, but you should see the hand gestures she aims at the director of music in her little CCTV screen. You should hear what she says to him and the precentor and the preacher. Iona would give Dr Rossiter a run for her money in the swearie department. All you are aware of, down there in your seat, is her sensitive improvisations, her mastery of Messiaen. She is twenty-seven, has crimson hair with bold black stripes, a dragon tattoo on her left biceps, and more piercings than Freddie May. Not your typical organist, you say? Don't worry, we solve this taxonomic puzzle by classifying her thus: family – Anglican; genus – a Character; species – organist.

Easter week drags by, a bit cold, a bit flat. Next Sunday will be Low Sunday; not the best moment for a first visit to your local church, should you be contemplating such a thing. The vicar will probably be away, and a retired priest will trundle out of hibernation. It is the day of the year when you are most likely to encounter a sermon that begins: 'When I was a young man on military service . . .' Rookie curates, local ordained or non-stipendiary ministers will be at the helm, and sometimes they will be celebrating Weird Intonation Sunday. The Lord BE with YOU. Lift up YOUR hearts.

But let's zoom in on Friday evening and check up on Jane and Freddie. When Susanna hinted to Jane that she might 'cherish' Freddie, Susanna probably didn't picture them sitting one at each end of the pistachio linen sofa drinking too much Malbec and rewatching series four of *True Blood*. But that's what they are doing. I'm a bit worried about that oatmeal carpet.

'Are you allowed up on the couch, by the way?' asked Jane, between episodes.

'Paul lets me,' said Freddie. 'If I'm a good boy.'

'Provided you don't jump up and lick his face, you mean?'

'Or hump his leg? This OK?' (He was giving Jane a foot massage.)

'Divine.'

'So yeah, what's happening with your hair, babe?'

'Babe? Don't oppress *me* with your patriarchal nomenclature, faggot.'

'Oh, sorry. What's happening with your hair, skank ho'?'

'That's better. Well, it's a work in progress. Long term, I'm aiming for the Cruella De Vil look.'

'Seriously? Wasn't she like, really skinny?'

'Watch it, you.' Jane shoved him in the chest with her foot. 'You can pour me some more wine.' He rolled round and reached for the bottle. (Careful, *careful*!) His black vest rode up. 'Hey! Tramp stamp! Is that new? C'm'ere, let's see.' She hauled him to her by his jeans waistband. It was a stylized serpent, coiled, head down, forked tongue disappearing. 'My, that's subtle. Paul seen it yet?'

'Nah.' He laughed, sat back up and refilled her glass, not meeting her eye.

'Cheers.' She checked out his upper arms. Ladders of scars. Freddie, Freddie, Freddie. And Maori bracelet tattoos. Like the ones Danny was threatening to get. 'Doesn't it hurt like hell?'

'God, yeah.'

'Then why do it?'

'Coz.' The smile. 'Hey, listen, Janey, can I cut your hair? Like really short?'

'Do you know how to cut hair?'

'Yeah, no yeah. Aw, c'mon, how hard can it be? Suze cuts Paul's. We'll use her clippers? G'wan. You'll totally look like Judi Dench?'

'No! No way.' She reached for the remote. 'Shut up. Episode three.'

'*I wanna do real bad thangs with you!*'

'I'm not letting you.'

'You *so* are.'

The Hendersons arrive home the following afternoon. Paul admires Jane's new haircut.

'Yes, I've decided to become a lesbian,' says Jane, stroking her stubble. It feels like a bus seat. 'Freddie recruited me. It's a lifestyle choice. Golly, I hope I don't tear apart the fabric of society and undermine the institution of marriage.'

But Paul just looks at her, patiently, until she feels bad.

Ah, damn it. 'Sorry.' And now she's got to own up to Susanna about the carpet as well.

Chapter 16

Dominic hears about it from Jane. He's at the crem, having just taken the funeral of an old lady who died of a stroke. The last mourners have gone when his phone vibrates. 'Ding dong, the witch is dead!' says the text. Oh my God, oh my God! He checks the BBC website. It's true! Maggie's gone. He looks round for someone to clutch, to exclaim with. But he's alone now outside the chapel. At his feet red carnations spell out MUM. Wreaths. The casket tribute of lilies and roses. A white cross made of dahlias.

Already the next set of mourners is in the chapel behind him. *Sheep may safely graze* has started up. He feels ... He presses a hand to his heart as if to check. Another old lady dead of a stroke. Has everything else dropped away now – the miners' strike, poll tax, Section 28? He's surrounded by death. The scent of lilies is in his nostrils. We are all going to die, he thinks. There's nothing we can do, nothing. Dominic has sat by countless deathbeds, held the hands of the dying; but priest though he is, he's still clutched now and then by Donne's 'sin of fear'.

I'm going to die. No, really, I'm going to die. He thinks of the hymn they've just sung: 'Death will come one day to me; Jesu, cast me not from thee.' Cast me not away, cast us not away. *Miserere nobis*. He's astonished to find tears welling. Now this he would not have predicted. Solidarity at the last with the Iron Lady. He shakes his head and walks to the car park. The row of poplars, planted to screen the uncomfortable truth from Renfold, sways in the wind.

'Who's Mrs Thatcher?' asks little Leah Rogers at teatime.

Marion is in London at the Deans' Conference when she finds out. She thanks the Lord that she is dean of Lindchester, not of St Paul's.

Meanwhile, back at home, her husband Gene smiles when he hears the news. He puts a magnum of 1990 Lanson in the fridge – 1990 being a year he remembers fondly in the career of that staunch friend of apartheid. He'll invite a few carefully selected people round tonight. Not the Hendersons. True, the bishop speaks up in the Lords against welfare reform. He may not be a toadying Tory sycophant, but Gene's still not prepared to deviate from the law that you don't waste vintage champagne on Evangelicals.

Giles the precentor, cut off from civilization while typing up the music list, does not hear until Gene phones to invite him round for a glass of something this evening. Giles immediately sets about crafting suitably eirenic prayers for evensong, prayers that will cater to both the grieving and the gleeful in Lindchester. Make me a channel of your peace, he thinks. Perhaps we'll be able to reclaim the prayer of St Francis now.

I ought probably to mention – lest the tendentious reactions of my characters are giving a wrong impression – that the diocese of Lindchester is made up largely of safe Tory seats. The truth is nuanced, but you will forgive me if, for simplicity's sake, I paint the political landscape with bold expressionist swathes of blue, and tell you that the region is populated by people who can discern the iniquity of benefit fraud more clearly than that of tax avoidance. People, in short, who think Maggie did a jolly good job. They get behind community projects, tirelessly volunteering for charitable causes and as Friends of This and That. If their good deeds have a strong local bias, who are we to judge? Which of us is not (secretly) more exercised by the threat of a high-speed train route ploughing through our back garden than by the plight of the shadowy poor we have never met? Radicalism, when it does surface within diocesan borders, has a right-wing flavour, as anyone who has ever proposed building a mosque round here would be able to tell you.

Linden University, it goes without saying, is a bit of an exception. Ravaged though the natural hairy leftie habitat is by the depredations of Management and the evil machinations of the vice chancellor, a pocket remains in the Fergus Abernathy building.

It was 11 a.m. on Tuesday. Jane locked her office door behind her and headed down the corridor to the disabled loo. Sorry, the accessible toilet. As she entered, the air freshener emitted a squirt of citrus toxin. Agent Orange, probably. It didn't quite mask the smell of fag smoke. Hey, Spider! Back from study leave. Well, hoorah for that. He was always too idle to go down six floors to smoke in the leper colony. Simeon E. Dacre, poet and creative-writing lecturer in the English department, was the closest Jane had to a kindred spirit in the Faculty of Arts and Humanities. (That is its name: it is not called the Faculty of Farts and Inhumanity.) Jane had her wee, deployed the liquid soap ejaculator and washed her hands. She then stooped to check her reflection in the low-placed accessible mirror. Oh, well. At least she still had her teeth. Bonjour, Fantine! How's that dream working out for you?

The tall, spindly shape of Spider was silhouetted against the big window at the tea point. He flinched at the sight of her. 'Jane? Oh, fuck, Jane. Was I meant to know about this?'

Jane toyed with the idea of stringing him along, but this was a piece of behaviour too vile even for her. 'No, God no, don't worry. Just a grim warning to us all: never let a drunk cut your hair.'

'Thank fuck for that. Thought it was chemo.' He looked her over to make sure, eyes magnified behind the blue lenses of his glasses. He thrust out his long skinny arms. 'Hug.'

She was clamped into the weird hollow chest, then pushed away again. 'Let's get out of here and go and get coffee,' she said. 'And celebrate.'

'You bet.' They set off for the lifts. 'State funeral, Jane. State fucking funeral!'

'Well, of course – like Clement Attlee,' she said. 'It's only fair. Oh, wait, he didn't get a state funeral.'

'Attlee! What did that bastard ever do for the country?'

'Yeah, apart from create a culture of dependency!'

'Present government are still tidying up after him. Bastard.'

We will leave them to their embittered socialist grousing as they head for the vegan restaurant. Perhaps you are wondering what I am up to, introducing a new character a quarter of the way through my novel. Aren't there rules against that type of thing? I hope you will permit me to hint that I am the writer, and I can do whatever I bloody like. My purpose here is to wean you off solipsism: just because you, reader, have not seen him before does not mean Simeon E. Dacre has not existed all along.

This, I trust, will prepare you for the following surprise: there is another bishop about to make an appearance in this tale. He is the suffragan bishop of Barcup. Even now he is winging his way towards us, in mid-air, somewhere over the Atlantic. He has been in the partner diocese in South America on sabbatical for the past three months. You will be saddened to learn that the Rt Revd Bob Hooty is a thorn in Paul Henderson's flesh. Paul has prayed the Lord rather more than three times that He would remove it from him. Still, the Lord's grace is very nearly sufficient for Paul.

The issue is this: the bishop of Barcup is a 1970s style Christianity-and-politics-from-the-bottom-up-type liberal. The two bishops are unfailingly courteous to one another. But there is not much collegiality. Bob's been in the diocese four years longer than Paul, doing the donkey work of licensings and confirmations, and he still has two years to go before retirement. At this point Paul will be able to appoint someone he is better able to work with. I'm afraid Bobby Barcup will come home to discover that Paul and his stooges have advanced the (decidedly top-down) Diocesan Growth Strategy significantly in his absence. But we will leave the poor man in ignorance of this for a little longer, happily flexing his toes in his flight socks and sandals to stave off DVT, and reading Francis Spufford's *Unapologetic*. It is such a good book that he keeps reading excerpts out loud to his wife Janet, who is sitting beside him reading something else. Discreetly on her Kindle (to see what the fuss is all about). If he doesn't stop interrupting her with bloody Spufford she's going to read him a toe-curler of an extract in retaliation.

In his suffragan's absence, the bishop of Lindchester has been doing more of the donkey work himself. It is Friday evening and he has just got back from confirming a dozen young teens and adults in one of the farthest flung corners of the diocese, on his day off. Bad bishop. Susanna has forgiven him, and is ready in the kitchen with a plate of sandwiches for him and Freddie, who was driving.

'How did it go?' asked Susanna, once they were seated and eating.

'Fine,' replied the bishop, in the off-hand manner of a child describing a day at school.

'Did your sermon go down well?'

'Hope so.'

'Did he preach well, Freddie?'

Freddie paused just a heartbeat too long before saying, 'Awesome?'

The bishop laughed. 'Now tell me what you really think.'

'Aaaw, c'mon. Man. You can't ask me that?' He crammed the sandwich into his mouth to avoid answering.

Susanna – who bowed to no one in her ability to feel bad about things for which she was in no way responsible – began to panic. 'I'm sure it was fine, darling. Freddie's teasing you.'

'No, he's not. He doesn't want to hurt my feelings.' He removed the plate of sandwiches from Freddie's reach. 'Come on, I'm genuinely interested in what you think.'

Freddie slumped over forwards and thumped his forehead on the table. 'No-o-o-oo. Oh, OK, fine, then.' He sat up. 'So yeah. Here's the thing. When you're preaching you're like, doing this jigsaw? Only it's like I've got this killer hangover, yeah, and you're all, look how it fits together? See? This is God's amazing plan, it all fits together, and it makes sense and therefore God loves you? Only I'm like, dude, yeah, totally, I so agree with you, only I've still got a headache and I'm gonna be sick?' There was a pause. 'Know what I'm saying?'

Paul stared at him.

'So you're saying Paul's sermons don't quite hit the spot for you, emotionally, as it were?' translated Susanna, to fill the terrible yawning chasm that had opened in her kitchen.

This chasm, dear reader, was caused by a momentary fit of abstraction on the part of the bishop. He had just benefited from his first glimpse of Freddie's tramp stamp when he slumped forwards, and had not in fact heard a word Freddie was saying.

'Sorry. Run that past me again,' he said.

Freddie coloured. 'Hey. It's cool. Forget it.'

Oh, bishop! That was your moment to own up and make light of it! Paul could see he'd just squashed Freddie and made him feel like a complete idiot. Another couple of seconds passed and the opportunity was well and truly butter-fingered and dropped. Say something! But nothing came to mind. The bishop castigated himself. And then, I'm sorry to say, began to find it amusing. He frowned in an effort to repress this.

And in that frown poor Freddie read disapproval. He checked his phone: 10.20. What the fuck. It was Friday. He got to his feet. 'Catch you later, guys.'

Susanna tilted her head in pastoral anguish as he left. Oh dear! The front door opened, and closed.

'Is he all right?' she asked. 'Should we . . . ?'

'Freddie's an adult,' said Paul.

Outside in the dark palace garden a fox wailed, lonely, cold, like the lost soul of a family pet.

Chapter 17

Spring? Surely we dare breathe the word 'spring' in the diocese of Lindchester? The first chiffchaffs have been heard along the banks of the Linden, cross-stitching the air with song; the water meadows are filling with Shakespeare's flowers, daisies pied and violets blue, ladies' smock all silver white.

Bob Hooty, back from his sabbatical, has missed the worst of the English winter, lucky man. He is in his kitchen now, looking out at his garden. His magnolia is nearly out. A blowsy yellow haze dusts the pussy willow buds, where a bee potters. Barcup is a village near the site of the ancient Saxon shrine of Sexfrot, or some equally implausible saint. But the bishop doesn't live there. He lives in the town of Martonbury, in the south of the diocese. This is the lot of suffragan bishops. The lines fall to them in suburban places. Not for them the oak-panelled be-moated idiocies inflicted upon diocesan bishops – in which their poor sofas and Billy bookcases look like doll's house tat – but posh detached houses, probably with an extra downstairs loo and a side door, so visitors and PA don't have to walk through the house to reach the bishop's office.

I like Bob. He's a good man. Look at him standing in his kitchen on Monday morning, with his All Saints' Martonbury 150th Anniversary mug of Fair Trade coffee, shaking his head at Radio 4. Ten million pounds for the funeral. He thinks about the poverty he's just seen. He sighs over austerity measures and the *Belgrano*. He ponders Spufford and sin, the HPtFtU. And yet outside his kitchen window a blackbird is singing in the magnolia, and the bee still potters in dusty golden bliss. All's not right with the world, but it's not all wrong, either. Hope remains. He's not an empty-tomber, but Easter is what makes the difference.

Bob is wearing a grey suit and a purple clerical shirt (under his jumper), because he's going to get in his car and drive to Lindchester for the senior staff meeting and give a brief presentation about his sabbatical. He goes through his little stack of A5 cards one last time. (Bishop Paul uses an iPad.) Bob's shirt is one of the four he bought when he was consecrated nearly twelve years ago: a little faded at the edges, but still going strong. He's not quite in sandals and socks, but his brown shoes have a distinct sandally air about them. You can glimpse sock through the little cut-out bits. He has a beard, nicely trimmed, not wild and mage-like. His varifocals are not stylish. Having been bullied by his children into trendy frames in the 1980s, Bob has stuck loyally with them ever since.

His wife Janet appears in her dressing gown and offers him a cooked breakfast. He declines. She starts cutting the rind off the bacon with a pair of recycled episiotomy scissors, because she's a midwife. (Don't worry, they've been sterilized.) She makes enough for him too, because he'll change his mind the minute he smells the bacon cooking.

'I bet Voldemort's taken over the entire diocese in your absence,' she says.

Voldemort, you will be relieved to learn, is not Janet's name for Bishop Paul. No, Voldemort is the archdeacon of Lindchester.

The ARCHDEACON! (Sulphur fumes and menacing discords on cathedral organ!) The word alone raises certain expectations in a work of this kind. It is customary for writers to have fun with their archdeacons; to give them a short fuse and a string of expensive hunters, or a secret boyfriend and black leather gloves. We unleash archdeacons as the bishop's enforcers, to strut across the page striking terror into the hearts of feeble-minded clergy. That said, a novelist has a duty to avoid clichés. You perceive the tension here? I ought to subvert the stereotype and present you with a mild-mannered godly archdeacon, free from foibles and eccentricities. And yet the stereotype exists for a reason: however lovely you are, you don't get to be an archdeacon unless you have at least a hint of Rottweiler in your psychological make-up. Archdeacons are not paid to be popular. They are paid to get things sorted.

And that, dear reader, is all the permission I need.

But you will have to wait a little longer to meet Voldemort. There are, in fact, two archdeaconries in the diocese of Lindchester. One is currently vacant, which gives Bishop Paul the opportunity to appoint yet another stooge. Sorry, to enhance collegiality in the senior staff team. Thus the evil Hendersonian master plan gathers momentum, to go into all the world and make disciples of all people.

And how is Bishop Paul? You will remember we left him in a not entirely happy frame of mind. He seems to be locked into a pattern of bungling his dealings with Freddie. What Freddie craves is his attention. Paul knows this, but Paul is deeply resistant to being manipulated. In fact, the best way of ensuring that Paul Henderson won't do what you want is to tiptoe round him hinting and angling. So he refuses point-blank to reward Freddie's attention-seeking behaviour. Unfortunately, the more he withdraws in steely disapproval, the more Freddie ups his game. At what point will Paul's strategy of taking no notice become negligence? For example, after walking out on Friday night, Freddie did not return till Monday lunchtime. Paul did not enquire where he'd been, but his PA (who always finds these things out) put him in the picture: Freddie hitched to London, scene of his earlier adventures. This is not a welcome development. Paul sees that he urgently needs to find some appropriate way of paying attention on his own terms, not on Freddie's. He wonders briefly whether to raise this with his trusty archdeacon. He's seen the two of them together and observed that Matt achieves some secret alchemical mix of banter and boundaries when dealing with Freddie. A light touch and a firm hand – *this* is what always eludes Paul. But no, the archdeacon is a busy man. Not worth troubling him with this. We will allow Paul a few more days to ponder this, then pop into his office on Thursday afternoon and see how he gets on.

Paul was due to reappear at any moment from a finance subcommittee over in the diocesan offices. Freddie was sitting at Martin the chaplain's desk, watching YouTube clips on Martin's computer while he waited for orders. This was allowed. Penelope was in the room, and Freddie was legitimately logged on under his own user name. He couldn't get up to any mischief because he did not know Martin's password. Thought Penelope. Freddie jiggled in his chair, rattled his tongue stud along his teeth, sorted his boys out.

'You're such a fidget!' said Penelope. 'And do you want a tissue? You're driving me mad sniffing like that.'

'Huh?' He pulled an earphone out. 'What'sh that, Mish Moneypenny?'

Penelope lobbed a box of tissues across. 'Stop sniffing!'

'Sorry.' He grabbed a bunch and tossed the box back. 'It's the blow.'

'You'll rot your septum, you silly boy!'

Fish in a barrel. Literally? Penelope had no bull-ometer. He grinned at her and returned his attention to the screen. I'm sorry to tell you that YouTube was not the only tab open. Freddie was in the episcopal diary again and seriously considering booking Paul and

Martin in together for a Swedish massage and pedicure at the local health spa.

Nah. Probably don't do that? But Martin, my man— Chaplain1? Time to rethink your password, maybe?

Footsteps crunched across the gravel. Freddie logged off quickly. The office door opened and Paul and Chaplain1 came in. Freddie gave them a sunny smile. 'Hey.'

'I'd like my desk back,' said Martin.

'Please,' prompted Freddie.

'Please.'

Freddie scooted the chair backwards across the office. 'All yours, dude.'

'And my chair. Please.'

Freddie sighed and trundled the chair back over to the desk with his feet. He stood up close to the recoiling Martin and whispered, 'Just keeping it warm for you.'

Paul observed all this with an expression that said he'd like to knock their heads together. 'Freddie, do you have a moment?'

'Sure.'

'Could you cast your eye over this and give me your perspective on it?' He had a print-off in his hand. 'Published last week by the Faith and Order Commission.'

Freddie was reaching out when he glimpsed the title: *Men and Women in Marriage*. 'No. No way. Man, you can't ask me to read that. Get *him* to read it, I'm not reading it.'

'I've already read it, actually,' said Martin, without unclamping his teeth.

'I'm specifically asking *you* to read it, Freddie,' said Paul, 'because I'd value your reactions.'

'Yeah? Well, this is my reaction. Not reading it.'

The distress flares were screaming up into the sky. But he hadn't stormed out. Paul risked edging the conversation on a little further. 'Are you . . . able to express why you don't want to read it?'

'Nope.' Freddie took hold of the back of Martin's chair and spun it round.

Paul waited, willing Martin to keep his mouth shut.

'So yeah, no, it's like all the grown-ups discussing me in the head's office, and I'm sent outside the room?' muttered Freddie. 'Totally does my head in.'

'Forgive me, but if you refuse to engage with the process, what can you hope to achieve?' asked Martin.

'I can achieve not having to listen to a load of hate from assholes like you.'

'Excuse me? It's not—'

'Thanks, Martin,' said the bishop. 'Freddie, I've upset you. I didn't mean to do that, and I'm sorry. But I'm genuinely interested in what you think and feel.'

'Yeah, well. But what's the point? Not like you're gonna change, are you?' Freddie gave the chair another twirl. 'So. Anything else you want me to do?'

Paul turned to Penelope.

'Gavin's got flu, so the vergers are short-staffed,' said Penelope. 'They're behind on the mowing.'

'I'm all over it,' said Freddie.

'You're still banned from using the sit-on mower,' Penelope called after him.

'La la la!'

The door banged. 'Honestly, he's hopeless,' said Penelope.

Excellent. That went well, thought Paul.

Actually, Freddie had read the report. He had plenty of thoughts and feelings about it. Like, why did it sometimes say '*we*'? Who is this *we* who *knows* this stuff about marriage? The Faith and Order Commission? People in general? Not Freddie, that was for sure, sitting outside the head's office permanently in the wrong. Plus, why's it all about *difference*? Why does nobody think marriage is about sameness? Yeah, coz why did Adam go, 'Here at last is bone of my bone, flesh of my flesh'? Unless Eve was someone *like* him? Adam was all, yay, at last, another one of me! But no way was Freddie saying any of this with Fuckwit1 in the room.

He collected the big petrol mower from Dave the head verger, who sent him to mow the palace lawn. 'Keep it nice and straight,' said Dave. 'Clippings in the brown bin. Straight lines, not round and round.'

'Straight lines. I hear you.'

Father Dominic has not read *Men and Women in Marriage*. He probably should, but hasn't quite mustered the strength. He knows there's nothing new in it that he wants to hear. What does he want to hear? Oh, he's an old softie. He wants it to be like that YouTube clip of the New Zealand parliament, when they announce the passing of the same-sex marriage bill, and the room erupts spontaneously into a Maori love song. He would like to hear the archbishop of Canterbury cry, 'Unlock the doors!' and General Synod breaking into song, and the song flooding the entire C of E. But that's not going to happen any time soon, is it?

Freddie mows the palace lawn all afternoon in the sunshine. As he mows he sings. It's the same Maori love song, because he was watching that YouTube clip on Martin's computer earlier, too, and now he has an earworm. *Pōkarekare ana*. He knows the words from Sing Up! concerts years ago, when he was a chorister.

> The waves are breaking, against the shores of Waiapu,
> My heart is aching, for your return, my love.

Because in the end, that's what it's about, no? Love? I mean, seriously, fuck everything else. Because what else is there? In the end, what else is there but love? Love love love love love?

The following morning the bishop opens his bedroom curtains and stares down at the palace garden. Freddie has not kept it nice and straight. The entire lawn is one giant heart.

Chapter 18

St George's Day. His cross flies from the cathedral flagpole. The fields and roadsides of the diocese of Lindchester are bright with dandelions. In years gone by, this was the auspicious day to go out collecting to make your dandelion wine. Now the shaggy golden heads are simply mown into oblivion as weeds.

The bursar of the Cathedral Choristers' School is making the most of the patchy sunshine and mowing the sports field. Like the vergers, he's overworked, but he has a long memory. Need any help, Mr Hoban? No, thank you, Mr May. Because I remember when you broke into the shed and wrote in fertilizer on the school lawn. Spring of 2003. No amount of mowing that summer got rid of it. But Mr Hoban is grinning as he drives the tractor up and down the field (keeping it nice and straight). Word's got out, of course. Ha! What Mr Hoban wouldn't give to see my lord's face if he'd woken to find SUCK MY COCK mown into his lawn, instead. Got off rather lightly, had the bishop, in Mr Hoban's humble opinion.

But that's quite enough about the scapegrace Freddie May – who, even as I write, is experimentally stapling his thumb, then dripping blood all over this morning's post and being cuffed by an exasperated Penelope. I know you will be far more interested in the archdeacon of Lindchester. You have been very patient. I had contemplated describing Voldemort in his office in William House brooding over this month's Lee List; or enumerating his duties and the endless meetings and interviews and installations he must attend; or even detailing the Quinquennial Inspections for which he is responsible (the latter being an Anglican pursuit so recondite that Word has no spelling suggestions to offer). But come with me instead, on the viewless wings of fiction, to a newly vacant vicarage in the centre of Lindford, where I will introduce you to the Venerable (for thus we style our archdeacons) Matt Tyler.

'Has he trashed the place?'

'Well, it's a bit of a mess, I'm afraid, archdeacon.' Geoff unlocked the front door with the new keys.

'All righty. Let's see the damage. Bloody hell.' The archdeacon stuck his porkpie hat on the stairpost knob and surveyed the hall. He opened the door to his right, put his head in. Laughed. 'Yep. This qualifies as a bit of a mess. They kept pets, I take it? OK, get a cleaning firm in. The diocese will pay.'

Geoff looked at Pauline.

'You can have that in writing,' said the archdeacon. He opened his iPad. 'I'll just get a record of this little lot.'

He went through the whole vicarage taking pictures of dangling light fittings, kitchen unit doors wrenched from hinges, filthy carpets, gouged plaster, ripped wallpaper, cracked sinks. The two churchwardens followed in tense silence. They can't believe he's really gone, thought Matt. They're scared he's going to burst out of the airing cupboard screaming threats. The archdeacon's Doc Martens crunched on broken glass. You bet your ass you'll see me in court, matey, he thought. He closed his iPad and tucked it behind his braces.

'Okey-dokey. That's me done.' He stuck his hat back on his shaved head and beamed at them. 'He's gone, folks. He's really and truly gone. Bishop Paul will be writing to you, but he wanted me to thank you today for all you've done. It's been hell, we know, and you two have borne the brunt of it. Once the dust's settled we can start thinking about the future. Promise you won't have a long interregnum. But in the meantime, you have official permission to par-tay!'

Geoff and Pauline exchanged glances again.

'Afraid the diocese can't foot the drinks bill, though,' said the archdeacon.

Well, I don't know what I was expecting, but it wasn't that. I think I'm going to like the Venerable Matt Tyler. He gets into his car. It's a sporty black Mini, and he's rather a large man for such a small car. He's wearing black jeans, and a black and white checked clerical shirt made out of the kind of fabric used for chefs' trousers. If I wasn't already warming to him, I'd say this makes him look like a complete plonker – which is certainly the view of many in the diocese. He's forty-eight, and one of Bishop Paul's 'bold appointments'. He's not really like Voldemort. The bishop of Barcup's wife only calls him that because of his shaved head. You'll be cheered to learn that, unlike Voldemort, the archdeacon has a nose. It's a classic busted-up rugby-player's nose, but he definitely has one. It's only Janet Hooty who calls him Voldemort. Everyone else calls him Matt the Knife.

He zooms off like a cab driver in his little car round the back streets of Lindchester, nipping through gaps in the traffic. He does a quick scan for traffic wardens, then takes his usual cheeky little dink up a one-way street to cut off a loop. Just twenty yards, nothing's com—

Shit!

OK. She's fine. Didn't hit her. The archdeacon pulls up, heart booming. He whips his dog collar out and stuffs it in the glove compartment. He's getting out of the car when – uh-oh! – he clocks the look on the pedestrian's face. He scrambles back in and locks the doors.

She bangs on the window. 'You fucking moron! Are you drunk? What the fuck are you doing? This is a fucking one-way street! Get out of your car!'

The archdeacon shakes his head.

The woman looms close and terrifying. 'Get out *now*!'

The archdeacon cracks the window an inch. 'No. You'll hit me.'

She tries the handle. Snarls. 'You could've fucking killed me! What's your name? I'm reporting this!' She snaps the door handle a few more times. 'I've got your number plate. I'll find you.' She glares at him through the crack. 'What are you, some kind of chef?'

'A chef,' repeats the archdeacon, neither confirming nor denying it. He reads the ID card swinging on the scary woman's lanyard. 'I'm sorry I nearly killed you.'

'You will be! I'm going to find out where you work. I'm going to hunt you down, arsehole. The police will be on your doorstep. I'll . . .' She runs out of threats. 'Yeah, so watch out, you overgrown nob-head boy racer.'

And now the archdeacon makes a mistake: he blows her a kiss.

Oooo-kaaay.

He watches in the rear-view mirror till she's safely gone, then gets out to check the damage. Yep. Good call, staying in the car. He can get the ding in the panel popped back out at the body shop, no probs. Which would not have been true of his crown jewels. He starts the engine and drives very sedately to Lindchester Cathedral Close, and parks outside William House. When he's at his desk he googles 'Linden University, Dr Jane Rossiter'. A wise archdeacon knows his enemies.

The Season of Easter nurdles gently along. This Sunday will be the Fifth Sunday of Easter (that's the Fourth Sunday After Easter in old money). The daffodils are past their best now, and at last the loveliest of trees is hung with white along the bough. In every park and field and garden in the diocese blackbirds sing joyously (like the first bird): *Piss off, this is my tree, tirra lirra!* Willow buds are bursting all along the Linden. The newly hatched leaves cling like green dragonflies to the fronds. Lulu plods faithfully along with Father Wendy. Yes, Lulu's still with us. The giant cloud factory toils apocalyptically on. In Renfold the food bank continues to dispense food and debt counselling. In Lindford the homeless with their paper cups beg outside coffee shops. They don't expect much, barely the change from your flat white, the difference between a regular and a large latte. But they are invisible. Anyone sitting on a pavement is invisible. Anyway, they'd probably only spend it on drugs. We'd love to help, but what can we do? Donate to Shelter, maybe? Yes, we'll do that. Must remember to do that. Oh dear, it's all so sad! And we nip into M&S and cheer ourselves up with some of those pastel-coloured mini macaroons.

Today, as everyone in the parish of St John's Renfold acknowledges when they ring him on Friday, is Father Dominic's day off. He's standing on his bombsite of a patio with a mug of coffee. It's not raining, so he ought to mow his lawn. But then he'd have to shift that bloody ladder which is still lying there under the laurels with nettles growing through the rungs. As far as he knows, the lead thieves never came looking for it. Maybe his psychotic priest act was a deterrent after all. Dominic knows he probably can't stop the thieves if they are really determined; but he can make it easier for them to target someone else's church. Yeah, go and nick the Methodists' lead! thinks Father Dominic, ecumenically. He stares at the lawn a bit longer. No. It really isn't going to mow itself. He finishes his coffee and lugs the ladder back next door to the churchyard, clipping gates and walls with the end he's not watching, tripping, getting wedged, like an impromptu homage to Charlie Chaplin. After another comic interlude – during which he amusingly extracts the Flymo from a garage so hilariously small that if he drives into it, he cannot then open the car door – he is happily mowing. He mows nice wavy lines, because he's the vicar, it's his day off, and he can do what he bloody likes.

On Saturday Jane wakes with a lurch. It's a moment before she works out she hasn't overslept, there is no cricket training to pack her great lump of a son off to; in fact, there is no lump of a son. He's been gone nearly four months now. Four months! How has she stood it?

But that's a third of his gap year done. Maybe she should tackle his room? She opens his door on the way to the shower. The museum of adolescence is unchanged. There is still a dent in the pillow. The last mug of tea she brought him on Boxing Day is by the bed, sealed with a disk of mould. She can still smell him. Her boy cub. She shuts the door. Let the bugger tidy it himself when he gets home.

Jane sits with her toast and coffee. Her boiler has been fixed. Radio 3 is playing, because Radio 4 is too shouty. She's checking her diary for the week ahead and not really listening, but then an a cappella song starts. I know this, thinks Jane. An old hymn, from the dusty old chapel of memory. 'What can wash away my stain?' Nothing, she tells the radio. 'Nothing but the blood of Jesus,' the voices reply. 'What can make me whole again? Nothing but the blood of Jesus.' The arrangement is out of kilter, somehow. Jane is not musical, but she can hear the harmony not quite coming back home, but yearning, yearning for resolution. It twangs at her heartstrings and tears start in her eyes. 'No other fount I know.' *Because there is none!* Jane wants to shout. There's nothing. Nothing. Nothing. 'Nothing but the blood of Jesus?' The music trails away, still asking, teetering on the brink of hope.

'That was the Dorian Singers, from their latest CD, *Nothing but the Blood*,' murmurs the presenter.

Ah, dammit. Jane wipes her eyes. She's going to be singing that all bloody week now.

MAY

Chapter 19

Coloured placards bloom on tree and lamppost across the diocese of Lindchester. Local elections this Thursday. Oh gawd, is it really? Again? Did I get a polling card? Damn, I suppose that means the school's closed and I'll have to make childcare arrangements. Yes, yes! Local elections, when the nation traditionally punishes the government by voting for nutcases! If we can be arsed to go to the polling station, that is. Our great-grandmothers chained themselves to railings for the right to vote for nutcases, but we aren't sure we can be arsed.

The weather has turned lovely. Of course it has – it's the revision period. The baby lime leaves tremble on their twigs. Wild garlic sprouts long and lovely and lush, and dread begins to shadow every heart, even the hearts of those who sat their last exam half a century ago.

Jane and Spider are having lunch in Diggers, the vegan restaurant a stone's throw from the Fergus Abernathy building. The coffee is excellent there, and they deserve a treat. They are recovering from an exam invigilation training session. Despite years of sustained and systematic incompetence, they've yet again found themselves on the rota. This time Jane is only down as reserve chief invigilator. This ought by rights to mean that she can sit in her office for the duration of the exam, on standby. But the chief invigilator is Dr Elspeth Quisling, who is in an advanced state of ill-humour with Jane. Jane is betting that Elspeth will schedule a revenge migraine of her own that afternoon; and Jane means to deprive the Quisling of her fun by calmly stepping up and making no fuss. Hence her attendance at the refresher course – during which it has emerged that, contrary to Spider's suggestions during the brainstorming session, the qualities looked for in an ideal chief invigilator do not include suave good looks, a background in the Special Forces and the ability to see through walls.

Spider stared at his flat white as though the fern pattern were a Rorschach test. 'Fuck, Jane. Invigilation. Why? Why?'

'Because we're bad people being punished, comrade. We must hang on to the thought that it's better than *sitting* exams.'

'Except we were mostly stoned in exams.'

'I wasn't. I was a good girl back then. I used to underline my titles with a ruler.'

'And ask for extra answer books? I would've hated you.'

'And I would've tried to convert you.'

'Really? To what?'

'Jesus, of course. I was in the God squad.'

'The God squad! Hard core.' He looked at her for a long time, eyes magnified behind his blue lenses, as though some mournful giant were imprisoned inside him, watching the world through a letter box. 'Don't you kind of miss him? God?'

'No,' lied Jane.

'I miss him.'

'I suppose I miss forgiveness.' What can make me whole again? Nothing? 'Being . . . put right.'

'Mended.' Spider sighed. 'Before we face the one true Chief Invigilator.'

'*In mortis examine*,' said Jane.

'The examination of death! Nice one. Never thought of that.'

'Yeah, that mother of all finals.'

There was a silence. Jane saw herself turning over the paper and thinking, I'm screwed. I can't answer a single question.

'I feel a poem coming on,' said Spider.

'I need cake,' said Jane.

We will leave Jane and Spider to wallow in eschatological vegan doom, and turn our minds to a ticklish question: what's happening about that vacancy at York? You will remember that The Most Revd Dr Michael Palgrove's translation to Canterbury means that we currently have no archbishop of the northern province. I hope you also remember that this narrative has eschewed all dabbling in affairs outside the boundaries of the diocese of Lindchester? All the same, we must interest ourselves somewhat in this matter, as it impinges upon one of our chief characters, namely the Rt Revd Paul Henderson. All you need to know at this point is that the mills of God (otherwise known as the Vacancy in See Committee and the Crown Nominations Commission) have cranked into action and are grinding exceeding fine. Consultations have occurred, submissions have been invited, names have been mentioned, paperwork has been updated, and testosterone levels in the House of Bishops are running high. As to process, well, senior clerics will not be locked up in a chapel and starved into consensus in the Roman manner. Instead, a series of meetings will take place. These will escalate from rather tedious to very interesting indeed – not to say top secret – at which point the press will know all about it and be in a position to tell the C of E exactly what it's done wrong. And what of our friend Paul? I will simply say this: he has thought and prayed, and *he has not ruled himself out.* (Let the reader understand. And if the reader does not quite understand, I have successfully conveyed the semi-transparency of the process.)

But enough of this constitutional cobblers. Let's have some sex. Or the next best thing in Anglican circles: baking. Who is baking today? Susanna, of course. I have stated before that this narrative will not intrude into clerical bedrooms and anatomize marital relations. That said, perhaps I ought to hint that these days Susanna expends more time and energy on her culinary than her other wifely skills. By contrast, Ulrika Littlechild, the precentor's wife, is (how shall I put this?) not famed for her light touch with pastry. Nor for that matter, is Marion the dean. Goodness, my toes are curling. Quickly, back to the palace kitchen!

It's Thursday. Susanna (having dutifully voted) has a loaf of bara brith in the oven, and she's now making walnut and cherry shortbread, because the charity she works for is holding a fundraising coffee morning this Friday. She will move on to gluten-free parkin, lemon drizzle cake and flapjack, and call it a day. She'll then get up on the crack of dawn tomorrow and make a batch of triple choc chip cookies as well, because it will suddenly occur to her at 2 a.m. that five kinds of cake and biscuit is nowhere near enough.

Miss Barbara Blatherwick has been baking too. She's made a batch of Chelsea buns, because she's going to persecute poor Freddie and make him tell her how the job search is going. By now he ought to have heard if he's got interviews for those choral scholar posts she made him apply for. The buns, bursting with fruit and spice, oozing honey, will be withheld until he has given an account of himself.

Freddie was ambling back to the Palace round the Close when the text arrived: 'Wöuld you like to come før tea © 4pm this ãfternoon¿ Chelseã buns. BB'.

Ah cock. Fuck it. Freddie tried to beat off the swarms of panic. He'd had an email last week inviting him for interview at Barchester, and he'd been meaning to get onto that. Gah. Chelsea buns. Evil woman.

He didn't notice the sporty black Mini kerb-crawling him, until a voice said, 'Afternoon, tarty-pants.'

He spun round and bent to look in the car window, bestowing taut vistas of *Men's Health* perfection on the lucky occupant. 'Well, hel-lo-o-o, Daddy!'

'Nice tits,' said the archdeacon. 'Hop in and I'll drive you round to the palace.'

'Oh, man. Are you gonna be strict with me again?'

'Would you like me to be?'

'Fuck, yeah.' Freddie got in.

But the archdeacon drove in silence. He pulled up on the palace drive, killed the engine. Then he turned and looked at Freddie.

Freddie looked back over the top of his orange mirror Aviator Ray-Bans.

The archdeacon shook his head. 'Why are you still here? It was meant to be for a year. Martin's got his licence back now. What's going on?'

'So yeah, about that. I've been applying for stuff? Got an interview coming up?'

'Congratulations. When?'

'I'm like, you know? Still firming up the dates?'

'Need any help? I know you're allergic to admin.'

Freddie retreated behind his shades. 'I'm good.'

'Well, give a shout if I can do anything,' said the archdeacon. 'Seriously. This isn't doing you any good, Freddie, hanging round playing errand boy. You're bored, you're getting into trouble—'

'I know, I *know*, OK? Man, you're so mean to me. Wanna blowjob?'

'Always,' said the archdeacon. 'But not off you.'

The archdeacon prefers girls. Sad, because he might have been rather good for Freddie. But there it is: writers don't always wield as much power as they'd like. Heck, even archdeacons don't wield as much power as they'd like. The Venerable Matt Tyler is not a bit happy about the Freddie May situation, let me tell you. There are those in the diocese who refer to Freddie as the bishop's catamite. When Matt flagged this up with Bishop Paul after Christmas, he got a *ve-e-ry* chilly reception indeed. Like an industrial-sized fridge had opened in his face. Hmm. Looks like Matt needs to man up, don his thermals and tackle the bishop again. Because why the hell is it being allowed to drag on like this? Susanna's doing, maybe? It's not like Matt suspects anything inappropriate is going on, but there's something . . . off. Something just a tad out of key.

Then again, if Freddie really has got an interview, it will sort itself out without any need for confrontation. So the archdeacon goes and talks strategy and growth with the bishop instead this Thursday afternoon.

Across the diocese people go and vote, or not. In church halls, parish rooms, primary schools, they go and stand in plywood booths and put their cross in boxes for nutcases, or serious candidates, or not. Outside a blackbird sings in the horse chestnut tree, or kids in hoodies skid bikes in the gravel. An ice cream van jangles by. Tomorrow we will hear that the Conservatives retain overall control. But you won't be too surprised to hear that UKIP will have some modest success round here as well. The diocesan communications officer will be briefing the bishop, in case his opinion is sought.

Polling closes. Father Dominic gets his church hall back at last. Blossom from the cherries in the churchyard confettis down on him. He walks home along a pathway of pink, and catches himself singing: 'Why am I always the bridesmaid?' Day off tomorrow. Where will he go? Bluebells, he thinks. I'd like to see bluebell woods, glorious, glorious bluebell woods, like the kind I remember from childhood. From the coach window on the way to swimming.

He lets himself into the vicarage, and he's back at the open-air pool, aged about ten, seeing the yellow and blue cubicle doors. He's climbing to the top of the high diving board, skinny legs, big baggy navy trunks, not Speedos like the other boys, all wrong. 'Hur hur, Todd's got his dad's trunks on!' High as the trees. He flinches as house martins zoom at him, screaming. Now it's his turn. Too high! 'Jump, jump, Todd, you spaz!' No! No, he daren't. Tries to retreat. But a hand shoves him in the back, and he's over the edge, arms, legs windmilling, down into the brutal spank of water.

Dominic hopes, really hopes, it's a bit easier growing up gay nowadays. That there's someone there to scoop up the poor spaz in the wrong trunks. Scoop him up and say, 'I've got you. Don't cry. It's going to be fine. I've got you, darling.' Come unto me, all you who are weary and heavy laden, and I will give you rest. Isn't that, thinks Dominic, what the Church should be saying?

Chapter 20

O freakish bank holiday weather! No good will come of you! All across the diocese of Lindchester people haul out their lawnmowers and barbecues; they wrestle with deckchairs and loungers. A day of sunshine is all it takes to germinate the seeds of optimism. Hoorah! It's going to be a gorgeous summer after all! Aren't we owed one? Don't we deserve one? Above the water meadows of Cardingforth (all sweet with lambs and Shakespeare's flowers), the cooling towers spell out the answer: *mene, mene* . . .

Where are all our friends on this fair bank holiday morn? Dominic opens his sunroof, puts on an Ella CD and drives off on a sentimental journey. Gonna set his heart at ease. He drives far beyond the reach of this narrative, to the Chiltern bluebell woods of old me-e-m-o-ries. He will visit that open-air swimming pool, and find it derelict. I happen to know that the yellow and blue cubicle doors hang crooked now on broken hinges. A filing cabinet lies in the airy deep end, ragwort sprouts between poolside paving slabs. Dominic will gaze up at the turquoise skeleton of the high board and murmur, 'Oh my God, oh my God!' Now there's a sermon illustration if ever he saw one. Sentimental jo-o-urney home.

And where is our lovely dean today? I'm happy to report that Marion is flying high. Quite literally. She's having a gliding lesson. This is the bank holiday treat the ingenious Gene has cooked up for his beloved, to help her put Lindchester Cathedral into perspective.

Martin the bishop's chaplain is driving. Driving, driving, driving. Yes! Not epilepsy, after all. See? He knew all along it wasn't. He told everyone it was just that virus, on top of the stress of marital problems. His life took a decided turn for the better the day he was able to say to the little git, 'I'll have the bishop's spare car keys back now, if you don't mind.' The little git kept claiming he'd 'lost' the keys, until Paul blew his top and barked, 'Then find them, and get out of my sight!' Martin genuinely tried not to gloat.

But Martin has made a rod for his own back today, I'm afraid. This journey is too long. His girls were wild with excitement – 'The seaside, the seaside! Yay!' – but now they're moaning in the back. 'No, sorry, we're not nearly there yet. Listen to Harry Potter, please.' After an hour, Jessica wears him down with her whining and he hands over his iPhone so she can play Angry Birds. Within fifteen minutes she's sick all over herself, the seat, the car floor and her pink backpack, just like Daddy said.

Sometimes it is scant consolation to be proved right about something, Martin.

And what of Paul and Susanna? Well, they nipped off on Sunday evening to their little bolt-hole in the Peak District. *No! Of course they're not taking Freddie May with them!* Sorry, sorry, sorry. Susanna was just being silly when she raised that possibility. Freddie will be fine. Miss Blatherwick has taken him in hand, bless her. And Giles says they'll be falling over themselves to have a tenor of his calibre in Barchester. So she's trying not to fret. Anyway, Paul needs a complete break, poor darling. All this Crown Nominations Commission stuff, it's just so unsettling.

They wake to blue sky and the burbling call of curlews. Just the two of them. In bed. With the day stretching ahead of them. Susanna leaps up at once to bake special marmalade breakfast muffins, to atone for her insensitivity.

The bishop eats the muffin he doesn't want, and walks out over the moor with his book of verse, dusting off that New Year's resolution to read more poetry. He hasn't managed to leave his troubles behind. But God willing, by September – barring wilful self-sabotage – Freddie bloody May should be someone else's headache. If they can only nurse him through the last few months without major scandals or disasters. Damage limitation, that's all this year's been. Paul knows that he and Susanna haven't managed to help Freddie in any meaningful sense. Maybe no one can? Not until Freddie decides he wants and needs to change.

Well, this is one mistake Paul won't be making again. Leaving it to Susanna to choose tenants, and being too busy to interview a new employee and delegating it to the diocesan secretary. Couldn't either of them hear the warning klaxons, or see those whopping great letters flashing 'Trouble!' over that golden head? Extraordinary. And yet Paul was to blame as well. A craven impulse, and the moment for bailing out slipped away. Or was it compassion? Once again Paul sees Freddie standing there in the palace hallway, shivering with misery.

Leave off. Leave it alone, he tells himself. He wills his soul to unclench. But into the vacuum rush thoughts of York. They also serve who only stand and wait. Each passing day sears that deeper onto his spirit. The secrecy, the hints, the manoeuvrings. But above all, this intolerable passive waiting. It's finding him out. He knows he's being short with people. He's close to throttling his chaplain, he explodes at Freddie, he even snaps at poor old Suze, who is only ever doing her best. All these years she's put up with him, loved his unloveliness, gone wherever his job has taken them, never once berated him. She deserves better, God knows. He reminds himself that his first calling is to be a husband. He takes a deep breath. Juniper, heather, bracken. Come on, Henderson, relax. A curlew call goes lassoing up into the blue. Paul sits on a rock and opens his book.

Hmm. I'm not sure Shakespeare's Sonnets are your best bet for banishing a beautiful golden young man from your mind, bishop. But I appreciate you are a completer finisher, and you started this volume back in January.

> . . . O, what a mansion have those vices got,
> Which for their habitation chose out thee,
> Where beauty's veil doth cover every blot,
> And all things turn to fair that eyes can see!
> Take heed (dear heart!) of this large privilege:
> The hardest knife ill-used doth lose his edge.

Hang on in there, bishop. Only fifty-nine sonnets to go and you can flee to the grumpy cloister of R. S. Thomas's collected poems.

We must press on. Today is Thursday. Here on Planet Church we mark a festival that slips past unremarked elsewhere: Ascension Day, when we celebrate our Lord's return to heaven after forty days of resurrection appearances. Early in the morning the choristers of Lindchester (bursting with excitement) are shepherded up on to the cathedral roof to sing from the base of the spire. At evensong tonight the anthem will be Finzi's 'God is Gone Up' (oh, those heart-cramping melodies!). But for now, let's pop across to Lindford, where Jane (oblivious to Ascension Day) is at her desk in the Fergus Abernathy building, opening her post.

What the hell? A Mars bar? She looked inside the padded envelope and pulled out a plain postcard: 'I was going to send flowers, but I spent all my money getting my car door fixed. Matt xx'. And a mobile number.

Matt? That chef! Jane laughed. Then she went cold. How the hell had he got her name and address? Whoa, not liking this. Unless . . . oh! he must be employed by Poundstretcher, in one of the various student eateries! Obviously he knew her by sight and asked someone. She studied the postcard. Well, it was funny, rather than stalker-ish, she had to concede. But he seriously thought she was going to phone him? She tried to picture what he looked like. Shaved head. Late forties? Big. Hiding in his stupid Mini. Not interested, mister.

She made a cafetière of coffee. The Mars bar would hit the spot, actually. She unwrapped it. Wait. Did he think she was a greedy pig? Was that what this gift implied? Pah. Jane seized a paperknife (embellished with Lindford County Council crest, God knew why she had it) and stabbed the poor chocolate through its innocent heart. She got out her phone, took a picture of the dead Mars bar, and texted it to the number on the postcard.

The archdeacon was in William House. He did a spectacular nose trick with his coffee. The bishop stared. The dean stared. The entire committee stared. The archdeacon mopped his agenda and apologized. Memo to self: no more cheeky text-checking during finance meetings.

Meanwhile, over in the bishop's office, Freddie was juggling balls of screwed-up paper.

'Do you mind?' snapped Martin, as one bounced off his head.

'Yes, stop it, Freddie,' said the bishop's PA.

Freddie started fiddling with the stapler instead.

'Tell me more about this audition,' said Penelope.

'So there's like, sight-reading?' He stapled his T-shirt hem to her desk.

Penelope removed the stapler from him. 'Well, you can sight-read, can't you?'

'You betcha. I can sight-read the ass off a thing.' He prised his T-shirt free. 'And then, I'm thinking I could maybe sing the "Queen of the Night" aria?'

'What, from *The Magic Flute*? But isn't that a soprano role?'

'Yeah, no, yeah, but if I practise I reckon I can ace it?'

'He's just winding you up,' muttered Martin.

'The fuck I am!' Freddie tore screamingly into *Der Hölle Rache kocht in meinem Herzen!*

'Shut up!' shouted Penelope. 'That can't be good for your voice!'

'It'sh a work in progresh, Mish Moneypenny,' admitted Freddie. 'But when I was a chorister, hey, I was all *over* that fucker. Literally. I was that good? Back in the day, I'd totally have ended up a castrato. Lucky escape, yeah, Martin? Still got my boys. Here, wanna check?'

'Oh, stop that.' Penelope belted him with *Alpha News*. 'You'll go blind.'

Father Dominic has been off on a wild goose chase this afternoon, looking for a non-existent address where one half of a marriage couple purports to live. Not many sham weddings round this way, but he had alarm bells ringing from the moment they first contacted him. Sure enough, there is no 89a Windermere Gardens in Renfold. He drops in on the food bank, to cheer on the volunteers. He just has time to swing by Waitrose on his way home, to buy a little Day Off Eve treat to crack open after the Ascension Day Eucharist tonight.

(Clergy everywhere, look away now. You will not like this next bit.)

He's back from the service. He's about to get the Chablis out of the fridge when he remembers. *Fuck!* Oh, dear God!

Dominic slides down till he's sitting on his kitchen floor. The vicarage answer phone will be molten with messages. He daren't check. Oh, let this not have happened! Rewind, rewind. He'll say he was taken ill! He was in a car crash!

No. He knows what he must do. He must go now and face the family and tell the truth: I forgot. I just forgot. She died at the age of forty-eight from breast cancer, and I forgot her funeral. He rests his head back against the fridge. He hasn't got a single rag of an excuse to cover his nakedness. He sees the coffin glide away, the curtains close. Had they found someone to step in? *Let light perpetual shine upon her, rest in peace, rise—* oh, dear God, forgive me, I'm so sorry.

Ascension Day incense lingers in the dark cave of Lindchester Cathedral. Silence. Rain patters on the roof. Freddie stands alone in the crossing. He rolls his shoulders, relaxes, fills his lungs.

Outside, Giles the precentor pauses as he walks home from the director of music's house. Good God! Can that be Mr May, actually bothering to rehearse for once? *Jephtha*. Not a bad choice. He stands and listens.

The vicarage door closes. Dominic gets in his car and sets off. Can it be mended? Even this? Oh, scoop me up, carry me, carry me.

Rain falls in the silent crematorium, on the letters spelling MUM.

> Waft her, angels, through the skies
> Far above yon azure plain, far above yon azure plain
> Glorious there like you to rise, there like you for ever reign ...

The last note fades. Well, that's the choral scholarship in the bag, thinks Giles.

Chapter 21

Father Dominic has not been forgiven. I'm afraid the fall-out was as bad as he feared. Terrible betrayed tears. Letters to the bishop. Threats of legal action. And on top of that, the lead's gone from the church roof again. The bastards used the same ladder, the one Dominic had helpfully replaced in the churchyard when he mowed the vicarage lawn. The archdeacon is not going to be very forgiving with Father Dominic, either, is he?

Nor can Dominic forgive himself. How, *how* had it happened? How could he not have checked his diary? In all his years as a priest he's never forgotten a funeral! His unpreached sermon, their accusations, the door shut in his face – round and round they go on the carousel of his conscience. Comforter, where, where is your comforting? He has had a kind letter from the retired Methodist minister who stepped in and took the service for him; he's had nice supportive messages from clergy colleagues. His congregation has been lovely.

It will pass. He knows this. But right now – Mary, mother of us, where is your relief?

'I'm bo-o-ored,' moaned Freddie on Monday morning. 'Got a top shecret mission for me, Mish Moneypenny?'

'You can go and put these up for Giles.' The bishop's PA handed him a pile of posters. 'Tea shop, visitors' centre, cathedral notice boards. All the usual places.'

'K.' Freddie glanced at them. 'Wait, the Dorian Singers? Fuck, the *Dorian Singers*? They're coming here? Omigod, omigod! They're singing with our choir? How come I didn't know this?'

'Well, I really couldn't say, Freddie – since it's been common knowledge for months. Honestly, you're such a dilly daydream.'

'Yeah. Probably it's all the meth?'

'The what? You don't!' Freddie grinned at her. 'You're being naughty. Anyway, it's a choir fundraiser. They're coming as a special favour, because Giles was a chorister with their director.'

'He was?' Freddie hugged the pile of posters to his heart. 'Like. Whoa. Fuck? I'm yeah, major, major music crush here? Met him once. I'd be like, eleven? Three Choirs Festival?' He subjected Penelope to a detailed analysis of the Dorian Singers' repertoire; their technical brilliance; the awesome musicality of their director. In his excitement he lapsed into complete coherence. 'Seriously,' he concluded. 'I fucking *love* that guy. Wanna marry him and have his babies.'

They both glanced at the bishop's office door.

'Well, you'll probably meet him,' whispered Penelope. 'You'll be singing, won't you?'

'Yeah, right. Like I'll get to dep for something like this.'

The director of music, dear reader, has a bit of a dilemma here. Freddie is quietly acknowledged to be the best tenor around, but he is not a member of the cathedral choir. Timothy can't bring Freddie in and give him showy solos without the cathedral lay clerks exercising their historic medieval right to be a bunch of grumpy old men.

Freddie set off round the Close with the posters. They were all inventing jobs for him to do now that Fuckwit1 had got his driving licence back. They were like, 'Oh, Freddie, Freddie, Freddie, what are we going to do with you? How are we going to keep you out of mischief till you're finally off our hands?' Yeah, no, that wasn't fair. They wanted the best for him, was all. Miss Blatherwick, driving him to Barchester, I mean, literally driving him there, to make sure he didn't fuck up again? Getting his suit dry-cleaned? Man, he hated that suit. His 'ooh, look at me, I'm the defendant, I'm the bishop's chauffeur, I'm a total failure' suit. God, what if he did fail? What if he cocked up the sight-reading? What if his voice didn't measure up, or they asked him like personal stuff, and he went blank?

Freddie blu-tacked a poster to the cathedral notice board and tried to remember those careful sentences Miss Blatherwick had come up with. Unhappy phase. Behind him now. Focused on— Fuck, what was he meant to be focused on?

Yeah, but what if he didn't fail and actually got the scholarship? He'd be starting over where he didn't know anyone. Having to find part-time work. Sharing a flat with the other scholars. He'd have to always be responsible for shit. The whole time? Gah! He was meant to be an adult, he was meant to be cool with this! He could not go for the whole rest of his life letting people carry him, like he was twelve? I mean, God, it was embarrassing now, think when he was thirty, forty?

Seriously. He couldn't tell what freaked him out more: failing, or succeeding.

Janet Hooty, wife of the bishop of Barcup, is delivering Christian Aid envelopes on her four streets in Martonbury. These are in the 'rougher' area, on a housing estate where other members of the congregation of St Mary's Martonbury are a bit reluctant to stray. Janet has no time for this kind of nonsense. She and Bob have worked in parishes that make the Hollyfield estate look like Postman Pat's Greendale. She feels a bit of a pang: this will be her last year in this patch. There's a new congregation on the estate, and they've said they will take over next year. It's a church plant from St James's, the big thriving Evangelical church in Martonbury. Much more Paul Henderson's cup of tea than Bob's, but he gave the initiative his blessing.

Oh bum, now Janet's going to have that tune going round her head. Their children have taught the grandkids to sing 'Bob the Bishop, can he bless it?' Never a dull moment round here. Once she got £39 entirely in coppers, in empty cat food tins. And last year a bloke answered the door stark naked and said, 'Sorry, can you come back, love? I'm in the middle of something.' Donations from these streets are generally higher than those from the nice areas (where residents have been known to say, 'Oh, I don't do charity'). Same with church offerings, according to Bob: the poorer the parish, the bigger the per capita donation. Interesting, that. Janet bends – oof! getting old – to stick an envelope through yet another ankle-height letter box. Blimey! Nearly got her fingers. She watches through the glass as a yappy little terrier tears the envelope to shreds.

It's Pentecost this coming Sunday (the festival formerly known as Whit Sunday). Another knees-up on Planet Church that passes the secular world by. Across the diocese of Lindchester Pentecostal preparations are in train. If you wander round the Close late at night you may hear Laurence, the cathedral organist, practising Duruflé's *Choral Varié sur Veni Creator Spiritus*. The cathedral choir are busy with the Lassus *Missa Bell Amfitrit' Altera*—

Stop. Enough of this 'ooh, father, your maniple's crumpled' poncing about! What's going on in the real world, some of you are asking. What about Renfold, what about Lindford, what about Cardingforth? Forget the cathedral. What about all those unglamorous places where the clergy just peg away, week after week? Where overstretched lay people put in long hours – helping run Alpha courses, toddler groups, food banks, after-school clubs, men's breakfasts – maybe on top of their demanding jobs? Do the fires of Pentecost not fall there too? Are they not also Anglicans? Yes! I will go further still: even the good folk gathering for café church, who egregiously sing 'Be thou my vision' in four/four and 'wanna see Jesus lifted high' – they too are Anglicans. And so yes, I say, yes! Let Pentecost come to the C of E: in flash paper and Prinknash incense, in vestments and WWJD wristbands, in Latin and tongues, in Fresh Expressions and eight o'clock BCP. Thy sevenfold gifts to us impart. Shine, Jesus, shine! Whatever. We'll take it.

But that's not till Sunday. Today is Friday. Friday, as we know, is Father Dominic's day off. He ought to take this opportunity to get right out of the parish and regain some perspective. Better still, let his hair down with some old friends. But these things take energy, they take organizing. I'm afraid Dominic is sitting in his kitchen giving way to self-pity. He wonders why someone else doesn't organize something and invite him, for a change. Why do none of his friends seem to think, 'I know, let's drag Dominic along too, that would be fun!'? Especially now, when he's had such a horrible week. Don't they care about him? He knows they do, but when you're single you tend to slip off people's radar. Everyone's so busy being child-friendly and family-friendly, they forget to be spinster-friendly. Is that what he is – a spinster? He tries it on for size. Spinster of the parish of St John the Evangelist, Renfold. It has a Jane Austen-y vibe. Dominic Todd, spinster. Could he inhabit this?

Just then the doorbell rings. God. If this is a bloody parishioner saying, 'I know it's your day off, but . . .' He goes to the door to give them a piece of his mind. Some instinct prompts him to check through the spyhole first.

Shit! Dominic recoils, heart bouncing in his chest.

Would you like to know what has caused such cardiac capering in our poor friend? Oh, go on then. I am all indulgence, am I not?

Help! It was the Prat in the Hat! Did he hear me coming down the hall? Does he know I'm in? Dominic risked another peep. The archdeacon loomed close and did a finger-waggle wave. Aargh! He has X-ray eyes! Dominic wiped his palms on his trousers as though he were about to share the Peace, and opened the door.

'Goodness! Hello there, archdeacon!'

'Morning, father.' He tipped his porkpie hat. 'Busy?'

'Well, actually, it's my day off, so, um.' The archdeacon appeared to be nursing bailiff-like intentions of shouldering his way in. 'But I can probably spare a minute.'

'Cheeky pint?'

Dominic waited to see if this utterance would dis-encrypt itself. 'Sorry?'

The archdeacon mimed having a swift one. Beamed encouragingly.

'Oh! You mean . . . now?'

'Why not? I'll buy you lunch.'

'Um.' Beware of archdeacons bearing gifts! 'Is this about that funeral?'

'Nope.'

'Oh God, it's the lead, isn't it?'

'Nope.' The archdeacon beamed again. 'Do you give up?'

'What?'

'Never mind,' he said. 'Grab a coat. I'll drive.'

They got into the black Mini and the archdeacon drove to a country pub overlooking the River Linden. On the way Dominic blurted explanations about the funeral and the lead. He couldn't stop himself. Why was he justifying himself to a plonker who wore checked clerical shirts? That pathetic playground dynamic was kicking in again, wasn't it? Trying to ingratiate himself with the rugger-buggers so they wouldn't chuck his schoolbag on the gym roof and call him a poof.

The archdeacon let him talk. He parked, and they headed into the pub. I bet he's a real-ale buff, thought Dominic. And sure enough, the archdeacon had a pint of Bishop's Legover, or some such, while Dominic asked for dry white wine. They ordered baguettes and found somewhere to sit. The archdeacon took a long pull of his pint and leant back. Oh shit, here it comes, whatever it is, thought Dominic.

'How long have you been in Renfold now?'

'Nearly eleven years,' said Dominic.

'Happy?'

'Yes.' The archdeacon was watching him closely. Dominic rubbed his face for stray breakfast crumbs. 'What?'

'Your mouth turned down when you said that. Which normally means "not happy".'

'I'm very happy,' said Dominic. And burst into tears.

Saturday night. Pentecost eve. A car creeps slowly past the vacant vicarage in the centre of Lindford. The trees thrash in the wind.

Raindrops crack on the windscreen. Was it time for a move? Could he imagine himself here? Dominic peers through the wrought-iron gates. One of tomorrow's hymns plays in his mind:

> Ready for all thy perfect will,
> My acts of faith and love repeat,
> Till death thy endless mercies seal,
> And make my sacrifice complete.

Chapter 22

The cherry blossom is past its best. Father Wendy smells rotting petals as she plods with Lulu along the bank of the Linden. It's like a tiny autumn. Still, the hawthorn blossom is out now instead. It clots the hedges and fills the air with a sweet whiff of corpses. Or so they say. That's why the hawthorn is thought to be an unlucky tree. The rowan, on the other hand, means good luck. Plant one by your house to keep the witches away. Wendy has no idea how she knows all this folklore. 'How do I know all this?' she asks Lulu. Lulu turns her old head up to listen. And there: a crab apple tree in bloom! Right by their bench. They sit.

Wendy thinks she can't sing – she was poked in the back when she was six and told to mime – but there's nobody listening, so she sings anyway because her heart is singing:

> I'm weary with my former toil,
> Here I will sit and rest awhile:
> Under the shadow I will be,
> Of Jesus Christ the apple tree.

A coot calls. There he is, busy with nest-making among the rushes. The fast train scythes through the fields in the distance. On the opposite bank, pounding feet: the young blond man again. Bless, bless. All the blessings of this life on him, on the folk on that train, on her parishioners, on poor old Dominic, on that funeral family, on us all.

As it happens, Paul Henderson is on the train that Wendy is busy blessing. He's off to the House of Bishops.

'What will you be debating?' asked his chaplain as he drove him to the station.

'Oh, stuff, as usual.'

My word, he was grumpy, wasn't he? You'd think he'd be relieved to have Martin driving him again. But no; perversely, the bishop found himself thinking that life was never dull with Freddie May at the wheel. He missed shouting at him to slow down. He missed the constant stream of lunatic suggestions. 'A circus! Awesome! We could go to the circus! Let's get an ice cream, let's get shit-faced, why don't we skinny dip? Hey, bouncy castle! Let's climb that tree, wanna play on the swings?' At least Freddie had a sense of humour. Even though the bishop spent half his time deliberately not getting Freddie's jokes. ('Body piercing studio – cool! You should so get yourself a PA!' 'I already have Penelope, thank you.') If Paul were to look out of the train window, his heart might be rejoiced at the sight of apple blossom, may blossom, rowan blossom, horse chestnut blossom; oh, the whole heaven-on-earth of an English spring morning! Instead the Rt Revd Testy Henderson is reading. What is he reading? Oh, I don't know. 'Stuff,' as usual.

Bear with me for a moment: I'm about to dump a bunch of Anglican facts on you. All bishops are in the College of Bishops, but not all are in the House of Bishops. The House of Bishops is made up of all the diocesan bishops, plus seven suffragans, four from the Province of Canterbury, three from the Province of York. The lovely bishop of Barcup (Bob the Bishop, can he bless it?) is one of those three. Together, these gentlemen constitute the House of Bishops. Oh, not forgetting the bishop of Dover (stunt double for the archbishop of Canterbury at diocesan level). But before long there will be women participants of the House of Bishops, too. Actual women. After the narrow defeat back in November of the measure to allow women bishops, 'the House decided that eight senior women clergy, elected regionally, will participate in all meetings of the House until such time as there are six female members of the House'. Whether you shout 'huzzah' or feel patronized by this is entirely a matter for you. And now back to the story.

The train stops at Martonbury station. Bishop Bob spots Paul in the quiet coach with empty seats around him. Oh no! But fortunately Paul is reading and hasn't seen him, so Bob abandons his reserved seat and heads to the opposite end of the train to Coach A instead. He feels bad about this, but he honestly can't face the whole journey to York making polite conversation with his diocesan.

In the quiet coach Paul steals a glance out of the window and sees Bob disappearing down the platform. Thank the Lord. He feels a bit bad about this, but he really didn't relish the thought of making polite conversation with his suffragan all the way to York.

The young blond man reaches the old bridge, the halfway point of his long run, and crosses it. He's running for the endorphins, running to fill the horrible hours of waiting, running so he won't have to sit around with nothing to do, obsessing about tomorrow's interview. There's nothing out here but the pounding of his music, the pounding of his feet, the pounding of his heart. Nothing, nothing, nothing.

It is Monday afternoon. Reserve chief invigilator Dr Jane Rossiter is invigilating an exam because, yes, chief invigilator Dr Elspeth Quisling has a 'migraine'. Dr Rossiter and her team of paid invigilators – who seem to know what they are doing, thank God – are invigilating not just one but five different exams simultaneously. There are 218 students in the Luscombe Sports Hall this afternoon, scrawling, staring into the distance, sniffing, swigging water. Undergraduates all swig water these days. They have to, obviously. Because climate change has transformed exam halls everywhere into the Gobi Desert, thinks Dr Rossiter.

I really hope Dr Rossiter does not get bored. I hope she doesn't sneak out her phone and follow the Commons debate on the Same Sex Marriage Bill and end up thinking: Aggressive homosexual community? What's that supposed to mean, dickbrain? The fags are arming? They're herding us into *Sound of Music* sing-alongs at gunpoint? Oh, for fuck's sake – a stepping stone to something further? Like what? The outlawing of heterosexual marriage? Compulsory queering lessons in all state schools?

I really hope Dr Rossiter is not doing this, as it would not conform to the qualities looked for in an ideal chief invigilator.

On Tuesday morning a little red car pulls out through the gatehouse of Lindchester Cathedral Close. It is driven by Miss Barbara Blatherwick. Beside her sits Freddie May, white-faced, in his newly dry-cleaned defendant's suit. So far he's held it together. He managed – just – not to go out and get off his tits last night. But he's jittery, feels sick, like he's hungover all the same. He leans his head back and shuts his eyes.

Well, wouldn't you be terrified? Isn't that your idea of a nightmare, having to stand up in front of people and sing a solo? But that's not the problem. You could stick Freddie in front of a packed Albert Hall and he'd say 'Bring it on!' He's an adrenaline junkie. To him, performing is a rush, like bungee jumping, like black-water rafting.

Miss Blatherwick negotiates the four-by-fours heading up the hill towards the Choristers' School. Freddie keeps his eyes shut. He has suspected for a while that he's wired up backwards. He's phobic about shit normal people take in their stride. But it's just this minute dawned on him that he's even more terrified that people will spot his phobia, and despise him. Suddenly he hears his dad's voice at all those karate gradings and contests: 'Stop being such a girl! Man up, son! Fight back!'

Yeah. Way to go, Dad. So here's your grown-up son: he can kick the shit out of anyone who starts on him, but he can't fill out a fucking job application by himself. I mean, hello? A seventy-eight-year-old woman is having to drive me to an interview! I'm still a girl, I've just learnt to hide it behind my 'Hey, everyone, I'm a brain-fried fuck-up!' act. Shit, Dad, I *can't* man up, I just can't do this reality thing, I want someone to look after me. Please. Please.

Miss Blatherwick – once they are safely in the Lower Town – reaches over and squeezes Freddie's arm.

'Ah nuts. Now you made me cry. Miss B, what am I going to do without you?'

Freddie doesn't know, but Miss B has been plotting. She's arranged to meet an old friend for tea in Barchester. She will confide in Christine. If Freddie gets this choral scholarship, Miss B can rest assured that there will be someone on hand who will take no nonsense, feed him homemade cake, and keep a special eye on her boy.

And what about our boy Dominic? Who is keeping a special eye on him? Why, the archdeacon, of course. He's not feeding him homemade cake, that's not really his style, but he's got a plan. It's now Thursday afternoon. The archdeacon is in his office in William House, playing Hearts in the few minutes before Dominic is due to arrive. He does not play against Pauline, Michele and Ben. The archdeacon plays against the pope, the AB of C and Dr R. Dr R is currently winning. She kicks his door panel in, she murders his Mars bar, and now she's whipping his ass at Hearts. The minx. But here's Dominic.

God, thought Dominic as he entered. *Please* not a harlequin patterned clerical shirt! 'Afternoon, archdeacon.'

'Afternoon, father. Take a pew. Get you anything? Coffee? Tea?'

'I'm fine, thanks.' Dominic sat. The archdeacon beamed. Like a bloody sunlamp. Shine, Jesus, shine! 'Well, I took a look, like you suggested.'

'What do you reckon?' asked the archdeacon. 'Think it might be a fit?'

Dominic hesitated. 'Well . . .'

'Bearing in mind this is not a good time to leave St John's.'

Dominic stared.

'It's never a good time to leave. Not if you're doing your job properly.'

'I'm not sure I am,' said Dominic.

'Aha, that funeral. Yep. Had a cracking green ink letter about that.' An even broader beam. 'Want to see my reply?'

'No!'

'Sure? I was very supportive.' He stretched his long legs and crossed his ankles.

Dominic spotted he was wearing black and white bloody harlequin socks to match his shirt.

The archdeacon noted him spotting this, and laughed. 'Look, friend, I may be a prat, but I know the difference between a good parish priest and a bad one. The folk at Lindford have just had first-hand experience of a real baddie. I'll fill you in on that some time. Now, Bishop Paul's been wanting a lively Evangelical Charismatic church— Wait,' the archdeacon raised a hand. 'I know you aren't. Paul's been wanting a Charismatic presence in Lindford for some time now. It's daft that there isn't one in a university town. But after this, nope. These folk just need someone to love them. Love them to bits. You da man, Dominic.'

'I . . .' Dominic felt tears surge up again. 'That's what the bishop wants?'

'That is indeed what the bishop wants,' said the archdeacon. 'Though it's possible the bishop is unaware of it.'

Trinity Sunday. Another arcane jolly on Planet Church. Consubstantial co-eternal. Who can we get to preach? Who gets the short straw? Can we use flash paper again? No, you can't. This week you must use water, ice and steam to illustrate the mystery of the Three-in-One. You may also catch your congregation out with the hymn 'I bind unto myself today', which changes tune halfway through without warning.

It is now late on Sunday evening. The bishop (still unaware of what he wants) is unwinding with a well-earned glass of wine. House of Bishops: over. Trinity Sunday sermon: over. Catching up on admin: over. Freddie May problem: over. (He got the choral scholarship – thank you, Lord!) The bishop's mobile rings. Local number, unknown caller. He very nearly doesn't answer.

'Is that the bishop of Lindchester? Sorry to bother you, sir. It's the police. We have a Freddie May here.'

Chapter 23

The journey home from Lindford Police Station went like this.

'Listen, I'm sorry, Paul. I'm sorry, OK? I'm really sorry.'

'Freddie, for the last time, you have nothing to be sorry about. I know it wasn't your fault.'

'Was literally a hate crime, man. They fucking ... Yeah. Hey, faggot – bam! They fucking did that.'

'I know, Freddie.'

'Telling you, hate crime. You're not mad at me?'

'Of course I'm not mad at you.'

'I love you, man. Fucking love you.'

'Yes, we established that. Are you sure we shouldn't go to A and E?'

'Nah, 'sjust a broken nose.'

'I'm more worried about concussion.'

'No, look, listen, it's— Listen. Thing is, I'm kinda wasted?'

I'll say, thought the bishop.

'Ow. My fucking nose really *hurts*.'

Pause.

'So they're like, hey, faggot. And I'm like— Hunh. Can't re'mber the, the, ah nuts.'

Pause.

'So yeah. Wossname. Busted his knee. Other guy, he goes to hit me, and I'm, block, turn, *boom*! With, with, with, yeah. Only, *jodan*, na mean?'

'What? Sorry, are you talking about karate?'

'Fucking hate crime. Hey, faggot – bam!'

'Yes, but are you telling me you retaliated? Freddie?'

'Fucking love you, Paul. Seriously. Do anything for you.'

The bishop pulled the car over and turned on the light. 'That was *not* in your statement, Frederick. You said one of them punched you, then you managed to run off! Come on, this is serious. Look at me.'

But Freddie's eyes were tracking an invisible tennis lob in ultra-slow motion. 'Wha-a-a'?'

'Tell me what you just said. About this guy, whose knee you "busted".'

'I busted his knee? Awesome!' Pause. 'Why've we stopped? You wanna fuck? Whoa. Prolly we shouldn't do that, Paul? Seriously, whoa.'

Give me strength! The bishop snapped off the light and wrenched the car into first.

'What I do? Hey! Do not lay your passive-aggressive shit on me, Paul! I do not enjoy that shit.'

Trust me – you'd enjoy my aggressive-aggressive shit even less, thought the bishop.

Normal bank holiday weather has been resumed. A glorious Trinity Sunday, true, but as half term commences we are back to our customary misery. The cathedral choir is on holiday. The Choristers' School is closed. It will be evensaid, not evensong this week. Dean and Chapter have taken advantage of the traffic lull on the Close: scaffolding will be going up on the south side of the cathedral on Wednesday. Where is the money coming from for the restoration work? I'm glad you asked that question. Just to set it in its context, we have been working very hard with our various partners on a wide-ranging ambitious five-year development plan, which includes education and missional projects, the redevelopment of our visitors' centre, investment in the choral foundation, urgent fabric repairs, along with a range of exciting new enterprise and outreach initiatives, with various funding bodies coming together, including we hope HLF, to—

'Don't bullshit me, Deanissima,' says Gene, 'the money's coming out of the endowment funds.'

'Only in the short term,' says Marion. 'It's all above board. We've got permission from the Church Commissioners.'

'Because the bastard thing's about to fall down.'

'Not on my watch, it's not.'

'You go, girl! But – just to clarify, if I may – the bastard thing could now go bankrupt on your watch instead.'

'Thanks for that cheery thought, Gene.'

'Well, let's not worry about it. You'll have a few years' leeway before it goes tits up, and who knows? You could even be bishop of somewhere by then, so it'll be the next dean's problem.'

'I'm glad I have you in my life. You are always such a support.'

'You're welcome. I also dance exceptionally well. Would you like me to show you my dance moves?'

'I've not heard it called that before,' says the dean.

June, it's nearly June. Danny's nearly halfway through his gap year, thinks Jane, and I still haven't cleared the bugger's room. Probably teeming with rats and roaches by now. This time last year I was on his case about revision. And then it was the Jubilee, whoopee-doo, pissing with rain, and we—

Jane calls herself to order. You can Skype him tonight and gloat about the cricket. This is not getting these suckers marked. (Marking! What a way to spend your bank holiday.) She picks up the first script: 'There were many causes for the Enlightenment, such as the influence of philosophers and cultural and intellectual influences as well as the political environment.' Should she read to the end? Or just drink bleach now?

Her phone buzzes. Well, well. A text from 'wazzock chef'. (Which reminds her: she still hasn't tracked down where he works.) The text contains a picture of two foaming beer glasses, and it's followed by a question mark. I'm afraid Jane then wastes rather a lot of valuable marking time on Google images, searching for a riposte.

'In this essay I will show that the impact of the scientific revolution also impacted on the Age of Enlightenment as well, when many new discoveries challenged traditional concepts of nature and man, such as for example deism.' Jane's forehead makes contact with her desk. That beer is starting to seem very tempting indeed.

The archdeacon of Lindchester – sitting in Costa in Lindford – snorts coffee all over his iPad. He'll take that as a no, then. He wipes down Lara Croft with his sleeve as she flips him the bird.

Susanna is optimistic about getting the bloodstains out of Freddie's clothes. The trick is a long soak in cold water first, followed by a forty-degree wash with Vanish. She secretly prides herself on her stain-removal skills. She even got that red wine stain out of the oatmeal carpet, though she'd despaired at one stage, thinking Jane had actually managed to set it in her desperate efforts at removal. Blot, not scrub. Never scrub. She hasn't told Jane that, of course. But Freddie's shirt and jeans won't be a problem. She still can't believe that Paul didn't wake her last night! Poor, poor Freddie! Oh dear, oh dear! Oh, let the police catch the brutes who did this!

'Do you think CCTV footage would show anything?' she asks Freddie. 'Have the police checked? Did they say anything about CCTV? Maybe they'll be able to identify them.'

'Could be, Suze, could be.' Fuck, his head hurts. He swigs down the painkillers she is handing him. Ow, fuck, his nose hurts. Fuck.

'Well, let's hope so.'

Or not, thinks Freddie.

Because there's this blurry line? Where self-defence stops being self-defence and starts being, yeah, kind of more stomping the shit out of your attackers? No-o-o-oh. What has he done? It happened so quick! Ah c'mon, it was totally self-defence – there were two of them, they started on him for no reason. It was a hate crime. He's got the right to defend himself against homophobes, no? It's not like he set out to injure them. It was pure reflex. Muscle memory? Except when you're that blitzed, there's no control, is there, no knowing how hard you're going in. What if—? Ah shit. But no. Police would be after him by now if it was serious.

Wouldn't they?

'Can I make you some breakfast, Freddie?'

'No. Really, no.'

The bishop is not a happy bishop. Freddie May is devouring ten times his fair share of the episcopal emotional energy right now. It's nearly lunchtime on bank holiday Monday, and Paul has promised to take Suze to hell's amusement arcade, the Outlet Village, to browse the bargain Le Creuset. He's offered this because he knows he's been too busy. He's been grumpy and neglecting her, his poor old endlessly forgiving Suze. He is trying to have his Quiet Time first, so he won't 'lay his passive-aggressive shit' on her for the duration of her retailing treat.

He reads his Bible. He prays. He tries to hold his soul still under the patient searchlight of grace. Why is nothing *ever* straightforward with Freddie May? Paul re-experiences that visceral shock from last night, when he saw him covered in blood. Then the rage, the *rage* that seized him. How dare they do this to my— My what? My employee? Friend? House guest? My something-not-covered-by-any-of-those-categories. Paul has no word for what Freddie May is to him. My boy? The word trembles. He tests an unacceptable idea: that Freddie is the son he and Suze didn't manage to have? He has never let himself articulate the thought that his daughters are not enough. Is this it? He wants a son. Even now his heart flinches from it. Could this be why he stonewalls Freddie's desperate need to be fathered? Because it's inadmissible?

Next, he climbs back on the anxiety treadmill that kept him awake last night. He prays for wisdom. He can hear himself saying, 'I want this flagged as a hate crime. And I'd value your reassurance that you'll do everything you can to bring his attackers to justice.' Standing on the dignity of his office, for once.

But now – because this is Freddie bloody May – everything's got complicated! Should he march Freddie back to the station to emend his statement, or leave well alone? Is it his business? It's not! Yet he can't do nothing and hope it goes away. But the Le Creuset! Come on, think. Why can't he think clearly? Right now he simply does not have the time or the mental space to deal with this. His diary for the coming month is a nightmare. There's the Lords' debate coming up, not to mention the York thing hanging over him. So he does what he probably should have done last night: he rings the archdeacon. He feels a fool, but Matt has the knack he's never mastered – of dealing with Freddie.

Then he resumes his Quiet Time. Oh dear. He is still making heavy weather of Shakespeare's Sonnets, I'm afraid.

> What's new to speak, what now to register,
> That may express my love, or thy dear merit?
> Nothing, sweet boy; but yet, like prayers divine,
> I must each day say o'er the very same . . .

No. This really isn't helping, is it, bishop? But it will be over soon. Freddie's off to Barchester, and there are only another forty-six sonnets to go.

Hmm, thinks the archdeacon. He rings off and asks himself the obvious question (which the reader has doubtless been asking for a while): is Paul gay? The archdeacon does not know. He's inclined to think not. But for whatever reason, Paul's got a pretty big bee in his mitre about the lovely Mr May. So, looks like a little trip to the police station is in order. See what he can glean about last night, and how much trouble the Close tart's in this time. Probably none. Sounds to Matt like reasonable force in response to an assault-query-hate crime. And they're talking ABH, if he's had his nose bust. But good to check it out all the same, because if the bishop ain't happy, ain't nobody happy. And then he should probably track down young tarty-pants and get his version. See how he's coping.

The archdeacon orders another flat white. He mulls the conversation over again. Hmm.

May draws to a close. Lilacs drip in suburban gardens. Insomniacs hear blackbirds belting out their repertoire at 2.30 a.m. Half term flits by, too fast, too fast!

Unless you are a single mum at your wits' end, that is, and trying to be civilized to 'the children's father'. Especially when the children's father is being as difficult as he possibly can be without ceding the moral high ground. Poor Becky Rogers! And poor Martin, too. Theirs was one of those marriages where both partners are secretly convinced that they are the only one who ever empties the bin. Habits of resentment take some unlearning.

Thursday is Corpus Christi. Father Dominic burns his thumb on the thurible because he's not concentrating. He's thinking: *This could be my last Corpus Christi in Renfold . . .*

JUNE

Chapter 24

This time the bishop is relieved it's his chaplain driving him to the station. He's off to the House of Lords for the Same Sex Marriage Bill debate, and he can do without getting into a futile argument now, there'll be enough of that later. He has a short speech prepared, but it won't be needed. Others will make the point that the bill is a bodged job, it's too rushed, it fudges questions of adultery and consummation. 'Equal marriage' is a snow-plough being driven at full throttle by monomaniacs, thinks the bishop. It's shoving everything out of its path, brooking no questions or qualification, no nuance.

Martin drives in silence. He would like to know what the bishop plans to say in the Lords, but prefers not to be snubbed with 'Stuff, as usual,' thank you very much. He knows perfectly well that Paul would rather be driven by the little git, but he's afraid that's just unfortunate, isn't it.

Martin pulls into the drop-off zone unaware that the little git's popularity has this very second taken another nosedive. The bishop, puzzled, has just felt around behind him on the front seat to see what he's sitting on. *Liquid Gold*? One of Suze's aromatherapy thingies? Then realization erupts. That little—! If he's been stealing my car again—!

Paul pops the vial in his suit pocket before Martin sees, and gets out, dropping – argh! – his iPad. In the ensuing fluster – is it broken? Is it? It looks fine – the other matter slips his mind.

It's now June. Can it get any greener, any lusher? Each day proves it can. The sweetness of an English June morning! (Have, get, before it cloy!) Mountain ranges of horse chestnut rear against the sky, white candles, pink candles. The palace garden has a laburnum walk, a secret tunnel of swoony gold poison. Susanna won't let the grandchildren anywhere near it: forbidden bliss, thrice forbidden! And lilac, and roses fill parks and gardens; while red campion, stitchwort, ragged robin, plantain, dog daisies, cow parsley, buttercups (of yellow hue) do paint the meadows around Cardingforth power station with delight.

We will whisper this very quietly in case we jinx it: the weather has turned lovely. There are those in the diocese of Lindchester who (confusing 'global warming' with 'Middle England warming', and 'climate' with 'weather'), will remark, as if coining the drollery for the very first time, 'Well, if this is global warming, I'm all for it!' They have read a book, perhaps, or at any rate heard someone talk about a book, and have satisfied themselves that climate change is a complete fabrication because scientists are divided. And they are quite right. It is our duty to remain open-minded and give equal weight to the dissenting two per cent. Remember how scientists were divided on the links between cancer and smoking, and on the depletion of the ozone layer, on acid rain and all the toxic hazards of leaded fuel? So you go ahead and enjoy this lovely weather with a clear conscience, people of Lindfordshire who have heard about a book that flies in the face of ninety-eight per cent of serious science.

The scaffolding is up on the south side of the cathedral. It will be a busy week for the precentor and the rest of the choral foundation. This coming Sunday Lindchester Cathedral will host a big service to celebrate the sixtieth anniversary of the Queen's coronation (deferred from last Sunday, because of choral half term). Giles looks forward to the usual clash of cultures that occurs in joint shindigs with the military and the mayor's office. He will always treasure the memory of that sergeant barking, 'Hat off in church, cunt!' the time the Princess Royal visited.

There's a tenor crisis looming. One of the lay clerks has laryngitis, and unfortunately, it looks as though the lovely Mr May is out of the picture. That broken nose makes him sound bunged up. Pity. Oh, and pity for Freddie's sake too, of course, poor lamb. After this service is out of the way there's the ordinations, and the Dorian Singers' concert. But then the end of term will be in sight. 'Nearer and nearer draws the time . . .' warbles the precentor as he continues with his meticulous ceremonial notes. Are you curious? They read like a game of liturgical chess: Cross party and Choir from East, Bishop to throne, Dean to pulpit; Lord Mayor verged from stall to lectern.

At this moment, the lovely Mr May (sporting two lovely black eyes) is mowing the grass on the south side of the Close. He mows moodily, smoulderingly, back and forth, back and forth, beside the cathedral. Man, is it hot today? Halfway up the scaffolding a workman leans out to watch as the flamer down there languorously peels his vest off. Eye contact occurs. Shall I pretend I haven't noticed that? Oh, not to worry – the head verger has just noticed for me. He tells Freddie to cover himself up, then sends him to water the hanging baskets on the far side of the Close. That's all right, then.

Thursday night. It's Day Off Eve, woo hoo! Dominic feels like celebrating. Actually, he felt like celebrating the moment the bill got through the Lords, but he had a PCC finance subcommittee that night. So now he's sitting in Jane's rather depressing kitchen (that gal doesn't have a domestic bone in her body) eating strawberries and drinking Taittinger Brut Rosé. He knows he will end up blurting out his possible move to Lindford, but for all her other faults (and he could write you a comprehensive list), he knows Janey is totally a hundred per cent discreet. His secrets have been safe with her for over two decades. Right now, however, she is manifesting one of her less charming traits: pissing on his reason to celebrate.

'It's completely market-driven,' said Jane. 'I can't believe you've been suckered! You don't want equal-with-breeders marriage, you just want a big fat white wedding – and you only want that all of a sudden because someone pushed your buttons by shouting "Human rights! Human rights!". Of course our consumerist society is all yay for "equality"! They're wetting themselves about the shit-load of money they're going to make out of you guys. Because basically, there'll be two bridezillas, both wanting their perfect romantic colour-swatched special day!'

Dominic considered a range of counter-arguments to this merciless analysis, before settling on: 'Fuck you.'

'You're welcome.'

'You drink my champagne, you're nice to me – that's the rule, you tragic lonely embittered old crone sitting in your ghastly 1990s kitchen with a moustache.' He topped up her glass. 'Damn, I forgot fat. And *fat*.'

She stroked her moustache and laughed her filthy laugh. 'Oh yeah? I have an admirer, I'll have you know.'

'No! And? Well, go on – tell me everything! Fatty.'

'Well, shrimpy, there's not a lot to tell. He's a chef. He nearly ran me over, I kicked his car door in, and now he finds me irresistible. We are currently conducting a drawn-out and rebarbative courtship via text message. But other than the door-kicking incident, we've not actually met.'

After Jane had told him all about her big bald suitor, Dominic told Jane all about his big bald archdeacon and the new job possibility in Lindford. (Eventually they will find out that they were talking about the same person.) Then they ordered a curry, drank a bottle of Malbec and descended into fond reminiscence about their theological college days, back when everyone agreed that, one way or another, homosexuality was a problem to be solved. An abomination to be repented of; or an immature phase to be got through on the path to heterosexual wholeness; or else a paternal love deficit that could be rectified by chaste manly hugs.

And now we're trying to solve it with equal marriage, Jane did not say. She had no faith in marriage's power to solve anything. It hadn't solved female subjugation or male aggression, had it? As far as Jane could see, the only thing equal marriage might address was good old-fashioned sin. After centuries of being called sinners – even if you believed neither in God nor in sin – being able to rock up to the altar to be blessed, to be told you're acceptable just as you are, yes, she saw that would help. That just might mend some of the hurt. God, we could all use a bit of mending.

'Paul Henderson's views haven't actually moved on since he was in Latimer,' said Dominic. 'He's just trained himself to sound more PC and caring.'

'Well, some people are homophobes – get over it.'

'Shut up. He votes against the bill, then he turns round and laments the C of E's appalling track record with gay people on "Thought for the Day"! Did you hear him? Thanks for your pastoral support *there*, bishop. Fucking hypocrite!'

'Oh well.' Jane yawned. 'The Church moves at the pace of the slowest.'

'Excuse me? Did I just hear you defending the Church?'

'Did you? You did. God, I must be drunk.'

Jane was not really listening to herself. She was wondering whether Paul still believed that there was an element of choice in sexual orientation. Whether that friend of his – the one who had wrestled through his teens, before applying himself successfully to project heterosexuality – whether this friend was still joyously married and utterly fulfilled. And whether the friend had in fact been Paul himself. She yawned again, stretched, and said nothing. Dominic was right: secrets are safe with Jane.

The big bald archdeacon has been on a gleaning mission to Lindford Police Station, where he has friends. This is not surprising, as he was himself a police officer before he went into the ordained ministry. He's learnt that the incident involving Freddie May has indeed been flagged as a hate crime, but there is no CCTV footage. An off-the-record chat established that the police have a fair idea who the perpetrators are, but no witnesses other than Freddie, who was, um, hazy in his recall of events. It probably would not be worth the CPS's time trying to bring it to court. Even further off the record was the reaction, 'Way to go, poof!' when the archdeacon touched on the matter of Freddie's robust martial arts-based self-defence. A flavour of this conversation has been conveyed by the archdeacon to young tarty-pants, who'd been busy convincing himself he was guilty of manslaughter. Freddie sobbed with relief into the archdeacon's checked clerical shirt, then offered him a quickie. Numpty.

We are now in Ordinary Time. Or what passes for ordinary on Planet Anglicanism. Father Wendy is on her way to London for the Enough Food IF rally in Hyde Park. You are a good woman, Wendy. No wonder the bishop is sending you a curate to train. I'm sorry that the curate is prickly and still very put out that you will be her training incumbent, rather than the rector of Risley Hill, as originally planned. You may need to dig deep to make this relationship work, I'm afraid.

Chapter 25

Father Wendy needs help with the curate's house in Carding-le-Willow. She's trying to keep this in proper perspective – and after her weekend in London, she ought to be able to do this, surely? To bear the G8 Summit in her thoughts and prayers? But oh dear, it's turning into such a scramble to get everything ready in time for Virginia's deaconing at Petertide.

Here's what has happened: the PCC pays annually into a decorating fund, which the diocese then matches, but this has only stretched to getting a firm in to do the downstairs. But what about the upstairs? The diocesan housing officer can find money for paint, but not for labour, and asks whether parishioners could lend a hand? But Wendy's parishioners tend to come in three categories: they are either at work, or looking after small children, or liable to fall off a ladder and break a hip. This leaves Madge, a nurse who's just taken early retirement, and even Madge the Miracle can't get it all done before the date when Virginia intends to move in. And Virginia is very clear about her intentions. So Wendy (feeling pathetic and a nuisance) picks up the phone and calls the archdeacon.

Ah, gone are the days when curates could be expected to move uncomplainingly into houses that the diocese has yet to decorate, rewire or indeed purchase. Gone, too, are the days of low-key training by example and general encouragement. It's all form-filling and targets and reviews now. Yes, the world of management has invaded the C of E. Unfortunately, it has not brought with it the financial and personnel support required by such professionalization, so the structures rest upon wafer-thin admin. Which means archdeacon Matt works his checked socks off keeping the diocesan plates spinning, with only 0.5 of a PA.

Still, the archdeacon is very happy to troubleshoot in this instance, because Wendy is cheerful, hard-working and low maintenance. (And because he suspects her new curate may prove to be a royal pain in the arse if the house isn't sorted.) So he tells Wendy he'll send her a volunteer worker for the week. All she needs to do is provide lunch and point him towards the rollers and cans of magnolia. It's not really magnolia – it's the closest match Wendy and Madge could find to Virginia's Farrow and Ball choices: 'Lime White', 'Matchstick', 'Dimity' and 'String'. Or, as Madge thinks of it, 'Fifty Shades of Pus'.

It's Monday morning. Madge is standing in the avocado bath in 16 Lime Crescent, Carding-le-Willow. The bathroom window is open. She can hear the raindrops pattering down onto the overgrown garden, and music coming from the main bedroom where the archdeacon's volunteer is supposed to be sanding down the woodwork. Madge cannot hear much sanding going on, but she's not prepared to police him. Not her problem. She did not just bail out of the whole NHS nightmare in order to run around shouldering other people's responsibilities.

She goes back to scrubbing the grouting. Damn. Nothing's going to shift that mildew. She'll have to re-grout, or Miss Virginia Farrow-Ball will be complaining to the archbishop. A blackbird sings in the lilac tree. Madge breathes in. Lilac and bleach. Next door her co-worker starts singing along to his music. 'Don't worry, be happy!' That would be nice, thinks Madge. I used to be happy. Till the shit-storm of work got to me. She looks down at her bare feet in the bath. Hey, remember when we used to dance, feet? We'll do that again sometime, OK? But right now there's grot to bust. She starts humming along. Be happy.

Virginia is not the only new deacon-to-be who will shortly arrive in the diocese of Lindchester. At the end of June Bishop Paul will be priesting last year's eight deacons on one Sunday, and the following Sunday he will ordain nine men and women deacon. I'm aware that ranks and orders in the C of E can be very confusing to outsiders. How does Anglican hierarchy work? Who ranks higher, a dean or an archdeacon? That's a trick question in a way: both are priests. I will now lean forward confidentially and murmur an explanation in the reader's ear.

There are only three ranks in the C of E: deacon, priest and bishop. The order of deacon these days amounts to little more than a probationary year, after which – unless the deacon blots his or her prayer book or jumps ship – priesthood automatically follows. An extremely gifted and well-educated priest, with clear leadership potential and a willy, may then progress to the office of bishop. And that's it. (An archbishop is just a bishop, only with more knobs on.)

These, then, are the three orders of the C of E. Three orders, but many jobs. Here's where the fun starts. A priest might be employed in any of the following jobs: rector, vicar, cathedral canon (precentor/chancellor/custos), chaplain (hospital/armed forces/school/prison), area dean, cathedral dean, archdeacon, prebendary, priest vicar choral, team vicar, priest-in-charge, diocesan education officer, theological college tutor/principal, director of ordinands, and so on. Priests may be stipendiary or non-stipendiary, they may be OLM (ordained local minister) or free range. They may retire, but they still remain priests and can lurk in the crem and take funeral services. It is indeed very confusing.

And now it's Tuesday. St Barnabas Day. Barnabas, Son of Encouragement. I'm afraid our friend the bishop is not busy encouraging Matt by appointing a fellow archdeacon to share the load. No, he is off for a top-secret interview about which I can tell you nothing. Not even his chaplain or Penelope his PA know where he's going and what it's about.

Paul is aware that at some point during this mysterious interview he will be invited to spill the beans about anything in his background that might be a problem should the press get hold of it. (My son is a loan shark/drug addict. I was done for drunk driving back in the 1980s. That kind of thing.) Paul's problem is that he can't think of anything. He had a great-uncle who was an alcoholic. One of his daughters married a Baptist. This is footling, but that's genuinely all there is. He does not even have a problem with booze and internet porn, for heaven's sake! Yes, there is a real gap in Paul Henderson's CV in the wild oats section.

All this will happen in a secret venue outside the diocesan boundaries, and therefore beyond the remit of this tale. However, as your author, I am willing to use my discretion and tell you briefly how it will play out. It will go something like this.

At some point as he sits facing the panel, Paul will remove his jacket (the room will be warm). He will drape it across a chair and begin to confess that he has nothing to confess. Whereupon *something* will tumble out of his suit pocket and roll across the floor in front of the astonished gaze of his inquisitors.

Fortunately for those of us who care about Bishop Paul, this something will prove to be a pink plastic yoyo out of a cracker, because Paul has not worn this particular suit since Christmas Day. You panic far too easily, dear reader.

It is a bit odd that Susanna hasn't found the yoyo and removed it, mind you. She is usually meticulous about going through pockets before hanging up or laundering her husband's tossed-down clothes. (Now *that* is a grave fault Paul might have confessed, had he thought of it. Many marriages have foundered on the rock of tossed-down clothes.) Susanna has rescued all manner of stuff in the past. Coins, £20 notes, orders of service, mobile phones, wallets, vital business cards, slices of cake wrapped in paper napkins. She's checking his pockets right now, in fact, before sending off his charcoal grey pinstripe to the dry-cleaners.

Liquid Gold? What on earth can this be? Susanna pops on her reading glasses. *Room Odorisor*. She unscrews the lid to see what it smells of. Sweetish, yet slightly—

What—? Oh, goodness!

Heaven pounces upon the bishop's wife. There's a madman at the dial of her pulse: he ratchets it up higher, higher, faster, faster. She's going to die! She staggers to the bed. A minute or two later it all subsides, but the poor thing is left with such a blinding headache she has to spend the afternoon sleeping it off.

We will tiptoe away and leave her in peace, and see how the decorating is going over in Carding-le-Willow on the afternoon of day two. Let's find out how Madge is faring with the Son of Encouragement the archdeacon has sent.

'That's not clever!'

'But ma-a-an, is it big.'

'How old are you? Eight? You paint over it right now!'

'You don't like it?'

'No. And turn that down. Why aren't you working?'

'Jus' waiting for the undercoat to dry. Hey, dontcha love this song?'

'I don't believe this! You're stoned.'

'Nope. No way. Not me. *Hallelujah!*'

'Don't lie to me, sunshine. I know weed when I smell it.'

'Nu-uh! That's paint fumes. Wanna dance? Aw, c'mon.'

Madge thrust the roller at him. 'I'm serious! Stop laughing.' Damn. He was setting her off now. 'Paint over that thing now, or I'm calling the archdeacon.'

'*God bless Mother Nature!*'

Suddenly Madge felt a nostalgic tug of yearning for a toke, for those years when she was a student nurse in London and it rained men, it actually flipping did. She tossed down the roller. 'Freddie May, you're a ba-a-ad influence.'

'Yeah! Work it, girlfriend! Nice moves for an old lady! *Hallelujah!*'

Wendy hesitates on the doorstep with the key. She looks up at the open bedroom window. How long is it since she's heard Madge laugh like that?

'Well, Lulu, shall we just leave them to it? I know, we'll pop to the shops and get them some cake and come back at teatime.'

Lulu thumps her tail twice at the word 'cake', then hauls herself up and hobbles back down the garden path after Wendy.

It's raining. Not men, just rain; rain over the whole diocese of Lindchester. The river is rising. Rain gets in under the perspex on the cathedral notice board and runs down the Dorian Singers' poster, buckling it.

Rain rolls down the palace windows. It's Saturday and Susanna is baking again. She is surrounded by cooling muffins. She'll take one to Paul once she's iced them. He's upstairs in his study preparing a sermon. Freddie is off out somewhere.

Oh, if only she hadn't googled it! She knows she should say something. And she will! It's just finding a tactful moment. Paul's under such pressure. Oh, it's probably just her being silly as usual. There will turn out to be a perfectly innocent explanation, and they'll both laugh at her getting into a tizzy about nothing again!

But Susanna has yet to come up with the innocent explanation for the bottle of amyl nitrite hidden in her husband's pocket. Believe me: she's tried. (Medication? Paul is keeping a secret heart condition from her?) Which leaves . . . Which is clearly nonsense!

The rain switches sharply to hail. It clatters and bounces against the kitchen window. What was the song she used to sing to their little girls?

> Rainy, rainy, rattle stones, don't rain on me.
> Rain on John O'Groat's house, far across the sea.

Decorating done. Next week, the garden. Madge locks up at 16 Lime Crescent and gets on her bike. She cycles home in the rain. As she pedals she laughs. She laughs and sings. Hallelujah! It may be painted over, but she will always know that there's a giant todger standing to attention over Miss Virginia Farrow-Ball's bed. Amen!

Chapter 26

Midsummer. Wild roses scramble up embankments and over hedges. Down by Gresham's Boats tourists clash punt poles on the Linden. The tea shops of Lindchester are bustling. Undergraduates, released from exam bondage, make day trips to Historic Lindchester to picnic on its riverbanks and chunder on its cobbles.

The Dorian Singers' concert this coming Saturday is sold out. I fear we must attribute their popularity as much to the theme music for *that* TV drama as to their technical brilliance. Many of our favourite people will be there in the audience. Some will have complimentary tickets and sit on the front row covertly reading a Bible commentary; others will be unable to afford a ticket, and will sell programmes instead, then lean on a pillar, gaze hungrily at the director, and drift off into Dorianland for a spot of choral sex.

Wendy will be there. She's bought a ticket for Madge as well, to say thank you for all her help with the curate's house. Jane and Dominic are going, but sitting in the cheap seats a long way from the stage. This may not matter too much, because it is the Dorian Singers, and who knows where those nutters will sing from? The cathedral administrator, a very nice gentleman called Terrence Hodgeson nearing retirement, has risked life and limb inching along narrow walkways up in the clerestory with the canon precentor, whimpering 'Health and safety!' and begging Giles not to allow the Dorian Singers up here.

It is Monday. Freddie – nose mending and black eyes faded to a pair of dark circles – is back in the bishop's office after his week of painting and decorating. Penelope has already confiscated the stapler and told him to step away from the guillotine. In desperation, she's given him the Dorian Singers' photocopied programmes to fold.

'No! Hugo Milton-Hayes? No way! I was at school with him. How come *he's* in the Dorian Singers? Fucking drama queen counter-tenor. Huh.'

'Is it Dorian as in Dorian Gray?' asked Penelope.

'I'm guessing Dorian mode? Like the white notes, D to D on the keyboard?' Freddie sang it for her.

'How on earth do you know? Have you got perfect pitch?'

'Nah, I can just like remember what a D sounds like?'

'That *is* perfect pitch,' hissed Martin without looking round.

'No, Marty, it's *actually* pseudo-absolute pitch.' Freddie prowled across to where Martin was sitting.

'Freddie, *leave*!' shouted Penelope, in her best dog-training voice.

'Wha-a-at? I was just going to give him a back rub.'

'Well, don't. You know he doesn't like it.'

Must we go through this soap opera every single day, thought Martin. The pathetic 'Look at me, aren't I a naughty boy?' routine, which Penelope simply colludes with. Martin clenched his teeth so hard his ears started ringing.

'What can wash away my stain? Nothing but the—'

'Excuse me?' Martin snapped. 'Some of us are trying to work.'

But Freddie raised his voice till it filled the office. 'What can make me whole again? Nothing but the blood of Jesus.'

For a moment everything stood still. Penelope replaced the receiver she'd just picked up. Martin's forefingers stopped their vicious pecking at the keyboard. The bishop, behind his closed door, paused and listened.

'No other fount I know. Nothing but the blood of Jesus.'

It's so wrong, thought Martin. Why would God squander such an incredible gift on that little shite? It was like the proverbial gold ring in a pig's snout.

Silence. 'Man, I love what they do with that hymn. The harmonies?'

'Oh, Freddie!' Penelope wrung her hands. 'I'm sure you're good enough to be in the Dorian Singers. Why can't you just focus and sing properly like this all the time?'

'Boys just wanna have fun, Mish Moneypenny.'

Certainly the precentor's boys just wanna have fun. Even now, at the eleventh hour, Lukas and Felix Littlechild do not want to revise for their A-levels and GCSEs. Normally Ulrika cracks down on idleness in all its teen forms, but on Friday her vigilance is impaired by pre-concert stress. Mr high-maintenance Dorian himself will be staying in their guest room. She's already had one row with Giles about this. ('Book him into a hotel, for God's sake!' 'No, he's an old friend!') So now she's got to find time to hoover behind the wardrobe, and make a supermarket trip to stock up on the sodding bloody organic soya milk and San Pellegrino bottled water and whatever the bloody hell other stuff he has to have. Grrrr. She slams the front door and devotes long compound nouns in her mother tongue to Mr Dorian as she drives to Waitrose. My colloquial German is rusty these days, but I can tell you that *Schwein*, *Scheiß* and *Schwanzlutschen* are all in the mix.

I will also tell you a secret: Ulrika is a tiny bit scared of Mr Dorian.

The lawn of 16 Lime Crescent, Carding-le-Willow has been mowed. Well, ploughed, really. But it will improve. The shrubs have been hacked back. There is a nice bouquet of flowers and a homemade cake waiting in the kitchen. I do hope Virginia feels cherished by her new vicar and parish when she moves in on Saturday. It is a pity that her curacy arrangement at Risley Hill didn't work out. (Matt the Knife pulled the plug on that one after the rector of Risley Hill fell so disastrously in love with the wife of the bishop's chaplain.) We must hope that Virginia does not feel like she's been fobbed off with second best. Personally, I think Wendy will make an excellent training incumbent. Would the rector of Risley have baked Virginia a cake that is both gluten and lactose free? I doubt it.

Timothy Gladwin, the cathedral director of music, has been working hard this week. So has the cathedral choir, men and boys (still no girl choristers at Lindchester, I'm afraid). If you wander past the Song School you may have your withers wrung by snatches of 'For the beauty of the earth'. This concert – a fundraiser for the choir trip to Germany in the summer – is a very big deal indeed. Timothy feels the pressure keenly (he too is a bit scared of Mr Dorian). Thrilling to perform with the Dorian Singers, of course, even though they'll mainly be doing cheesy Rutter numbers and crowd-pleasers. The Hallelujah Chorus, for God's sake!

Gene, the husband of the dean, is looking forward very much to this concert, and the post-concert bash afterwards. He was most disappointed to hear that Timothy's distinguished predecessor, Sir Gregory Laird – normally a stalwart of these concerts – had arranged a prior engagement the instant he heard that Mr Dorian was performing. Shame. Gene had been looking forward to some choral fireworks. (Cf. Laird's even-handed review of the latest Dorian Singers'

CD: 'Dumbed-down and toe-curlingly meretricious in its sheer saccharine awfulness.')

Well, Timothy need not have worried. The concert was a riotous success and nobody plunged to their death from the clerestory. I will now hurry my readers off to the post-concert party, where Freddie May will do what Freddie May does best – take aim and shoot himself flamboyantly in the foot.

Quickly, now. Shoulder your way through the crowds unfurling their umbrellas. We're heading to the deanery, where the performers are already mingling with the great and the good. The bishop is being talked to by the high sheriff. There's Susanna, head tilted pastorally as she listens to the headmaster's wife. Gene is pouring drinks and stirring up trouble wherever he can. Come.

'Freddie May! As I live and breathe! How the fuck are *you*?' Hugo Milton-Hayes hugged him. 'Guys, guys, I was at school with this nob-head.' Freddie was introduced to several other younger members of the Dorian Singers who were stationed by the booze. 'Hey, can you still do that Buddhist monk thing? Listen up, guys, you gotta hear to this!'

'Seriously, you don't want to?' But Freddie allowed himself to be persuaded. That tortured drone emerged from his lips again, like bagpipes warming up.

The noise drew the attention of the director himself. Picture a serial killer styled by Tom Ford and you have him; in his early fifties, tall, lean, silver-dark, with psychotic pale grey eyes. He crossed the room, like a shark slipping between surfers and positioned himself in front of Freddie. Freddie broke off, and blushed to the roots.

'Do that again.'

Freddie obeyed.

Mr Dorian looked as if a puppy was widdling on his trouser leg. 'Dear God. Please stop.'

'How are you even *doing* that?' asked Hugo.

Freddie, stuttering with hero worship, blurted something about Tuvan throat singing? Harmonics?

'And freakishly virtuosic breath control,' said Mr Dorian. He favoured Freddie with a long sociopathic stare. 'Well, well. Little Freddie May, all grown up.'

A jolt passed through Freddie. Remembered! By the great Mr Dorian!

'Who's your voice teacher these days?'

'Um, so yeah, I like, um, I haven't actually got one right now?'

'Really? What stage are you at?'

'Right, ah, so it's complicated? I'm like, I've taken time out? But I've got a choral scholarship at Barchester?'

Mr Dorian dismissed the eavesdroppers with a wave, then perused Freddie's face, taking in the broken nose, the fading black eyes. 'How's the voice? When you're not murdering it.'

Gene drew near, scenting the makings of a good row. He watched with interest as Freddie stood on one foot tugging his hair, as if he were in a school corridor explaining why his homework was late.

'Oh, you know?'

Mr Dorian indicated that he did not know.

'Like, it's kind of average? You know, a nice tenor sound, but it's never going to be anything special?'

'How can you possibly know that?'

'So yeah, someone warned me I couldn't expect my adult voice to like . . . yeah.'

The director pounced. 'Who was this?'

Silence.

'Because I'd question the credentials of anyone who told a twelve-year-old boy that.'

'Yeah? Well, actually I was more like fifteen' – ooh! a promising spark, thought Gene – 'and I think he knows what he's talking about?'

'Aha, I discern the presence of the sainted Gregory hovering! Yes?' The director swirled his San Pellegrino in its glass. 'And, what? You internalized Laird's godlike pronouncement and simply rolled over?'

Go, go! urged Gene. He saw Freddie's jaw clench. High time someone gave Mr May a boot up his cute little arse.

'Purely out of interest,' went on Mr Dorian, 'why not try to prove the old bastard wrong instead? Why this pattern of self-sabotage Giles has been telling me about? Pre-empting the possibility of failure?'

To Gene's delight, Freddie's switch tripped. 'Look, *fuck* you, asshole! Seriously, go fuck yourself. Don't fucking analyse me. You know nothing about me!'

The director allowed a glacial pause. Then he leant close and said very, very quietly, 'What is your problem, exactly, Mr May? Care to enlighten me? It seems to me you've got it all – you're a born performer; you're blessed with youth, looks, and talent; you have the technical grounding, the connections. People would kill for your advantages – yet you stand there like a big girl bleating, "I'm only kind of average".'

By now Freddie was ashen. The director waited for a response. None came.

From the other side of the room the bishop saw something was amiss.

'Well, Freddie, this has been lovely,' said Mr Dorian. 'Let's do it again some time. Here,' he tucked a card in Freddie's shirt pocket and patted it. 'If you're ever looking for work, get in touch. I can always use a good tenor. All the best in Barchester.' He inclined his head. 'And now I'll go and fuck myself.' He sauntered back to where the precentor was standing.

Gene watched him go, savouring the bouquet of this encounter. When he turned back, Freddie had vanished.

'Dr Jacks,' said Giles, 'I do hope you weren't being a brute to poor Mr May?'

'I certainly was. Mr May called me an asshole.'

'You *are* an asshole, Andrew.'

'While this is undoubtedly true, I don't have to take it from him,' said the director. 'I have music stands older than that little prick.'

The bishop, still trapped in conversation with the high sheriff, watched, helpless, as Freddie flung himself out through the deanery door into the night.

Chapter 27

Sunday morning. All across the diocese of Lindchester people are up early. It's a big day. The eight men and women who were ordained deacon last year will be priested. Loyal parishioners will come from those eight different parishes to the cathedral to support them. They have slain the fatted sausage roll for the bun fights in church halls later. Posh frocks will be donned, fascinators deployed. Teenage boys will be scolded out of trainers. Middle-aged men will be perplexed to discover that their best suit trousers have shrunk.

So why all the fuss? What does priesthood mean? Well, this being the C of E, the answer is a resounding 'it depends'. In high-church circles it is taken with hushed seriousness. The day when you celebrate your first Mass is etched on your memory like a wedding anniversary. You might even have little cards made announcing the date. For vulgar low-church types, however, priesting just means 'you get to do the magic bits'. It will be possible to spot the low-church ordinands at the service today. They'll be the ones in black preaching scarves, not white stoles. The stole/scarf battle is by no means as bitter as it was thirty years ago; but believe me, Sayre's Law about university politics applies to the Church: 'The feuds are vicious because the stakes are so low.'

Training incumbents pack their robes bags. Great: a Sunday when they don't have to do anything other than rock up in the cathedral. Our friend the archdeacon will be there to give the liturgical thumbs up to the bishop that, yes, the ordinands have taken the necessary oaths and made the Declaration of Assent.

The suffragan bishop of Barcup puts his crosier into his car. It's a genuine shepherd's crook, made of honest wood and iron. Bob puts it in the car all by himself, because he does not have a chaplain to do it for him. Janet will not be accompanying him. She'd rather go to her parish church. Last time she went to a big cathedral bash one of the stewards bounced her with the words, 'You can't sit there, it's reserved for the bishop's wife.' Susanna leapt in and intervened, before Janet could say, 'Listen, mush, I *am* the bishop's wife!' Bob the bishop puts on a CD of Taizé chants and drives to Lindchester, sunning himself in the goodness of the Lord. What a nice man he is.

But not everyone is happy on this happy day. Timothy, the cathedral director of music, has a back row crisis. His tenor choral scholar has gone down with gastric flu. So have two of the tenor lay clerks. (I ought perhaps to mention that gastric flu often strikes after a choral night on the town.) Freddie May isn't answering his phone, probably because he got comprehensively wasted too, after flouncing out of last night's party. Who on earth can Timothy find to busk their way through Schubert in G at this notice? The tenor solo line! With the best will in the world, the two tenor lay clerks left standing will struggle. Don't say he's going to have to ditch the *Benedictus*!

Virginia Coleman wakes in her new home in Carding-le-Willow. Fresh paint in the air and boxes piled in every room. This time next week she'll just have finished her ordination retreat and be heading for the cathedral to be ordained deacon! Can she do this? Is she really cut out for this? All by herself? She barely knows her training vicar – oh, if only the first arrangement hadn't fallen through! It's never so lonely for ordinands with spouse and family. Virginia watches the clouds through her curtainless window and feels very small, stripped of the skills that took her to senior management in her old life.

All at once the task of unpacking and making a home in this 1960s box feels undoable. She needs to get out. To IKEA? But who will help her make her Billy bookcases? To church? No, she's in limbo. It would be awkward to turn up to worship before she's officially the curate. The cathedral? She could go to the priests' ordination. Hide at the back, anonymously. That way she'll be more able to get her head round next week. Picture where she'll be sitting, standing, kneeling. Yes, that will help. It will be all right. He who calls you is faithful, she reminds herself. He will do it. There, hanging on the back of the bedroom door, are her new robes. Cassock, surplice, white stole, black preaching scarf. It feels absurd. As if next Sunday will be World Book Day at school, only this time she'll be dressing up as a vicar, not as Hermione Granger.

Timothy tries Freddie again. Still no answer. Nobody's answering. He leaves desperate messages for every half-decent tenor he can think of, then canters across to the Song School. He'll have to start the practice and hope someone gets back to him before the service.

The cathedral has already come to life. The stewards are putting 'Reserved for Ordinand's Family' signs on the front rows. The flower guild are spritzing the large yellow and white floral displays. Techie guys in black prowl like ninjas, trailing cables and checking the CCTV cameras and screens. Where are the vergers, though?

The vergers are in their vestry taking a break and eating choc-anana muffins. Susanna has just popped over with a batch still warm from the Aga, to thank them for all their hard work. This pisses Ulrika off when she finds out, because it feels like a criticism: why didn't the *precentor's wife* make muffins for the vergers, eh? But sodding heck, Ulrika is not getting into all that rubbish! They get paid, don't they? Bad enough that she has to find organic sodding bloody peppermint tea for Dr Picky-Picky Jacks. And then he asks, 'Is it filtered water?' (*So eine Frechheit!*)

I think the vergers deserve muffins, personally. (And even if they don't, the quality of home-baking ought not to be strained. In the course of justice, none of us should see triple choc chip cookies.) I happen to know that the vergers worked far into the night dismantling the concert stage and rearranging the entire cathedral floor space for this morning's service.

We will leave the vergers to their muffins and duck instead into the chapel of St Michael, where Dr Picky-Picky Jacks is kneeling. He has just finished saying the Morning Office. Does that surprise you? It's been a decade since those noviciate years, but their routine is now carved deep on his soul.

His chilly stare is locked onto the Annunciation above the altar. He's troubled by the light in it. The way it evokes that sense of the Other breaking in. As he stares he feels a presence draw alongside; some Being far beyond even his monstrous capacity to control, intimidate, destroy. So it's back again, is it? This stubborn love that just will not give up on him; this rock he cannot believe in, yet which he must always return to and shipwreck himself on and be saved. The divine No, which is also the Yes.

This Annunciation is more a threat than a promise. Unsurprisingly, given the artist. He knows her well; may even have been around when this huge canvas was painted, for all he can remember. God, these lacunae, these drink-corrupted files.

Behind him in the cathedral the organist begins to practise. Widor. His hands briefly play a phantom manual on the hymnbook ledge. Vestigial muscle memory. He looks at the scar on his left forearm, a souvenir from that black, black night fifteen years ago, when he fell through a plate-glass window and severed those finger and thumb tendons.

Ah well.

Coloured light pools on the stone floor. He raises his eyes to its source. To be a window, through thy grace! The blond Burne-Jones angels glow. He thinks of the lovely Mr May. And smiles. Then shakes his head at that impulse of his to torment, manipulate, spoil, simply because he can. Yes, you are an asshole, Jacks. He stands, crosses himself, and leaves the chapel.

Already the candidates' families and parishioners are arriving for the 10.30 start. Giles is in an advanced state of control freakery over the choreography. He bitches under his breath about the bishop's liturgical illiteracy. He's already been forced to issue a stern disciplinary warning to the lay clerks about smirking during the Evangelical worship songs Paul has insisted upon having during the administration of communion. Fortunately Giles saw off the abomination of desecration inflicted by Evangelicals upon 'Be thou my vision' – Slane! in four/four! – last week, after a head-to-head with the bishop's chaplain.

The bishop, in all his liturgical illiteracy, is about to head across to the cathedral to greet the ordinands and pray with them. As he stands in the palace hallway in front of the mirror to slip in his dog collar, he hears the familiar sound of Freddie May retching on the drive. Excellent. Paul sighs. What am I going to do with that boy? Nothing. I'm going to do nothing. This is not my problem. In a couple of weeks we'll be off on holiday. Then it will be August, and in September he'll be safely in Barchester, thank the Lord. The bishop gathers up his robes and heads out of the house.

And now he must repent. Freddie did not go out and get wasted last night after all. In fact, he has just come back from a ten-mile run. The bishop rebukes himself.

Freddie is doubled over, hands on knees, panting, sweat dripping. But he glances up and grins.

Paul smiles back. 'Good run?'

'Meh.' Hand wobble. 'Bit slow.'

'Your phone's been ringing.'

Thumbs up. Another bout of dry-retching. 'Gah. Ffff . . . kinell.' He spits on the gravel.

'Lovely, Frederick.'

Freddie straightens, then peels up his vest and wipes his face with it.

'Right. Good. Well, do join Susanna and me for lunch if you'd like to.' The bishop sets off for the cathedral. As he walks he labours to erase that musclescape – abs! pecs! piercings! – from his mind.

And suddenly he remembers. Gropes in his jacket pocket. Pats himself down. Gone! It *was* this suit, wasn't it, the charcoal grey pinstripe? Never say it's fallen out somewhere! Has Suze found it? Oh, Lord! The awful hilarity of it seizes him. Later. He'll have to worry about this later.

It is not the intention of this narrative to visit evil upon its characters. We may rely upon the characters to run into trouble quite unaided. But for today, in Lindchester Cathedral in the Ordination of Priests, all is well. Virginia, hiding in a side aisle, watches Bishop Paul's face on the screen as he lays his hands on the head of each candidate in turn. She sees the care, the tenderness there. 'Send down the Holy Spirit on your servant for the office and work of a priest in your Church.' Next week, God willing, she will be able to approach that new doorway, knowing a friendly presence is waiting to greet her on the other side.

Yes, all is well. Paul gets the names of all the candidates right. Nobody gets a heel stuck down an aisle grating, or stands on the back hem of their cassock when kneeling. Nobody's phone goes off. The retired bishop who led the ordination retreat preaches well. The small person stating very audibly, 'But I have to go *now*!' gets there in time. Nobody knocks over a full chalice. No lay clerk is caught smirking on CCTV, even when singing the phrase 'vibrating love' (tune: Danny Boy).

During the *Benedictus* the terrifying Mr Dorian closes his eyes and smiles when the tenor solo line comes in. He breathes in – ah! – as though he can smell the apricots ripening on heaven's terrace.

Kind of average, my arse, Mr May.

JULY

Chapter 28

If the diocese of Lindchester were a dog, it would be panting in the shade with its tongue lolled out. Tarmac melts on the roads. Everywhere, the scent of lime blossom. The Close is woozy with it. Oh, the bees, the fainting bees! All the livelong day. And at night honeyed breath creeps through open windows, where naked bodies sprawl under thin sheets, un-Englishly. *Come slowly – Eden! Lips unused to thee –* The songbirds have fallen silent. No dawn chorus. Just the sleepy wheeze of the greenfinch, the scream of swifts, the *ke-wick! ke-wick!* and answering *hoo-hoo-hooo!* of owls in the dark.

This is the second week of the heatwave. Friday will be end of term for schools in the region. Too hot for those Leavers hoodies, but not too hot for egg and flour fights, or scrawling your name all over your classmates' white school shirt, or getting shit-faced behind the gym on vodka disguised in Pepsi bottles, mentioning no names but watch my eyes, Felix Littlechild. Or for jumping fully clad into the school pool and breaking your ankle: yes, you, don't look at your friend, Lukas Littlechild. (Why are clergy children always the worst?)

The ordination of deacons has taken place. Virginia is now curate of the parishes of All Saints, Carding-le-Willow, St Martin's, Cardingforth, St Mary's, Holy Trinity, and the King's Café Church, Lingmorton. That should keep her out of mischief. Father Dominic is busy preparing a ten-minute presentation for his upcoming interview, and getting weepy at the thought of having to break the news to St John's that he's leaving – if he gets the Lindford job, that is.

Choral term has ended. The cathedral choir is on holiday until their tour to Germany in two weeks' time. Visiting choirs, ranging from 'rather good' through to 'execrable', will hold the fort over the summer. The visitors traditionally offer two things: they sing the weekend services, and – by their lack of volume, or their hubristic choice of repertoire – remind everyone how excellent the cathedral choir actually is. Unfortunately (fortunately?), the choir scheduled for this coming weekend had to cancel. Giles has scrambled to arrange cover: Byrd's Mass for Three Voices will be sung by his loyal wife, a bass lay clerk, willing to sing for free(!), and the lovely Freddie May, basically a tart, willing to do anything.

At least it's cool in the cathedral. Dr Jane Rossiter, in her doctoral gown (that is what it is called; it is not called a Scarlet Whore of Babylon gown), is very glad that this is the venue for Poundstretcher University's graduation ceremonies. It is Wednesday morning. She sits with her colleagues and tries to keep the 'oh, for fuck's sake!' look off her face, in case the camera strays in her direction as the Dean of Faculty stumbles through the obstacle course of names. Böröcz, Knyazev, Zhōu.

Earlier the Close sounded like a film set for a Regency coaching epic, with the clopping of stilettos on cobbles. The chancellor looks each graduand earnestly in the eye, always the eye, as he shakes their hand. 'Congratulations, all the best for your future. Congratulations, all the best for your future.' His gaze never wavers to the skirt, which is often shorter than the heels are high.

What a carry-on, thinks Jane, whose degrees were awarded in absentia. New outfits, manicures, hair appointments, photos. It's like a bloody wedding. What has made these pieces of paper and their attendant ceremonies such a big deal again? Obviously, it's a monster fed by consumerism; but is there more? Some echoing emotional void here? The absence of proper local communities? Of God? Or is it just the generation pendulum swinging predictably back towards all things traditional?

Such are the musings of Dr Jane Rossiter during the Faculty of Farts and Inhumanities graduation. But then she is distracted by her phone vibrating. Mindful of the cameras, she waits till the new graduates are filing out in procession before she checks. Ha! a message from wazzock chef. A link to YouTube. She clicks on it. And snorts. Chris de Burgh's 'Lady in Red'. Jane concludes from this that wazzock chef definitely works at Poundstretcher, or else he wouldn't have known she'd be in her gown today.

The archdeacon of Lindchester is just arriving at Lindford for the interview, when his phone vibrates. A message from Dr R. A YouTube link: 'These Boots are Made for Walking'. He's still grinning as he enters the parish church hall, where the churchwardens are waiting with the candidate. By this evening Father Dominic Todd will have two things to celebrate: Royal Assent will be given to the Same Sex Marriage Bill, and he will have a new job.

Freddie May is wearing pink this afternoon. Yeah, take that, haters. The Queen fixes it for queens. He's in a pink vest and pink board shorts. He's very tanned. In fact, after many hours spent on the palace roof, he has (ssh!) no tan lines. Penelope is on annual leave and Fuckwit1 is off chauffeuring the bishop to something. Freddie is in the office alone.

Uh-oh.

But wait, Freddie May is actually behaving himself for once. He has done those admin tasks which he ought to have done, he has left undone the hacking which he ought not to have done, and is innocently running through his part for Sunday's Byrd Mass, when a hassled young mother arrives with two little girls in gingham school frocks.

It is Becky Rogers. She's early for hand-over time, but banking on being able to dump the girls on Penelope while she dashes to the dentist for an emergency appointment. Wisdom tooth. The poor thing is demented with pain and co-codamol. Here's what happens.

'She's on holiday? Oh no, this was the only slot they had! Um, when is the children's father due back?'

'Say five, maybe? It's cool, leave them with me.' Freddie saw her expression. 'Um, hello? I'm CRB-checked to death. The choristers?'

'That's not ... No! I didn't mean ...' Yeah, you did, thought Freddie, watching her go red. 'I don't want to impose on you.'

'No worries.'

Becky looked at her watch. Pressed a hand to her throbbing jaw. 'Girls, will you be all right with Freddie? Mummy won't be long.'

'Promise you'll bring us sweets and a comic?' said the older girl.

'Well, I don't know, we'll have to see.'

'Daddy always buys us sweets and a comic.'

'I *said* we'll see, Leah. Well, if you're sure, Freddie? Thanks. You're a star.' She pushed her hand through her damp hair, battling with tears. 'Right then. Mummy's going now, girls. OK? Don't pester Freddie. Just read your books and play quietly. They have my mobile number if there's a problem. Bye, girls. Be good. All right? Bye now.'

'Bye, Mummy,' said the little one. The older girl ignored her.

The door closed. Becky's footsteps crunched off across the gravel drive.

Freddie looked at his two charges. The older one was in Fuckwit1's chair pretending to read her *Horrible History* book. Man. Had she got that passive-aggressive shit nailed. The younger one was sucking her hair and gazing up at him.

'So, ladies. Whatcha wanna do?'

'We're not *ladies*, we're girls,' hissed Leah. 'And we're not talking to you, because we hate you.'

Back at ya, kiddo. He looked at the little one. Jessica? 'How about you? You hate me?'

Jessica gave him a heart-melting smile, shook her head. Then froze when big sis shot her the evil eye.

'So who's this?' Freddie squatted to look at the doll Jessica was swinging by the legs. 'Punk Barbie? Awesome haircut!'

'I did it.'

'You did? Awesome. Yep, that is one kick-ass Barbie. Maybe give her some tattoos as well?'

'She's not allowed,' said Leah from behind her book.

'Not allowed, huh?' Freddie shrugged at Jessica.

She shrugged back, then whispered, 'Actually, now I need a new Barbie coz I can't style this one's hair any more.'

'It's your own fault,' said Leah. 'You've got to learn.'

'Listen, tell you what – you can style mine.' Freddie sat cross-legged.

'She's not allowed.'

'She so is. Go ahead, Jess.'

Jessica opened her Barbie backpack and found a pink hairbrush. She stood behind him. He could hear her breathing. Then very gently, the plastic bristles touched his scalp. Tugged. Smoothed. He sighed. Man. How long since anyone had brushed his hair? Maybe Miss B, combing for nits back in the day? Or his mum, even? Brush, brush, brush.

Breath in his ear. 'Freddie?'

'Uh-huh?'

'Why have you got ear rings in your chest?'

Ri-i-ight. He rearranged his vest, smothered a laugh. 'Um, coz I like how it looks?'

'It's because he's *gay*, stupid.'

He felt the hairbrush flinch. 'I know.'

'No, you don't. You don't know anything, baby. You don't even know what gay means.'

'Yes, I do.'

'Liar. What does it mean, then?'

'Not telling.' The brushing started up again, double tempo.

'Ha ha ha. See? You don't know. It's when men have sex with men. They suck each other's willies and stick them up each other's bums, *that's* what it means. Ask him, if you don't believe me.'

'Hey, hey! *Way* out of order.' Ah nuts. Now the little one was gonna cry. 'First of all, that's *not* what it means, OK? It's about who you love, not what you do. And second of all, why don't I steal us each a Magnum from Susanna's freezer?'

'You're not allowed.'

Screw you. 'Is that right? Well, if you're scared, I'll steal one each for Jess and me, and you can just read your book.'

'I'm not scared, for your information,' said Leah. 'I want a white one.'

He cupped a hand round his ear. 'Magic word?'

Evil eye again. '*Avada kedavra.*'

A moment later he was hanging over the open chest freezer, soaking up the cold. Gah, un-fucking-*believable*! Eight-year-old girl, hating on me! Witch. Yeah, but to be fair, probably some older kid in the playground told her, and she was just passing on the joy to little sister, the way you do. Kind of, ha ha ha, there's no Tooth Fairy.

Ew, flashback! Hadn't thought about that for ever. Back when he'd be like, thirteen?

Ah, it was nothing.

Just this older guy, this grown-up? First real snog. No biggie. Except, even now he had no words for how wrong that felt. And the guy was all, 'Ooh, so you don't like that? Then don't come on to me, kid.'

Freddie fished out three ice creams and shut the freezer. But back then I *was* still a kid! Mother Nature suddenly gives me this totally insane new toy, and I'm, y'know, all, whoa! Flying skateboard, everybody! And figuring out what it can do? Then you had to slap me down. You had to be all, 'That's right, cry-baby – Santa's dead.'

Easy to forget how sick and scary the grown-up world feels to kids, thought Freddie, as he went back through to the bishop's office.

'Everything all right, Freddie?' asks the bishop, after Martin has gone home with the girls.

So what's he gonna do – grass up an eight-year-old girl for hurting his feelings? 'Yeah, fine, thanks.'

But the bishop, with his finely calibrated Freddie barometer, knows he is lying.

Hot, hot, unbearably hot. Little Jessica is twisty and weepy and she can't sleep. Daddy opens the window wide and gets her water with ice cubes. He takes away the duvet and tucks her up under just a sheet. She whispers a question.

'It's not true, is it, what Leah said?'

'What did Leah say?'

Jessica hides under the sheet and says it.

Martin tightens in shock. 'Oh, take no notice. That's probably something Leah heard some big children saying. She's got no business repeating it to you, because it's private grown-up stuff that little girls can forget about till they are a lot, lot older. Night, night, darling.'

Then he goes to confront Leah and tells her he's Very Disappointed.

'*I* didn't say that.' Leah doesn't look up from her *Horrible History*. 'Freddie told us.'

Chapter 29

Martin followed the correct procedure. He made a note of what had been told him. He did not investigate the allegation himself. He did not contact the alleged perpetrator. Instead, he waited a few days and rang Jan Lewis, the cathedral safeguarding officer. Jan was on holiday, so Martin was referred to the diocesan safeguarding officer. He reported the matter to her, and followed it up with an email summarizing his grievance. And then Martin took his daughters to Normandy for two weeks, to stay with his parents, his sister and her family, who had hired a farmhouse. Somewhere remote, somewhere with no mobile signal or internet connection. Because he really needed to get a proper break, away from it all.

We are now in the holiday season. The bishop and his wife have taken theirs early this year, so that they can be back in the country when daughter number three has her second baby in August. The Hendersons are in Corfu. They chose this destination because Susanna had always wanted to go there, ever since reading *My Family and Other Animals* in her teens. Insufficient research led her to pick Kavos as an ideal spot to begin their two-week tour. Freddie wept with laughter when he heard this. He was driving them to Birmingham airport at the time, and the bishop had to shout at him to watch the road.

He dropped them off. Thursday afternoon. He was supposed to drive straight back to Lindchester. But hey. Who was gonna know? He could go anywhere. Literally? Well, if he had any money, that is. Got his new passport – thanks, Miss B. Taken him in hand yet again, so he'd be able to go with the choir on tour, beef up the back row, lend a hand supervising the choristers.

Oops, not concentrating. Looks like he was on the M42 south by mistake. Might as well go to London. His phone rang, but he didn't answer it. Couldn't risk a ticket while twocking the bishop's car. Later, when he checked, it was only some HR person in the diocesan offices wanting to see him. It could wait till Monday.

And now it's Monday. Helene Carter is at her desk in Diocesan House. In front of her is Freddie's file. I should probably explain that Helene, the diocesan safeguarding officer, is new. Brought in two months ago from the public sector, to move the diocese on from the flawed child-protection practices of the past, in the teeth of offended parishioners muttering 'political correctness gone mad'. It is her duty, at all times and in all places, to implement current good practice, as outlined in *Protecting All God's Children*.

Our good friend the archdeacon has just had an email from Helene. He thunks his forehead with the heel of his hand. What's the Close tart been up to now? Great timing, with Jan on holiday. Normally they'd get this done and dusted with the minimum fallout.

Perhaps you have already begun to suspect that Matt has a bit of a tricky-Dickie reputation? He's sharp on process, as is seemly in an archdeacon, but he's capable of ducking and weaving. He's flexible in his definition of what constitutes a 'temporary' change to a church building, for example, when it comes to granting faculties. He is frowning now about Helene. High-powered lady – he'd been in on the interviews – but with the best will in the world, she's not had time to get her head around the C of E. She doesn't speak the lingo or get what makes people tick yet. All righty. Time to bring her up to speed on the background here. He sets off for her office on the other side of William House. We will listen in on their conversation.

'Thank you for coming, Matt.'

'No probs,' said the archdeacon. 'But before we kick off – just so you're not blindsided – you're aware there's a spot of history here?'

'Yes. But as far as I can see, Matt, none of it's germane to the issue.' She ran her eyes down the list. Credit card fraud, theft, unauthorized taking of a motor vehicle, affray, possession of Class B drugs. 'No record of any concern about his fitness to work with children.'

'Good.' He sat. 'But I meant history between Martin and Freddie. Basically they hate each other's guts.'

He watched her make a note of what he had just alleged. Ooo-kay. Nothing was off the record, then.

'Thank you. But we have to keep an open mind.'

'For sure.'

Helene then outlined the diocesan safeguarding policy for him.

Now, the archdeacon was a big easy-going secure guy. It was not easy to patronize him. But heck, she was giving it a whirl. 'Yep. Got that, thanks.'

'I'm just underlining the fact that we need to be above reproach, Matt.'

'We certainly do, Helene.' He cracked his knuckles. 'All righty. Hit me with it.'

She handed him a print-off of Martin's email. It had bullet points. The archdeacon was not overfond of bullet points. It alleged that Freddie had violated good practice by:

- undertaking to supervise two young girls alone without another adult chaperone
- inappropriate language
- emotional abuse in discussing subject matter beyond the developmental capacity of six- and eight-year-old girls, i.e. giving explicit descriptions of oral and anal sex between adult men
- inappropriate behaviour by exposing himself and showing them his nipple rings
- encouraging inappropriate physical contact by inciting them to brush his hair
- rewarding inappropriate behaviour and encouraging secrecy by giving them ice creams.

Martin, Martin, Martin. Really? The odd cheeky expletive, maybe. But explicit descriptions of oral and anal sex? Getting his tits out? That didn't sound like Freddie. (Well, not to an audience of little girls, anyway.) Then again, was it likely Martin would fabricate that? Or his daughters? Clearly something must have gone on. Hmm. The archdeacon had encountered the Rogers girls more than once. Older one was a right little madam.

'Well, for what it's worth, my hunch is that this will prove groundless. Out of interest, is this what *both* daughters allege?' He watched her make a note of his hunch. 'Or just the older girl?'

'I'm afraid I don't know the answer to that.'

'Well, can we find out?'

'Not for a fortnight, Matt. They're away on holiday in France. Martin made it clear he wouldn't be contactable.'

Dumping the bombshell then scooting off. Nice. 'Well, let's get Freddie in and hear his side of the story.'

'I've been trying to get hold of him. We have to suspend him immediately, of course, pending investigation.'

'From what? Folding the hymn-sheets? Mowing the cathedral lawn? Come on.'

'No, Matt. From any role that involves contact with children.' She consulted Freddie's file. 'My understanding is that he's a "choir chaperone", which is why we have a CRB certificate for him.'

'Fair point.' Yep. Probably no wiggle room there. Lucky it was the vacation.

'The issue is the choir tour next week.'

Oh, bugger. The archdeacon rubbed his hand over his face. 'Look, any chance we can get this cleared up before then?'

'Well, that's going to be problematic, Matt, with Martin away.'

The archdeacon contemplated the situation. On the one hand, the fan. On the other, the shit pile. Lovely. He was beginning to think there must be a new sub-clause to Sod's Law: if something can go wrong, it'll go wrong to Freddie May.

'Look, assuming his account holds up, and we can get hold of Martin for some clarification, Freddie could presumably still go? Just thinking out loud here. Let's get the canon precentor in the loop. If he ensures there's another adult present at all times—'

'No, Matt. We have to suspend him immediately. You're asking me to bend the rules for one individual.'

The archdeacon reminded himself that shaking someone till her teeth rattled might be construed as bullying in the workplace. 'I'm not asking you to bend the rules, I'm suggesting you stand back for a second, use a bit of common sense and *interpret* the rules. Let's find a way to head this one off before it turns into a total mare.'

There was a silence. She made another note. 'Just for the record, Matt, my job is to interpret and apply the rules. That's what I'm doing. Protecting children is paramount.'

The archdeacon cooled his jets. 'Yep. Absolutely. Sorry if anything I've said implied otherwise. I apologize.'

'Accepted.'

'You're welcome.' He got up to go. 'Keep me posted. Let me know if there's anything I can do.'

Her expression suggested the only thing he could do for her right now was go and fry his face. 'I will. Thank you, Matt.'

The archdeacon headed back to his own office. He ran over what he'd said, saw how it sounded like he was suggesting they should sweep it under the carpet, just like the Church in the bad old days. He closed his eyes. Now he'd bollocksed things up even more comprehensively for young tarty-pants. He'd raised the stakes. Helene was going to do this by the book. To the letter. (Which was only right and proper.) And he couldn't even contact Freddie and warn him what was coming, because that would contaminate the process. All he could do was wait. And pray.

The weather has turned. The princess is admitted to the maternity ward. At evening prayer, the precentor has everyone saying the litany for once.

> That it may please thee to preserve all that travel
>   by land or water,
> all women labouring of child,
> all sick persons, all young children;
> and to shew thy pity on all prisoners and captives,
> **We beseech thee to hear us, good Lord.**

The princess is delivered of a baby boy. Huzzah! Huzzah! But in the distance, at the edge of things, we can hear the muttering and trampling of thunder.

It is not till Thursday that Freddie returns and bothers to present himself at Helene's office. It's a total mare all right. When it ends – abruptly, with Freddie hurling himself out in tears – Helene turns to the archdeacon.

'Does someone need to be with him?'

'I'm on it.'

It's raining. A month's rain in an hour. The River Linden rises. Thunder rips the sky.

> From lightning and tempest,
> **Good Lord, deliver us.**

He caught up with Freddie at the palace door.

'It *so* wasn't like that? I would never do that! He hates me, dude. He fucking *hates* me. Coz I'm gay? Ah, fuck. That bitch *suspended* me? Un-fucking-*believable*! Like, guilty till proven—? Oh God, fuck, what am I gonna do, Matt? Everyone will be all, hey, what's wrong, why aren't you in Germany, Freddie?'

> From envy, hatred and malice, and all uncharitableness,
> **Good Lord, deliver us.**

'Listen to me: don't just hit the self-destruct button, Freddie. Let's get you off the Close. Got anyone you can go and stay with? Your mum?'

'Dude, she's in Argentina? That's like six, seven hundred quid?'

'True, I'd forgotten. Your dad—'

'*No!*'

'Hey, hey. C'mere. Man hug. I know, I know. It sucks.' He ran through a list of clergy good in this kind of crisis. Dominic Todd – older gay guy? Or a woman? Wendy Styles? Or who? 'Think of anyone?'

'No, I dunno, I'm— Maybe Janey? Ah, there's no point. She'll be on holiday. Ah shit. Why would he do that?'

'I know. But let's focus, OK? Let's try your friend and take it from there.'

Jane is standing at the door of Danny's bedroom. The light dims. Storm coming. She really should tidy the fecker. What's the big problem? She's acting as though he's dead, and this is his shrine, her last link to her boy. Does she fear, at some level, that if she tidies up, he will never return? Get a grip, you daft cow.

Lightning flickers. She counts. Just like she used to with Danny when he was little. Three, four, five. A rumble shakes the windows. How far away is five? She's never known.

No, she still can't do it. It'll take for ever. She knows she'll weep over every sock, every plectrum. Because she'll be packing away his childhood, and the whole of Project Motherhood. No. Come on, gal. Just blitz it. Bang. Done. Tidy. She needs a kick up the arse to get started, that's all.

And then her phone rings.

AUGUST

Chapter 30

ain. Rain over the whole diocese of Lindchester. Biblical rain. Gresham's Boats is closed for business until the River Linden returns to normal levels. The Lower Town is on amber flood alert. William of Lindchester, pray for us!

> The rain came down and the floods came UP!
> The rain came down and the floods came UP!
> The rain came down and the floods came UP!
> And the house on the rock stood firm!

Some of my readers may remember that chorus from Sunday school days. Father Wendy has resurrected it for a holiday club in Cardingforth this week, because it (sort of) fits the theme – Pirates. She had an email of complaint about the holiday club (the archdeacon was copied in), because:

- Piracy in Somalia is no joke.
- The Church should not be promoting robbery and criminal violence at sea.

But shiver me timbers, Father Wendy went ahead anyway.

It's Monday, day one. The church hall is transformed with rigging and Jolly Rogers. A CD of sea shanties plays. Cap'n Wendy (Ar-harr!) and First Mate Virginia (the new curate) (Yo-ho!) have a crew of fifty-seven Key Stage 2 scurvy knaves at their command, on board the Good Ship Yacki-Hicki-Doo-La. And a team of CRB-checked adult seadogs, of course, to help quell mutinies in line with current good safeguarding practice. No child will be flogged, keelhauled or made to walk the plank without a chaperone.

By midday, there is an atmosphere of barely contained anarchy in Cardingforth church hall, which is exactly how it should be. The parents and carers are gathering in the rain to collect their kids.

A rowdy chorus (pirated – rather appropriately – from an old music hall song) floats out to them as they jostle umbrellas and buggies:

> And I snap my finger HA HA HA HA!
> And I snap my other one HO HO HO HO!
> I don't care if it's rain or shine,
> I am my Lord's and my Lord is mine!
> So I shout for joy and sail away,
> No pirate could be cooler!
> And where'er I go I fear no foe
> On the good ship YACKI-HICKI-DOO-LA!

Two hours of childcare for a quid. For a whole week. Not bad, that. Say what you like about the Church, that's not bad.

Tuesday. The four-by-fours crawl round the Close at 6.45 a.m., tyres going *flippety-flippety* over the wet cobbles. Choir parents dropping off the choristers. The choir tour coach leaves for Germany at 7 a.m. The precentor explains: 'Unfortunately, Mr May has had to pull out for personal reasons.' The lay clerks roll their eyes. Good. Giles has been praying they'll assume Freddie's just gone off on another bender, and that the real reason doesn't get out. If only Freddie has the sense to keep schtum and not blurt all over Facebook! It's obvious to Giles that the allegations are groundless – malicious, even. But he knows how the taint can linger, even when someone is exonerated. Especially if that someone is gay. The process is all stacked in favour of the alleged victim. Hard to see how it couldn't be, admittedly. And fair enough, the safeguarding officer had no alternative. But the precentor is spitting tacks. He'd cheerfully strangle Slope with his own preaching scarf. Sanctimonious twat. And Mary Poppins is about as much use as a chocolate thurible when it comes to reining in his chaplain.

The door closes. The coach pulls away. Someone draws willies on the steamed-up window. Someone lets off. Someone pipes that he knows a song that'll get on your nerves. Twenty hours of this. Christ, have mercy.

But I am toying with you, reader. You will be wondering what happened to poor Freddie. Did Jane take him in? Why, of course she did. It gave her that kick up the arse she'd needed to tidy Danny's room. Took her a mere fifty-eight minutes, change of sheets, dusting and hoovering included. It also – as you no doubt anticipated – brought about a meeting between her and the archdeacon at last.

Jane was cramming the last bin-liner of crap into the wheelie bin when her doorbell rang. She raced back, scanned the kitchen in case the archdeacon came in for a cuppa. Shit. Not that she gave a toss about archdeacons, but quickly, shove dirties into dishwasher, sweep breakfast crumbs onto floor, kick them under the fridge, dust self down. Good. She went to answer the door.

There was Freddie with his holdall, looking so woebegone she took him in her arms. 'Aw. Poor baby. Really sorry you're having to deal with this.'

'Thanks, Janey. Love you.'

'Yeah, love you too. Come on in. I've put you in Danny's room.'

It was only then that she looked at the other man on her doorstep. The big bald man. She frowned and looked past him, to the black Mini. Then back at him, standing there in his checked chef's shirt. His checked *clerical* shirt. Oho! She folded her arms and waited.

He raised both hands in surrender.

Jane battled in vain with a smile. 'Well, hello, Mr Archdeacon. Nice to meet you. Won't you come in?'

The three of them stood for a moment in Jane's hall. 'Right. I'll get the kettle on,' she said. 'Tea? Coffee?'

'Janey, I'm— OK if I go for a run first? To like clear my head?'

'Feel free. Takeaway later?'

'Cool.'

Freddie's footsteps thumped up the stairs. That left Jane and the archdeacon. 'So. Tea, coffee?'

'Tea, please.'

They sat in the kitchen waiting for the kettle to boil.

'Kind of you to do this,' said the archdeacon.

'More than happy.' She looked him over. Did battle with that smile again. Of course – he must be Dominic's Prat in the Hat. 'So. Not a chef at all, then, eh, Matt?'

'Nope, not a chef.'

Jane bunged a couple of teabags in mugs. 'You lied. You said you were.'

'No, I just failed to deny it.'

'That's as bad as lying.'

'I was scared.'

Jane laughed her filthy laugh. The front door banged shut. Freddie, Freddie. 'I assume you can't discuss the allegations with me?'

The archdeacon shook his head. 'Probably not.'

Jane made the tea and sat again. 'So. What shall we talk about then, Matt? Oh, I know – let's start with how you got my name and email, shall we?'

He gestured. 'Lanyard.'

'Hah!' Bloody Poundstretcher. Completely anal about ID cards. 'Thought you must be a chef in one of our eateries, or something. Wait, you bloody saw me on the Close in my doctoral robes, didn't you? Stalker!'

He smiled.

Not very chatty, was he? 'Well, go on then – why stalk me? Were you coming on to me with those texts?'

'I was.'

'You were?' He was! Another filthy laugh. 'And why was that?'

He smiled again. 'Let's say, you got my attention.'

'What, by kicking the shit out of your car?'

'That tends to get a man's attention.'

'Damn! And all these years I've been wearing tight skirts and high heels!'

There was a pause. The archdeacon sipped his tea.

'And stockings,' added Jane. 'With—'

'Moving on,' said Matt. 'So how do you know Freddie?'

He's on the river bank, slithering, cursing. Then the path ahead vanishes under water. Freddie vaults the fence, and the field's a quagmire too. He slips. Ah fuck. Now he's covered in it. Can nothing go right? He gets up, sploshes across the cowfield and gets back on the road, where he pounds, pounds, pounds. On and on he goes, left, then left, then left, making a big loop. Thank fuck it's raining. Hides the tears. Man, he's such a cry-baby. 'Sticks and stones, son. It's not your fault you're gay, but it *is* your fault if you're a victim.'

Ah Jesus, but nothing hurts like words, Dad.

Why would Martin even do that? Ah fuck, what's he gonna do? Is Paul gonna believe him? Or will he take fuckwit's side? What if nobody believes him? What if they're all, Yeah, but why would a little girl make that up? You must have done *something*.

A car swishes past him. He can kiss the Barchester job goodbye, can't he? This'll be on his record like, for ever. Oh, what's the point? Janey and Matt are being sweet, but there's no point. Why even bother? When he knows he's just gonna get slapped down again? Ah God, he wishes he was dead!

'Why not try to prove the old bastard wrong instead? Why this pattern of self-sabotage?' Mr Dorian's words go round and round his head as he runs. 'It seems to me you've got it all. People would kill for your advantages.'

I so do *not* have it all, asshole. What do you know? Fuck you. Seriously, fuck you.

Suddenly the rain doubles. Fucking *mental*. Like someone up there's emptying baths, swimming pools. He hears the Dorian Singers: 'What can wash away my stain?'

Then it's Allegri: *Amplius lava me ab iniquitate mea.* Wash me throughly from my wickedness. And that's what the rain's doing. Literally? It's washing, washing, washing him clean. He sobs out a laugh. And then this weird thing happens? It's like someone's, y'know, *there*? Running beside him? Just for one moment, someone's there in the rain, not saying anything, just running with him.

It's Saturday evening. Father Dominic is standing in his study rehearsing what he's going to say. He's got it all written out, but it's not going well. So far he's got no further than 'I have an important announcement to make' before crumpling. He cried when he broke the news to his churchwardens yesterday. His mood tonight was not helped by an encounter in Waitrose with the family of the poor woman whose funeral he forgot. Ran slap into them in the cereal aisle. Made himself say hello and ask how they were doing, but they snubbed him comprehensively. *O clemens, O pia*. Pray for me. This failure will always be a sword through his heart. But on with life:

Ahem. 'I have an important announcement . . .' Deep breath. You can do this. 'I have—'

His phone rings. Aargh! The Prat in the Hat. 'Archdeacon! Hello!'

'Hello, father. All set for tomorrow? The churchwardens in Lindford are poised to make the announcement at their 10.30, so Thunderbirds are go, basically.'

'That's good.'

'All OK at your end?'

'Oh God, I don't know. Yes. No. I'm rehearsing my speech and it sounds like a Dear John letter! I know I'm going to burst into tears.'

'And does that matter?'

'What if I get the first sentence out, then stand there like an idiot, howling? They'll all think I've got terminal cancer, or I've been defrocked, or something!'

And that is why, on Sunday morning, the archdeacon of Lindchester attended the 10.30 Eucharist at St John the Evangelist, Renfold. After the service, before the final hymn, he stood beside the weeping Dominic, put a hand on his shoulder, and made his announcement for him.

A murmur of shock went through the church. Going? No! Father Dominic was going? But . . . but . . .

The archdeacon beamed at the congregation.

'Now, Dominic here is looking out at a bunch of people and he thinks he's letting them down and abandoning them. But I'm looking out at a bunch of people who know that he's loved them, worked with them and prayed for them faithfully for the last eleven years. In my role I get to see a lot of priests. The good, the bad and the ugly. And this is one of the good ones, people – as you know. So if you could all tell him that during his last weeks here, that would be peachy.' Spontaneous applause broke out. 'All righty, then. Let's sing the last hymn: "All my hope on God is founded".'

Dominic was still crying as he walked down the aisle, past the sea of smiling faces, through the hands reaching out to pat him, offer him wads of tissue, grasp him. They loved him, they really did. He was carried along on a groundswell of love.

Christ doth call
One and all:
Ye who follow shall not fall.

Chapter 31

Not much gets past the Venerable Matt Tyler. All the same, he's not infallible. When he dropped Freddie off in Cardingforth, Matt clocked that Sunningdale Drive rang a bell for some reason; but, distracted by the revelation that Freddie's Janey was the very Dr Jane Rossiter he had been textually flirting with for the past few months, he failed to chase it up later on.

Perhaps he might have remembered the following morning, had the thought not been driven from his mind by demon priest (formerly of Lindford Parish) lawyering up and taking him and the bishop to an employment tribunal for unfair dismissal and breach of contract. So he wanted to play rough, did he? The archdeacon had been ready for this for some time. Had a big old file. Pics of the vandalized vicarage, screenshots of defamatory rants on Facebook, list of witnesses to summon. Demon priest was going to discover that they don't settle out of court here in the diocese of Lindchester.

Please don't get the impression that our friend the archdeacon is normally a vengeful man. But it's true to say that he's still smarting from being suckered four years ago, by the person who threw this particular dead cat over the wall. Back when he was a rookie archdeacon. 'Why didn't you warn us the guy was a serial suer?' Matt demanded. His oppo, the archdeacon in Another Diocese (which will remain nameless), purred: 'But my dear archdeacon! You didn't ask.'

Moral of the tale: always ask. Ask: 'Is there anything which, two years from now, I'll be glad I asked?'

With all this caper going on, Matt failed to warn Freddie about who was living four doors down from Jane. Freddie discovered for himself about a week later.

He was on his way back from the corner shop with milk. The sun was out for once. Maybe, just maybe it would all be OK?

'Freddie! Freddie! Mummy, it's Freddie!'

He whirled round. Jessica. With her mum, on the front lawn. No! Don't say this was their house!

'Hey, sweetie!' He waved and tried to keep walking, but she came running after him.

'It was my birthday in France and I got a tent from Grandma and Grandpa!'

'Yeah, I can see. Awesome! Happy birthday!' Get me out of here – like now? Becky was coming over to bawl him out! Little witch was nowhere in sight, thank God.

'Freddie! What are you doing here?'

'So yeah, I'm like, staying with a friend? Look, it's cool, I'm off, no worries.'

'Come and see my tent!' Jessie was tugging at his shorts leg now. 'It's a princess castle tent!'

'Aw. Maybe later? I've got to take the milk back so my friend can have her coffee?'

'I've got a new Barbie, too! I'll get her!' Jessie ran back to the tent.

'It's OK, Becks.' He started walking. 'You don't have to say anything.'

'Wait!' Why was she looking at him like that? 'What's wrong?'

Gah, he can't *believe* this. 'Nobody's told you?'

'Told me what?'

'Look! Look, Freddie! This is my new hairtastic Barbie, so I can style her hair!'

'Whoa! Love that purple streak!' He squatted down. 'Listen, can you and Barbie do me a massive favour? Can you, um . . . pick me some flowers from your garden, so I can give them to the lady I'm staying with? Yeah? Awesome!'

He stood up. Becky was looking totally freaked now.

'Told me what?'

'Oh, man. I shouldn't— Listen, it's just, Martin made these, yeah, allegations? About when I looked after the girls that time?'

'What?! What allegations? Why haven't I been told?'

'Dude, I'm sorry, I have no idea why.'

'What's he been saying? Tell me *now*!'

'Probably I shouldn't do that? I've been suspended. There's like, this investigation process?'

'Investigation? I'm their mother!' Man, she was going mental here. 'I have a right to know!'

But now Jessie was back with her bunch of flowers. 'Hey, thanks! These are totally the best!' Jessie beamed up at him. 'Listen, you couldn't make, like, a card to go with them? You could? Yeah!'

'I'm going to use my Hello Kitty craft kit that I got from Aunty Helen!'

They watched her skip back to her tent. Ah nuts. Please don't let me start crying.

Becky put her hand on his arm. 'Freddie! I can't believe this! You're so sweet with her. What's the children's father been saying?'

So Freddie told her. 'I have no idea why Leah would say that? Coz I honestly did not tell them that, it was her? And I'm all, hey, out of order!'

'Of course you were! She must've heard it at school, then she was scared she'd get told off, so she fibbed.' She was grinding her teeth now, literally? 'He escalated it, stupid man. He is so heavy-handed! Oh, Freddie! Leah . . . Leah isn't a happy little girl at the moment, with . . . everything.'

With all due respect, lady, do *not* ask me to feel bad for your daughter, not right now.

Must've shown on his face. 'Well. I'm sorry. Look, she's at a friend's on a sleepover, so I can quietly get Jessica's version of what happened, without . . . I'll make sure this is cleared up as soon as possible, Freddie. I have no doubts about you. None.'

Uh-huh, right. Flashback to her face, when he said he'd look after them. 'Thanks.'

'I know what he's trying to do: he's trying to make out I'm an unfit mother. Well, it won't work!'

Ah cock. This isn't even about me, is it? It's all about them, fighting. Was she going to screw things up even worse by wading in on his side? But here came Jessie, waving a piece of pink paper. He bent down to look. 'Aw, that is so amazing?'

'It's a Hello Kitty mandala.'

'It is? Whoa! My friend's gonna love this.'

You will have inferred from this that Martin is now home. He has been contacted by the archdeacon, but he stands by his allegations. Is the archdeacon suggesting Leah's lying? No, he absolutely will *not* question either of his daughters further. They have suffered enough.

The bishop and his wife are home too. Obviously, the bishop has been informed that there is a safeguarding issue with Freddie. His opinion has been sought. The bishop would gladly have kept all this from Susanna (he routinely spares her the horrid stuff), but Susanna needed some explanation for Freddie's absence from the palace. Oh dear, oh dear! A spasm of baking occurred.

Marion, the dean, had to be brought into the picture, and she confided her frustration to her husband Gene. Bishop Bob Hooty has been informed, too. So, how many people now know? Let's see: the diocesan safeguarding officer, the cathedral safeguarding officer (back from holiday), the cathedral administrator (of course), the diocesan communications officer (just in case), the archdeacon, the precentor (and his wife), the bishop of Lindchester (and his wife), the dean (and her husband), the suffragan bishop of Barcup (who's told nobody), Dr Jane Rossiter (likewise), Becky Rogers (who sounded off to her mum). Not forgetting Martin Rogers' parents, sister and brother-in-law, because he needed someone outside the situation to tell him he'd done exactly right, and join him in lamenting Becky's poor judgement in leaving the girls in the care of an aggressive proselytizing homosexual. I make that nineteen. But they are all utterly discreet, and they have only told other people who are equally trustworthy.

Becky Rogers has a gentle little chat with Jessica about that afternoon.

'Mummy, Leah was being very, very mean to Freddie, ackshully, she said we weren't going to talk to him coz we hate him, but I don't hate him, Freddie's my friend, he let me style his hair coz Barbie's hair was all cut off. Leah said I wasn't allowed. And then Leah said he was gay coz he's got ear rings in his chest, and she said I'm stupid and a baby, and then she said a bad thing about gay and Freddie was upset and I was crying. Then he got us all a white Magnum. Then Daddy came.'

She can't say the bad thing, Daddy says she has to forget it, coz Leah shouldn't've told it to her.

Mummy says she won't be cross, promise, and she won't tell Leah. Or Daddy.

Jessie is allowed to put Mummy's scarf over her face. Mummy shuts her eyes and promises not to look. So Jessie whispers it: Sex. Willies. Bums.

'Good girl, I know that was difficult to say. Nobody's cross with you. And now, let's make chocolate crispy cakes!'

'Yay! Chocolate crispy cakes! We can have a picnic in the tent! Can we invite Freddie? Please? Oh, ple-e-ease?'

'Another time, darling.'

The aggressive proselytizing homosexual is now having kittens. Literally? Gah. He should never have told Becky all that. Should have just walked away. Ah nuts, he's probably broken like a thousand rules here! But why the hell had nobody told her? Man, what's he gonna do?

Ring the archdeacon, of course.

Matt puts the phone down and indulges in a brief fantasy of seizing the bishop's chaplain by the ears and head-butting him. He distinctly remembers saying to Martin, 'Becky needs to be informed. Is that something you feel able to do, or shall I contact her?' And Martin replied, 'You can leave that with me, archdeacon. I'm sure the girls' mother will contact you, if she has anything to add.' And that – as Dr Rossiter herself would say – is as bad as lying. The games people play. Matt drums his fingers on his desk. Gets out the paperwork. Yep, got a note of that conversation. All righty. He picks up the phone and rings Becky Rogers to get her version before the Spanish Inquisition meets.

Bishop Paul is not happy. Those restorative two weeks in Corfu have vanished like burnt flash paper. He's in his study, praying for everyone concerned. He casts his mind back to the bright, eager young man he appointed as his chaplain. A bit earnest, yes. A bit lacking in humour; but highly organized, generous, motivated, dependable, loyal. And what's left? A boiled-down distillation of Martin essence. A quivering wire of rage. How serious is this latest development? Was Martin simply reacting in panic and horror, the way any father might, blindly protecting his daughters? (Except, hah! The bishop has four daughters of his own, and knows that little angels are capable of telling the most astounding whoppers.) Or was this a calculated piece of vindictiveness?

Or – he must entertain this possibility – was Freddie so far lost to reason, so driven by his gay rights agenda, that he'd think it appropriate to speak that frankly to children about gay sex?

Freddie, Freddie.

Yet again the bishop finds himself caught between the pair of them. Whatever the outcome of the investigation, the emotional fallout will be ghastly. Is this his own fault? Ought he to have dealt decisively with their mutual antagonism much, much earlier?

Yes, he's failed them both.

But he sees how he let it come about: on any given occasion he'd judged it was not quite worth the hassle. Always so many more important and urgent things clamouring to be dealt with, and besides, Freddie was always about to leave. As he is now: about to go off to Barchester. In a matter of weeks. If he weren't going, it would be worth getting a mediator in, and sit the two of them down and make them listen to one another, properly. *Make* them understand each other.

Paul sighs. Yes, Freddie will soon be gone. He'll just have to keep him out of Martin's way for a couple more weeks. Maybe with Freddie out of the picture Martin will relax, become bearable again. And it won't be for long.

(Don't breathe a word, but it looks as though Paul will have a new job this autumn.)

He picks up his volume of R. S. Thomas poems, and reminds himself that the meaning is in the waiting.

Susanna (baking a batch of fairy cakes with pink sprinkles to take to Becky) is the only one who thinks: *That poor little girl. That poor, angry, unhappy little girl! Is anyone really looking after her?*

Chapter 32

August. Ragwort and rosebay willowherb crowd the verges and riverbanks and railway embankments of Lindfordshire. Thistledown idles by on the humid air. The first lime seeds helicopter down from the trees. Summer has rolled over and turned to face autumn. The shops all trumpet the same message: BACK TO SCHOOL! New uniform! Ring-binders! Pencil cases! Schoolbags! Tantrums in Clark's shoe shop! 'Too soon,' wail children and teachers. 'Not soon enough!' think frazzled parents, and people whose houses back on to parks or wasteland, where bored kids clamber on roofs, invade gardens, set fire to stuff.

A-level results on Thursday. University clearing week. Dr Jane Rossiter is on the hotline this year. Having weaselled out of this duty for the last decade, Confirmation and Clearing is a mystery, shrouded in a dense fog of acronyms. ABB HEFCE SCN-exempt. SCN countable home/EU CI or CF. WTF? But Dr Elspeth Quisling was in charge of the rota this year. She put her nemesis on duty at the crack of dawn on Thursday, when the calls were expected to come thick and fast. But wait – Jane has a hospital appointment on Thursday! She has already booked a day of annual leave. Dr Quisling may check that, if she wishes. Dr Quisling does indeed check. She would gladly check with the hospital too, but this is not possible; so she gnashes her teeth and puts Jane down for Friday morning instead, by which time the calls will have slowed to a mere trickle.

I'm sure my readers are not concerned about the state of Jane's health. They are more troubled – quite rightly – by her habits of mendacity. She has no hospital appointment. But as we shall see, the fates have decreed that she will nonetheless spend half of Thursday in hospital.

It's Thursday morning. Ulrika Littlechild, wife of the precentor, has driven Lukas up to school so he can get his A-level results. They already know he has not got the three A grades he needs for Durham, because his offer was not confirmed late last night when they checked on the UCAS website. *Ach Gott!* The question now is exactly how disastrously he's done.

She parks in a side street a tactful distance from the school and watches him amble away. Doesn't he care? Is this her fault for sending him to the local comp, rather than packing him off to a Harrow or Hogwarts or wherever the bloody hell, where bright but lazy boys are flogged till they work? Bad mother!

In her mind, good mothers sit at the table each night (not drinking wine) overseeing their children's homework, while Mozart plays in the background to make them brainy. Good mothers make their sons learn the piano or the violin, they make them practise an hour a day and take their grades, they do not let them just teach themselves jazz piano or bass guitar. If she had her time again, she would do it all differently!

No, she wouldn't. She knows she is a totally crep mother. Second time round she would still think, hey, lazy bums, I finished my Abitur back in 1984! I will not sodding well be doing your work for you! They have to learn to be independent. I can't be always there. They will have to learn to motivate themselves without Mutti or teacher standing over them cracking the whip.

High above the bank of lime trees there is a buzzard circling on the thermals. She hears its call. *Keee-keee!* And suddenly a rush of tears surprises her. He's leaving me. They will both be flying the nest in the next couple of years. I can't keep them for ever. All I want is to see them flying free. *Ach Gott*, don't let those results be too awful! How will my babies ever manage to be grown-ups? Oh, let them fly high and free as that bird!

She pulls out her mobile and glares at it. Come on! Text me, you little shit! Tell me what you got.

The minutes creep by. The buzzard wheels round above the restless limes. *Keee-keee!*

'Well,' says the diocesan safeguarding officer. 'I think we're in agreement, Matt.'

'I think we are, Helene.'

'We've followed procedure.'

'Yes, indeedy!'

Helene looks sharply at the archdeacon. He beams at her. 'It remains for us to feed back to the parties concerned. Perhaps if I contact

Martin, and you contact Frederick? Does that sound like a sensible course of action to you, Matt?'

'It does, Helene.'

There is a long silence. 'I'm sorry, Matt, but just occasionally I get the impression you're poking fun at me. Would that be fair to say?'

Matt considers making a note of this allegation on a pad of paper. Instead he bows his head. 'You could well be right there. Sorry.'

There is another silence. Is she about to send him on a professional development course to re-educate compulsive piss-takers?

She closes her file. 'Well, as I said, Matt, if you could contact Frederick as soon as possible?'

'Will do.'

Matt walks back to his office.

I'm sorry, Helene, but occasionally I get the impression you think I'm the HR office boy, not the chuffing archdeacon of Lindchester.

He sits at his desk, composes himself, then picks up the phone to ring tarty-pants. Tarty-pants is not answering. Uh-oh. Please don't say he's gone AWOL again.

Freddie has not gone AWOL. He's been having a horrible time, though. Janey is a star, but he feels bad for leeching off her like this. She's all, 'Don't be stupid'; but it's the 'Oh, Freddie, Freddie, Freddie!' thing again. Poor Freddie, he's so hopeless, so vulnerable, he's such a drama queen, he can't cope on his own. Same old. Gah, his whole existence is parasitic! Plus he, like, trades on his cuteness? He totally admits that. If he wasn't so fucking cute, people wouldn't be all, 'Aw, poor puppy, come and live with us, we'll look after you!' So what's gonna happen when he's not cute any more? He's gonna end up some fat lonely old queen, isn't he, hanging around the pretty young guys, asking to be loved?

Oh, *stop* that. Jesus.

It's this investigation hanging over him, freaking him out? He needs something to occupy him – but what? He stands at Danny's window looking out. Maybe sort out Janey's garden for her? He should totally do that. It is a fucking jungle out there. Literally?

So that's what he does. He rips out the brambles, hacks back the shrubs, gets Janey to drive him to the garden centre so they can hire a big bad boy petrol strimmer and reclaim the lawn.

Jane is more than happy with this scheme, incidentally. She gets her garden overhauled for free, she gets to glance up from the first draft of her Josephine Luscombe book and contemplate a gorgeous young man stripped to the waist, working his butt off. What, as the young people say, is not to like?

Once he's finished digging the beds over, they are going to go back to the garden centre and stock up on plants. He's thinking maybe potentillas? Lavender? Stuff even Janey can't kill. That's the plan for this afternoon. Freddie is just forking over the last bed when his phone rings. He stops, drives the fork into the earth. And clean through his right foot.

You will appreciate now why the archdeacon's call went unanswered.

The irony of spending four hours in A&E was not lost on Dr Rossiter. She whiled away some of the time wondering if she'd rather be on the clearing hotline after all; but no, another ride on the Freddie May rollercoaster just had the edge. She had a book, she had sandwiches (years of rugby had taught her never to enter a waiting room underprepared), she had company.

Freddie had been assessed, his wound had been irrigated, he'd been given a tetanus jab. Happily, the fork tine had missed the bone. They were now waiting for a doctor to stitch him up. Jane had been asked twice if she was his mum. Oh, for fuck's sake. How likely is that? Look at him. Yes, I'm his mother – and his dad was a golden meteor shower!

Freddie's phone rang. 'Hey, Matt.'

Jane's heart did a thump. Then Freddie reached out and gripped her hand. Oh shit – this must be the outcome of the investigation. She gripped him back. Tried to assess from his face if this was good or bad news. He was fighting off tears, but that could mean anything.

'Yeah. Uh-huh. K.'

Concerns . . . after discussion. Freddie was nearly breaking her fingers.

'So, like, no case to answer? That's it?'

That's it. All concerns allayed after discussion. Jane caught it that time. Well, thank God for that. She squeezed Freddie's hand again.

'I can come back?'

Of course. Whenever you like. The Hendersons are expecting you. Need a lift? Where are you now?

'O-o-ohh. So yeah, I'm up in casualty? I like stuck a garden fork through my foot?'

What? You numpty! Is Jane there looking after you?

'Yeah, she's right here.'

Excellent. Catch you later, tarty-pants. Take care now.

She heard him ring off.

'Good news?' Freddie nodded. 'So you're not a sleazy old nonce, after all then?'

There was a silence. Damn. Misjudged that one.

'Yeah, listen, could you please not joke about it, Janey?'

'Of course. Sorry.'

'No worries.'

A nurse called his name. Jane watched as he limped off to the cubicle where the doctor was waiting. He'd forgiven her, but argh. Bad woman, all the same.

Oh dear, oh dear! That poor boy is so accident-prone!

It's Friday morning and Susanna is in her kitchen whipping up a batch of millionaire shortbread, because she knows it's Freddie's favourite. She'll pop it round to him once the chocolate has set. It makes sense for Freddie to stay at Jane's a few more days, so he won't have to contend with four flights of palace stairs. Jane. Oh dear, Susanna hasn't had a proper chat with Jane for ages, and it's been on her conscience. How is she coping without Danny? It's been months since she last asked that. Susanna castigates herself as she spreads the caramel on the warm shortbread. This can be for Freddie, and she'll take Jane one of the little jars of Greek honey and nuts they brought back from Corfu. And a bunch of roses from the garden.

Oh, Freddie! Thank heavens Jane was around to look after him during the investigation. What a sad, sad business. Oh, Martin! Becky! The girls! Oh, Paul! Paul! So much on his plate, poor love! This dreadful waiting and secrecy. Still, next week he'll be telling his close colleagues on the senior staff team. That will be a relief for him, to have their support and prayers at last, not to have to pretend any more. She pops the tray into the fridge to cool it down.

Is there enough in the freezer for when she nips down to Bristol after the baby's born? Maybe she should stick a couple more lasagnes in, especially if Freddie's back – that boy eats like a horse! Claire's baby is already a week overdue. (Oh, let everything be all right!) She starts snapping the chocolate in pieces. She knows it's a bit naughty of her to use real Belgian chocolate, but it tastes so much nicer.

The archbishop elect (ssh!) is having his Quiet Time. R. S. Thomas's grumpiness is contagious. This is (O sternest of Evangelical disapprobations!) Not Helpful. The bishop has taken to reviving himself with Vesuvian nips of Emily Dickinson, like a dowager with a brandy bottle in her glove drawer:

> Come slowly – Eden!
> Lips unused to Thee –
> Bashful – sip thy Jessamines –
> As the fainting Bee –

But today his mind wanders. Freddie's latest mishap has merely postponed a tricky confrontation. Martin is furious about the safeguarding outcome. He is refusing to work in the office if Freddie is there. So Paul will have to ask Freddie to stay away. He can't afford a messy public rupture with his chaplain at this stage. But pragmatism always leaves a bad taste in Paul's mouth. He knows Freddie will have (in a phrase never applied to angry straight men) a monumental hissy fit. Oh, Lord.

As the fainting Bee –

Come along, Henderson. Concentrate!

Reaching late his flower,
Round her chamber hums –
Counts his nectars –
Enters – and is lost in Balms.

Chapter 33

Bob Hooty gazes through his study window in Martonbury. The first swallows gather on the telegraph wires. This afternoon he and Janet are going out blackberrying along the canal towpath. There is a whiff of September in the air now. New beginnings everywhere. Students, like those swallows there, about to take flight for other worlds. And now his colleague, off to York.

This preferment of Paul's has unsettled our good friend Bob, I'm afraid. It has overturned a stone in his psyche and all manner of stuff is scuttling for cover. Little earwigs of resentment, woodlice of indignation. He tries simply to observe them, not judge. Well, this is interesting, he tells himself. I seem to be angry. I seem to feel sidelined and overlooked. I seem to be saying, 'How come my younger brother gets the biggest piece?' I wonder why – when I've never had any ambition to be archbishop of York, and retirement is beckoning? Abruptly, a centipede breaks cover: 'I have never liked the man!' Aha, interesting! Bob leans forward to get a proper look. He's known all along about this little fellow, but this is the first time it has come out of hiding and shown itself properly. You don't like Bishop Paul, you say? 'No! I *hate* him!' The centipede stamps a hundred tiny feet. But Paul's always been very pleasant to us, hasn't he? Kind, professional, prayerful. Why do you hate him? '*Because he's a hypocrite!*' shouts the centipede.

The bishop of Barcup contemplates this accusation for a long time. He watches the swallows as they natter on the wires outside his window. Lord knows, we are all hypocrites. The inside seldom matches the outside. Why, Bob himself does not parade his menagerie of creepy-crawlies before the world. But there is something more than usually . . . closed-off about Paul. Maybe that's it? A deep reticence beneath his surface amiability, that makes you feel you will never really know the man. You get the feeling that although he plays his hand fairly, he's probably got a knave up his sleeve. In short, he's the calculating type, and Bob is not. So maybe, he suggests, Paul's just a strategist, rather than a hypocrite? But the centipede has gone to ground.

Flying away, they are all flying away. Lukas Littlechild (he got A, B, B for his A-levels) has decided to go and spend a gap year in Heidelberg with his Tante Birgit, improving his German, and rethinking his future. On Thursday Ulrika had a second stint of waiting in the car watching the buzzards circle, this time while Felix collected his GCSE results. A mixed bag of grades, but he passed them all. Apart from RE. Hilariously! The canon's son, failing GCSE Religious Studies! Both Littlechild boys are going off to Cornwall with a few friends this weekend, on a little beach holiday. Paddling, sandcastles, and picnics with lashings of ginger pop. Think Giles and Ulrika, without reflecting properly on the fact that it was Freddie May who recommended Polzeath.

Flying away. It took her a few months after waving Danny off through All Departures, but Jane thought she had pretty much got her head round the concept. Alas no. Turns out there was another cranking of the maternal rack in store for her. Danny has decided to stay down under and go to uni in New Zealand. Well, why wouldn't he? He has dual nationality, fees are a fraction of what he'd be paying here, and frankly, his grades are only ever going to get him into the likes of Poundstretcher if he stays in the UK. Who in their right mind wouldn't rather do their degree in Middle Earth than Thickford, Urbansprawlshire?

But fuck it. Why didn't he tell her that's what he was hoping to do? Why didn't he discuss it with her? That's what's killing her – the thought of him and Mickey cooking up their little plan and making sure it was a done deal, so Mum (bless her) didn't chuck a spanner in the works. Bastards. Is she really so unreasonable? Do they really think she'd ever stand in the way of Danny's happiness?

Which is probably why she gets on Freddie's case and rides him so hard about getting in touch with his mum. Little fecker hasn't emailed her for months. Turns out he's convinced himself he can't get an Argentine visa with a drugs conviction. For God's sake. Why get your knickers in a twist, when the answer is one click away on Google? Why this chronic inability to face stuff? Half her students are the same: failing to avail themselves of supervisions for two terms, then going into meltdown over their dissertations a week before the deadline. Your choice, my friends. I'm not going to chase you.

Freddie, however, is a different matter. Freddie she's prepared to chase mercilessly. After a bout of 'Gah, fuck, *no*! Don't ask! Get off my back, OK?' she extorts the truth and bullies him into accepting his mum's offer of a free fortnight's holiday on the ranch. Organizes the ass off him, that's what she does. Poor kid needs to get Close politics out of his hair before setting off for Barchester.

There. My good deed for the month, thinks Jane when it's over. She looks at Freddie, sulking at the other end of her ratty corduroy sofa. I will deposit you back at the Hendersons' tomorrow, and then maybe I can stop playing Mum and try my hand at Single Gal again.

'Yeah? What are *you* smiling at, slag-face?'

'You'll never know, my little slut-puppy.'

Jane is smiling at the thought of a certain archdeacon.

It's Friday morning and Susanna is happy. Yes, she genuinely is! As they drive to Bristol she cautiously patrols the borders of her life for trouble, and all she can find to fret about today is whether Paul will remember to water the African violets from the bottom not the top. (Not counting Global Warming, of course.)

Oh, thank you, Lord, for all your goodness! The new grandson has arrived safely! Seven pounds four ounces, neither too big nor too small to trigger anxiety. Freddie's foot is mending nicely, he's off to see his mum, he has a job to come back to, which was mercifully not wrecked by that safeguarding process (momentary surge of panic about Martin, but Martin will no longer be a problem when Paul takes up his new job – Susanna bravely renounces all Martin-related fretting for now). Paul has been able to share his news with his senior colleagues, so the burden of secrecy has been lightened. If only the announcement could happen! But the Queen is at Balmoral; they will have to be patient a bit longer.

She reaches across and squeezes Paul's arm as he drives. He turns and smiles at her. Oh, she's so lucky to be married to him! If only he could spend the weekend with them in Bristol, rather than driving back this evening. What a good man he is, so forbearing with her when she's being silly about nothing! That little bottle! She'd finally found a moment to mention it while they were in Corfu, and he'd explained. The relief, the sheer relief of knowing it was nothing. (Freddie is so naughty!) It didn't even matter that Paul had laughed till he cried nearly, when she owned up that she'd sniffed it to find out what it was.

Well, another time she's going to remember this, she really is, and not let herself be such a catastrophizer. She'd known from the start that when Paul was in his teens he went through a phase of being attracted to other men, he'd admitted it. These schoolboy crushes are terribly common, *but they pass* – it's not PC to say that, she knows – and she's never had reason to think that's still a problem. She feels awful now for even entertaining the suspicion. When had their marriage been anything other than full and rewarding? Still romantic, even if it was not quite as . . . Well, after thirty years, things steady down a bit, don't they? Looking back, she can't believe she was so silly. To carry that dreadful load of misery for no reason!

So yes – Susanna is happy!

I'll tell you someone else who's happy: our friend Father Dominic. He's spent a happy fortnight in France, he's happy and excited about his move to Lindford, and has just popped round to see his good friend Jane. That should cure him of his happiness. Let's be nosy and listen in:

'You've just missed the divine Mr May,' said Jane.

'What, the blond man-trap? Well, thank God for that!' He handed Jane a chilled bottle and some cheese. 'Now *this* you must try. My new discovery: Sauternes with Roquefort.'

'I thought Sauternes was the one that goes with Christmas pudding. When you're so pissed you might as well be drinking Buckie.'

'Ah, but this is what the French do. Glasses, plate, cheese knife.' He clapped his hands. 'Come along now.'

Jane obliged while Dominic drew the cork. 'Bet it's disgusting.'

'Well, it is a bit. But it's also *divine*.'

They sat at her kitchen table. Jane gave it a whirl. Savoured. Considered. 'Oh my God. So wrong – and yet so right!'

'And yet so right! Exactly!' He giggled like a schoolboy. 'Have some more! And tell me what you've been up to.'

'Well, you remember that chef? Mmm, salt, sweet, I love this! My admirer? I've met him.'

'No! And?'

'Turns out he's not a chef after all. I was misled by the fact that he wears a checked shirt.' She waited. Nothing. 'A black and white checked shirt. Made from that kind of chef's trousers fabric. Ringing any bells? Big, bald guy, wears a black and white checked shirt? No?'

'*No!*'

Jane did her filthy laugh. 'Yep.'

'No! *No!* You're boffing the archdeacon?!'

'I am not boffing anyone. I believe the term is, we are stepping out. Or we will be,' she emended (an academic habit). 'We are stepping out tomorrow. Literally. We are going for a walk, followed by a pub lunch.'

'Omigod, omigod, omigod!' Dominic fanned himself in agitation. 'Jane! I don't know what to *do* with this information!'

'Treat it like Sauternes with Roquefort,' she suggested.

'So wrong, and yet so ... *wrong*! I shall forbid the banns! You can't do this to me!'

'It's not about you, Lady Bracknell.'

'Omigod! But seriously? You ... like him?'

'Well, I'm about to find out, aren't I? *Slightly* wondering why he's still single.'

'His wife died, I think. About ten years ago.' Dominic topped his glass up.

'Freddie assures me he's not gay.'

'Well, Freddie would know, that's for sure.'

Freddie does not always know. Every couple of years a stealth plane gets under his gaydar. Come with me to the palace, where the bishop, back from Bristol, is in his study. There's a knock at the door.

'Come in.'

Freddie stuck his head round the door. 'Hey. Can we like talk?'

No, thought Paul. 'Of course. Come in.'

'Gah. Look. Listen. Paul, I don't want to mess you around, but I'm really not coping with this, this— So, yeah, can I just not come into the office next week? I just don't think I can stand to be around Martin? After, y'know?'

The bishop exhaled a long, long breath. Thank you, Lord. 'If that's what you want, Freddie. Of course.'

'You can find me like other stuff to do?'

He was tugging his hair. Looking as wretched as he had that first evening. Paul was overcome by his own uselessness. It was ending as it began. 'That's fine, Freddie. I completely understand. I'm really sorry about all this ... mess.'

'Yeah, no. Paul, I'm trying to like forgive him? Because Jesus? But I— what? Why are you looking at me like that?' He broke off. 'Ah, crap. You think I don't—? Look, I know I'm a total fuck-up, Paul, but I do believe and everything, I really love him, y'know? Man. Look, never mind.'

'Freddie!' Paul came round from behind his desk, reached out a hand.

A pastoral gesture gone wrong.

So wrong. And yet so right. At last, at last – this is bone of my bones, flesh of my flesh!

Salt. Sweet. *Come slowly – Eden –*

The bishop is like a man who leans against a wall, only to find it is a door. He plunges down, down, into the cellar he'd denied he owned. And finds it full of all the vintage wine sealed up decades before.

SEPTEMBER

Chapter 34

In the palace garden the wind wanders down the forbidden laburnum walk. All the gold has fallen. The dry pods whisper: *ssh, ah ssh*!

'Whoa. Wild! That I was not expecting. Seriously, Paul? Whoa.'

Up there on the ceiling a strand of cobweb lifts, falls, lifts. Suze must've missed it. Bible commentaries. Theology. Shelves of it. He can see it all looming there, way up above, over where they ended up.

Here on the carpet.

He hears Paul's breath. There's a catch in it, like a sob.

Ah, shi-i-it. Why does he *have* to be such a whore? When's he gonna learn to say, 'No way, nothing doing,' to the closet cases? Every time he forgets what a big deal it is for them. He's like, 'Oops, sorr-ee, knocked that vase over there!' And they're all, 'Omigod! No! That's priceless Ming dynasty!' Which kind of leaves him thinking, yeah? So another time maybe don't play ball indoors, dude? I mean, c'*mon*.

Freddie shuts his eyes. Gah. Here comes the whole 'I'm not gay, I can't believe I let you do that!' thing. Can't we like fast-forward over this part? To the bit where we go, 'Yeah, we shouldn't've – but know what? Actually, we did.' Followed by the bit where we do it again, and again, because, hey, the Ming's trashed now?

'So, yeah. That was intense there. Mmm, *mmm*. I'm guessing it's been a while?'

'Freddie, I'm not going to discuss my marriage with you.'

'Naw! Du-*ude*! I mean, since you've been with a guy?'

Nothing.

Outside in the dark he hears a fox wail.

Then it's like he's spilt an icy drink on himself. Oh Jesus. *Please* don't say I'm the first?

All over the diocese of Lindchester life goes on. The sun sets, it rises. Lives begin, lives end in Lindford General Hospital. Lawns are mown. New school uniform is bought. People put the bins out. Up above, planes slide across the blue. Food banks feed the desperate families who are counting the days till school breakfast club starts again. Clouds still billow from the Cardingforth cloud factory. Swallows congregate on wires, apples ripen and fall ungathered along railway embankments.

Yes, life goes on as though nothing has happened in the palace. Can we pretend nothing has? Can we pick up the pieces, glue them together again? Put the vase back on the shelf and say nothing? Hope nobody notices?

The following morning, the archdeacon – all unaware of his bishop's plight – showers, shaves carefully, then dresses in baggy shorts and a polo shirt, sticks his porkpie hat on and drives out to the pub where he has agreed to meet his . . . date? Is that the word for Dr R? What is the right vocabulary for this, when you're middle-aged? Middle-aged! He feels like a fourteen-year-old! Nudging his friend and daring him to go and say, 'My mate says to tell your mate he fancies her.'

Nobody looking at the big sunshiny man in his little car would guess at the freak adolescent storms tearing across his inner landscape.

Likewise, Jane is in a bit of a stew. What price your feminism now, Dr Rossiter? The bed is heaped with every garment she owns – tried on, then flung aside for the crime of making her feel fat. Now she regrets her snooty resolve not to grace the . . . date? occasion? date (was it a date?) with a new outfit. Fa-a-ark. Now what? Get the legs out, maybe? Black T-shirt dress? Denim skirt? But that will involve some urgent shin topiary. Time for the (yikes!) ancient epilator? No, shaving's less painful. Does she have any razors, though? And what about her moustache?

Shut up, you silly mare. How come you're even having this conversation with yourself? Where will this madness end? With a Brazilian? Oh lordy, lordy, do blokes expect that nowadays? Not the middle-aged ones, surely? No, middle-aged blokes are probably still perfectly happy with your basic traditional lady-sporran. Unless they watch a lot of porn. Which archdeacons don't, presumably.

Or do they?

Will you shut up? We're talking about a walk and a pub lunch, not a dirty weekend, for God's sake.

Anyway, forget the skirt: lardy pallid legs, and no skirt-appropriate summer footwear. Still too sunny for boots, more's the pity. If only it were autumn! Fall, leaves, fall! Die, flowers, away! True, the youngsters all seem to wear trainers with frocks, but Jane knows she'll feel like a mad woman if she tries. She could go the whole hog, get a plaid shopping trolley, a fleece with cats on, and about two hundred badges on her lapels to pull the look together. Not an ensemble famed for its sex appeal, however. So maybe—

Shit! The time!

Khaki linen trousers, black top, big silver jewellery, film-star sunnies. It'll have to do. She bangs the door shut and leaps into her car and drives to the canal-side pub where the archdeacon is already parked and waiting under a fig tree, like an Israelite in whom there is no guile.

Shall we tag along?

Matt was the veteran of too many sharings of the Peace to be fazed by Jane's greeting. She'd decided in the car: a peck on the cheek. No, both cheeks. Suavely, insouciantly, in the French manner.

She negotiated the first side successfully, but then bumped jaws, noses. How hard, how indescribably hard it is to be English! Simply *garstly*. Jane's mood veered towards hysterical as she finally landed a peck on his other cheek.

'You've shaved! I haven't. That's why I'm in me kecks.' She plucked at her trouser thighs as if she was about to curtsey to him. 'I was thinking about shaving, but I've run out of razors, and I couldn't bring myself to use the mother-plucker. Sorry, too much information?'

'Mother-plucker?'

'Epilator. It's what Danny calls it.'

'Ah! And Danny is?'

'My son. Currently in New Zealand with his dad. But don't ask me about him, or I'll cry.'

Not surprisingly, a silence followed this embargo.

'So,' said Jane. 'What's your view on Brazilians?'

Equally unsurprisingly, there was another silence. I've gone completely mad, she thought.

'Well,' said Matt, 'I'm an admirer of their free-flowing fast-paced style of football.'

'Of course you are. OK, I'm shutting up now.'

He smiled, and began ambling along the towpath, hands in pockets. After a couple of paces he crooked an elbow at her. She slid her arm through his. They walked in silence. A narrow boat puttered by trailing a cloud of blue smoke.

We're stepping out! I'm stepping out with an archdeacon! Arm-in-arm!

Cabbage whites lolloped round a purple buddleia. She could smell the dank water, a whiff straight from childhood. Long nature walks with Mum. Their version of a summer holiday, because there was no money to go away anywhere. Mum dinning the names of plants into Jane's head, Jane mulishly refusing to respond.

Still knew all the names, though. Dock. Deadly nightshade. Rowan. And that there was a hazelnut tree. She bit her tongue to stop herself bombarding him with botanical erudition. Why wasn't he saying anything? Argh. She glanced up at him and he smiled again.

Relax! It's called companionable silence. He hasn't throttled you and shoved you in the canal yet, so let's assume he likes you.

The opposite bank was a haze of pink, where puffs of willowherb seed crowded a field edge. A half-built house stood among nettles. They passed back gardens with neat lawns. A hammock slung between apple trees. Idyllic. Jane remembered how she'd almost bought a tiny canal-side cottage back when Danny was on the way. But someone had pointed out that she'd never relax: toddler, deep water. So she'd bought the house on Sunningdale Drive instead.

She could move now, though, couldn't she? Start over anywhere she liked. Her world no longer bristled with sharp edges and sudden drops. Blind cords! Toppling wardrobes! Plastic bags! It was time to decommission the klaxon of maternal alarm. Ah, but even so, it was still a death-trap, this planet of ours.

They passed under a brick bridge. The archdeacon had to duck his head. They emerged into the sun again.

'We're never more than a phone call away from heartbreak,' she said.

He squeezed her hand with his arm. 'No, we're not.'

She remembered: his wife died. Isn't that what Dominic had said?

'How's young tarty-pants doing?' he asked.

'A bit pouty. Probably because he couldn't go running. Or dogging, or whatever he gets up to. But anyway, he's mobile again, so I dumped him back on the Hendersons yesterday. Then he's off to Argentina next week for a fortnight. I bullied him into it.'

'Good work, that woman.'

'Yep. I should perhaps mention that I'm extremely bossy. What do you say to that, Mr Archdeacon?'

'Whatever you tell me to say, ma'am.'

'Is the correct answer!' She felt him squeeze her hand with his arm again. 'So what does archdeaconing entail?'

'Basically, I'm the bishop's leg-breaker.'

'Ha! I'd say Paul's quite capable of doing his own leg-breaking. In his quiet steely way.'

'You know Paul?'

So Jane ended up confessing her shady religious past.

'Shame the Church couldn't keep hold of you,' said Matt.

'God no! I'd've made a terrible priest! I'd be drunk on *vino sacro* by eleven in the morning, and punching the old ladies. Does this pub do real ale, by the way?'

'You're a real ale kind of gal?'

'Certainly am.'

He stopped. Laid a hand on his heart. 'Dr Rossiter, will you marry me and have my children?'

'Well, I've had my tubes tied and I don't believe in marriage, but with those caveats in mind, broadly speaking, yes.'

'Peachy,' said the archdeacon. And kissed her.

Father Dominic is sitting among cardboard boxes in his study. Spragg's Haulage of Lindford are moving him. Of course they are. Clergy who are moving in the diocese of Lindchester are required to get three quotes, one of which must be Spragg's Haulage of Lindford. The diocese will then choose the cheapest. Which will be Spragg's Haulage of Lindford. Old Mr Spragg, young Mr Spragg, and the boy. Dominic is terrified that old Mr Spragg will have a coronary while attempting to lift something. He will be found crushed and lifeless under Dominic's pastel green Smeg fridge. Yet if this is what it will take before the diocese allows its clergy to use Pickfords, then old Mr Spragg will not have died in vain.

He is packing his books himself, because he doesn't trust the Spraggs to do it properly. Young Mr Spragg had looked at all the shelves for a long time, ruminating. In the end he said, 'You've got a lot of books, your reverence.'

Lord, have mercy. How many vicars have you moved in your career? Yes, we do tend to have a lot of books.

His phone rings.

'I'm phoning to let you know how it went.'

'Not listening. La la la— What?!'

'I said, he asked me to marry him.'

'*No!* Tell me everything!'

So she does.

It's Wednesday morning. The bishop watches in the driver's mirror as Freddie walks away towards the station. Train to Heathrow, plane to Argentina. He will be back briefly in a fortnight to collect his stuff, but Paul has made it clear that he will be out when that happens. Miss Blatherwick will drive him to Barchester. And that will be it.

The vase is back on the shelf. The cellar door is shut.

Paul watches till the shaggy blond head has vanished through the station entrance. There. All done. He pulls away from the drop-off zone and drives home. He's only gone half a mile when he has to stop in a layby.

Thistledown breaks from the clumps and drifts off. The blackberries are ripe. Blond grass heads, blond, blond, bend in the wind. A lorry roars past, rocking the car.

Paul knows he's not having a heart attack. Only last month he underwent a whole barrage of tests in Harley Street at the Church Commissioners' expense. Routine for all senior appointments. So he knows he is in rude good health for a man of fifty-eight.

There is nothing wrong with the bishop's heart.

It's just that it is breaking.

Chapter 35

'So, who's your new boss going to be, deanissima?' Gene asks Marion. 'Who will be the next bishop of Lindchester, when our right-trusty and well-beloved Mary Poppins is translated?'

Marion sighs from behind the *Guardian*. 'I've told you, I don't know. The process won't even start until his move's announced. And then it'll take ages because of all the baby-boomers retiring. There's a backlog.'

'A backlog of bishops! Is that the proper collective noun? Sounds rather rude. Backlog. Or is that just me?'

'It's just you, Gene.'

'But will you have the power to veto any mad homophobic Evanjellybabies they try to appoint?'

'I'll almost certainly be on the Crown Nominations Commission. I can make my feelings known.'

'And if we translate that out of cathedral circumbendibus into English, does it mean "You bet your ass! I'm gonna veto the shit out of them!"?' The dean makes no reply. 'It still grieves me that you can't be the next bishop. I quite fancy playing bishop's wife. My first act of hospitality would be a cleansing ritual; an exorcism, if you will. I'd give the entire palace over to an epic three-day homosexual orgy.'

'You do womble on sometimes, darling. I'm actually trying to read the paper here.'

'There will be no more triple choc chip muffins in my glorious reign! I piss upon lemon drizzle cake! Ooh. Unfortunate visual. I will never regard lemon drizzle cake in the same light again. Well, never mind: when I preside in the palace, it will be all foie gras and fat juicy ortolans, served by naked altar boys. And filthy innuendo will be our lingua franca. Touch wood. Fnurr fnurr.'

The dean lowers her paper and gives him a headmistressy stare. 'Incredible. I never thought this possible, but you've just succeeded in making me glad that the women bishops measure failed to get through Synod.'

Gene bows. 'I am but your motley fool, my lady.'

Even as Gene is speaking, the smell of triple choc chip muffins fills the palace. Susanna is back home from her grandmothering duties. She is not a stupid woman. She noticed at once that there was something different about her husband. He looked . . . not quite himself. Younger, somehow. Had something happened to him? What could have happened to him?

Suddenly, she freezes, measuring jug in hand. The truth bursts upon her.

He's trimmed his eyebrows! Susanna smiles and heats the cream to make the chocolate ganache icing. Finally! Aren't men funny? It must be ten years since she ventured a little hint that his eyebrows were getting a bit bushy. And she'd got the distinct message to back off. As far as Paul was concerned, she could fill the palace with her cushions and rose-petal potpourri, but his eyebrows were his own. A last bastion of undomesticated masculinity. Like a shed. Bless him!

I invite my readers to say 'Amen' here, even if so far they have not warmed to Paul Henderson. Bless him now, in all his anguish. Despite his new metrosexual eyebrows the poor bishop is wrestling to subdue himself to the world of afternoon tea, with its bone china and petits fours. He must remember to sip and crook his little finger again and use the silver sugar tongs. Not easy, after those nights of mindless gluttony in the Freddie May eat-all-you-can carvery.

Outwardly he seems calm, but Paul is wandering in the smoking ruins of his soul's city. He's numb with disbelief at the Total. Sudden. Breakdown in law and order. His head still roars with the avenging mob. Roiling through his streets, sacking treasuries, torching libraries, profaning every altar.

How could he be so *stupid*?

At least he has some perspective: he's nobody special. He knows he is not the first middle-aged man to make a fool of himself over a pretty blond. He will not be the last. It happens all the time.

But ah, dear God, this is the first time it has happened to *him*!

And it must be the last. Get the army in. Curfews. Crackdowns. Go and sin no more.

You may be wondering, reader, what on earth he is playing at. Really, bishop? You are seriously proposing to sweep this under the vestry carpet? You think you can say a quick sorry to God, then proceed, without further reflection, to the archiepiscopacy of York?

You may be sure he doesn't think this. I don't believe there is a man in the Church of England today who keeps shorter accounts with God. Yes, he is currently shielding Susanna, but Paul is by no means trying to pretend nothing's happened. I would say he's temporarily paralysed. He cannot see what the godly course of action is, how to get out of this mess he has brought upon himself – and potentially on his family, his friends, the whole Church.

Can he trust Freddie's promise of silence? ('Dude, I so wouldn't do that to you! And hello? – you think I want the tabloids all over my past?') Oh, but maybe it would be a relief to be exposed, a severe mercy? Or must he bear this alone until his dying day? Hypocrisy! Martyrdom? If not silence, then who ought he to confess to? And what – dear God! – what *is* he now? What does it all mean? Well, whatever else he is, he's an adulterer. And betrayer of a vulnerable young man in his care. He has violated every pastoral trust. He's just the latest in a line of predatory older men in Freddie's life, isn't he?

Only one thing is clear at present: he must not panic and do what can't be undone afterwards, just in order to assuage this terrible guilt.

So never fear, reader. A lifelong habit of inward scrutiny will not permit the bishop to shrug this one off. As it happens, he had already planned a retreat to prepare for the next stage of his ministry. It has been in his diary for months. He will use those ten days in self-examination. He will hold that magnifying glass unflinchingly, focus the rays of truth on himself till sin and pride and self-deception are all burnt out.

And he will *not* indulge in thoughts of him. Ever. Will not linger over peeled-down garments, snagged breath – 'Oh yeah, Paul, that's it, oh yeah, ohh yeah' – nor consult ever again the compendium of acts committed; nor trail his finger down the inventory of sinews, of clefts, parted lips, limbs, each scar and freckle, pierced flesh and tongue, tattoos, he'll never retrace those serpent coils—

Eden –

Oh God, help me, help me, I can't— Because who's he in bed with now?

Whose hands, mouth—?

Ever again.

Old Mr Spragg, young Mr Spragg and the boy stand on Father Dominic's drive and scratch their heads. How are they going to fit it all in? It's a puzzle, all right.

Dominic (in his Marigolds) watches them through the kitchen window. He despairs. He honestly despairs. How many times did he say, 'This is the kettle. Don't pack it, or you won't be getting any more tea. Kettle. Not to be packed. OK?'

'Ooh, right you are, your reverence.'

And where is the kettle?

'Ooh, I don't rightly know, your reverence. Maybe we've packed it.'

Take me now, Lord. I'm ready to die.

Jane is stripping the spare bed ready for Dominic. Tomorrow she's going to help him move into his new vicarage. They'll make a good team. She'll just crack on and unpack his boxes, get stuff on shelves and into cupboards, and leave him to stress over where to put his Philippe Starck lemon squeezer.

Jane is hardly the most scrupulous of hostesses, but even she can see that fresh sheets would be polite. She flings the window wide so that poor Dominic will not be tormented by any lingering pheromones, bundles the bed linen under an arm, then scoops up the wastepaper basket with her free hand. Pair of knackered flip-flops on top, but she is not about to investigate further. She hopes to God Freddie remembered to check under the bed for any stray underpants. Et cetera.

Outside in the alley Jane up-ends the basket into the wheelie bin. The rowan berries are red, red, red. Autumn! Boots and jumpers! Huzzah! She's spent almost all her life locked into the rhythms of academe. September always feels like New Year, the season of fresh hopes, when her fancy turns lightly to the thought of love. And now she smiles at the thought of her big bald archdeacon, who is taking her to the pictures on Sunday evening. She's paying her own way, of course, but he has promised to buy the popcorn.

She goes back indoors and stuffs the sheets into the washing machine. A twinge of anxiety: they smell of Freddie. Silly mare. But in all fairness, the boy is fatally easy to love. Like a radioactive bush baby. Well, he's off her hands now. Let his real mum do a shift in the boiler room of maternal angst.

Jane goes upstairs and makes the bed, then squirts a spot of polish into the air to create the impression that dusting has occurred. She wipes her sleeve over the bedside cabinet to protect the impressionable Dominic from the stray skin cells of Freddie May, who by now must be halfway across Patagonia on horseback, or whatever. Well, let's hope he finds that smoking hot retired polo player to look after him from this time forth and for evermore.

But is anything ever going to be that simple for Freddie May? Just stay safe, you bad boy. And my own bad boy, down under, you stay safe too. Keep wearing that crash helmet. And your bad boy dad, he needs to stay safe as well. Oh, in fact, stay safe, you bad boys everywhere.

Would you look at that? It's almost as though she's praying again after all these years. She rolls her eyes, and goes downstairs to stick a bottle of prosecco in the fridge for when Dom arrives.

I'm not coping. I'm just not coping, thinks poor Becky Rogers. She has just screamed at Leah – in public, in the middle of Clark's shoe shop in Lindford.

'Right! That's *it*! You're going to school barefoot!' And yanked her out of the shop by her arm. Past all the people staring. Smirking. Looking sympathetic.

She's sitting in the car in the multi-storey car park weeping. Howling.

Leah kicks the dashboard. Sighs. Can we go now? Kick. Kick. Stop crying, you baby. Kick. Kick. But Mummy carries on crying. She's got snot and everything.

Then Leah has a horrible thought, icy cold. What if she never stops? What if she is having mental health issues? What if she gets out of the car and runs off and leaves Leah on her own?

Like those nightmares she gets. The grown-ups leave her and Jess alone in the car and the car drives off by itself, and Leah doesn't know how to make it stop because she doesn't know how to drive. She's only a child! How can she possibly control the car when she doesn't know how to drive? But she has to, she has to climb into the front and steer it, or the car will crash and she and Jessie will get killed. Jessie starts screaming, 'Stop the car, stop the car, Leah! Mummy's gone, Daddy's gone!' But it speeds up and speeds up!

This is like the dream, only she can't make herself wake up, because it's real.

'I can't cope, oh, I can't cope, I can't cope!'

Stop saying that! You're the grown-up, you *have* to cope!

'I just can't cope!'

'I'll have the stupid shoes, OK?' she shouts. '*I don't care, I'll have the shoes!*'

'Oh, I just can't cope any more!'

Leah opens the glove compartment and grabs the tissues they keep for when Jess is car sick. She shoves them at Mum. 'Here.' Nudges her arm. Bangs her arm. '*Here!*'

'Thanks, darling.' Mummy wipes the snot off, then blows her nose and wipes her eyes. 'Oh God, I'm so rubbish. It doesn't matter. We can buy the shoes on line. I'm sorry I'm such a rubbish Mum.'

'You're not rubbish.'

Is it OK again? Is it? She tries to think of something to add. Probably she should say sorry. But she hates saying it. Teachers and Brown Owl are forever trying to make her say it. 'Say it properly, young lady. Like you mean it.'

Mummy starts the car up and they drive home. Leah whispers it in her head all the way. Over and over. *Sorry. Sorry. Sorry.* Each time they pass a street light she says it inside her head.

There's a broken feeling in her throat, like she's fractured her voice-box. That can actually happen. It's been scientifically proved that you can fracture your throat, she might have read it on Wiki; so you have to be really careful and conserve your voice energy. Or she'd say it out loud, probably.

Chapter 36

A new year has started at Lindchester Choristers' School. Choral term began on Sunday with the 10.30 Eucharist (Howells, *Missa Collegium Regale*, for those interested in such things). Every morning and evening you may see the crocodile of choristers in their blazers and cherry-red caps again, as they file across the Close to the Song School. The four new spotty choral scholars (two altos, tenor, bass) moved into the squalory next to Vicars' Hall over a week ago.

Uh-oh. You know what this means, don't you? Freddie May has cocked things up already. Somehow he forgot the start of term date when he let Jane book his flights. Well, forgot, as in, didn't actually let himself think about it? Like, la la la, that would make it not be happening? His voicemail was *mental* with 'where-the-fuck-are-you?' messages when he turned his phone back on. He had to ring his new boss in Barchester the minute he got through customs. (Man, it would be good just once to walk straight through, but apparently he has this, like, massive 'Hey Guys, I'm a Drugs Mule!' sign over his head?) But finally they were done, so he could ring and grovel. Gah. Nice going. Established his 'I'm-a-useless-twat' credentials really early there.

The train hurtles towards Lindchester. Miss B will be there at the station to meet him. Grab his stuff from the palace, and he's out of here. Thank God, Paul's gonna be away. But Suze. Na-a-w. Let her be out. Oh man. Even thinking about Suze is like he just ran over Bambi? Please don't let Paul have done anything dumb – like telling her? He feels really bad about all this, *really* bad. Been shutting it out for a fortnight, coz he knows he semi-seduced him? Or *semi*-semi. And they're good people, Paul and Suze. Took him in. Gave him a job. Looked after him.

Freddie bumps his forehead on the train window. Why, *why* is he such a tart? Ga-a-a-ah. Will Paul be OK? Hard man to read, Paul. For a while back there things got pretty intense and he was, ah cock, *please* not the whole, 'I love you, let's run away into the sunset' crap? But no, so it's most likely all gone quiet. Probably Paul's sorted his head out by now. Poor guy. Kind of mean to pressure him, but he couldn't stop himself being just a little bit, hey, time to rethink your position on equal marriage, Paul? And he was all, 'I need to rethink my position on *everything*, Freddie.' So yeah, maybe some good will come out of it?

Probably he should delete the photos, though. Yeh, probably he should get on to that. Paul would totally freak if he knew.

Miss B gets into her little red car and sets off for the station. Oh, drat. Amadeus, the cathedral cat, is strolling along the high wall by the Song School with another goldfinch in his mouth. She raps on the car window at him. Bad puss.

'Oh! I'm going to miss that boy!' Penelope, the bishop's PA, blows her nose and sits down at her desk after waving Freddie off. 'I hope he does all right in Barchester. They'd better look after him properly, or I'll have a thing or two to say about it!'

Martin, at his desk, stays quiet. He knows that if he punches the air Penelope will probably come over and punch him.

For some reason – on this yearned-for day of the little shite's departure – he finds himself remembering the school coach park. The Lord of the Flies nightmare of it after the grammar school day. He can still taste the sick dread. Dave Felton and the others from his class. The Girls' High girls with their cellos and hockey sticks. 'Watch where you're going, you wally!' Feral packs of comprehensive kids, smoking, shrieking, shoving. Legs, love bites. 'What are *you* staring at, four-eyes?' Mud and trampled grass, juicy fruit, Lynx sprayed through shirt armpits after PE. 'Fight! Fight! Fight!' His desperate prayers to stay invisible on that ten-mile journey home. Worst of all, knowing that he was locked into this hell for seven years.

But there was one glorious day – he was fourteen – when a bus ran over Dave Felton's foot and he screamed, and the driver had to carry him on to the playing field. The driver was a bandy-legged Scot, tiny, but he carried Dave Felton – like a huge, screaming bride – on to the field. And everyone saw.

Penelope blows her nose again and says, 'Oh well.'

He hears her go and put the kettle on.

'There are some stem ginger cookies from Susanna to cheer us up,' she calls.

Martin curls his lip (cheer us up!) and continues to work through the bishop's inbox, fielding emails for him while he's on retreat. There's a broadside defending the sacked vicar of Lindford ('How can you call yourself a Christian, you hypocrite, when you've robbed a man of his livelihood?'). Huh, rallying support for the tribunal. Martin pastes a reply (cc-ing the archdeacon): 'The bishop has asked me to thank you for your concern, which has been noted.' He has no case! The idiot has no case! It's pure malice! How can anyone be so blinded by prejudice? But doubtless this will make the national press when it finally gets to court, whatever the outcome. He can see it now: Archbishop 'robbed man of livelihood', claims tribunal.

Martin tries once again to bask in the reflected glory of his bishop's elevation, to enjoy being in the inner circle of those who already know. But his eczema has flared up. It takes all his self-control not to scratch himself raw. Because what's he going to do? He'll have to find a new job. Everything is being taken from him. Wife, children, job, health! Sometimes he feels like giving up. Sitting in his life's ash heap, and scraping himself with potsherds like Job.

Penelope puts a mug of coffee and a biscuit on his mousemat. He winces and moves the mug onto a coaster, puts the biscuit onto a postcard, and sweeps the crumbs into his bin. 'Thank you.'

You try so hard to be a good man, a good husband, father, priest. Then it all gets flung back in your face. Suddenly Martin hears how he must sound. No wonder nobody likes him. Oh, he doesn't want to be this way any more! Let me hear joy and gladness, Lord. Let the bones that you have broken dance. How can I begin again? What must I do, Lord?

He waits. And something like a gracious question mark begins to hover in the margin of his mind. Against the little-shite section.

Oh, I can't. I just can't. Anyway, it's too late now. He's gone.

Apart from that, what must I do?

'Martin, will you please stop scratching?' cries Penelope. 'You'll only make it worse.'

At his desk in William House on the other side of the Close, the archdeacon sprays coffee over his iPad once again. To the best of his knowledge, the bishop of Lindchester has never called himself 'a Christina'. Either Martin has not spotted the typo, or (more likely) does not find it amusing. The archdeacon knows someone who will appreciate it, however.

Dr Rossiter – locked in a departmental training day – startles everyone with her filthy laugh during a colleague's PowerPoint presentation on electronic marking.

Sloes stud the hedgerows like blue beads. Strands of bryony berries trail over elder and hawthorn. Fairies' necklaces, that's what we used to call them, thinks Father Wendy. She's walking along the river bank, and yes, there's Lulu, still hobbling beside her. How much longer can this be borne? Oh, a little longer, please say a little bit longer? Until the pain of watching her suffer outweighs the pain of her letting go. Is this just selfishness? Cruelty? Is it? Lulu lifts her old head and cries. Oh, darling! Not long now, not long. Here's our bench.

On the opposite bank a heron waits. Will the blond young man run past today? It's been a while since they've seen him. Perhaps he's starting uni somewhere? Wendy watches a green dragonfly dart and zoom. Laura would have been twenty-two this summer. She'd be a graduate. Starting work. A new bride, even! I would be having to learn how to let her go, whatever, by now.

Wendy reaches down and strokes Lulu's head. Memories race like time-lapse photography – that mad puppy, all huge scrambling paws; the years of naughty food-raids and running off; then the steadying down. And now, old age and pain and weariness. A whole lifetime in those thirteen years since Laura was killed. Not filling Laura's place, of course not filling her place. But offering loyal companionship along this stretch of life, day in, day out. Well done, Lulu, good and faithful servant.

Will dogs go to heaven? Father Wendy does not know the answer. But she believes in a kingdom where not a single sparrow falls unnoticed, where no cup of water is given in vain. Where, against all the odds, the last word is kindness.

Who will be kind to Leah Rogers, though? The little madam who told whoppers about poor Freddie and who bullies her little sister so spitefully, and drives parents and teachers to distraction. Who will find it in their heart to be kind to her, when she so clearly deserves a slap?

I confess to a soft spot for Leah, having occasionally been a spiteful little fibber myself. I think the poor child is terrified. Terrified by the power she can wield. She wants to be stopped. Somewhere,

somewhere there must be a big policeman figure to blow a whistle and say, 'It ends here, young lady. You're nicked.' And then the world might feel safe again.

Her mother Becky is nearly aware of this. In the wake of the great school shoes meltdown, she consulted her Clergy Spouses' Handbook, and got in touch with the diocesan pastoral care and counselling officer. A session has been arranged for Becky and Leah to talk to someone together on Saturday morning. Just a gentle exploratory chat with a nice middle-aged woman counsellor. Well, good luck with that. I'm of the opinion that Leah will make mincemeat of any nice middle-aged woman who crosses her path.

Not all middle-aged women are nice, however.

Stupid, stupid, stupid. Stupid car not starting. Stupid Mummy leaving the lights on. Stupid lady they were meant to be going to chat to. Who cared if they couldn't go? Oh, boo hoo, we don't get to chat to the *lady*.

Leah kicked open the gate – clang! – and stormed up the path of number 16. There was tape stuck over the stupid doorbell, so she banged the knocker: BAM, BAM, BAM. Come on, you big stupid. Answer your stupid door.

Someone was coming. Leah could see through the pebbly glass. The door opened. A giant woman with short grey-y hair stood there eating toast.

'Yep?'

'My mum says can you bring your car round to ours at number 10 so she can jumpstart it.'

But the woman narrowed her eyes like a wicked witch and carried on munching her stupid toast. Like she was stupid. Or DEAF.

'I *said*, MY MUM SAYS CAN YOU—'

'I HEARD YOU.'

Typical. What's the magic word, nyeah nyeah nyeah. 'Ple-e-eease.'

'Meh.' The old witch wiped her fingers on her T-shirt. 'Can't be arsed. Bye.'

And she shut the door!

Now what was she meant to do? The old witch was just standing there. Leah could see her through the glass! She hesitated. Now Mum would come and ask herself, and she'd tell on her. I *hate* you, you stupid old witch! Leah jigged from one foot to the other. I'm *not* saying *sorry* to *you*! Up the street, Mum was still trying to get the car bonnet to stay lifted up, and going, 'Oh God, oh God!' Leah looked back at the door.

The weird woman was kneeling now and staring through the letter box at her! 'Psst!'

Leah bent down, but she was ready to jump back, coz maybe it was a trick. 'What?'

'I don't know what the rules are round your way,' whispered the wicked witch, 'but in my world, if you play nice, I play nice. So. Let's try again, shall we?'

Chapter 37

Acts of kindness: the waybread of pilgrims. When the road is rough and steep (or for my more Catholic readers, when the night is dark, and you are far from home) the kindness of fellow travellers may keep despair at bay.

But who will be kind to Bishop Paul Henderson? That I cannot tell you. He has strayed temporarily beyond the boundaries of the diocese of Lindchester, and thus outside the scope of this tale. I believe it is a very nice retreat house, comfortable if remote (no wi-fi or mobile phone signal). There's homemade cake in the afternoon, and plenty of walks along a rugged coastline. I could tell you where the retreat house is, but then (like Martin the bishop's chaplain), I would have to kill you.

Yes, Martin's lips are sealed. The bishop has extended his retreat by a further five days. This has meant some juggling of the diary by Penelope, and several suave phone calls by Martin to explain the situation without explaining anything. Martin is in his element here. But he must be constantly discreet, because Penelope does not know about Paul's imminent elevation. Thinks Martin.

You may be sure that Martin will defend his bishop's privacy to his last breath, against vulgar curiosity and intrusions from the media (and there is increasing speculation in the run-up to the announcement). Martin is also shielding him from the clamour of diocesan affairs and 'any nonsense from disgruntled former employees'. Those were Paul's exact words. So the former vicar of Lindford can take a running jump. Martin enjoys being in adversarial mode and fielding the nonsense relating to the tribunal. He also enjoys (despite eczema and panics about the future) being part of the inner circle. He is important-by-proxy; he is in on the secret. It flushes his daily routines with the glow of power. He could nip to the bookies and have a flutter on who'll be the next archbishop of York! Of course, he'd never dream of doing any such thing. But oh, the hints he could drop, if he chose to . . .

But to return to my question: who will be kind to Bishop Paul Henderson? Hang on, you say: does he actually deserve kindness after such a crass sexual lapse – not to mention his gross dereliction of pastoral duty towards a vulnerable employee? Well, that might depend on what he decides to do – though perhaps kindness ought to depend upon nothing at all, and, like the sun, dawn on the righteous and the unrighteous alike? I will leave such matters to the experts, who can explain it all to you from the pulpit in three alliterating points and one amusing illustration. I imagine that the good people who run the retreat house are being kind to the bishop. Were he to confess his sins to a spiritual director, or the archbishop of Canterbury – who I take to be his line manager – I have every confidence they would be kind to him, too. But he might decide against doing that. We will have to wait and see.

There is one person who will categorically not be kind to Paul Henderson, however – and that is Paul Henderson.

Autumn is in the air. Can you smell it? Fat wood pigeons gather in the stubble; while in other fields a haze of wheat lies already like green chiffon across the furrows. Lime seeds pop underfoot on pavements. Here and there among the tired cherry leaves there is a flash of the fire to come. Hedgerows groan with nature's bounty: hips and haws, filberts and cobs, crab apples and rowan berries. Marrows swell rudely in allotments up and down the diocese of Lindchester, competing for prizes in local shows, or for pride of place in the harvest festival.

They still do harvest festival properly round this way. There are plenty of farms in the diocese. Agricultural imagery still resonates here, while in other places I fear that ploughs have become as quaint a notion as spinning jennies. You may walk into a church in darkest Lindfordshire and confidently expect to sing 'We plough the fields and scatter'. There will be a big harvest loaf in the shape of a wheat sheaf, egg-glazed and gleaming. The smell of childhood harvest festivals will greet you as you walk through the door. Apples, leeks, potatoes, damsons and greengages, bunches of dahlias, chrysanths as big as footballs. Yes, 'All is safely gathered in, ere the winter storms begin.'

In Cardingforth Primary they are rehearsing 'Cauliflowers fluffy and cabbages green', an atheist-friendly harvest hymn that will offend nobody with menacing talk of Final Harvests and angel reapers. It can be made offensive by ingenious little girls, however. Leah Rogers is sent to stand outside the head's office for teaching her class to sing 'Broad beans are sleeping in their wank-ety bed.'

'My-mum-says-to-give-you-these-to-say-thank-you-for-starting-our-ca-a-aaar,' droned Leah.

Jane was about to set off to Poundstretcher University. With a gusty sigh she seized the box of Celebrations and droned back, 'Tell-your-mum-thanks-very-mu-u-uuuch-and-she-didn't-ha-a-aaave-to.'

They glared at one another. Good grief. A reincarnation of her eight-year-old self, sent as a punishment! 'Here.' Jane put down her briefcase and opened the box. 'Want one?'

The child hesitated.

'What's the problem? All the yucky coconut ones on the top? Have a rummage.'

'You're not allowed. You have to take the nearest.'

'Says who? I always eat all the Malteser ones first before anyone else gets to them.' She saw the girl's eyes widen at this glimpse into her depraved moral universe. 'Which do you like best?'

'Caramels.'

Jane shook the box at her. Leah took one. 'G'wan, g'wan, g'wan. Have two.'

'You're not allowed two the same.'

'Really? Who's the boss round here, I wonder? Oh, that would be *me*.'

Leah rooted around for another.

'Stop that, you greedy pig!' The girl froze. 'Kidding.'

She gave Jane the evil eye and took a Malteser one. That'll teach me a lesson, thought Jane. 'So. How's school?'

'School sucks.'

'Of course it does. But if you study hard, in another trillion years you can leave and go to uni. What's your favourite subject?'

'Hate them all.'

'Well, duh, I know that. Because they suck. But which is the least sucky?'

The girl's chops were now bulging with chocolate. 'History.'

'History, you say!' Jane laughed her filthy laugh. Hmm. Yes, it still scared small children. 'Read the *Horrible History* books?' A nod. 'Got them all?'

'Most of them.'

'Tell you what, my big boy's left home and I'm slinging a whole bunch of crap out. Including a complete set of *Horrible Histories*. Why don't I stick 'em in a box and whizz them round? Take any you want, and your mum can give the rest to a charity shop. How's that sound?'

The girl scowled.

'Why, don't even mention it, child! You're doing me a huge favour taking them off my hands. No no, not another word. Can I interest you in *Murderous Maths*?'

'No way. Maths sucks.'

'Like the hoover of the Dark Lord himself! I couldn't agree more. But then, I would think that – I'm a history lecturer,' said Jane. 'I *have* been known to help people with their homework in my time, if I'm in a good mood. Which isn't very often, admittedly.'

The girl looked as though she'd rather drink a cup of cold sick than ask Jane for help.

'Oh well, back to the coal face.' Jane picked up her case and crammed the chocolates in with her files and photocopying. 'Cheery-bye. And tell your mum tha-a-a-anks.'

You will be wondering, reader, how the romance is going. Have Jane and Matt been on any more dates (trysts? assignations?)? Is Matt now to be considered Jane's boyfriend (lover? OH?)? While Jane struggles to decide upon an appropriate lexis for their relationship, I will confide that she is stupidly in love with the archdeacon.

Her colleagues have noticed a change. Good God, Dr Rossiter! What brings you to a compulsory staff training day? Do you not have an urgent migraine to attend to? Is that a new pair of boots you are wearing? Have you culled your collection of knackered leggings at last? And are our eyes deceiving us, or have you paid for an actual haircut for once, rather than waiting to get attacked in a dark alley by a deranged sheepshearer?

Even as I write this, Jane is driving to work with most of a box of Celebrations to share out over coffee. She is singing as she drives. What is she singing? She is caterwauling, in a terrible Mockney accent, Nancy's song from *Oliver*: 'As long as 'e neeeeeds meeee!' I'd love to tell you she's singing it ironically and rolling her eyes like the hairy-legged feminist she is. But Dr Rossiter has bought a Venus razor (five blades, hugs every curve).

Have no fear, dear reader. Jane's choice of song is not my way of dropping a dark hint that in some future episode the archdeacon will viciously murder her. Apart from his thick-set calves and a certain fondness for ale, he is nothing like Bill Sikes. True, he features as the villain in some circles. He is, after all, the archdeacon; and if an archdeacon is beloved wherever he or she goes, you may be sure that we are not in the C of E any more, Toto.

And what of the archdeacon? Is he stupidly in love with Jane? Yep. Drove his sporty little Mini straight into a bollard in the car park of William House yesterday, because he was wondering about taking her to Paris. What better proof could you require?

We are now going to pay a long-overdue visit to Carding-le-Willow, where the new curate, Virginia, lives. How is she getting on? Her summer was a strange one. After a packed theological college course, followed by the chaos of moving house and the thrill/terror of ordination, those first weeks in the parish seemed a bit empty. She struggled to fill them, in fact, and felt a bit guilty because she didn't feel she was working hard enough.

(We will now pause and allow all the ordained people reading this to laugh like hyenas, because they know that come Christmas Virginia will look back on this slack period and decide she must have dreamt it.)

Things are beginning to crank up now. We are in the third week of September. So far Virginia has taken her first funeral, preached her first sermon, started her first confirmation class, attended her first deanery synod, and been snubbed for the first time on gender grounds by both a high- *and* a low-church colleague. The C of E – an equal bigotry employer! It is Thursday evening. Virginia is getting ahead of the game and preparing next Wednesday's primary school assembly. As this will be her first attempt, she's pouring a lot of effort into it. She's got out her marker pens and is busy making a ginormous party invitation, with the intention of tying this in with Back to Church Sunday, the week after next. (This coming Sunday ought probably to be 'Sit in a Different Pew' Sunday, so that the regulars don't get flustered by newcomers taking their seat.)

Well, we will leave Virginia to get a bit squiffy on marker pen fumes, happily planning what she will say to the boys and girls of Cardingforth Primary. We will shield her from the knowledge that she will be pre-empted by some smart-arse saying, 'At Jeee-sus's party everyone's invited.'

There. She's finished her visual aid. We will allow her a glass of Day Off Eve merlot in front of a boxed set of something, then pack her off to bed, where she will sleep all unwittingly beneath Freddie May's whopping painted-over boner. Sweet dreams, Virginia!

And sweet dreams, Paul Henderson, wherever you are. I'm really sorry, but it looks as though someone on the Crown Nominations Commission has broken ranks. Yes, your name has been leaked to the press, and right now, in far-off London Town, a journalist is writing a big feature on you, the ex-public school Conservative Evangelical anti-gay next archbishop of York.

Chapter 38

The bookies have shortened their odds on Paul Henderson. The diocesan communications officer is fielding calls left, right and centre from journalists and producers. Colleagues on the Close have been approached for their reactions. Former curates and parishioners have been interviewed. Paul Henderson's past has been ransacked. What a good thing he sowed no wild oats as a young man.

You must be wondering how Susanna is faring in this ordeal. She has been all alone in the palace while Paul's been off on retreat, remember. Goodness, she misses Freddie! It's true, he could be a very naughty boy. (She's pretty sure that was cannabis she could smell when she came to clean his empty room. And she found a condom wrapper under his bed, despite their 'no overnight guests' rule!) But oh, it was such fun having him around the place. She longs to hear him leaping down the stairs again and vaulting over the banisters. To hear his incredible singing voice echoing in the hallway.

Not that she'd have been able to say anything to him about Paul's new job, of course. It's just that the palace feels so empty without him! She senses that deep down even Paul was sad to see him go; though he made a point of saying (quite fiercely, she thought!) that they'd have to make sure they never take in any more waifs unless he's met them personally beforehand.

Oh, it will be such a blessed relief when the waiting is over and she can talk freely to people. She's rather cross that someone leaked the news early, because it's actually been jolly hard for her not being able to confide in her daughters or her closest friends, even. Paul got a letter from Downing Street several weeks after he'd been told he'd got the job, which stressed how hush-hush it was. 'You may, of course, discuss this with your wife,' was the only concession. Honestly! As though Paul would keep a secret of that scale from her!

But the thing that makes her crossest is their girls being pestered by the press. What a way for them to find out! It put her and Paul in such a horrible position. Their nearest and dearest were practically the last to know – simply because she and Paul had played it by the book. And then, lo and behold, someone else thinks the rules don't apply to them! Their youngest had to lock her Twitter account, because journalists started following her! So naughty.

And all this time she and Paul haven't even been allowed to go and look round Bishopthorpe! She knows it shouldn't really matter (the foxes have holes, the birds of the air have nests, and all that), but this is how Susanna always copes with having to up sticks – she focuses on making a home in the new house. So this time she's had to content herself with little secret trips to wander round John Lewis, daydreaming. (And buying a new frock and shoes for the big unveiling. Ssh!)

But she mustn't grumble. One nice thing about all the gossip and rumours is that people on the Close have been really lovely and supportive. Even Gene, the dean's husband – normally a bit prickly, bless him!* – popped round with a bottle of wine.

Oh well, Paul will be home the day after tomorrow. And then they will head to York for the official Downing Street announcement on Friday morning. Finally! After all the delays with medicals and CRB clearance and then the Queen being away at Balmoral. It really will happen, Susanna tells herself. Not long to wait now. She picks up car keys and handbag and leaves the palace. She's going to the hair salon. Goodness, she's actually feeling quite excited at last!

Well, dear reader, we will leave Susanna to go and get her highlights done, and make our way to the deanery, where we will join the canons residentiary of Lindchester. Once again, I apologize for the language.

The canons are having canons' coffee. They all know about Paul's preferment, of course; though only the dean knows officially. The rest know because the precentor has just asked the dean if Paul is definitely the next archbishop of York, and Marion has replied, 'I'm afraid I can't comment.'

'"Paul Henderson, 58, bishop of Lindchester, widely tipped to be the next archbishop of York . . ."' Mr Happy, the canon chancellor, was skimming the newspaper article. '"Conservative Evangelical . . . links with Anglican Mainstream"** . . . Really? Urgh!'

---

* 'Bless him!' is Evangelical for 'Bastard!'

** Bless them!

'Surely not!' said Philip, the treasurer.

'"... vigorous campaigner in the House of Lords against the same-sex marriage bill ..." What! "Currently in seclusion"?' Mr Happy glared at his colleagues as if they were his tutorees, and guilty of sloppy research. 'He's on retreat! "In seclusion" means he's fucked up and the archbishop's about to sack him.'

'Oh, that's journalists for you.' Giles was doodling on his agenda. 'They get church terminology nearly right, but not quite.'

'Yeah, but this guy knows his onions. It's a deliberate slur!'

'He knows his onions?' repeated the treasurer. 'Oh, surely you can render that into German for us, father, so we can take it seriously as an academic statement?'

'*Er kennt sein Zwiebeln!*' shouted Giles in a mad SS officer voice.

'I think you'll find the term is *Zwiebelnwissenschaft*, actually,' corrected the chancellor.

'Bitch, please!' said Giles. 'So who is this so-called expert?'

'Roderick Fallon.'

'Roderick Fallon!' Giles threw his biro down in disgust. 'I was at Oxford with that tosser! He's always been a poison toad.'

There was a silence round the table. They were perilously close to closing ranks and defending Mary Poppins against poison toad attacks. Paul might be a bigot, but he was their bigot. Gene glided in with another cafetière.

'Isn't it a bit early for a hatchet job?' asked Philip. 'He's not even in post yet.'

'Is it ever too early for a hatchet job on a fag-hating Bible-basher?' enquired Gene.

'Thanks, Gene. I think that's everything,' said Marion.

The door closed softly behind him.

Mr Happy was still shaking his head over the profile. It was a big full-page job, with a photo of Paul on the day of his consecration as bishop fourteen years earlier. He was posing with his brand new mitre and crosier on the steps of St Paul's Cathedral, with the then archbishop of Canterbury. Some trick of the camera gave him a slightly louche matinée-idol look, as though he might be about to pat a pretty bottom. Which was no doubt why this picture had been chosen from the files.

'This is completely tendentious!' Mr Happy threw *his* biro down in disgust. 'He's gone out of his way to present Paul as ultra-conservative, and he's really not.'

'I'm afraid Roderick Fallon's world is a bit binary,' said Marion. 'The equal marriage switch is either on or off as far as he's concerned.'

'Well, let's look on the bright side,' suggested Philip. 'Maybe the *Daily Mail* will leap to Paul's defence?'

‘God, that’s all he needs,’ said Mr Happy.

‘Well, people, lots to get through, so shall we make a start?’ said Marion.

We will tiptoe away now and leave them to such knotty matters as volunteer car parking spaces, should male visitors to the cathedral be asked to remove their hats, and whether there was enough money to stop the spire crashing down through the nave roof.

So that, perhaps, goes some way towards answering my question: who will be kind to Paul Henderson? Not the liberal press, clearly. Roderick Fallon lives in London, and is therefore safe from any personal remarks I might feel inclined to make about him. Let me just say that a well-informed reader would be capable of reading between the lines and concluding that Fallon has an axe to grind. The majority, however, will simply believe that the C of E has appointed yet another brontosaurus to be archbishop – and in its walnut-sized brontosaurus brain there is but one thought: *God hates fags*.

It is Wednesday, late afternoon. Tonight is Father Dominic’s big night, when he will be officially licensed as the new vicar of Lindford parish church. The service will be taken by the lovely bishop of Barcup, Bob (Can he bless it? Yes, he can!) Hooty. The archdeacon will be there too of course; as will Dominic’s old mucker, Dr Jane Rossiter. This will be the first time the three of them have been in company together, and I am rather looking forward to seeing how that goes.

A great deal of baking is currently occurring in the parish of Lindford. It is a fact universally acknowledged that a single priest in possession of a modest stipend must be in want of approximately seven tons of pastry goods. Tonight in the parish hall, as fast as one plate is emptied on the trestle tables, another will appear in its place. In fact, it will be like the feeding of the five thousand: there will be more left over at the end than they started with, and Dominic will have ice cream cartons full of quiche and sausage rolls pressed into his hands when he tries to go home. This is how we express affection in the C of E. We do genuinely love one another, even though we find the Peace an awkward business. Ah, how much easier Holy Communion would be if the priest said, ‘Let us offer one another a piece of flan’!

I will leave you with that consoling vision and whisk you back to the Close. There is no choral evensong on Wednesdays. The canons residentiary are saying Evening Prayer in the chapel of St Michael with a small band of the faithful. Miss Blatherwick is there, and so are a few retired priests. I wish Miss Blatherwick had bunked off for once, because then she might have been in when Freddie May hammered on her door.

Yes, Freddie May is back. He's read that piece by Roderick Fallon, and he's incandescent. He hitched to Lindchester and went straight to the palace to have it out with Paul, but there was no answer. He tried the bishop's office and found Martin.

No, Martin could *not* tell him where Paul was. No, he could not pass on a message. No matter how 'desperately urgent' it was. Why? Because Paul was on retreat, and he had specifically said that he did not want to be bothered by 'any nonsense from disgruntled former employees.'

What?! What the fuck? Disgruntled former employees?

'Fuck you, Martin. Seriously, *fuck* you. And you can tell Paul fucking Henderson— Jesus! I don't believe this shit! Disgruntled—? Arsehole! He's going to be so— Fuck this.' He slammed the office door and stormed round the Close.

Oh Jesus, un-fucking-*believable*!

And now Miss B was out. Ah fuck, where was everyone? I'm losing it. Any nonsense?! Disgruntled former employees? Seriously, is that all I am? Is that *it*, Paul?

Like fuck that's it!

Freddie flung himself on a bench by the school and pulled out his phone. His hands shook. Twitter. Search. Fallon. Yeah, that was him.

Ah nuts, you can't do this.

Yeah, I can, trust me.

But you love that guy! Freddie doubled over and began to sob. Paul, Paul, you were going to rethink that stuff. You promised me, and you lied. Why would you even do that?

Just then a black Mini approached. Uh-oh, thought the archdeacon. What's young tarty-pants doing back here? Clearly in a state about something. Matt glanced at the time. Meant to be meeting his lady, already running late. And to be honest, he didn't have energy for another episode of the Freddie May soap opera right now.

So the archdeacon drove past.

Freddie sat up and wiped his eyes on his sleeve. And tweeted fifty-five characters to @Roderick_Fallon: 'I can tell you a whole bunch of stuff re Paul Henderson.'

OCTOBER

Chapter 39

Shock as Bishop of Lindchester Resigns Over Gay Sex Scandal
Archbishop Elect's Nights of Gay Shame: Exclusive Pictures
Exposed: Criminal Past of Bishop's Rent Boy Chauffeur Lover

That is so nearly what happened. I'm convinced that if the archdeacon had not sighed a weary sigh and reversed his black Mini back round the Close to the bench where Freddie was sitting, these are the kind of headlines we would all have been reading.

'Hop in, blondie. What's the problem this time?'

Freddie got in the car. 'Matt. Oh God. It's— Oh fuck. Oh God. I've got to talk to him but he, he, he's—'

O-o-okay. Looked like that cheeky pint with Jane was off. Matt gave Freddie's knee a squeeze and a pat. 'All righty. Let's get off the Close and talk.'

The archdeacon headed out of Lindchester with Freddie weeping beside him in great wrenching sobs. They stopped at the first convenient place, an empty car park in a trading estate. Matt texted Jane his apologies.

'OK, then. Let's have it.'

'I'm, oh God. I'm, listen, it's—'

Matt leant close. 'Sorry, what?'

Freddie whispered it again: '*Paul.*'

'What about Paul?'

More choking sobs. 'He's going to be the next arch— arch— Oh, God— total betrayal? You know? In, in the, in the, paper? Fuck. Why would he say—? Like he hates me?'

'Course he doesn't, you numpty. Look, Fallon dug those quotes out of an interview Paul gave back in the early 90s. I don't recognize the Paul I know in Fallon's piece.'

'Yeah, no, yeah, but he's against equal marriage! He totally is, Matt!'

'For sure. But you've always known that.' The archdeacon waited. Nothing. 'Why the big drama all of a sudden?'

Freddie was white. Hands up his sleeves. Shuddering.

'What's the problem? Talk to me. C'mon, sweet man, talk to me. Talk to Uncle Matt.'

'Gonna puke.' Freddie got the door open and staggered off.

Oh no.

Matt climbed out too. Oh, no no no. Not that. But it was, though, wasn't it? Had to be. And now part of Matt felt like he'd known all along. He went over and rubbed Freddie's back as he retched onto the tarmac.

After a moment Freddie straightened up. 'Gah. Sorry 'bout that.'

'Water?' Matt handed him a bottle.

'Cheers.' He drank.

It was beginning to get dark. Somewhere a lorry beeped as it reversed. Crows were swirling and gathering in a distant clump of trees.

'Matt . . . Ah nuts. I shouldn't . . . Look, thing is, right before I left – while Suze was away? Me and Paul, we . . . yeah.'

Matt closed his eyes.

'I'm sorry, OK? I'm really sorry. Don't be mad at me, Matt.'

'I'm not mad at you. You're saying that you and Paul had sex?'

'Oh God.' Freddie stood chewing his lip, tugging at his hair. 'I promised I wouldn't tell?'

'We're way past worrying about that.'

So Freddie told him. Told him the lot. Showed him pictures no archdeacon wants to see of his diocesan bishop.

'OK, Freddie, what's the plan? Going to sell these to the tabloids?'

'Wha-a-a'? No! Omigod, Matt, why would you even think that?'

'So you took them, why, exactly?'

'Like, oh, to remember? You know? Coz he's a sweet guy and I dunno, maybe kind of love him?'

'Well, seeing as he's a sweet guy and you love him, how about deleting them?'

'Yeah, probably I should do that?'

'How about doing it now?' Matt held the phone out. 'Before you lose this, or someone nicks it.'

'Hnn. Good thought.' He went to work with his thumbs. 'Done.'

'Show me? What about this one? And this?'

'What the . . . Jesus, Matt, that's someone else, OK? Give me that. Hey! Don't slut-shame me, asshole! Yeah, you totally are – you're doing your "I'm Very Disappointed" thing.'

'Freddie, more than happy to have this fight later,' said Matt. 'But right now I need to know, are there any copies anywhere? Think. On your laptop? Albums? Photo stream? Flash drives? Facebook?' Freddie shook his head. 'Good. Talked to anyone else about all this?'

'Um, nah.'

'Sure about that?'

Freddie's gaze wandered off to the reversing lorry. 'Yep.'

Excellent. So who else knew? Matt rubbed his face with both hands, then clasped them behind his head. He stood numb, like a defender who could not believe the other team had just scored. This was A. Total. Chuffing. Mare.

'Well, Freddie, I think the best thing is for you and me to hop back in the car and tootle down to the retreat house. Now. Have a chat with Paul and see how he wants to play this. You OK with that?'

'Oh man. Yeah, no. Do we have to? Yeah, probably we should do that.'

'Okey-dokey. Let me make a few phone calls.'

'Cool. Listen, sorry I started on you? Can I . . . get a hug here?'

'All right. C'mon, trouble.'

Freddie locked his arms round Matt's neck and clung on. Matt held him tight. The blond head burrowed into his shirt. He could still feel tremors running through him. Poor kid. You poor screwed-up kid. What the hell was Paul thinking? OK, fair enough – probably *thinking* wasn't uppermost.

'Thanks. Love you, man.'

'Back at ya.'

'Only, yeah. Matt, listen. Um. Don't be mad?'

'Now what?'

'Promise?'

'Promise.'

'Only . . .' Tiny whisper.

'What? *You tweeted Roderick Fallon?!*'

'Naw, dude, you promised!'

This was last Wednesday. The formal announcement of the next archbishop of York was scheduled for Friday. However, this date was secret and had not been formally announced. The day for announcing the announcement (Thursday) came and went. Friday came and went likewise. Of course, everyone knew unofficially that Paul Henderson was to be the next archbishop of York and that this would be officially announced on Friday. But because nobody knew anything about this officially, no formal announcement or explanation about the lack of announcement was necessary.

I hope you followed all that.

A great cloud of Anglican obfuscation now shrouds the matter. Naturally, it teems with gossip. What? What's going on? I thought Paul Henderson . . . ? Wasn't the announcement supposed to be on Friday? He's withdrawn?! Ssh. Totally off the record. Why? Some scandal? What, squeaky clean Paul Henderson? Surely not! Maybe he's ill? Apparently he'd been looking strained. Oh no, poor guy, let's hope it's not cancer. Stress? Depression? Marriage in difficulties? So who's the next archbishop of York now?

Good question. Behind the scenes we must suppose that the number two candidate is being scrambled through his CRB check and medical, and fed into the Anglican/Downing Street machine to be mumbled in its ponderous and marble jaws and cast up again as an archbishop. We will have to wait and see, but I reckon we can look for an announcement in around three weeks. As far as I know, the withdrawal of an archbishop elect so close to the wire is unprecedented. The church powerbrokers are probably making it up as they go along. In unseemly haste! Like a stout ermined duchess being obliged to gallop for a bus. She can do it if she has to, but she'll be A Bit Cross, I can tell you.

I was not privy to those anguished discussions which occurred in the retreat house, after Paul was called down from his room to find Matt and Freddie there waiting in the hallway. However, I can hazard a guess that during his stay Paul had been pacing like a groom with cold feet. The closer the wedding loomed the more urgently he needed to bail out, but the more impossible it became to contemplate. The cost! The guests! The devastating hurt! The gossip!

Naturally, everyone now wants an explanation. None is forthcoming – other than a short press release from the diocesan communications officer stating that, contrary to recent speculation in the press, the bishop of Lindchester is not to be the next archbishop of York, and that Downing Street would be making a formal announcement regarding the vacancy in due course.

We may safely conclude that the Most Revd Dr Michael Palgrove knows what happened. The Crown Nominations Commission, well, perhaps some of them know what Paul Henderson's 'personal reasons' for withdrawing were. Do the senior staff of the diocese of Lindchester know? The dean and chapter? No. Only Matt knows. And Susanna, poor Susanna. Not all the cakes in all the kitchens in all the homes in the Anglican Communion worldwide can put this one right – no, not if we baked from now till Christmas.

The Hendersons are spending a few days in their little bolt-hole in the Peak District. Good people of Lindchester, let's not discuss them. That is the kindest thing we can do for Paul and Susanna right now. When our friends are called to pass through the deep waters, surely the kindest thing we can do is not talk about them? For however compassionately, however prayerfully, forgivingly, sensitively, scrupulously we discuss their situation – in what hushed tones, with what tears in our eyes! – our talking can never match the simple elegance of shutting up.

How true. And yet how irresistible the urge to talk! How else can we make sense of the baffling actions of our fellow human beings?

We ought to spare a thought for Matt. Long years of confidence-keeping mean that silence goes without saying here. But there are times when he feels like a landfill site for everyone else's crap. Be nice to take a holiday, get the stink out of his nose, take a break from beating off gannets the whole chuffing time. Or, once in a blue moon, offload on to someone else. Not been able to do that since Jen died, really. Bit soon to start dumping work stuff on Dr R. He owed her a drink, mind you. Gotta love a gal who doesn't give you grief when you stand her up. Take her somewhere a bit special, then. And our archdeacon is a bit of an expert on the local watering holes.

'So what's this place, exactly?' asked Jane. 'A prohibition bar?'

'Yep.'

'This can't be right. It's derelict. It's boarded up.'

The archdeacon pushed open the black door. A thread of blues wound out. And there it was: a secret speakeasy! In Lindford! Narrow and dimly lit, with a mahogany bar and a piano. Smaller than Jane's seminar room in the Fergus Abernathy building.

'I've worked here years and I had no idea!'

Matt installed his lady in a snug corner and bought them both whisky sours.

'How's the world of archdeaconing?' she asked.

'Right now? It's a mare.'

'Paul?'

The archdeacon paused, whisky halfway to lips. Shit. Freddie? Susanna? Or Paul himself even? He felt her hand on his thigh.

'Don't worry. Shot in the dark. I've heard nothing.'

But she'd guessed, hadn't she? 'Right. Well. How's the world of lecturing?'

'Meh.'

He felt her hand slide higher. 'Um. You might want to stop doing that, Jane.' And higher.

'I say, Mr Archdeacon! I hope you've got a faculty for that.'

'No need. It's not permanent. Mmmargh. Please, Jane!'

'Ooh! Unexpected item in bagging area!'

Well, we will leave our archdeacon to be felt up in a speakeasy like the naughty man he is, and turn our attention politely elsewhere.

The reader will not have forgotten Roderick Fallon, I dare say. Did he get Freddie's tweet? Indeed he did. In far-off London Town he studied the trashy blond avatar and he scented major scandal. Oh, yes. Oh, yes. He tweeted @choirslut90 back: 'Interested! Tell me more?' But because Fallon was on an urgent deadline for another piece, he didn't keep an eye on his timeline. You may picture his disappointment when several hours later he found the following: 'Soz, ignore that!! My mate got hold of phone lol :)'. He checked. @choirslut90 had locked his Twitter account.

Hoorah for the archdeacon!

But a day or two later, when his unnamed source murmured to Roderick Fallon that Paul Henderson had withdrawn for undisclosed 'personal reasons', Fallon smiled. He smiled like a crocodile on the banks of the Zambezi who hears the distant wildebeest approaching. Yeah, come to Daddy, @choirslut90.

Chapter 40

In the palace garden in Lindchester the apples and pears ripen, then fall. They rot in the grass, thrumming with the last drunken wasps of summer. Gavin the verger mows them to mush. He keeps it nice and straight, up and down, up and down. Straight lines now, where Freddie May once mowed his big heart. This year in Susanna's pantry the rows of Kilner jars stand empty. The palace stands empty. The Hendersons are still away.

'Oh, all these crab apples, just going to waste!' she says. 'And the blackberries! Why didn't I bring a basket? Stupid, stupid! I ought to come back and pick them and make blackberry and apple jelly!'

He takes her hand as they walk down the country lane and says, 'Darling, you don't have to. It's all right.'

'And the sloes! Look at them all. It's such a bumper year – that heatwave, it must be the heatwave – and now it's all going to waste! Oh, Paul, Paul, I can't bear it,' she says.

'I know. My poor darling.'

'Oh, what are we going to tell people?'

'We don't have to tell them anything.'

'No, you're right. Oh, but the girls, what will we tell the girls?'

'Nothing, for the moment.'

So far, all they have told the girls is that after much heart-searching, Paul decided that the Lord was not calling him to accept the York job. He was not the right person, and therefore he could not in all conscience proceed.

He will resign as bishop of Lindchester, of course. For personal reasons. It will be announced next month. He'll be gone by Christmas to start his next job in January: principal of a new Anglican training college in South Africa. Will Susanna go with him? Oh, she doesn't know, she just doesn't know. She adores South Africa – all those visits when it was their partner diocese, before they moved to Lindchester.

But the girls! The grandchildren! Perhaps she will divide her year between the bolt-hole and South Africa?

She thinks: if only the baby had come on time, if only she'd been at home when— Ah, if only she'd never clapped eyes on that Freddie May!

How could she not have noticed? All these decades of lovingly looking after . . . oh, an heirloom, a Chippendale sofa. Polishing its wood, plumping its cushions, lifting any stains, making sure everything was perfect. Only to be told out of the blue it was just a reproduction! Was it still worth polishing? Was she a bigger fool to stop now, or to carry on? Because hadn't she loved the old thing for itself? Wasn't it *her* sofa, her old friend? Wasn't that what counted? The love of the old thing, worthless though it suddenly was? Please say all those years of love made this marriage worth something after all?

But sometimes she can't bear the sight of it. She'd like to plunge her dressmaking shears into its upholstery. Rip it to ribbons. Gouge its fake varnish. Kick it, stab it, burn holes in it. Oh! Then collapse on to it weeping with despair. Because where else can she go? What other support is there?

'Oh, Paul, it's such a waste. It's all so sad.'

'I know, darling. I know. I'm so sorry.'

Later that afternoon he goes out walking on his own, leaving her with her box set of *Downton*. He climbs a hill among the dingy bracken and sits on the same rock he sat on in the spring. When the green fronds were unfurling. He remembers it. How manfully he tried, with his volume of Shakespeare's Sonnets, to fend off thoughts of Freddie. Now, like Susanna, he asks himself, How could I not have noticed? Wasn't it *obvious* that he had fallen comprehensively, catastrophically in love with that fair youth? And that it could only end badly? But out alack, he was but one hour mine!

A far-off curlew calls. The wind mourns in the dying heather. How nearly, nearly it didn't happen at all! But for that freak set of circumstances – Susanna away, Freddie distressed, a pastoral hand reached out – it might never have happened. (You fool, to fall like that, a yard from the finishing line!) Yes, were it not for these things, Freddie would have gone, Paul would have escaped all this shame.

Or would he? Maybe there would have been some worse lapse further down the road. So perhaps this shame *is* the escape? He has been saved, but only as through fire. Hauled out of his burning folly by the archdeacon, in the nick of time.

Yes, perhaps he's been saved. He ponders that strange wash of relief when he saw them standing there in the hallway. Like a fugitive, caught at last. Found out. Brought to justice. The running's over. He's been running all his adult life. He's run round his entire globe and come back to the beginning, to find the same thing waiting for him. The worst thing imaginable: it is men he is attracted to, not women.

The curlew calls again. He looks down at his hands. The two rings: wedding ring, episcopal ring. Ah, he should take them off – he's worthy of neither. Not worthy to be called either a husband or a bishop.

But then some words float into his head: *Put a ring on his hand.*

He knows the quote. The prodigal. 'But when he was yet a great way off, his father saw him, and had compassion, and ran, and fell on his neck, and kissed him. This my son was lost and is found.'

Not found out. Found. He hears the old hymn:

> Perverse and foolish, oft I strayed
> but yet in love he sought me;
> and on his shoulder gently laid,
> and home, rejoicing, brought me.

He has squandered everything. Everything. Wasted it all. But he is home at last. For the first time in all this hell – the first time in decades – Paul breaks down and weeps.

Someone, somewhere, is praying for Paul Henderson. I can tell you who it is: it is our good friend, the suffragan bishop of Barcup. He's standing in his kitchen in Martonbury, waiting for the kettle to boil. It's a grey afternoon here, but his back garden is lit up by the cherry tree and necklaces of Virginia creeper trailing from the high wall. The glory, the glory! Bishop Bob thinks clergy-type thoughts about the fact that it is only death and decay that causes this symphony of colour. How the cloth of our life is woven of joy and sorrow together.

Sorrow. This is what turns his thoughts to Paul. He does not know what led Paul to withdraw from the archbishopric. He would not dream of intruding into those personal reasons, tries not to let himself speculate, even. But he prays.

He is not a Conservative Evangelical, so he is not compelled to school his prayers into words. He does not now, for example, say, 'Dear Lord, we pray for Paul, bishop of Lindchester, who has recently withdrawn from the post of archbishop of York, for personal reasons. We lift him before you at this difficult time. We pray also for his wife Susanna . . .' Bishop Bob is inclined to think that God is probably already up to speed on the biographical details. And not being a Charismatic Evangelical either, he hesitates to give the Almighty matey advice in the subjunctive mood. 'So yeah, Father-God, we pray you would, yeah, sovereignly overrule in Paul's situation?

And would Paul and Susanna just know your presence right now, Lord, and would their home be a place where your spirit is, yeah, mightily at work? Mmm. We just claim that promise right now, Lord. And would this truly be a season of awesome blessing for them?'

Instead, Bob thinks about Paul. He sees him as he's often seen him: in Lindchester Cathedral, sitting on his big throne. And then he pictures the Lord coming and sitting beside him. There's room for two on that throne. In his mind's eye he sees the Lord put his arms round Paul. Bishop Bob holds this picture in his thought. And all he thinks is Love. *Ubi caritas et amor, Deus ibi est.* Love, love, love. And there is a yearning, barely clothed in words: be with him, be with him.

And as he stands in his kitchen thinking, yearning, Paul starts to weep up on that hilltop far away.

But what of our friend Father Dominic? I'm afraid we abandoned him rather rudely a couple of weeks ago, just when he was about to be installed as vicar of Lindford. I'm pleased to report that right now Father Dominic is a happy bunny. He has not been in post long enough to cock anything major up, and any small cock-ups will be forgiven in his first year. That is the usual rule at parish level. In Dominic's case, I reckon he has at least two years' grace, on the grounds that however badly he cocks things up, at least he is not a monster like his predecessor.

I say he's a happy bunny, but right now, Dominic is in a bit of a strop. It's Friday. Which we all know is his day off. He's been shopping, and now he is facing the single person's flatpack hell. 'IT IS ADVISORY TO BE TWO PERSONS DURING ASSEMBLY,' say the instructions. How, exactly, is he to assemble his Bølløks bathroom cabinet if he is only 'one person', and he has no wife or girlfriend, like the lucky gentleman in the illustration, to hold the tall bit while he wields the Allen key? What is a gay bachelor supposed to do? Clone himself? Why is there no flatpack Grindr, where frustrated chaps with Allen keys can help one another out?

Right on cue his doorbell rings. He's had a constant stream of people bearing jars of jam and chutney to welcome him to Lindford. Enough jam and chutney to last him the rest of his life! He should buy a Bølløks jam cupboard, too! But with a bit of luck, this jam-bearing parishioner will help out with the vicar's DIY dilemma.

It is not a parishioner with chutney. It's his good friend Jane. With whisky. Now we're talking.

Amid much foul language and hateful personal remarks – unlike the illustrated girlfriend, Jane proved incapable of mutely holding the tall bit, she *had* to interfere and offer advice – the cabinet was constructed. It was not perfect, but then, what is? Jane and Dominic were now celebrating their DIY skills with an Indian takeaway.

'More chutney, vicar?' asked Jane.

'Shut up. How's the archdeacon? Have you done the deed yet?'

'Shut up.'

'You shut up.'

'I can't tell you anything if I shut up.'

'Good point. Well, go on then. Tell all.'

Jane rested her elbows on the table and her chin on her hands. She scowled.

'That would be a no, I take it,' said Dominic. 'Janey! You're not crying, are you? Don't cry, darling!' He dropped his fork and went and hugged her.

Jane rubbed her eyes. 'Fuck. Sorry. It's just—'

It was some time before she managed to explain what it just was. An impasse. Seemingly. The archdeacon could not go around wagging a stern finger at fornicating priests if he himself was getting his leg over.

'We-e-ell, he has a point, there,' said Dominic.

'*I know he has a fucking point!*' She grabbed some kitchen roll and blew her nose. 'Sorry.'

Dominic patted her hand. 'You've got it bad, girl.'

'I know.'

'You're going to end up marrying him.'

'Piss off, you fat ponce,' said Jane. 'And pour me some whisky.'

Now it is Saturday. The late bell is chiming for evensong. A black Audi convertible parks on Lindchester Cathedral Close. A tall man gets out. He is ungainly, all awkward angles, as he hurries down the steps to the cathedral. His flat feet slap on the flagstones. He disappears through the north door.

A choir dad, you think, rushing in late to hear his son sing his first solo? No, I'm afraid not. That, my friends, was Roderick Fallon on the trail of @choirslut90.

Chapter 41

Roderick Fallon did not find @choirslut90 in Lindchester Cathedral, of course. You might be wondering why he was looking for him here and not in Barchester. The explanation is simple: Freddie failed to update his Twitter profile when he moved in September. I'm relieved to say that he has not been suckered by any of the fake Twitter accounts set up to lure him into permitting access. So all Fallon had to go on was that slutty selfie, the name and the location. (And he acknowledged that, yes, he did wish his boyfriend was hot like @choirslut90.) Google cast up a single nugget: a Lindchester Cathedral Choir CD from 2003, which featured a certain Frederick May as treble soloist. This seemed to clinch Lindchester as a good starting point. Hence Fallon's appearance at evensong last Saturday.

He clattered in late and folded his awkward frame into the last vacant stall in the quire, then a moment later lurched back to his feet like a self-erecting music stand when the choir processed in. He scanned the back row boys of *can* and *dec* as they passed. @choirslut90 was not among them. Fallon did not clock the tall, wild-haired precentor as he glided by.

The wild-haired precentor clocked Roderick Fallon, however. He had time to move from, 'Oh Lord, what's he doing here?' to a creeping fear (that hostile article, Paul's unexplained withdrawal from the York job), through to strategies for heading off any unhelpful lines of journalistic enquiry, should they arise. All in the space of the psalmody (Day 12: Psalms 65–67, 'Thy clouds drop fatness').

Roderick Fallon was aware that he might have to contend with evasion and ecclesiastical rank-closing. But there was a bigger problem he failed to take into account: that a rapacious newshound who strays into the liminal space of a large medieval cathedral might suddenly find a Hound on his own trail. It was a while since he dusted off his Francis Thompson, I fear. Even the most determinedly lapsed of lapsed Catholics, the most vitriolic hater of The Cloth, really cannot expect to breeze into Byrd's Second Service sung in an ancient hallowed space and escape unscathed. The non-being he so devoutly disbelieved in picked poor Roderick up in the *Mag* and *Nunc* and twanged his heartstrings like a banjo. He was sitting right in the middle of the front row. There was no escape. He consulted the music list, and saw Byrd's *Ave Verum Corpus* looming in the anthem slot. *Fuck.* He ground his teeth. Cursed the Jesuits who got hold of him at seven. Conjured up the most blasphemously pornographic images at his command. Even got out his phone and checked his emails. Still those strong feet followed, followed after.

You may know from experience, dear reader, that trying not to cry in church is as futile as trying not to laugh. You plead, you bite the inside of your cheek, you make wild vows of future good behaviour. But the more you castigate yourself, the more you fan the flames. Roderick hung on till the first *miserere mei* before he crumpled. Oh God, let the gloom hide him! He doubled over as if in prayer. *Miserere mei.* Maybe he could pass it off as contact lens trouble? *O dulcis, O pie, O fili Mariae!* I hate you, don't do this to me, you make-believe bastard!

He was still rather distrait when the service ended. And then, before he could compose himself, he was buttonholed by one of the canons. Some Einstein-haired Trollopian fuckwit, who obtruded his blithering hand-wringing pastoral concern right into Fallon's face. No, I'm *fine*, no, you can't help me, thanks. Unless you can tell me where I can find Freddie May. But the lanky twat was unable to say with certainty where young Mister May had taken himself off to. Bolivia, possibly? Gap yah? Volunteering? Sorry not to be more help.

And because he could still hear (deliberate speed, majestic instancy!) those fecking feet coming after him, Fallon got the hell out of there, without pausing to ask anyone else if they knew the whereabouts of Freddie May. He hared back to his black Audi convertible to find the vergers had given him a parking ticket.

Welcome to Lindchester Cathedral, Mr Fallon.

The reader is not, I hope, too shocked by the precentor's behaviour. He did not precisely lie to Roderick Fallon, although it was a piece of blatant misdirection, admittedly. And in his defence, had Fallon wished to open his heart to the blithering canon, Giles would have heard his confession in all gentleness and sincerity, and absolved him in the appropriate manner.

Giles left the cathedral and crossed the Close to his house putting two and two together as he went. Never! But no matter how he ran this particular calculation, the gobsmacking four he kept getting = the lovely Mr May and his diocesan bishop in some kind of flagrante. This branch of mental arithmetic was rightly discredited, he knew. Probably letting his imagination run away with him. But all the same, should he mention to Paul – when he came back – that Fallon was sniffing round the Close after Freddie May? Text Freddie to alert him? Or just butt out and mind his own business? Oh Lord. In the end he decided to inform the proper authorities: that is, he went and told his wife. In strictest confidence, of course. He stressed that. As did she, when she discussed it with the treasurer's wife. Who very discreetly mentioned it to her husband. Who in all conscience, felt it incumbent upon him to murmur something to the dean.

It is Wednesday morning and Dr Jane Rossiter is swearing at her car radio as she drives to work.

No, you ineffable Tory tosspot, more people are not using food banks because the Trussell Trust is opening more food banks. More people are using food banks because they are fucking *starving* in this green and pleasant land as a result of your evil policies! Yeah, that's right – and I bet if you chucked more lifebelts into the sea, more drowning people would use them too. What, you think people treat food banks like a free McDonald's? Oh, I fancy a takeaway tonight, Chinese? Curry? Ooh, I know, a new food bank's opened round the corner, let's give that a try!

Actually, now I come to look over that rant, it's on the mild side in the swearie department for Dr Rossiter. One tosspot and a single f-word. Perhaps the steady mildness of our friend the archdeacon is working its magic on her vocabulary?

Oh. I spoke too soon. Dr Rossiter is now trying to park. The old staff car park has been closed as part of the university's redevelopment plan. It will be landscaped into a calm little garden. There is alternative car parking provision in a derelict lot behind Tesco. The alternative car park is full. Dr Rossiter drives round and round the streets of Lindford looking for a space within walking distance of Poundstretcher. She gets later and later for her lecture. (The Victorians: Gender and Sexuality.) OK. As you were. Dr Rossiter is as flamboyantly foul-mouthed as ever she was.

Meanwhile, another of our favourite characters is responding in a more temperate manner to her radio. Father Wendy is in her kitchen feeding poor old Lulu. Lulu is not hungry. She sniffs her food and mumbles a mouthful out of politeness, then lets it drop back into the bowl. Wendy sits beside her and strokes her old head.

'What are they saying now, Lulu?' she asks. 'Well, I suppose it's true. There are more food banks and more people are using them – but what were they doing before? That's what we have to ask, isn't it?' Father Wendy knows the answer, at least in her cluster of rural parishes. Country living is not all swishing off to Waitrose for quails' eggs in your Hunter wellies and shiny four-by-four. Some people are choosing between mum eating, and the kids eating. Between heating the house and buying food. 'Thank goodness for our lovely curate, eh, girl. Thank goodness for Virginia!'

Virginia, with her professional background in HR, has been a tower of strength for parishioners who fell through the welfare reform cracks. Virginia lives and breathes Process. This can make her a pain in the bottom at PCC meetings – and in those endless red tape-y personal development review thingies that go with being a training incumbent these days – but her skills are an absolute godsend when someone's benefits get suspended.

'Thank goodness for Virginia, eh, girl?' Lulu thumps her tail once in agreement. 'We'll just have to love those prickles off her,' Wendy says. Then she frowns at herself. Perhaps Virginia is only prickly with Wendy? Maybe Wendy is the problem? Oh dear. And besides, maybe people should be allowed to be prickly; perhaps they should be loved, prickles and all? Like Mrs Tiggywinkle?

'Oh bother. I shouldn't have thought that, should I, Lulu?' From now on she will never quite be able to banish the image of that bustling little Beatrix Potter hedgehog from her mind when she thinks of Virginia.

Meanwhile, Dr Rossiter has found somewhere to park. The archdeacon's drive. Arse and feck. She really does not want to presume upon him, not right now. With things being, as the young people say, complicated. She texts him as she walks: 'Parking hell. Left my car on your drive. Hope that's OK. Jx'. She's now fifteen minutes late for her lecture and still five minutes' brisk walk away. Plus she's got to lug all her crap uphill to the sweet FA building. Stream of consciousness narrative has much to commend it, but I believe we can dispense with Jane's inner monologue at this point.

It's Thursday. The Hendersons are back on the Close. Susanna bakes. Paul picks up the reins of the diocese. We will pay a visit to the office and listen in.

Martin, the bishop's chaplain, talked him through the weeks ahead. Filled him in on what he'd missed. Was there an elephant in the room? No. They had conspired Englishly to banish the elephant. But it was there, just outside the office window, its large grey flank blocking out the light.

'Looking ahead to late November now,' said Martin, 'we have the . . .'

Paul stared at the episcopal diary on the screen while Martin talked. I'll have resigned by then. We'll have to start emptying the house. Getting rid of stuff. So much stuff.

He came to. Martin had just asked him something. 'Sorry?'

Martin repeated his bullet-pointed question, but by the time he reached the end, the beginning had eluded Paul.

'I'm afraid I don't know, Martin.'

There was a long silence. Paul saw him thinking: how can you not know the answer to a straightforward question?

'Is . . . everything all right, Paul?'

There at the window the huge head bowed. A wise sad eye peered in at them. 'Yes, sorry, yes. A bit distracted. I'm . . . I find myself having to adjust to a new set of expectations, of course.'

'Of course. I see.'

'But there we are!' Paul clapped his hands on his knees. 'Where were we?'

'The employment tribunal,' repeated Martin. 'I was asking you which of the following four considerations—'

But here they were interrupted by Penelope, the bishop's PA, who came in bearing a plate of millionaire shortbread from Susanna.

'Oh, I do miss Freddie! These were always his favourites!' Penelope burst out, as if Freddie were dead, rather than just down the way in Barchester. 'I worry about that boy, I really do. What's he been up to *now*?'

A pause. 'How do you mean?' asked Paul.

'Well, with that horrible journalist looking for him. He came snooping round at evensong on Saturday apparently. You know the one, him, oh, what's his name?'

'Roderick Fallon?' suggested Martin.

'That's him!' said Penelope. 'Oh, I hope Freddie hasn't done anything stupid!'

'I'm sorry if this sounds callous, Penelope,' said Martin, 'but I'm sure Paul will bear me out when I say that Freddie May is no longer our problem.'

Chapter 42

Martin was wrong. Freddie May was still Paul's problem. He would always be Paul's problem. If Paul took the wings of the morning and dwelt in the uttermost parts of South Africa, even there would the thought of Freddie May pursue him. Or so it seemed to Paul, as Penelope stood with the plate of millionaire shortbread fretting over that boy.

'Excuse me a moment.' Paul stepped out of the office on to the gravel drive of the palace. He rang the archdeacon to see if he'd heard this rumour about Roderick Fallon. Of course the archdeacon had heard the rumour. He had also heard the first whispers linking Paul's name with Freddie's in all this.

'I'll be honest, bishop. This still has the potential to go tits up on us. How are you doing? Coping?'

'I'm fine.'

The car was right there. He could drive to Barchester now. Find him. Say, 'Get in, we're leaving. Come with me to France. To Timbuktu. To the moon.' Help me, God, help me, help me, God.

Martin was watching through the office window. He saw Paul walk up and down under the huge copper beech, head bowed, talking on the phone. Something was wrong. Badly wrong. Penelope was still chattering on about the little shite. Up and down, up and down the drive. Then he saw Paul finish his conversation and put his phone away. Rest a hand on the car roof, the other on his heart. He hunched over suddenly, as if—

'I'm sorry, excuse me, Penelope.' Martin raced outside and crunched over the gravel to Paul.

He wasn't moving.

'Bishop? Are you ill?'

Paul shook his head. He opened his mouth to speak, but a moan, a whoop of pain escaped.

'Come on, you need to sit.' He steered him to the wooden seat near the beech. Martin was first-aid trained. Shortness of breath, cold sweat: coronary?

Paul had already slipped his dog collar out and was fumbling his top button undone.

'How are you feeling, Paul? Any tightness in your chest? Tingling?'

Paul shook his head.

'Are you feeling faint?'

'Not my heart,' he gasped.

'Good, good,' said Martin, 'but let's get you checked all the same. Let me drive you up to—'

'I'm gay.'

'Casualty—'

In the silence that followed a squirrel rippled over the gravel with a beechnut in its mouth. They watched it dig a little hole in the lawn, bury the nut, then pat the earth back into place. Then it whisked past them and up the great grey bole of the beech.

No first aid for this. Say something. Quickly. *Thank you for telling me.*

The cathedral clock chimed the half hour. Martin's hand crept out and found the bishop's. It was not grasped, but nor was it flung off. He let it rest there on top of Paul's. There was an eye in the beech trunk, where a branch had once been. *This must be hard. If there's anything I can do.*

'I'm afraid I've made a fool of myself. I'm resigning . . .'

'No!' Freddie May. I *knew* it.

'. . . from my role here. It will be announced in due course.'

A handful of leaves rolled over and over across the lawn. 'Paul, I'm so sorry.'

'I've been invited to take up the post of principal. New theological college. South Africa.' He gave another horrible whoop. Tried to disguise it with a cough. 'I've accepted.'

Martin gripped his hand. The pain was catching. It clenched his own heart.

Paul cleared his throat. 'So if I can count on your discretion over the coming weeks. Trying desperately to contain this, this— consequences of my— stupidity! For the wider Church. My family. And of course, the— Protect the other person involved. Susanna and I would greatly appreciate it.'

'Of course.' He should strategize. Prioritize. But Martin was numb.

'This will turn out for my deliverance,' whispered Paul at last. 'That's what I've come to believe. In the end, this will be for my deliverance.'

Martin had won Scripture Knowledge prizes as a boy: 'Philippians 1.19.'

'Yes.' Paul's hand writhed under his. 'It *will* be for my deliverance. It just doesn't . . .'

It just doesn't feel that way now.

Martin knew. The gravel drive and the beech trunk swam. The hardest thing is to love someone, and know you can never be with them, ever again. Shortness of breath. Chest cramped like a vice. Dear God! I'm going to die!

'I'll do everything I can to support you in this, Paul.'

'Pray for me.'

'Of course.'

'And him. Pray for him, too.'

'Yes. I will.'

The archdeacon put the phone down and prayed as well. Then he acted. Choral half term. They did *not* want the devil finding work for idle hands in Barchester, so he got young tarty-pants out of there, pronto, before Fallon rocked up and schmoozed him into telling everything. Freddie was devastated. 'Omigod! You *still* think I'd do that?!' Well, call him a cynical bastard, but the archdeacon could not entirely rule that possibility out. Which is why Freddie spent half term mooching about the archdeacon's house in his underpants hitting on him now and then out of sheer boredom. (Yeah, no, and coz Matt was hot, he would totally do him in a heartbeat?)

'Hey! What are you doing here, Janey?'

'Parking my car. What are *you* doing here?'

'Aw. Y'know?' Freddie panted, getting his breath back from his run. 'It's like half term, and yeah, Matt invited me?'

'Oh.'

Tum-te-tum. Neither was entirely keen to launch into lengthier explanations here.

'Well, hey, girl. Can I get a hug?'

'No fear. I don't want your boy sweat. Argh! Get off me!'

He smeared his cheek against hers. 'Yeah! Testosterone for ya.'

'Eurgh!'

'C'mon. Kiss kiss. Makes the ladies less cranky. Been scientifically proven.'

'God! Now I need a slag jab.' Jane peeled him off and wiped her face with her sleeve. 'Listen, I'm late. Management's bollocksed up the staff parking, and Matt lets me park here, so um.'

'Yeah?' He grinned at her, rattled his stud round his teeth. 'Ha ha ha, you're blushing. You so are. Are you two getting it on?'

'No. Are you two getting it on?'

'I wish. Hey, we should maybe get a drink after work one night this week, and you can tell me everything?'

'Huh. You should maybe come and finish my garden, sunshine. It looks like the Somme.'

'Cool. I can do that. Gimme your car keys?'

'Are you insured?'

'Dude, I was the bishop's chauffeur. I've got insurance coming out of my ass.'

Jane narrowed her eyes. 'You're not covered to drive *my* car, though, are you, you lying tart. Oh, hi, Matt.' Dammit, she was definitely blushing now. 'Sorry, got to fly, guys. Late for a lecture. Mwa mwa.'

Jane stomped up the hill to the Fergus Abernathy building swearing at herself, at Freddie, at the archdeacon, and for good measure, at God. No point travelling any further down this road. Dead end ahead. Turn around where possible! Make a U-turn! Your destination does not even exist. Oh, for fuck's sake, Rossiter, get over it. An institution that treats women like chattels! Who *gives* this woman? Excuse me? How can any thinking person buy into this cornerstone of female oppression?

It's true. One of the hardest things of all is loving someone you can't be with.

I'm afraid that Jane will not even be cheered by thoughts of the royal christening this week. Or, more properly, the royal baptism. Up and down the diocese of Lindchester clergy and churchgoers are seeking to explain the difference, or the lack of difference. Perhaps I can be of some assistance here? Generally speaking, if the post-ceremony party venue is booked first, and the church service second, then it is called a christening. If the prospective godparents candidly tell the vicar, 'Oh, I don't believe any of that, but I'm happy to say it!' it is a christening. A baptism is simply a christening whose significance has been properly understood.

Poor old Virginia, Father Wendy's curate, is making heavy weather of explaining the significance to the young couple who want their second child 'done'. There is a clear process. Three sessions of baptism preparation are required before the baptism can take place. The couple are pointing out that they did all that when the first child was christened. Well, it clearly didn't sink in, thinks Virginia, as you've not darkened the doorway of the church since. They also insist they want a private ceremony. 'I'm afraid we don't do that,' says Virginia. All baptisms take place during the main act of worship. The couple say that this is not true in other churches. 'Well, it's our policy here,' says Virginia.

I don't want you to think that Virginia is implementing a policy just for the sheer jobsworth joy of it. (Though she has that streak in her, I will admit.) She can feel the nasty crunching of gears between policy and pastoral need. On a sudden impulse she says, 'Tell me about your little boy.' And it all comes out. The string of miscarriages, the complicated pregnancy, premature birth, the harrowing weeks in the Special Care Baby Unit. The mum is crying. Virginia just sits and listens.

And then she says, 'We'd love to welcome Nathan into the church and celebrate his safe arrival.' She is about to use her discretion and boldly waive the baptism preparation sessions (and worry about precedent-setting, and explaining it to Father Wendy later) – when they agree to come along!

So baptism, christening – same difference. But when his parents bring little Nathan to church, I suspect it will be a baptism.

It's late October now. The shops and pubs are fettled up with pumpkins and bats. The clocks go back. The nights reek of rotting leaves and gunpowder. Whizz bang scream. Please to remember. Or might we not, in this enlightened age, decide it's time to forget treason and plot at last? And in a spirit of ecumenism, quietly discontinue the practice of burning Roman Catholics in effigy?

A couple of young chancers call at Lindford vicarage on Thursday evening and ring the bell.

'Penny for the guy?'

Dominic stares in astonishment at the contents of the buggy parked on his step. 'What? It's not Bonfire Night yet! It's not even Hallowe'en! And that's not a guy! Who's this?'

'Ryan.'

'Hello, Ryan!' The toddler grins.

The two bigger boys grin up at him too. 'He's our little brother.'

'You're not going to burn Ryan, are you?' They look shocked. 'Well, he's not a guy then, is he? A guy's made of old clothes and straw. You're supposed to put your guy on the bonfire on bonfire night and burn him. Like Guy Fawkes? You know, Guy Fawkes? Who plotted to blow up the Houses of Parliament and the King? No?'

They shake their heads.

'Do your parents know you're out collecting?' They nod. Ooh, little fibbers. 'Tell you what, we're having a bonfire party here in the vicarage garden. Want to come?' He gives them a flyer. 'Now you go straight home before your mum and dad get worried, OK?'

After they've gone, Dominic gets in his car and follows at a distance till he sees them disappear safely into a house on the Abernathy estate. Jesu mercy!

I suspect Father Dominic has forgotten the things he got up to at the age of eight, which to this day his parents don't know about. Raking the streets on dark evenings after the clocks went back. Knock down ginger. Dare you, dare you. We've probably all forgotten. We will never know how many times someone watched from a distance till we were safely home again.

Chapter 43

Batten down the hatches! There are storms on the way. Storms like the hurricane of 1987, which turned Sevenoaks into Oneoak overnight.

When the St Jude's Day storm strikes (patron of lost causes, pray for us!) southern England bears the brunt of it again. Nonetheless, across the diocese of Lindchester wheelie bins frolic, trees fall, the Linden rises. In the canon chancellor's garden the huge poplar splits in two, and half of it crashes into the school playground next door. The high wall is demolished, but nobody is hurt, thank the Lord. (Yesss! The canon chancellor punches the air. Next year's firewood sorted!) It will be a busy week for Ecclesiastical Insurance.

Susanna watches. The garden she has so lovingly nurtured is lashed and threshed. She stares through the palace window as if at news footage of some distant disaster. It's terrible. She ought to care. Rain slashes the pane. Rainy, rainy, rattle stones, don't rain on me.

But they have. They *have* rained on her, not on John O'Groat's house, far across the sea, where it would have been terribly sad, but not really her problem.

Paul is upstairs in his study. The storm has prevented him driving off to see his counsellor. Why don't you get in your bloody car and drive off to your *lover*? I know you want to! Susanna stops short of picturing a tree falling and squashing him flat. Because that's not what she wants. She doesn't really want him dead. But she wants to run Freddie May over! Then reverse back over him, and run over him again. No, no, poor Freddie! No, she doesn't want to do that.

What do you want, Susanna?

Oh, I don't know, I don't know!

What do you want, Susanna?

The question has been padding round after her for weeks, like a dog. Go away! It's no use, I don't know the answer. She just wants it not to be like . . . this. Not to hurt so much. She wants to pour a huge tumbler of sherry and drink it down in one go. To rush up to Paul's study and slap his face. She wants to know what they did. Where they did it. Whose bed. How many times. No, she doesn't. She wants to walk out of her life for ever, disappear without explanation and start all over again, like the woman in that novel they did in her book club, who was it by? That would teach him.

Oh, she can't cope with not being the silly one, the one in the wrong. She's always been in the wrong. Paul is never in the wrong – that is one of the rules!

Everything is broken. The stupid announcement dress hangs in the wardrobe, unworn. Suddenly she realizes: somewhere, in some other palace, there's another wife busy planning her outfit for the Big Day. Some other bishop already knows he's the next archbishop of York. Any day now there will be an announcement. We will sink without trace. It was all for nothing. Apart from her girls, everything she's ever done is pointless! The nursing training she's never used. The homemaking. The stupid unpaid part-time job that brought Freddie May into their home. I should have done something with myself. And now it's too late!

What do you want, Susanna?

I want to die, she thinks. Not to kill myself, but to be dead. I want it to be over. I want to be at peace.

The branches of the ancient cedar churn in anguish.

I just want to be at peace.

Our good friend the archdeacon is also housebound by the storm. Bloody weather. Means he won't get a glimpse of Dr R today, parking on his drive. He feels an urge to be a total bastard. Wants to throw his archidiaconal weight about, close a bunch of churches. Whack some useless nobs into disciplinary measures. (Don't worry: he's got it reined in.)

Young tarty-pants tried his patience to the limits last week, pestering him to help sort out Dr R's garden for her. As if, given an ounce of encouragement, Matt wouldn't cram her garden with red roses! Dig her a pond, stock it with koi carp. Lay York stone slabs, plant apple trees, strawberry beds, build her a henhouse, fill it with broody chooks. What would Matt not do for his lady?

'G'wan, g'wan, g'wan, Matt. You know you want to. Let's do it while she's at work. Surprise her? C'mo-o-on, why not? Dude, she's totally into you, I can tell.' In the end Matt snapped, 'If you don't shut up, I'll spank you.' Face-palm. Memo to self: think your threats through.

The rain pounds on his study window. So, three possible solutions: (a) Dr R relaxes her position on marriage; (b) Matt relaxes his position on extra-marital relations; (c) Matt resigns from active ministry.

He can't ask (a) of her. He can't ask (b) or (c) of himself. Not looking too good, really, is it? No wonder she's backed off. Sensible woman. He's always been Captain Sensible himself. Blue Peter badge. Deputy head boy. D of E Gold. Police Bravery Award. But right now he'd rather be round the back of the bike-sheds, being a bad lad. Doing seventeen kinds of rude thing.

He could list them.

Fifteen . . . Sixteen . . . Seventeen. Yup.

But anyway. Work to be done. He opens his inbox and slogs through his work emails. He keeps at it for forty-five minutes, then he cracks. He fires off an email to Jane: 'Darling, I can't stand this. Can we meet for a drink ASAP so I can tell you how deeply, madly, hopelessly, etc. I love you? We can work this out. Matt xx'.

He goes off to make a mug of coffee, comes back. She hasn't replied. There you are: she's a sensible woman. Just an email from the bishop of Barcup's wife: 'Immensely flattered to be addressed so passionately by the archdeacon of Lindchester, but something tells me that this is meant for someone else. Janet Hooty'.

Damn you, auto-fill.

The storm passes, as storms will. Then there is the aftermath to face. We must save what can be saved, tie up our broken plants, mend our fences and roofs. Then we must say farewell to what is beyond repair. Let it go. Tree surgeons come and fell what is left of the canon chancellor's poplar. They leave a huge ragged hole behind in the sky above the garden. A stunned absence of tree. But the eye will accustom itself. The squirrels and stock doves and wood pigeons, the owls, all the young magpies and jackdaws, the long-tailed tits, the green woodpeckers, the hawk moths, grubs, beetles – they will find another home. It's not the end of the world. It really isn't. It just feels – My aspens dear! All felled, felled, are all felled! – that way right now.

Susanna was correct in her surmise: there is another bishop somewhere who already knows he will be the next archbishop of York. The number two candidate was hastily tapped up. And yes, his wife has made a little trip to John Lewis for a new frock and shoes. The announcement will be next week. We must be patient a little longer.

It's Thursday. Hallowe'en gurns in at us through the windows. The police will be kept busy tonight. Trick or treat, smell my feet!

Father Wendy (who can't be doing with the celebration of darkness) and her curate Virginia (who can't be doing with lawlessness) host a Super-Hero Party in Cardington church hall, inviting all the kids who came to the holiday club in the summer. Father Dominic (who can't be doing with party-poopers) doles out sweeties to the callers at the vicarage, along with flyers for his bonfire party. Undergraduates test the boundaries of good taste with their fancy dress outfits, get bladdered in the bars of Lindford, and jeopardize future careers by immortalizing it all on Facebook.

Jane turns off the lights and doesn't answer her door. Why hasn't she heard from Matt? Because you told him nothing doing, silly mare. Yes, but *why* haven't I heard from him? He could at least argue with me! Try and talk me round. *Fuck off and stop ringing my doorbell, you little shites!* Come morning she'll find her porch and car have been egged and floured. Next year she must enter into the festive spirit, and hand out muffins laced with broken razors.

For all the saints . . . We feebly struggle, they in glory shine.

On All Saints' afternoon, Bishop Paul drives off for his rescheduled appointment with his counsellor. He knows – who better? – that he is feebly struggling. We will not intrude into their session. For a start, it takes place in a small village just over the diocesan border, where this narrative has vowed not to stray. As he drives back in the late afternoon past empty pumpkin shells on gateposts, he thinks about the anarchy of Hallowe'en, the rising up of the unholy dead in gruesome carnival. Cheek by jowl with All Saints. His counsellor has invited him to reflect on Jungian shadows. To ask whether Freddie burst into his life as an incarnation of everything in himself that he had believed was dead and buried. To ponder that recurring dream of his, in which he finds he's wandering in a house he knows well from childhood, but there is another room, and then a whole other wing, that he didn't know existed. And when he looks out through an attic window he sees in the sky huge combine harvesters, gigantic cranes, earth-movers, all floating past overhead, silent and serene.

With God nothing shall be impossible.

The bishop does not need his chaplain here to tell him that this is Luke 1.37. The angel Gabriel to the Virgin Mary. But why has it popped into his head now? What does it mean? That he will be overshadowed by the power of the Highest? That this new thing being born in him in so much agony and bitter shame will be called Holy? Son of God? How can this be?

With God nothing shall be impossible.

The sky is charged with sudden light. The road ahead blazes silver. Sheep graze transfigured in eerie emerald meadows beside the burnished Linden. Nothing is impossible. Nothing is impossible.

Is it even possible that the heart of the bishop's chaplain might gradually relent towards Freddie May? I wonder. You will remember that Martin promised Paul he would pray for Freddie. He goes into the cathedral, to the chapel of St Michael and All Angels, to fulfil his promise. An odd choice for Martin, but I suspect he doesn't want the little shite invading his personal Quiet Time in his study at home.

'Dear Lord, please bless Freddie May.'

This is uttered as though 'bless' were some kind of synonym for 'visit hideous plagues upon'. But there. He has done it. He has prayed for his enemy.

Up in the quire they are rehearsing Duruflé's *Requiem* for tomorrow. Martin has no truck with all that pre-Reformation All Souls nonsense. All God's people are saints.

He tries again. 'Dear Lord, I pray that you will be close to ... be with ...'

I warned Paul! I told him he had a blind spot! But he just slapped me down.

'Help him to ...'

It all made sense now, the blatant favouritism, his constant refusal to confront Freddie's bad behaviour. I will never be able to think well of Paul again. The thought makes him panic. Ridiculous! Surely he knows that all God's people are sinners, too, as well as saints? Why can't he accommodate Paul's lapse? It's not about works. He knows we can't earn God's love.

So why does it feel the whole time as if he has to? Why does he spend his whole life trying to stay on the right side of God?

In the distance the choir begins the *Agnus Dei*. Martin glares at the macho bronze Michael. He loathes it. Legs splayed, fists raised like a triumphant athlete, the distinctly unangelic crotch bulge. That thing should never have been allowed in here.

'Please let Freddie—'

It's pointless. I'm sorry, Lord. I hate him. What can I pray, when I hate him so much?

In the distance the choir answers: *Agnus Dei, qui tollis peccata mundi, dona eis requiem sempiternam.* Lamb of God, who takest away the sins of the world: grant them eternal rest.

NOVEMBER

Chapter 44

'I just want to get my best dressmaking shears and snip it to ribbons!'

'Do it.'

Susanna gasps. 'Paul! I couldn't possibly! It's a brand new dress.'

'If it'll make you feel better, snip it up.'

'But it was really expensive!'

'So?'

'No, no, I couldn't. I was just being silly. I'll give it to a charity shop.'

They fall silent.

'I haven't dusted in here for ages,' she says. 'There's a cobweb up there.'

That strand still rises and falls above his bookshelves.

All your precious ruddy books, she thinks. 'I suppose you'll be taking them to South Africa?'

'Yes.'

The work she'll have to do. Getting rid of stuff. Thanks to you! Her gaze scorches round. 'You need a haircut. And another thing: your eyebrows need trimming again.'

He flushes.

Freddie May! *He* trimmed them! I'd been offering for ten years, but no! 'Well! Would you like me to do it?'

'No. To be quite frank, I'm not sure I trust you with a pair of scissors at the moment.'

'Oh!' She tries to laugh the sob off. 'I wouldn't do anything really.'

'Well, I'd rather the dress gets it than me.'

'Don't be silly!' She wipes her eyes. 'So the announcement's this week. Do we know who it is yet?'

'Yes. Unofficially. It's Rupert Anderson.'

'Oh! Rupert and Cordelia. Well, they're lovely people. They'll be very good,' she wails. 'Oh dear.'

'Come here.' He takes her in his arms. 'My poor old Suze.' He rocks her, rests his cheek on the top of her head. 'You could always send the dress to Cordelia.'

She wants to thump him, but her arms are trapped. 'She's not my size! She's actually quite *fat*!'

'Have you decided about South Africa? Please come. I'll be lonely without you. And the girls won't understand if you stay here. Nobody will.'

'Then why don't you *explain* to everyone? Get yourself a boyfriend if you're so lonely!' She can't stop these dreadful things bursting out! 'Tell them you're gay all of a sudden. They'll understand that!'

'I'm married to you. I can't get a boyfriend any more than I could keep a mistress.'

'What if I divorced you?'

There's a long silence.

'Is that what you want?'

'I don't know what I want!' She weeps into his shirt.

'Then why not come with me to South Africa? At least to start with? See how it goes?'

'No. Oh, oh, all *right*.'

'Truly? You will?' He tries to check her face to see if she means it, but she won't oblige. 'Ah, they'll be so pleased. They love Mama Bishop.' He hugs her tight.

'I'm sorry I was mean just now. I know you can't help being . . . gay,' she tells his shirt. 'But even so, Paul, I'm sorry, but part of me can't help feeling that you've behaved like a complete *shit*.'

(You must forgive her: she's very new to swearing. She pronounces it in italics.)

She feels him quiver with laughter. It infects her. They laugh till they cry.

In the end she gasps, 'Oh dear! Would you like a cup of tea?'

'Yes, please,' he whimpers. 'Shall I make it?'

'That would be lovely. There's chocolate tiffin in the green spotty tin.'

'Um, I don't know how to tell you this, Suze, but I really don't have a sweet tooth.'

'What?' She pulls away, astounded. 'But I only make all that stuff for you!'

'I know you do.'

'All these years! Why didn't you say something?'

'Well, you kept on baking things, and I didn't want to hurt your feelings.'

'Oh dear!' They leave the study. 'Cheese straws? I could make you—'

'No! Suze, look, you don't have to do anything for me. Just— Just love me. If you still can?'

'Of course I can,' she sobs. 'Oh, must we tell the girls tonight?'

'You know we must, darling. Before the press release.'

'Let's not say you're . . . gay. Can we not say that? Oh, is that cowardly?'

'I don't think we need to tell anyone that yet.'

They go down the grand palace stairs, holding on to one another like strangers who have survived a shipwreck.

The press release is prepared. It is timed to coincide with the announcement at York, to be eclipsed by it. With luck it will tidy up that lingering question mark about the bishop of Lindchester. Yes, what was all that about? Oh, I see – he's off to South Africa to head up a new theological college. The press release will talk of a strong sense of calling, Paul's historic links with that region, a desire to serve where the need is great. Good-hearted folk will conclude that Paul has humbly renounced flight path A to church glory, and they will respect him for it. Others will think there's something fishy going on. If they dare, they will pump the dean, the archdeacon, the suffragan, the bishop's chaplain, anyone, for information. In far-off London Town Roderick Fallon will curl his lip. Strong sense of calling? Pah! But it looks like this is one scoop that got away. He will just have to vent his spleen by viciously contesting that parking ticket he got on Lindchester Cathedral Close.

Out of professional courtesy, the bishop informs his senior staff a few days before the press release. He receives their congratulations and good wishes. Giles promises to scramble together a cracking farewell service, with all the choral bells and whistles. (Argh! when, though? When? Advent is almost upon them! The cathedral diary is already a nightmare!) The senior staff will all sing from the same hymn-sheet when the pumpers come to pump them. In private the pumpees may scratch their heads and turn the hymn-sheet over and over to see if they've missed some crucial explanation tucked away in a footnote. But in public they will sing in sweet unison.

The burden of running the diocese for the next year will descend upon the shoulders of our kind and gracious friend the bishop of Barcup. Does Bob Hooty not deserve to be taken into Paul's confidence?

It would never occur to him to think that. And Marion, the dean – surely Paul owes it to her to be a little more candid? How can he carry on pretending? Isn't this hypocrisy? And what about the gay clergy in his diocese? What about Father Dominic? In fact, what about gay people the world over – he's betraying them! Doesn't he have some sort of responsibility to out himself, tell the truth, recant his earlier homophobia, and stand alongside the outcast? Come along, bishop, has that hilltop epiphany faded so fast?

Ah, you think Paul hasn't been asking himself all these questions? Of course he has. These and many others. Yes, the Transfiguration on the mountain! But the exodus passes through Gethsemane and Golgotha all the same. Questions, anguished questions, but no answers. So he remains silent. Having kept the secret from himself for forty-odd years, keeping it from his daughters and close colleagues isn't hard.

He regrets those two words he blurted out to his chaplain. 'I'm gay.' Isn't that too simplistic? Do four days of homosexual activity make you gay? Why? Why don't forty years of heterosexual activity make you straight? Who's to say his bedrock is gay, with a thin straight topsoil, rather than the other way round? True, he does find men attractive; but in his time he has found women not unattractive, too. Hasn't he? Until all this, was his marriage not committed, tender, genuine? Ought he not rather describe himself as bisexual?

The truth is, he's probably nothing at all. He's asexual. He's been a cold fish all his life.

Cold? Cold? When he burns like this? He *burns* for men, past all reason! Of course he's gay!

> Perjured, murd'rous, bloody, full of blame,
> Savage, extreme, rude, cruel, not to trust.

Except, no. No no no, not true. It's not *men*, it's one man. Just one.

> My love is as a fever, longing still
> For that which longer nurseth the disease ...

Ah, he's *ill* with Freddie May: demented, queer in his head, in his bones and marrow! But he cannot see that this excuses him from his marriage vows.

Even if he could excuse himself, there's no future here. It would be a suicide pact, not a relationship. All accelerator, no brake. Crash and burn. He knows this. But if Freddie walked in now and smiled that smile, he'd probably toss him the keys anyway. O wretched man that I am! Who shall deliver me from this body of death? Please. Please let this pass. It will pass. It must. He's going to a place where this self-absorbed agonizing will look like a luxury. He will cast it off like a cashmere smoking jacket, and take the form of a servant. He looks again, and again, and yet again to Jesus, the author and finisher of his faith, correcting his course every moment by that unwavering North. It will pass.

Meanwhile, Martin obediently takes his soul into the carpenter's workshop every day and gives it another whirl on the lathe of intercession. Little by little it is becoming clear to him that he has probably not behaved entirely well. That safeguarding business? Sawdust flies. Yes, but. I mean. Oh, come on! He catalogues Freddie's manifold sins and wickedness. And gets John 21.22b in reply: 'What is that to you? Follow me.'

'So, has the bishop been bumming the lovely Mr May all this time?' asks Gene. 'That's the real question.'

'No, Gene, that's not the real question.'

'Well, it's *a* question.'

'No, it's idle gossip,' says the dean. 'The real question, regardless of what may or may not have happened, is: how can we help the Hendersons to leave well?'

'Yes, of course that's the real question. And we'll do everything we can to help them. But I'm still slightly interested in the idle gossip,' says Gene. 'Aren't you, deanissima? Slightly?'

The dean sighs. 'If some very dear people are now able to stop living a lie, then in the end that will be a good thing. That's the only part that interests me in all this.'

Gene comes close and studies her grey eyes. He sees they have tears in them. 'You are a good woman. And I am a worm and no man. I'll go and find them a nice Sauternes.'

'That would be very kind.'

'My pleasure.' He inclines his head. 'Am I allowed to sympathize with Paul? Hypothetically, you understand. Because it must have been hell. Hypothetical hell. Mr joy-of-man's-desiring May oozes availability from every pore. Heavens to Betsy, I'd bum him myself, if I were even the *tiniest* bit gay.' He frowns. 'Which, oddly, I am not.'

'I realize that, darling. You're just ridiculously camp. It must be very confusing for you.'

'Well, Miss Bennet, there certainly was some great mismanagement in the education of those two young men.' Gene does a pirouette on his way to the cellar. 'One has got all the gayness, and the other all the appearance of it. An exquisite 1989 Barsac coming up. Oh, go on then, two. I'm feeling frivolous.'

Bonfire Night. Father Dominic's party is a riot. Sixty people turn up and eat hot dogs and cinder toffee, and watch Dominic's feeble display of jammed Catherine wheels and widdling sprinkles called Golden Fleece, but which might better be named 'Was that *it*?' He has inflicted a whole boxful of premature ejaculations on his parishioners! What must they think of him? I can tell you, reader: they love him to bits. It was a good old-fashioned bonfire party like they remember from childhood. And they have had a good nose round the downstairs of the vicarage into the bargain.

When they've finally gone, he gets out his squeegee mop and cleans the muddy footprints from his kitchen floor. Janey didn't turn up. He checks his phone. No text. Not like her. He rings and leaves a message.

Jane is standing in the dark at her bedroom window watching the fireworks. Just like she used to when Danny was small. Ooooh! Aaah! Her phone vibrates. She checks, but doesn't answer. Wrong man. He's not going to call. Ever. Which is why Jane has decided to spend Christmas in New Zealand.

She watches the last rocket zip across the sky and die in flowers of sparks. Ticket booked. She'll apply for jobs when she's over there.

It's finished.

Chapter 45

Giles the precentor makes the first coffee of the day. 'And next, the Dorian Singers,' murmurs Radio 3. Oh, God. More Victorian schmaltz. Why do you persist in inflicting this maudlin tosh on us, Jacksie? Get back to Lassus and Palestrina, from whence you came!

> When peace like a river, attendeth my way,
> When sorrows like sea billows roll;
> Whatever my lot, Thou hast taught me to know,
> It is well, it is well, with my soul.

Giles blows his nose. Damn. He can hear that the great Mr Dorian isn't even being ironic for once. No smart-arse harmonies subverting the text, no camping it up.

It is well, it is well, with my soul.

Well, Lord knows, enough sea billows have rolled over Andrew Jacks in his time. There have been points, frankly, when Giles was braced not to see him again this side of glory. Great Scott, man! Do you have the liver of Dorian Gray? No, this isn't cheap happy-clappy grace he's singing about here. Giles blows his nose again like the trump of the angel. Suddenly he decides: we must have this at Paul's farewell service. He gets out his phone. A voice drawls: '*C'est moi*. Leave a short and coherent message after the tone.'

'I'll give you short and coherent, you insufferable old queen. Listen, can I have the music for "It is Well with My Soul"? Just heard it on the radio and you made me cry. Bastard. Anyway, hope it is well with you. *Ciao bello*.'

Typhoon Haiyan rolls in across the Philippines. What do we know of storms and sea billows? The cloud factory in Cardingforth toils on. Our high streets fill with Yuletide luxuries and tat. Treat yourself, spoil yourself. Get one free. Why not? A rising tide lifts all boats! All boats? Yes, and houses and trees and villages, towns, lives – all lifted by the rising tide of global prosperity and swept away. And while we Keep Calm and Carry On Shopping it rains on John O'Groat's house – low-lying, poor, powerless, far across the sea.

It is not really well with Susanna's soul right now. But it is slightly better than it was. She has gone at last to talk to a counsellor. You might wonder why she didn't do so before this – the offer was there – but that would be to admit there was a problem. It would be like getting a cleaner in because you weren't coping with all the dusting and tidying, and Susanna has never done that, not even when she had four little girls under the age of six running her ragged. Or like bursting into tears and admitting the ironing pile is now as big as Mount Everest and even if she irons till her dying day she will never get on top of it, she must have help.

I must have help! I can longer make everything perfect. The York announcement is this week. My husband does not have a sweet tooth. I can't bake the problem away, I can't tidy it up, straighten it, or sing to it and cuddle it, lift those stains, or make scatter cushions and throws to disguise the fact that I have failed, and I cannot make everything lovely again.

The counsellor listens, a tender sounding board, now and then bouncing back something Susanna has just said. Failed? Perfect? Lovely? The counsellor has one question: what is Susanna afraid will happen if she does not make everything lovely and perfect again?

Susanna is not ready to answer that yet. Because all she has is a wrong answer. Susanna needs to give the right answer. She gets in her car and sets off for home. The wrong answer is: she's afraid everyone will find out. Everyone will know that the perfect palace was never perfect, the perfect marriage was a sham all along. They will point and laugh. They will think she did it on purpose. She will get into trouble. She will get told off!

That's the worst thing! By now Susanna is wailing as she drives. Getting told off! When all the time you were trying your very hardest to be good, leaving nothing undone, no corner undusted, trying to anticipate every possible accusation and head it off! And still getting told off! Getting crushed and humiliated and having your light snuffed out. Oh, how silly is that! When people are dying in typhoons, to be scared of getting told off! Why would God, why would anyone have any patience with her?

When she gets home Paul is out, thank goodness. But what is this on the kitchen table, propped up against a vase of pink roses? A letter! He's leaving her! He's telling her off! She's in trouble; oh, please don't let it be anything horrid. She makes herself open it.

It is a list of a hundred and one things he loves about her. In his beloved handwriting.

The one-hundred-and-first thing is this: *I am a better person, after nearly forty years with you, than I could ever have been without you.*

It's official. The next archbishop of York is the current bishop of Barchester, the Rt Revd Rupert Anderson. There's a lovely photo of him and his wife on the Church of England website. You will see that Susanna was wrong. Cordelia is not fat. She's an M&S size 14. Which is not fat.

I hope you also noticed the announcement about the bishop of Lindchester? That's right: he's off to South Africa in January to help set up the new Anglican theological college. He has a strong sense of calling to this challenging and exciting post. His wife Susanna goes with him, and they are both looking forward immensely to this new stage of their ministry.

The archdeacon and the diocesan communications officer are on high alert all day. But it looks like all's quiet on the Western Front. Fallon hasn't crawled out of the woodwork, thank the Lord. Yep, good to avoid washing *that* little load of church laundry in public. Problem is, by Friday evening Matt feels like he's been drinking the dirty water from the C of E washtub. Never been a big fan of cover-ups. But it was the right thing – or the least worst – on this occasion, if only to protect young tarty-pants. Poor kid is barely twenty-three! Tabloids would be wetting themselves: drop-dead good looks combined with criminal record, drugs, escort work. Not forgetting the – God help us! – 'film career'. Nope, open that can of worms and you'd probably put the kibosh on Mr May ever straightening up and flying right.

So, is it well with the archdeacon's soul as he drives home? Yes, deep down.

That said, things are pretty grim in the love department, to be honest. You've got to assume the Lord knows what he's doing; but being a fixer himself, Matt gets frustrated when other people don't crack on and sort stuff out. Gets the urge to tell God it's not rocket science. Come on, we're crazy about each other! How hard can it be?

Answer (apparently): it's a total mare.

Paris? Daft idea. Does he really think Dr R would drop everything and come away for a non-dirty weekend? The combined lure of the

Eiffel Tower and his platonic company just isn't going to cut it. Plus there's the real risk he won't stay platonic longer than, say, thirty seconds. In which case, why faff around with Eurostar, why not go straight up to the Fergus Abernathy building, shoulder-barge her office door right now, do his seventeen rude things?

And then resign, with immediate effect.

Nope. Still not a goer. He keeps trying that possibility on for size and it's just not right. He's a round peg in a round hole in this ordained ministry malarkey.

And he respects her views. Not fair to pressure her, when he isn't prepared to shift ground himself. He'll pay her the compliment of taking her seriously. Not let himself bombard her with red roses. Or even send a plaintive little text: 'Remind me again why you're so dead set against marriage?'

'My mum says to say is it OK if I ask you about the Second World Wa-a-ar.'

'And are you remotely interested in the Second World Wa-a-ar?'

'No. But we've got ho-o-omework. We have to ask people about the Second World Wa-a-ar.'

'Excuse me?' Jane put her hands on her hips. 'Listen, Missy Muldoon, I can remember my son Danny doing this topic. You're supposed to ask your *grandparents* about their memories of the war! I'm not that old, thank you very much.'

'Yeah, but they live in Hemel Hempstead and Brighton and I don't know any other old people round here, do I, so how am I meant to do my stupid homework? Plus you said you're a history lecturer.'

In the nick of time Jane remembered she was a grown-up and ought to set a good example. 'Oh, all right. Come in.'

They went through to the kitchen. Leah held her nose.

'Now what?'

'Your house stinks.'

'Yeah? I'll tell you why. Because I was cooking coley last night. Know what that is?'

The girl shook her head.

'Fish. Cheap fish. They ate coley in the war because it was cheaper than cod or haddock. So what else did they eat?'

The girl shrugged. 'Who cares?'

'They ate meat three times a day. Sprinkled with sugar from a golden spoon. With a side order of sweets and tropical fruit.'

'No, they didn't.'

'Prove it.'

'There was rationing, durr-brain.'

Jane sneered. 'Sez you.' The good example thing was going nicely. 'Would you like a drink? Orange juice? Flat cola? A flagon of mead?'

'Has the orange got bits in?'

'No.'

'OK, orange.' Eye roll. 'Pleeeeeease. I suppose your dad fought in the war.'

'You suppose wrong.' She handed her a glass of juice. 'My dad was born in 1937. Do the maths. My granddad didn't fight, and nor did my great-uncles, because they were all coal miners and shipbuilders. "Reserved Occupations". Google it. Biscuit?'

'What sort?'

'Digestive.'

'Meh. Got any chocolate ones?'

'Actually, these were chocolate digestives, only I sucked the chocolate off. Want one?'

'You think you're funny and you're so not.'

'Wow! That's spooky! Danny always told me that as well.'

'Is that him there?'

Jane swivelled round and looked at the picture on the fridge. 'Yep, that handsome devil is my son. What do you think?'

'He's weird. Why's his *face* tattooed?'

'*Moko*. Traditional Maori tattoos. His dad's part-Maori. But it's not real, he just Photoshopped it to wind me up.'

'Why's he pulling that face?'

'It's a Maori warrior thing. Meant to be scary.'

'Well, it looks stupid.'

'Hah! I wouldn't tell that to the All Blacks.'

'You're not allowed to say that. It's racialist.'

'Since when? The All Blacks are the New Zealand rugby team. You into rugby? You're not?' Jane shook her head in sorrow. 'I understand. Girls these days! It's all My Sparkly Little Pony, and baking princess kitten cupcakes in your tiara and ballet pumps, isn't it? And boyfriends. Have you got a boyfriend?'

Leah poked her fingers down her throat.

'Attagirl!'

An hour later, Jane watched her sprint home along Sunningdale Drive. Not a great deal better informed about the Second World Wa-a-ar, but she could at least perform a creditable haka now. My work here is done, thought Jane.

She shut the door and went back into her fishy kitchen and stared at Danny's face on the fridge. The picture wavered. Silly mare. Coming to see you soon, baby boy. Just wish I could invite that sweet man along and introduce the two of you. Reckon you'd get on.

Could I invite him?

Hello, Matt, would you like to drop everything, compromise your reputation and come all the way round the world with me – at the most hideously expensive time of year – and get nothing out of it at all, because I'm not prepared to change my mind?

Or was she? She tried the idea on. Aargh! It felt like a Lady Di blouse with a piecrust collar, three sizes too small.

I've not come all this way – through all this, on my own! – in order to become someone's wife. Not interested.

And I'll tell you what: you can fuck your equal marriage campaign and try offering me equal civil partnership. Then we might be talking.

Over in Martonbury, the bishop of Barcup's wife is thinking about Jane, though she doesn't know it. She's thinking about whoever it was that Voldemort was trying to email so passionately that time. Janet Hooty is a bit of a fixer herself, too. So she has no qualms. Sort it out, please, she instructs the Almighty.

Chapter 46

Yes, but what is it, exactly? I'm glad you asked that question.

'The General Synod comprises the Convocations of Canterbury and York, joined together in a House of Bishops and a House of Clergy, to which is added a House of Laity. It meets in February in London and in July in York, and occasionally in November in London.'

This week sees one of those November occasions. You remember the storm in a tea urn last year, when the House of Laity dealt one from the bottom of the pack, and voted down the proposed legislation on women bishops? Well, Synod is back again to have another crack at it.

This will be Bishop Paul Henderson's last General Synod. A hasty email was circulated among his senior staff requesting information for the archbishop's farewell speech. 'Key points and amusing or telling anecdotes' – that's what the Most Revd Dr Michael Palgrove was seeking. We trust that such material was forthcoming and the speech goes swimmingly.

Invitations have gone out across the diocese to Bishop Paul's farewell service. It will be in mid-December, which is – shriek! – less than four weeks away! This Sunday is Christ the King (proofread carefully, O typers of pew sheets: we are not here to celebrate 'Chris the King'). In old money this is Stir Up Sunday, the Sunday next before Advent, named after the Prayer Book collect, 'Stir up, we beseech thee, O Lord, the wills of thy faithful people; that they, plenteously bringing forth the fruit of good works, may of thee be plenteously rewarded; through Jesus Christ our Lord. Amen.' It is, of course, the day on which good Anglicans traditionally order their luxury Christmas puddings from Fortnum and Mason.

Giles the precentor is up to his ears in Advent and Christmas music lists and rotas of clergy to cover the hundred and one carol services and concerts that the cathedral will host during this season. The next big thing on his horizon is the Advent Sunday 'Darkness into Light' service (again, proofread carefully: this is not a Procession with Carlos), which will be attended by up to 800 people. Such occasions offer delicious scope for liturgical control freaks to exercise their special skill set. Yesterday Giles found time to send a draft order of service to the bishop and catch a brief conversation with him, in which he enquired, very courteously, whether there was anything Paul would like to include.

'That's kind. Thank you for asking,' said Paul. 'I should very much like to sing "Be thou my vision". You know, to the modern lively setting of Slane? With Celtic drums. In four/four.'

'Well, father,' replied the precentor, very, *very* courteously, 'it is, of course, your farewell service, but since it will be Advent, I wonder whether we might need to explore alternatives?'*

'Ah, it will be Advent, will it? I was forgetting that.'

The precentor stared at him for a long moment. 'You're winding me up, aren't you?'

'I am,' agreed the bishop with a smile. 'No, the order of service looks wonderful. Thank you, Giles, for all your hard work at such short notice.'

As he walked back to his house – pausing to peer in the skip outside the school to see if it contained anything combustible – the precentor reflected that if he'd seen more of that playful side of Paul over the last seven years, he might have been able to love him a little better.

Christmas cards and Advent calendars are now on sale in the cathedral bookshop, along with pious baubles and meaningful chocolate. You will also find posh floral paper napkins, Celtic jewellery, fudge, lavender bags and the complete works of Tom Wright. The Cathedrals Measure of 1999 stipulates that all cathedral shops must stock these items. Why not get your charity Christmas cards there, too? The Friends of Lindchester Cathedral have produced a charming set of snowy views of the cathedral, taken by a local photographer. It includes an 'aw, bless!' shot of the snow choristers crocodiling into the cathedral. The one of the snow bishop on the cathedral rooftop was ruled out by the Friends of Lindchester Cathedral Christmas card consultation subcommittee. I fear the notion is

* Cathedral-speak for 'Fuck off!'

widespread that bishops have their sense of humour cauterized at consecration.

Please be patient with the nice assistants in the cathedral shop. You will encounter them, pecking at the till as though playing some terrifying retail version of Russian roulette that might trigger an explosion at any moment. These good folk are volunteers of retirement age, gamely battling with modern technology. Bite your tongue as they scan the bar codes with in-fin-ite care. 'Oh dear, oh dear, what am I doing wrong? It doesn't seem to be working!' They will proceed to check the scanner by turning it towards their face, momentarily blinding themselves with a scribble of red light. Don't smirk. My friend, you too will be old one day, and baffled by technology. And ask yourself: is your time really so precious that you cannot afford to spend five companionable minutes while someone attempts to Sellotape your Lindchester Cathedral glass paperweight into a piece of bubble wrap that is nearly, but not quite, big enough for the job? Get over yourself! Listen to the nice music playing. It's Lindchester Cathedral Choir's latest CD. Why not buy a copy? (Oh, fair enough, you don't want to trigger the whole agonizing routine all over again.) Order it online. It's rather good.

Across the diocese of Lindchester yellow leaves (or none, or few) are all that remain on most of the trees now. Silver birches still offer a splash of gold. Beeches glow russet. The leaves may have gone from the rowans, but the berries blaze red. Here and there the tips of the Lombardy poplars sport foliage, like paintbrushes dipped in phthalo or viridian green. Sunshine comes and goes between the rain clouds, and yes, there are rainbows. There is sprung up a light for the righteous, if they know where to look for it.

And light, light at the end of the long tunnel of sex inequality! Synod takes the next step towards women bishops. Proposals voted through 378 to eight, with twenty-five abstentions. Maybe next year the legislation will be passed? And which will be the lucky diocese to appoint the first ever woman bishop in England? Quickly, who's due to retire at exactly the right moment? Heads are scratched in dioceses that already have vacancies. Are they out of the running, or can they word the diocesan Statement of Need judiciously? The new bishop must be a year off retirement and/or have a dicky ticker?

We are far on in the night. Day is at hand. The Christmas lights are up in Lindchester and Lindford. Schmaltz oozes from speakers in high street shops. 'I wish it could be Christmas every da-a-a-ay.'

(Words you are unlikely to hear cathedral clergy singing.) Go and search diligently, and you may yet find an Advent calendar 'with a religious theme'. But it's mostly Christmas Countdown calendars these days, which, by the time of our Lord's Nativity, will be ransacked of their chocolate and cast aside. Do today's children know the thrill of opening the big window on Christmas Eve? Or the furious calculating that goes on in families of three children, to work out whether you need to go first, second or third, in order to bag the 24th?

Synod has completed its business. The Most Revd Dr Michael Palgrove has made his speech thanking those bishops who are retiring. There were no amusing or telling anecdotes about Paul Henderson. This is not because nothing amusing or telling occurred during his time at Lindchester. It is more that the person best placed to supply such anecdotes had not found it funny that time Paul substituted the parish for the candidate's name and said 'Confirm, O Lord, your servant Little Slapton, with your Holy Spirit.' Or put his mitre on backwards so that the lappets dangled in front of his face. No, Martin tended to treat such incidents as undermining his bishop's dignity, and best forgotten.

How is Martin faring? Is he still praying for Freddie May? He is! He began by firing vindictive little prayer arrows, only to find that they all rebounded. His poor conscience is now pin-cushioned like St Sebastian! He writhes and squirms, skewered upon the memory of that email he sent to the cathedral safeguarding officer. He's peppered by his own bullet points! Ah, deep down he knew at the time it was fuelled by spite and rage, though he would have died before admitting it. And then there was the last time he saw Freddie, and turned him away when he was in such distress! Oh, the appalling damage he almost did there, the scandal he so nearly unleashed!

Every Eucharist is a torment. Jesus said, 'Before you offer your gift, go and be reconciled.' As sisters and brothers in God's family, we come together to ask our Father for forgiveness . . .

Go and be reconciled, Martin. Go and be reconciled to your brother. Go. Go! But what's he meant to do? Email him? Phone him up? Drive to Barchester and find him? Oh, I can't, I just can't! He'll spit in my face, he'll . . . he'll taunt me! Ask something else of me, Lord!

Oh, Martin. What you have failed to realize is that Freddie is actually about as vindictive as a big bag of marshmallows. Go and find him, for goodness sake! I bet you will barely manage to blurt out the first sentence of your rehearsed apology before he falls on your neck and weeps for your misery. No? Very well. Then I fear you must wallow in that misery for a little longer.

I'm afraid that Matt and Janey are still wallowing too. Both of them keep nearly texting the other ('Come with me to Paris!' 'Come with me to New Zealand!'), then deciding it wouldn't be fair. Jane no longer parks on the archdeacon's drive, preferring to trawl the streets of Lindford for free spots, and relieving her feelings by getting into slanging matches with local residents. She will be taking strike action next week, with her fellow union members. I really would not want to cross any picket line with Dr R on it right now.

The music lists are done. The first orders of service have been printed. The precentor has spotted a missing apostrophe on page three of the Advent Carols booklet. But he bravely lets it go. Well done, Giles. He has, however, taken his eye off the ball slightly with regard to Paul's farewell service, and so far forgotten himself as to delegate partial control to the director of music. The result is this: Timothy has taken a look at Mr Dorian's four-part harmony score of 'It is Well with My Soul' and thought how lovely and fitting it would be to get Mr May back to sing the tenor part. He knows how fond the Hendersons are of Freddie.

DECEMBER

Chapter 47

The bishop of Lindchester wakes. All is silent, but for the wind mourning in the ruined cedar. Then the cathedral clock chimes three. Paul remembers when they arrived in the Close, how he heard every blessed quarter that first night. Impossible to believe that he would ever grow accustomed to it! Yet before long he slept through, and when he did wake, found the chimes reassuring, like a patient nightwatchman calling the hours. Three o'clock and all is well.

Is all well? No.

A fox barks. Susanna sighs in her sleep. He reaches out and strokes her hair. But it will be well. It is almost Advent, the season of Hope. For now is our salvation nearer than when we first believed. He will miss the chimes when he wakes unmoored, untethered, in a strange African night. Remember not the former things, nor consider the things of old. Behold, I am doing a new thing. Does he perceive it? Nearly. Sometimes he glimpses it in the distance. This new thing that lies on the far side of the deep waters, of this hell-fire he is having to walk through.

> Past three o'clock,
> And a cold frosty morning!
> Past three o'clock;
> Good morrow, masters all!

Freddie. Singing that carol on the way back from last year's Midnight. His voice carrying clear across the Close. Hours go by now in which Paul does not have to fend off the thought of him. The hours will become whole mornings, afternoons, evenings. And then days, weeks. How badly I treated you, sweet boy. Forgive, forgive me. If I had hated you, I could not have behaved worse. Because I hate that part of myself? Hated? Still hate?

Born is a baby,
Gentle as may be,
Son of the eternal
Father supernal.

What *possessed* me? You're younger than my youngest daughter! I could have held you as a baby! Baptized you. Paced the room, rocked you to sleep on my chest. Suddenly Paul thinks: I could have held the Christ-child, too. Rocked the Supernal to sleep, cradled his tender head to my heartbeat. Hush, hush. Daddy's here. All is well. Sleep, my darling. Paul could weep now for that babe, knowing what lay ahead of it: the hatred, the cross, the grave. How strange and giddying the incarnation is – to console the Creator!

Ah, but he would like to see him just once more before he leaves. To say goodbye properly. Apologize, make amends. But no. He is consulting his own need yet again, not Freddie's. Still wanting to offload this vast slurry-tank of remorse. Does Freddie waste a moment's thought on him now? Paul doubts it. 'Dude, you're a sweet guy, but lighten up.'

Yes, why don't you lighten up, dude? It's that curse of Evangelical egocentricity again, with its furtive delusions of grandeur: 'There is therefore now no condemnation!' (Footnote: except for me!) What a huge portentous meal he makes of his sinfulness. As though it were a surprise and a shock to the Almighty. As though Paul Henderson alone required some extra atoning provision.

Return, O my soul, to your rest; for the Lord has dealt bountifully with you.

Hush, hush, my darling. All is well. For a moment it is as if Paul can feel the babe in his arms, its weight on his chest. He could almost lay his cheek on the tiny pulsing skull. All the babes he has ever cradled. His own soul, cradled. And underneath are the everlasting arms.

The clock chimes again. Past three o'clock. Paul, strangely consoled, drifts back to sleep.

But what of poor Janey and the archdeacon? Is all well with them? Not yet, I'm afraid. The bishop of Barcup's wife – who saw Matt looking pretty woebegone at a licensing last week – rattles off another prayer. A prayer for that unknown gal (she assumes it's a gal) who, for whatever reason, is evidently giving Voldemort a hard time.

The gal has just got back from a day at Poundstretcher University. She scoops up the post from her doormat. Ha, the first Christmas card of the year! Aunty Brenda wins again. Bills, pizza flyers. And something from the diocese of Lindchester. Her heart does a barrel roll. She rips the envelope open. Not from him. OK, deep breath, wasn't really expecting it to be.

It's an invitation to Bishop Paul's farewell service. And to farewell mulled wine and mince pies in the palace afterwards. Shit. Can't *not* go to this, can she? But there will be no avoiding Matt. He'll be poncing down the aisle in solemn procession, won't he, and he's bound to be at the bash afterwards. Oh God. Can she beg off? Invent a prior engagement? The thought of Susanna's wounded face makes this impossible. Jane knows she has always been more special to Susanna than she deserves, more cherished, more valued as an old friend. God alone knows what's been going on in the Close in recent months – the York fiasco, the sudden announcement about South Africa. Jane, reading between unwritten lines, could hazard a guess that the lovely Frederick is not wholly unconnected with the mystery.

Argh. What a crap friend she's been to the Hendersons. Not even to get in touch, send flowers, anything. After all their years of patient, forgiving support! No, you're going to that service, you evil cow, so let's hear no more whingeing on the subject. She fires up her cranky old computer and RSVPs. Her thoughts stray to what she might wear. Buy a new frock? Red? She yanks them savagely back.

The following morning Penelope updates the list of acceptances to the Hendersons' farewell. She copies it to the archdeacon, because he has asked to be kept in the loop. The archdeacon is in a safeguarding meeting. He really oughtn't to check his emails in meetings.

Whoa! Dr R will be there! Matt shifted in his chair. Rubbed a hand over his bald head. Blushed scarlet.

'Forgive me, Matt,' said Helene, 'but I'm not sure I have your full attention.'

'Ah um. Yep. Nope. Sorry. Wandered off for a moment there. You were saying?'

When the meeting was finally over, Matt retreated to his office with a mug of coffee and tried to deal with the fact that he was going to be in the same room as his lady in a couple of weeks. Cool your jets. Plenty of time to get your act together, plan how to play this. Corner her and get a quiet word? Leave it to her to make the first move? Drop her an email in advance?

A tap at the door. Helene. Oh Lord. He got the choke chain on his temper.

'Helene! Come in, park yourself.'

She sat. 'Matt, I couldn't help noting your demeanour in our meeting back there.'

He raised his hands. 'You got me. Bad habit of mine, checking emails in meetings. Sorry.'

'I think this calls for some ——.'

Très what? French now? Latest HR jargon? But Helene had an open biscuit tin and was offering him something.

'Would you like some ——?' she repeated.

'Oh! Tray bake! Um, well, cheers.' He took a piece.

'Is everything all right, Matt? Only in recent weeks you've seemed . . . not quite yourself.'

He sat back, a bit stunned. She came in peace! Tray bake, not humble pie! 'Yep, that's possible. I've been up to my axles in the whole . . . Paul's move. And now there's the upcoming vacancy, obviously. Plus an employment tribunal in the New Year. So it's all been a bit of a mare, to be honest.'

'Matt, as you know, I'm new to the Church, as an organization. But as I understand it, the bishop is your line manager?'

'He is.'

'And can you clarify for me: what support structures are there in place for you, if that relationship becomes complicated? Or indeed, if the bishop retires and there's a vacancy? Who looks after you, Matt? Who do you turn to?'

'Well, colleagues on the senior staff team. And I have a spiritual director, obviously. So, yes, that's about it.' Nobody, he thought. At the end of the day, when I get home, there's nobody. Well, what do you know – he could feel tears pricking in his eyes. She'd hit a nerve there, obviously.

'I know you and I got off on the wrong foot, Matt,' said Helene. 'In that I find your sense of humour occasionally marginalizing. But I'm concerned for you.'

'Well, thanks. Much appreciated.' He finished his pecan tray bake. 'Mmm, this is a bit good. Did you make it?'

'Yes.' She smiled. 'Have another piece?'

He smiled back. Quite a nice-looking lady when she smiled. Nice dark eyes. He was a sucker for dark eyes. He took a second slice.

'You're entitled to support if you're experiencing stress in the workplace.'

'No no. Goes with the territory. It's more . . . Ah. Look. Actually, spot of old-fashioned girl trouble, basically. So . . .'

'Tell me about it.'

There was a pause. 'You want me to tell you about it?'

'No, Matt. It's a figure of speech.'

Another pause. 'Oh! OK, gotcha.' He ran a quick scan to check how big a nob he'd been over the last six months. 'Well, maybe we should go out for a cheeky pint some time and compare girl troubles?'

'I may take you up on that, Matt.' She got to her feet. 'But in the meantime, if there's anything I can do?'

'Well, you could leave that tin behind.'

'Sorry, Matt.' She whisked her tray bake away. 'I'd have to do a risk assessment first.' The door closed behind her.

Head-desk.

Yep, small wonder they'd got off on the wrong foot. He probably represented everything that hacked her off: straight white male bastard, oozing smug privilege, acting like the rules don't apply to him. Serious player in an institution with a pretty poor track record on women and gays. He'd probably even tried to deploy the old charm offensive on her as well. Oh, Lord.

Plus his sense of humour was occasionally marginalizing, of course.

But anyway. Other things to think about: Pilling Report to get his head round. Looked like the old working group on human sexuality had managed to piss off both extremes of the spectrum. Which probably meant they were talking calm good sense. He sighed and cracked on with it.

December. Quickly, open the first little window! What is it? Ooh. Um. A pudding, maybe? Or a very fat robin – wait, a round robin! Ho ho ho!

Yes, my friends, those Christmas round robins have started arriving through the post. Pedants, mount your seasonal hobby-horse and remind us that this is not what 'round robin' means! Tell us, friends, O tell us of the achievements of bright and talented offspring! The foreign holidays!! How the extension is going!!!

Today is Advent Sunday. The precentor is wearing purple socks. At least this year he won't need to install a bucket in the triforium because the person singing the O Antiphons is hungover. (Yes, thanks for that, Mr May.) Giles has drafted in a nice reliable soprano from the Cathedral Chamber Choir instead.

Father Dominic arrives at the cathedral while *Wachet Auf* is playing on the organ. Why isn't he taking his own service? you ask. Why, because there is no Sunday evening service in Lindford parish church. Abolishing it was one of his predecessor's many unpopular acts. It will be resumed in the New Year, but for now, Father Dominic is secretly glad to attend an act of worship for which he has no responsibility whatsoever.

The lights go off. Silence settles. In the distance, way down at the west end, a voice:

> I look from afar: and lo, I see the power of God coming,
> and a cloud covering the whole earth.
> Go ye out to meet him and say:

And the choir responds:

> Tell us, art thou he that should come to reign over thy people Israel?

Father Dominic's eyes strain to the east, where the faint glow of the floodlights is just visible through the great rose window. In the dark he hears the voices weave in and out of one another. It is as though they are reweaving the fabric of his yearning soul.

Chapter 48

Lulu, Father Wendy's faithful old Labrador, is housebound now. At some point, a month or so ago, they had their very last totter along the banks of the Linden. To her shame, it slipped by without Father Wendy even noticing it. Like so many last moments. How we would have treasured them, if we'd only known.

Wendy sits now on the kitchen floor stroking Lulu's head. A day like any other day. That's what the end of the world is always like. Eating, drinking, marrying, giving in marriage. And the flood came and took them all away. I must decide, she thinks. I can't let her linger on any more like this. Saturday? Yes.

Saturday is Father Wendy's day off. She will ring the vet. Yes, she knows she must.

Oh, Lulu.

Lulu is too tired now to lift her head. But she cries softly for Wendy's pain.

Susanna is lightening the ship. Endless trips to the charity shop, to the municipal dump. How can they have so much stuff? What are they going to do with it all? They can't possibly transport all this to South Africa. Well, they'll just have to put it all in storage.

But why? When they retire, what will they do with all the stuff they have stored? The bolt-hole is already bursting at the seams. They don't need it, do they? Why is she hanging on to it? Because she's loved these things so much. They symbolize the home she's made. Now she's dismantling it all and putting it in the metaphorical loft, because she can't bear to let go of it completely. Isn't that what she's doing? Like the girls' soft toys. They are still there in the actual loft, in a plastic crate. Big Ted and little Ted. Panda bear. The knitted crib set from a church bazaar.

It's ludicrous. Suddenly she sees how ludicrous it is. Storage, indeed! Think of the cost of storing it all for years and years, when she's never going to need any of it again! She might as well pile it all on the lawn and set fire to it, for all the good these things will do her.

But my antique French storage jars! The grandfather clock!

Maybe one of the girls will want them?

Oh dear, oh dear. The pagoda, the plants. The garden tools. The tubs and planters. Whatever am I going to do? Something in her whispers: 'Give it away, cast it off, be free!' But she can't, she just *can't*.

One by one the little windows are opened and the chocolate is scoffed. Dean Marion has a homemade Advent calendar. It was lovingly constructed by her husband Gene. It features an innocent woodland nativity scene with furry creatures kneeling in homage among much glitter. There is no chocolate, but each little window opens upon a different aspect of Gene's naked person. The dean believes she can already guess what lies behind the big window; but she must wait, as must we all, for the 24th. Don't forget to hide the calendar when the choristers come to the deanery for their Christmas party, Mrs Dean!

Wander with me through the Cathedral Close on Wednesday night, and you will hear the strains (I use that word advisedly) of Handel's *Messiah* being rehearsed, ready for the big performance this Saturday. Timothy Gladwin, the director of music, is doing his best to coax out/rein in the talents of the Cathedral Community Choir. Bless them. Let no stout soprano fall off the stage on The Night! Let there be no rogue extra 'Ha—' from the tenor section in the closing bars of the Hallelujah Chorus! And, O Lord, O Lord! Please let the bass soloist not be totally up himself and a complete nightmare to work with this time!

And so the year draws to a close. Where has the time gone? It seems only a minute since I was wafting you on the eagle wings of Anglicanism in the twilight of 2012, over the oxbow lake towards Renfold! Let us retrace our journey now.

Yes, the Christmas lights of Renfold are up again. Blue icicles dangle from eaves, Santas clamber over rooftops once more like thieves in the night. St John's vicarage stands vacant now. Father Dominic's cassock and biretta no longer hang on the peg in the hall. However shall we manage without you, Father Dominic? But they have managed, the doughty parishioners of St John's Renfold. Never underestimate the power of lay people to manage without clergy. Or the amount of money that the diocese will save on stipends during an interregnum.

There are storms again on Thursday. High winds whip away the clouds from the Cardingforth cloud factory. The Christmas lights in Lindford wag and bob above the streets as shoppers battle bravely on. And still it rains on John O'Groat's house, far across the sea. We shut ourselves in and batten down the hatches, cuddled under blankets with a glass of wine in front of the TV, tweeting irritably, drolly, shoutily, trivially. And then we cease. We will always remember that this is where we were when we heard: his long walk to freedom is complete. RIP Nelson Mandela.

'We refused to buy Cape grapes,' said Jane.

'Yeah. And we boycotted Boerclay's Bank,' said Spider. 'Back in the days when students were radical. When did they last organize a sit-in at Poundstretcher?'

They sighed and shook their heads. They were in Peggoty's Pie and Ale Parlour in Lindford.

'Bitching about their tutors on Facepalm is about as radical as they get.'

Silence.

'Can't believe he's gone.'

'No.'

More silence.

Simeon the poet watched Jane through his blue-tinged glasses. 'Everything OK, Janey?'

'Nope.'

'Well, comfort-eat, lass. You've lost a shit-load of weight.'

'Yeah, it's the misery diet.' Jane prodded at her festive game and cranberry pie, then looked up. 'It's—'

'It's what?'

'Nothing.'

Spider turned round to see what she was looking at. 'What?'

Jane focused on him and smiled. 'So! I'm off to New Zealand on the twenty-first. See my baby boy. Get a bit of vitamin D. Watch a few whales, climb a few glaciers.'

'Hunt a few orcs. Eat some man-flesh.'

'That kind of thing.' She raised her pint. 'Nelson Mandela. May he rest in peace.'

'Mandela.' Spider chinked his glass against hers. '"You will achieve more in this world through acts of mercy than you will through acts of retribution."'

'Acts of mercy,' repeated Jane. 'More of those, please. Though retribution has much to commend it.'

He hadn't seen her. So that was it then. She managed to eat her pie. She drank another ale. Her eyes didn't stray, not once, to the booth where the archdeacon was sitting with another woman.

And now it is Saturday. Father Wendy gets up and makes her way downstairs. Today is the day. Another small end of the world. She will put poor Lulu in the car one last time, and—

But Lulu, with exquisite tact, has slipped away in the night. Father Wendy stumbles to the basket, creaks to her knees and lays a hand on the cold fur. Oh, Lulu! Good girl, well done, old girl. There, there. All done now. You made it. She closes her eyes and sobs. Oh, what will I do, what will I do without you? Then she sees, clear as a video clip, Lulu bounding ahead of her along the river bank, young again, away, off into the distance, where a tiny figure is waiting to greet her. Laura? Oh, let it be so! Wait for me? Because one day I'll be joining you, my darlings. Not long now.

A silver Aston Martin DB9 purrs on to the precentor's drive. The bass soloist gets out. He retrieves his bespoke tail suit and overnight bag from the boot, then saunters to Giles's front door. Does he look totally up himself to you? Yes, I'd say that's a fair description. But he is resolved to behave and not to be a compete nightmare to work with. Provided they've remembered his San Pellegrino water.

The bishop has been insanely busy. He is busy in the office and around the diocese; he is busy when he gets home, where he is called upon to make urgent decisions about carnival glass bowls and Lloyd Loom linen baskets. I am glad about this. Paul is too prone to bouts of lacerating introspection. He can hide from the thought of Freddie May in the exigencies of his diary and domestic decision-making. Space does not permit us to anatomize episcopal affairs. Let us content ourselves with the vague idea that handing over the reins of a busy diocese is a vexed and time-consuming business. His trusty chaplain is on hand at every turn with things to sign, lists of bullet points to action, people to thank, practicalities to redirect to the suffragan bishop of Barcup or the archdeacon.

How is Martin faring? you ask. Martin is still barbecuing himself on the brazier of conscience. He has not yet found a way to make peace with Freddie. He drafts and redrafts emails in his head. He rehearses phone conversations. He googles the route to Barchester. But he is too busy to do anything about it. Far too busy. He has a new job to look for now as well, remember. He hides from the thought of Freddie May behind the *Church Times* classifieds.

Ah, Handel's *Messiah*! If you are *au fait* with matters choral you will know to despise it. The rest of us can have a jolly good time. Our souls will travel that great narrative arc of salvation which is Jennens's libretto. The bishop and his wife, sitting on the front row with the chain gang, will hear those familiar words – 'Comfort ye, comfort ye my people' – and they will be comforted. They will get to their feet in the Hallelujah Chorus and once again be wafted to heaven's throne room. Even the snooty bass will stand, in acknowledgement of a majesty exceeding his own. 'King of kings, and Lord of lords!' Higher, higher climb the valiant voices of the Community Choir. Light winks off sequins, sweat glints on bald heads. 'For ever, and ever, hallelujah!' In that beat of silence (there is no stray 'Ha—') before the last 'Hallelujah', the world holds its breath.

There was mulled wine and mince pies at the deanery afterwards, it goes without saying. The precentor approached the bass and handed him a bottle of San Pellegrino and a glass of ice (made with mineral, not tap water).

'I'd like to thank you from the bottom of my heart for not killing anyone.'

'I am all docility these days, Giles. That said, there were some priceless tenor moments going on behind me.' The soloist scanned the throng. 'Mr May not here?'

'He's left us. Our loss is Barchester's gain. Why?'

'Well, it's not often I'm told to go fuck myself. I found it rather energizing.'

'Very happy to oblige in his absence.'

'Thoughtful.'

'Seriously, what's your interest in Freddie?'

The bass turned his arctic stare upon Giles. 'Professional. Of course.'

'Of course! But you do realize you look frighteningly like the child-catcher off *Chitty Chitty Bang Bang* in that coat?'

Mr Dorian (for it was he) left before he started drinking, or killing people, or both, and walked back across the Close to the precentor's house alone. Funnily enough, his motives in this instance were pure. He'd been praying for Freddie May on and off for over ten years. Ever since that little flamer came to his attention at a North-West Three Choirs Festival, and he saw something of himself in the brilliant and desperately unhappy child.

Chapter 49

There is no category of person upon whom we lavish more care and forward sartorial planning than an ex. Even a clandestine lover comes a poor second. New haircut, new frock, new shoes, new hosiery, accessories, perfume, a manicure – all these are needed to demonstrate unambiguously that we have not wasted a moment's thought on him since the break-up.

Jane has surveyed her wardrobe and spotted a gap. She does not own an 'I am so over you, you bastard!' dress. It is now crucial that she acquires one before the Hendersons' farewell service next week. She sits in her kitchen swearing and googling like a woman possessed.

Don't even bother raising the possibility with Jane that Matt might have been out with a work colleague. Because she saw him place a hand on the small of her back and laugh down into her upturned adoring cow face as they disappeared into their secret lover booth.

That's it! The Dress. Yes, yes, yes! It is red, it is stretchy, it will flatter an (ahem) hourglass figure! It is knee-length, it has tactful ruching over the stomach region, it plunges just enough. And – ladies of a certain age will sigh in understanding here – it has sleeves. Jane leaps up from her desk and hunts the house for a tape measure to check her new misery diet vital statistics. Not being of a dressmaking bent, all she can find is a retractable steel one (cold! shriek!). She calculates that, in terms of the frock website, she is . . . Large?! Pah. Overlooking this piece of unpardonable rudeness, she orders the dress.

Take that, Mr Archdeacon.

The precentor of Lindchester Cathedral eschews the habit of singing Christmas carols in Advent. But ever at our backs we hear bankruptcy's chariot drawing near, so he bows to the inevitable. From now till Christmas it will be two or three carol services a day. Schools, voluntary organizations, civic groups, charities, hospitals, hospices, police, fire service – they all want their own carol concert, and such a brisk revenue stream may not be sacrificed upon the altar of liturgical purity. So the verger team arranges chairs this way, that way, erects stages, dismantles them again. The flower guild spritz holly and ivy on the Advent ring. The Holy Dusters chisel spilled wax from floors. Stewards polish their badges and smiles. (You can't sit there, it's reserved. Don't forget to use the Gift Aid envelope.) Cathedral Chapter clergy take it in turns to climb up into the pulpit and say a few words of welcome and allude to Christ.

This year sees a huge regional gathering in Lindchester of Townswomen's Guilds. The Close bustles with grey-haired women in court shoes and jolly red winter coats. Some cock-up with the rota means that both the canon treasurer and the canon chancellor turn up for the concert. It is Mr Happy's first ever brush with the Cowboy Carol, can you believe it? (Pink-a-pink pang pong!) He is completely incapacitated by *fou rire* when the choir of septuagenarians gets to its feet and warbles, 'Yoi, yippee!' and vows to climb up to the saddle and ride the trail. Every time he masters his mirth, the treasurer on the opposite side of the aisle leans out from behind a floral display, catches his eye, and deliberately sets him off again. (Those of you who were there and wondering, that is why you glimpsed one canon beating another about the head with a service booklet afterwards.)

'This is my favourite moment of the church year,' said Giles. 'We are now at the farthest possible point from another performance of *Messiah*. You survived the malevolent Dorian stare, Timothy?'

'Well, I couldn't really see him, the way the staging was set up. But I could sense him there, in my peripheral vision.'

'Yet your baton never wavered!' Giles gripped the director of music's shoulders and gave him a shake. 'Stout work, my man. I'll see you get a bravery award. Everything in hand for Paul's farewell service?'

'Yes, I hope so.'

'Excellent,' said Giles.

'Freddie's confirmed he can sing, so we're—'

'*What?* You've asked Freddie May back?!' Giles suddenly recollected, strangled the explosion, tried to relaunch it as delight. 'What a *lovely* idea!'

Timothy retreated a pace. 'Um. Well, that's what I thought. To sing, "It is Well with My Soul". But if it's a problem . . . ?'

'Not *at all*!' Aaargh! 'It will be *lovely* to see him again! But warn him from me: if he rocks up here off his face, I'll have his balls for christingles.'

'He is? That's nice,' says the archdeacon. 'Sorry? No, no, I'm sure the Hendersons will be really touched. No probs. Okey-doke. Cheers, Giles.'

Holy crap, Batman. He dials tarty-pants.

'Well, hell-ooo, Daddy! How's it going?'

'You're coming to Paul's farewell.'

'Huh? O-ohh. Yeah. They asked me to sing?'

'Freddie, think for just one moment. Is this a good idea?'

'Wha-a? Listen, Timothy's like, will you come, it would be really nice, and I'm, hey, you bet? Fucksake. What am I gonna say – ooh, sorry, dude, it's *complicated*? Paul and me have *history*?'

'It didn't cross your dozy mind to say you were busy that night?'

'Yeah, no. Actually, it didn't. Know why? Coz it's not that big of a deal!'

'Not for you, maybe.'

Silence.

'What, he's still . . . ?' More silence. 'Ah nuts. Seriously?'

'Seriously. Engage brain, Freddie. How's he going to feel?'

'No-o-oo. Aw, c'mon, Matt, please don't make me bail now? I'm trying so hard not to be flaky, you know? And Timothy, he'll be all, typical Freddie May!'

'You may have to suck that one up, my friend.'

'No, yeah, it's just, I've got this new thing going? If I like commit to something, I actually do it? That make sense? Someone, ah, he kind of called me on this a while back, on the whole self-sabotage thing, and I'm, yeah. Trying to address that?'

Matt rubs his face. Oh, Lord. 'Well, that's good to hear, Freddie. I don't want to stomp all over your good intentions, but . . .'

Silence. 'Yeah. But probably I should get laryngitis?'

Why, thinks the archdeacon suddenly, is it all about Paul's feelings? What about Freddie? Who's looking out for him in all this mess? 'Actually, no, you come. We'll deal with it.'

'Seriously? Cool! Can I stay at yours?'

'Yes. Just don't crawl into my bed at 3 a.m.'

'But I get lonely!'

'Too bad. I'm pushing the chest of drawers over the door.'

'Man, you are so-o-ooo strict with me!'

'Somebody needs to be.'

'They do. They so do. How's Janey?'

'Bye, Freddie.'

Father Wendy walks along the banks of the Linden alone. She hunts for a hanky and discovers she still has poop bags in her coat pocket!

Tears roll down her cheeks. Lulu, Lulu. Oh dear. The reed heads bow and shush in the wind. On the opposite bank the big woman is out jogging again. Has she lost weight? And where's the young blond man? She's not seen him in months. Well, bless them, bless them.

Lulu is buried in the back garden. Well done, good and faithful servant. Come the spring Wendy will plant a laburnum over her. Silly word association: Labrador, laburnum. But she'll enjoy the cheerful blossom each year, the sweet scent on the breeze. A sunshine tree. That's what Laura called them. What was the Song of the Laburnum Fairy? Something something yellow flowers, hanging thick in happy showers? And then in the summer, maybe, maybe it will be right to start thinking about another dog? A rescue dog this time. Yes. Or a retired greyhound. She turns to call, 'Here, girl!'

Ah, it takes time. Father Wendy knows to be kind to herself. And to others. Being kind to others helps a bit. She starts plodding again in her floral wellies, praying for friends, family, parishioners, Virginia her curate, refugees, the debt-ridden, those close to death, women in labour, the homeless.

A kingfisher darts past – oh! And the dark December world flushes with joy.

The big Christmas tree is up, lit and duly blessed in front of the cathedral. Fairy lights twinkle in round and square and arched windows all about the Close. If you wander past the deanery this evening, you will hear the racket of sixteen overexcited choristers as they play team games (*can* versus *dec*) involving balloons. They are not as hyper as last year, much to matron's relief. June – unlike her predecessor, Miss Blatherwick – is not a member of the Freddie May fan club. Thank God he's not here instigating belching contests and luge races down the deanery stairs in bin-liners, or teaching them dirty limericks – to cite three specimen charges. So far, the naughtiest thing anyone has done is arrange his chipolata sausage and cherry tomatoes in a rude and amusing way on his plate.

Before long they will gather in the drawing room and sit on the carpet by the Christmas tree while the dean reads them a Christmas story. Welcome back to the 1950s, ladies and gentlemen. This is the cue for Gene to excuse himself and slip off upstairs to change, scooping up (oops!) the forgotten Advent calendar as he goes. Hope none of the little cherubs saw that, or he'll have dykey Dora from diocesan house safeguarding the bejasus out of him. Timely reminder – be careful to wear the right Santa outfit, not the slinky one with the saucy cut-outs. Ho ho ho! Me-rry Christmas, little boys! Look what Santa's got for *you*!

'Mrs Dean, Mrs Dean,' pipes Ollie Bowerman, 'every year Mr Dean has to go to the toilet and he misses Santa!'

The older boys snort with hilarity.

'I know, Ollie, it's a real shame. But we can tell him all about it afterwards,' says Marion. 'Now then, settle down boys. Thomas, will you stop being silly, please.'

'Sorry, Mrs Dean. But Harry Bianchi just snotted everywhere.'

'Eurgh! Gross! Eurgh! Gross!' squeal the choristers antiphonally.

'I dare say. No! Use a tissue, Harry! Oh, thank you, June. Sssh! Simmer down, boys. One cold winter night, many years ago . . .'

We will leave poor Marion trapped in a Joyce Grenfell sketch and tiptoe across the Close to the palace, where Susanna is sitting in despair on the grand staircase. The stuff. She just wants to get rid of it all. But she can't. What will Paul say? And the girls – these things are their childhood!

Paul is in his study trying to write his farewell sermon. He turns his thoughts towards South Africa. That beloved country looms like a place of exile. Almost as though the Church had decreed him not worthy to be archbishop of York, and packed him off to minister to the natives instead, where it wouldn't matter. The implied racism—

Stop, stop this! He knows it's not like this; he is responding to a genuine call. But Paul is trapped in the diver's helmet of his own consciousness. He just *cannot* get out of his head.

Then a memory breaks the surface: that time he got hopelessly lost trying to find a church in a black township. Night coming. White man, hired car. No map. Driving, desperately driving. Finding himself going down a dead end. Men appear and block his escape. They gather round and bang on the car roof – his heart hammers even now as he remembers! – then faces at the window, beaming at him. 'Welcome, bishop! Welcome, brother! Come, we are waiting for you.' And they lead him into the church where they are singing and rejoicing.

This son of mine was lost and is found.

Paul has his sermon.

The two little Rogers girls are writing letters to Santa. Jessie writes hers in sparkly gel pen and decorates it with stickers.

'I'm putting Barbie Mariposa and the Fairy Princess castle playset, a Hello Kitty duvet set, and a Hello Kitty onesie.'

'That's so lame. I want an iPad, and a karate suit. You've spelt Mariposa wrong. What's that last thing? Get your arm off it, I want to see.'

'It's a secret! No! Mu-u-um!'

'Girls, be nice!' calls Becky from the kitchen.

'Huh!' Leah flings the letter back. 'Anyway, I was going to put that. I thought of it first.'

'Did not! Mu-u-um, she's copying me!'

'Girls!'

Well, ha ha! It won't happen, because there's no such thing as Santa, you big *baby*. Leah only thinks this, because you mustn't be mean when it's nearly Christmas. She shields her letter with a crooked arm and adds another wish. It's not copying. Because she thought of it first.

Please can we have Christmas with Mummy and Daddy and be a family again.

Paul finds Susanna on the stairs. He sits beside her.

'Is it all getting on top of you, darling?'

She smiles bravely. 'A bit.'

Let's get rid of it all, he wants to say. But he can't. It would belittle a lifetime of homemaking.

'Oh, Paul! I know it's silly, but let's get rid of it all. We don't need it. Let's just . . . just sell it and, I don't know, give the money away!'

The bishop's heart soars. Extraordinary! It takes to the sky like a Chinese lantern, up, and away. He feels it go. For the first time in months he laughs. 'Yes,' he says. 'Yes!'

Chapter 50

It's half past midnight. Jane's phone rings. Mickey. Danny's dead.

'Danny's fine! Danny's fine! Danny's fine! Hey, babe. How are you?'

'I'm having a fucking heart attack, you moron! I was asleep! It's half past fucking midnight!'

'Hey, no fair! I said he's fine! First thing I said, like you told me to, eh. Danny's fine.'

'Hi, Mum, I'm fine,' calls Danny in the background.

'Sorry, thought you'd be up. Happy Christmas, Janey. Peace and good will?'

'Yes, all right, happy Christmas, you nob. What do you want? Don't ever do this to me again. This had better be important.'

'We-e-ll, kinda. Me and Sal are making honest people of each other while you're over here, and Danny says you'll kill me if I don't warn you. I know, let's blame Danny, eh. It's Danny's fault.'

'Whoa whoa whoa – you're getting married?'

'Nah, nah, just a civil union. No suits, no hats, very low key. Just a quickie ceremony followed by a barbie.'

'Well, God, listen, this is great, Mickey. Congratulations! I'm disappointed you won't be in a white tux, though.'

'With a white sombrero?'

'Exactly. And white cowboy boots.'

'Sweet. I'll run that by the committee, but my guess is it'll be a no.'

They banter for a bit longer and rang off.

Civil union? Wait. Could foreign nationals—? Stop that, you silly mare. Matt's found someone else, remember.

Jane turns the light out. Slowly her heart rate returns to normal. The wind whines in the telegraph wires. Rain batters her window. Danny is fine. Mickey and Sal are getting hitched, but Jane already has a killer 'I will survive!' red dress she can wear. It's all fine. Fine, fine, fine. These are tears of joy.

All across the diocese of Lindchester the hedgerows are decked for Christmas. Old man's beard drapes its silvery swathes over red-studded hawthorn. Here and there you'll see apple trees, their leafless boughs decked with gold baubles. The holly and the ivy (both full-grown), trim gardens and graveyards. Snowberries, pink spindleberries, yellow and orange pyracanthas, red dogwood shoots light up the municipal embankments. And look – there on the River Linden – seven swans a-swimming! The shopping mall hath not anything to show more fair.

In Lindford and Lindchester, in Cardingforth and Renfold, in Martonbury and Barcup, the lights are up, the trees are decorated. The good folk of Lindfordshire make their house fair as they are able. Schools and colleges squeeze out their last week of term, wrung from the dregs of teacher-energy. At Poundstretcher University the staff lecture to half-empty theatres, counting down the days till they can compose their out-of-office auto replies. Students slump across desks, crushed beneath the twin tyrannies of deadlines and partying. What a long term this one has seemed. There are mince pies at the final history department meeting of the year. Staff are urged to wear Christmas jumpers. Dr Elspeth Quilter wears one that plays a little festive medley when pressed. The reindeer's eyes light up red as if demon-possessed. I dare say it is fortunate that Dr Rossiter gets another of her migraines and has to send apologies.

This is the week of the Amazon box. Small, large, flat, square, they flock to Lindfordshire. You could build a cardboard city with the Amazon boxes of the diocese. Off to the lofts and secret cupboards with them, before small children come a-poking. Women of a certain age, I admonish you to make a list of what you've bought, and where you have hidden it all, and thus avoid a last-minute panic dash to the roiling hell of the high street to find something for someone it turns out you've already bought for. (Ah, how motherhood and menopause lay waste to the memory!) And be careful with that one-click buying, or you will end up with two of everything.

Christmas is coming, the goose is getting fat! Please to put a penny in the old man's hat! Or, in these modern times of ours, make a donation to your local food bank. Here in the blue-swathed Tory heartland of Lindfordshire we rather reject the notion that benefit cuts are in any way linked to the rise in food bank use. It is simply a coincidence, a blip, like climate change. Nonetheless, the good folk of the region are moved to donate tins and packets on their way out of the supermarket, where once they donated cat food. Because they can't bear the thought of other people being cold and hungry and miserable over Christmas. It's not on, is it? Not at Christmas.

If you haven't got a penny, a ha'penny will do. If you haven't got a ha'penny, God bless you. Can there really be people without a ha'penny nowadays? People with literally no money, not just no money in the current account? No! Seriously? MPs snigger in the food bank debate.

Father Dominic works a shift at the food bank in his new parish. He pops in and encourages the debt advisors. He organizes hampers for asylum-seekers, and notes that the poorest of his parishioners on the Abernathy estate have come up with toys and sweets to add to the collection. Virginia, Father Wendy's curate, supports her parishioners when they have appointments at the benefits office. She's like the importunate widow of the parable. Except the staff there are not really like the unjust judge. They are doing their best. Even so, there will be parents not eating this week, so that they can buy a present for the children. There will be cold houses, where they can't afford both heating and a frozen turkey crown. There are even people who'd be glad of our Amazon boxes, glad of our ha'pennies. In John O'Groat's invisible house, in a parallel universe sealed off from our own, right next door.

Help! Christmas is next week! What have you forgotten? Goose fat, present for the postman, pudding wine? Chocolate coins for the children's stockings? Sprouts still on a stick in the currently fashionable manner (yeah, that'll be less work on Christmas morning). Extra tin of Quality Street for the person who springs an unexpected present on you? Where did you put the roll of turkey foil last December? Have you missed the last posting date for second class? (What would happen if you sent no cards this year? No! No! Don't even think that.) Who the hell are Derek and Christine? Derek and Christine? Oh, wait, was this meant for next door? What are Phil and Vicky Hollings's sons called, darling? Oh never mind. Phil and Vicky and the boys.

In the cathedral chancellor's house Mr Happy snarls his way through his Christmas card list.

'Honestly, Mark, why don't you use the new address list I've done?' asks his wife. 'I can print the address labels for you.'

'I prefer my old address book. It has more dead people in it.'

And while we are on the Close, dear reader, let us tiptoe to the palace and see how they are faring. The tasteful wreath (made of real twigs and berries and cinnamon sticks) adorns the big front door like a posh Christmas card, as ever it did. Perhaps all is well within?

Perhaps. Susanna, that world champion of the Perfect Christmas, is doing things differently this year. They are having their big family meal early – tomorrow, in fact. All the girls are coming with husbands and children. The palace will be full of Hendersons one last time. A big festive lunch, and then Bishop Paul's farewell service in the evening. It will be their girls' chance to choose the pieces of furniture they would like, the vases and jugs and clocks and much-loved books and pictures of their childhood, before the firm of auctioneers comes on Thursday to take everything else away.

Susanna bakes. She sears. She grates. She stuffs and bastes and chops. The pudding rattles and chuckles on the Aga. A CD of carols plays. 'A great and mighty wonder, a full and holy cure.' Is she happy at last? Now she is losing everything, will she find her soul?

Oh, how different it will be next year! A South African Christmas. She cannot imagine how it will be. And how different from last year. Ah, last year all . . . *this* still lay ahead of them. Freddie May. Freddie May. Of all the young offenders we might have taken in, it had to be you.

Then, in a sudden burst of clarity, she sees that this was her own doing. She had not tried to rescue one of the dull ones, the spotty, pasty, talentless ones with awful accents, had she? No. She'd picked the beautiful Mr May. A boy from the right kind of background. A perfect boy for the perfect palace. Isn't that true? Oh dear, oh dear! Perhaps it *is* true. And yet, and yet. Hadn't she genuinely wanted to be kind? Is this what comes of wanting to be kind? Part of her still wants to be kind to Freddie, in spite of everything. To hug him and forgive him and say goodbye properly. To leave this place not harbouring resentment. To let that all go, along with everything else.

The antique French storage jars look down from the dresser. Goodbye, *Farine*, goodbye, *Sucre*! Well, she has enjoyed them long enough. Someone else can have pleasure from them now. She can't take them with her, can she?

No, we can't take any of it with us. When we finally rest from our labours, only our deeds will follow us. Maybe those acts of kindness – grubby with compromise, ambiguous, flawed though they generally are – maybe they will be the things that make it through the fire to the other side? Like wonky Christmas gifts made by primary school children, they will be treasured up long after we have forgotten we ever made them.

Paul is in his office polishing his sermon when he overhears the news through the half-open door: Penelope telling Martin how lovely it is that Freddie May is coming back from Barchester to sing at Paul's farewell.

The blood rushes to his face. Coming back! He masters his breathing. Calm down, this is what he's been praying for – the chance to act honourably, say goodbye properly. It's a relief, isn't it? It would appear that Freddie has forgiven him.

Ha, probably Freddie thinks there's nothing to forgive. No biggie. Lighten up, dude. I was nothing to him, thinks Paul. Just another nice guy.

> Thus have I had thee as a dream doth flatter:
> In sleep a king, but waking no such matter.

Well, he's awake now. Yes. Yes, this is . . . doable. He tests the strength of his resolve, like St Peter stepping out of the boat. Will he sink? The wind, the waves! He can't do this. Don't look at the storm; look to the Lord who calls you, whispers a voice. He steadies his soul once more. Look to the Lord, look to the Lord.

And even if, like Peter, he wavers and sinks, the hand will be there to haul him up again. You of little faith, why did you doubt?

In the office next door Martin sits in despair. So, the Lord has lost patience with his feebleness. Martin won't go to Freddie? Very well, Freddie will be brought to him. A last opportunity. He must and will apologize. Even if Freddie slaps him down. It will probably be horrible, but, like a plateful of sprouts before pudding is allowed, he *will* get through it somehow. Then maybe he can enjoy Christmas.

It's getting dark now. Outside the bishop's window a robin bursts into song. Sweet and yearning. The last cadence fades away, tinged with sorrow like a Chopin nocturne.

It is Tuesday evening. Over in Martonbury the bishop of Barcup puts his crosier in the boot, along with his vestments. Then he gets in the car and waits for his wife, who is doing her customary five last-minute things that he has long since ceased to reproach her with. No matter how much warning he gives, she will always be doing five things at the last minute.

Back in the pantry Janet is injecting her Christmas cake with another shot of brandy from a syringe. She makes a note on a chart of how many mls she's given it today, because she's a midwife. Then she dashes into the sitting room to turn off the fairy lights so the house doesn't burn down. (They might get away quicker if he lent a hand instead of just sitting in the car, but she's long since given up expecting him to grasp this fact.) Finally she kicks off her slippers in the hall and puts on a pair of court shoes because she's in bishop's wife mode tonight. Coat, keys, handbag, phone – phone? phone? – oh, it's in her handbag. She sets the burglar alarm, locks the door, goes back and checks she's locked the door, then hurries to where her husband is waiting patiently for her on the drive.

By the end of the evening our good friend Bishop Bob will have assumed responsibility for the diocese of Lindchester. Before the final hymn, Bishop Paul will symbolically hand him the historic Lindchester crosier and pray that God will bestow upon Bob the wisdom, love and courage he will need to lead God's people until a new bishop is appointed.

Let us follow the crowds toiling like medieval pilgrims up the hill to the cathedral. The big Christmas tree (how lovely are your branches!) shines. In windows all around more trees wink and twinkle. The bells peal. We will enter through the south door, and accept a service booklet from a smiling steward. The cathedral is full. Who is here? Friends of the Hendersons from way back, family, clergy, members of congregations from all across the diocese. Looking around, I believe all our old friends from this tale have come. There's Jane in her red dress. Fathers Wendy and Dominic are here too. And there sit the Rogers girls with their mother Becky. (At the end of the service Becky will manage to invite Martin to share Christmas Day with them, so that the girls' wish will be granted.)

The precentor is busy herding cats at the west end as he gets the procession – all bewigged, gowned, mitred and cassocked, with many a sparkly buckle and stocking – into the right order. Readers, chaplains, college of canons, chapter clerk, diocesan registrar, chancellor of the diocese, archdeacon, visiting bishops and clergy, ecumenical guests, and on and on, the dean, the suffragan bishop of Barcup, until right at the very end (the first shall be last) we find the bishop of Lindchester. On the front row, in the reserved seats for the very last time, sits Susanna and her family, with chapter clergy spouses, assorted chain gang members, high sheriffs, and Lords Lieutenant a-leaping.

I will not detain you, reader, with a detailed account of the service. Suffice it to say that all goes smoothly, with much merry organ-playing and sweet singing in the choir, and so forth. Bishop Paul preaches from the heart and many are moved, including Gene (to his surprise, Mary Poppins not being his cup of lapsang suchong). There are suitable tributes and presentations. Intercessions are offered.

The end of the service approaches now, so permit me to waft you briefly, on our scriptural eagle wings, up to the triforium, where Freddie May (stone-cold sober) and his three fellow singers are poised to begin their piece.

Man, please let it go OK? Don't let him choke up? It's the tenor part that carries this. They'll fall apart if he chokes. He remembers standing here as a chorister, belting out Allegri, nailing those top notes. Fearless, back in the day. Gah, then there was last Advent, total disgrace, puking between the antiphons. This *has* to go well. He needs to prove to himself he can do this. And he kind of owes it to Paul? Wa-ay down there on his throne. OK. Prayer finishing now. We're on. He rolls his shoulders. Relaxes. Fills his lungs.

'When peace, like a river, attendeth my way . . .'

Down below the congregation turn to see who's singing. Like a field of sunflowers turning to the sun. Who *is* that? Wow, what an *incredible* voice!

About sodding time, thinks Ulli, the precentor's wife, up there singing the alto line. Finally he stops pissing about and takes himself seriously.

From his throne way up in the chancel Paul recognizes the old hymn. He knows after the first line that he is going to break down. He bows his head. Covers his face.

'Though Satan should buffet, though trials should come . . .'

Freddie, up in the triforium, sees the bishop of Barcup get up from his seat and cross the chancel.

> My sin, oh the bliss of this glorious thought!
> My sin, not in part, but the whole,
> Is nailed to the cross, and I bear it no more,
> Praise the Lord, praise the Lord, O my soul!

The bishop of Barcup climbs the steps to the huge throne, sits beside Paul Henderson, and puts an arm round his shoulders.

> It is well with my soul,
> It is well, it is well, with my soul.

And now the service is over. Let us linger up here among stone angels and rude sculptures carved by disgruntled medieval masons that nobody ever sees. The procession glides back down the aisle, with the bishop of Barcup now bearing the Lindchester pastoral staff. The organ plays something vast and French. People throng and mingle, saying their farewells. There, you almost missed it: Freddie

May being hugged by Susanna. And now by Paul. How small they seem from up here. Yes, that passed off all right. You can follow that blond head through the crowds. He's leaving now. Wait, someone else has stopped him. Can it be Martin? It's Martin. Now *they* are hugging! For a moment there I thought Martin was struggling to escape – he's dropped the bishop's robes – but it looks fine. Freddie is rubbing his back for him. I can't really see from up here, but I think Martin is crying. Maybe they are both crying. It is well, it is well.

I will now hurry you to the palace for mulled wine and mince pies, as I sense you are impatient to see how Jane and Matt will conduct themselves.

Jane ignored the archdeacon thoroughly. Even though he was wearing a daft Santa hat. Never before had an archdeacon been so ignored. She ignored the heck out of him as she chatted to the Henderson daughters and worked the room. She continued her robust policy of ignoring him for forty-five minutes, then said her farewells to Paul and Susanna and went to collect her coat.

It is difficult to ignore six foot four of archdeacon if he is blocking your exit from the cloakroom, however.

'Well, good evening, Mr Archdeacon. Are you well?'

'Yes, thanks. You?'

'Yes, thanks. All set for Christmas? I suppose you're staying here?'

'Yes.'

'Well, I'm off to New Zealand on Saturday. Seeing my baby boy.' He offered no comment. 'Want to come with me?'

'Yes.'

'No, you don't. Don't be ridiculous. It'll cost a fortune and I'll be vile company. Danny's father is getting hitched. Civil union. They have them out there, unlike this benighted country. What would you say if I asked you to be my civil partner?'

'Yes, please.'

'No, you wouldn't. What about that other woman? The one I saw you with in the pie and ale place?'

'Work colleague. What about the tall skinny bloke I saw you with, the one who looked like a complete tit and I hate him?'

'Work colleague.'

A smile dawned on the archdeacon's face, like the dayspring from on high. 'Well, he seemed like a decent bloke. Nice frock, by the way.'

'It's my "I'm over you, you bastard" frock. What do you like about it?'

'The zip down the back.'

Jane laughed her filthy laugh. 'Well, I like your Santa hat. Is that mistletoe on it?'

'You bet your shapely derrière it is.'

'Oops, excuse me!' Janet Hooty retreated. She could nip to the other loo instead. Goodness. Well, there you go. Looked like she could cross the archdeacon off the prayer list now.

But where is the lovely Mr May? Is he standing outside the palace, face pressed wistfully to the window like the little matchgirl? Or has he found a silver fox to whisk him away in his convertible for a night of disgracefully rude hotel sex? Or is he, perhaps, with the lay clerks, getting off his tits? None of the above. He's with someone who loves him. Someone who is even now plying him with home-made game pie and Christmas cake, and admonishing him to be good, ring his dad and accept that invitation to spend New Year with him. Yes, Miss B is looking after her boy one last time this year. Freddie does as he's told. I can't believe how good he's being, frankly. He will make up for it later on, by plaguing the archdeacon, with whom he is spending the night. The archdeacon will sit at his study desk and try to book flights to New Zealand. Such are our hero's levels of concentration that he will manage this, despite a (by then) extremely drunk Mr May straddling him, crooning 'Santa Baby' in his ear and begging him to hurry down his chimney tonight.

And so Christmas comes. All across the diocese of Lindchester people go to church. They go to crib services and christingles, they go to carol services, to Midnight Mass, to the Eucharist on Christmas Day. Hail, Lord, we greet thee, born this happy morning. They go not only to the cathedral, where one might expect it, but to ordinary parish churches in towns and villages, on housing estates, in pubs and community centres and schools. And not just in the diocese of Lindchester, but right across the nation. And the Church, so long accustomed to decline and further decline, cannot quite make sense of it. The clergy, those watchmen on the walls of faith, strain their eyes to the east. Is it . . . can it be . . . ?

And now with the ever-circling of the year we come back to where we started. Later on our friends will gather in their various groups and houses across the diocese to see in the New Year. Father Dominic will be in his new vicarage, not with his old friend Dr R this year – she is already on the other side of the world, with the archdeacon in hot pursuit. Don't worry, though: Dominic has his lovely mum with him. He is wearing his new Christmas jumper which she bought him. It has reindeer on. Dominic and Mum have had a little chat about this, and decided to believe that these are acrobat reindeer in the early stages of building a reindeer pyramid. And that Mum probably needs to get her eyes tested. Although, yes, it's a lovely cheerful colour!

In the deanery Gene has already put a couple of bottles of something rather gorgeous in the fridge. His beloved is asleep on the sofa in front of the fire. What will this coming year bring? Is he destined to be the first ever bishop's husband in the UK? Heavens to Betsy, he'll need an entire new wardrobe! His jackets will all be lined in mauve silk! His cufflinks will all be cabochon amethysts the size of gobstoppers! He will drink nothing but aviation cocktails! Bleugh. No, he won't. Crème de violette is a bridge too far. Besides, one wouldn't want to be too matchy-matchy. He smiles down at Marion as she sleeps. Darling deanissima. I love you dearly. Pissed though I fear I am.

Over in the precentor's house Ulli is swearing as she tries to wedge another bottle of cava in the overstocked fridge. What the bloody heck is all this crap? Why is she the only one in this house who ever chucks stuff out? *Um Gottes Willen!* She may as well just put all the cava in the hall. It's a bloody walk-in freezer in there anyway.

All is quiet in the canon chancellor's house. Mr Happy Junior has mastered the art of sleeping at last. Quiet, too, is the house of the canon treasurer. They've nipped off skiing for a week.

The palace is empty now. If you were to go and peep through the windows, you'd see bare walls, oatmeal carpets bearing the imprint of vanished furniture.

At 11.55 p.m. tonight people will spill out of houses on the Close and gather in front of the cathedral and wait for Great William to toll in the New Year. Fireworks will blossom, Chinese lanterns will sail by trailing wishes. Hands will be linked and 'Auld Lang Syne' will be sung. We are all a little older, and maybe a little wiser, than we were twelve months ago.

And so we say farewell to our friends in Lindchester. Bless you all. May all the lights before you turn green. May it be well with your souls.

It is late afternoon. Rooks stream to their roosts and settle. A lone figure walks home along the banks of the Linden. It is Father Wendy. The sun slips below the earth's rim. Bright sky lies in tractor ruts as if the earth were charged with light from below. The shell has cracked and the glory, the glory seeps through. There in the west the folding star winks. Star of wonder. All along the horizon ancient trees stand leafless, black filigree against pale gold, their clinging ivy, their clumps of mistletoe, the ragged magpie nests all etched in patient detail.

Not long now.

Listen! A fluting in the distance, like imagined shepherd-pipes in long ago Bethlehem: a mistle thrush carols in the December dusk.

If you've enjoyed
Acts and Omissions,
here's a chapter from the sequel

UNSEEN THINGS ABOVE

SPCK
978 0 281 07236 1
June 2015
£9.99

Chapter 1

In homage to our esteemed forerunner, we commence this ecclesiastical tale with the question: Who will be the new bishop?

Back in the year of 185— when this same puzzle absorbed the good folk of Barchester, appointing a new bishop appears to have been a pretty straightforward affair. To be sure, there was some Oxbridge high-table-style manoeuvring behind the scenes. There were raised and dashed hopes, with the press confidently (and, for the most part, wrongly) naming names; and then the prime minister made his choice. Dr Proudie, we read, was bishop elect 'a month after the demise of the late bishop'. A month! I fear, by contrast, we will still be asking 'Who will be the new bishop?' for many months to come, while the Crown Nominations Commission ruminates.

Ruminates? Dare I apply so bovine a metaphor to this august body – evoking as it does an image of a herd regurgitating and re-chewing what has already been swallowed and partially digested? Do I wish my reader to picture jaws rolling, rolling, strands of saliva swinging, heads turning ponderously this way and that as the process of discernment toils on? And how – if we pursue this alimentary metaphor to its logical conclusion – are we to characterize its outcome?

No, we had better eschew rumination.

And anyway, they are not an august body. They are just a bunch of ordinary Anglicans operating as best they can in this awkward limbo that the C of E currently occupies (somewhere between 185— and the real world). These days it takes a very long time to appoint a new bishop. It feels especially protracted for those caught up in the process and zipped by oaths into the body bag of confidentiality.

So who will be the new bishop of Lindchester? I have no idea. If you're keen to know early, your best bet is to keep an eye on

Twitter. It is possible that someone will award themselves a smiley sticker on the wall chart of self-aggrandisement by being the first to blab what others have appropriately kept under wraps.

We rejoin our Lindcastrian friends just before Low Sunday, that is, the first Sunday after Easter. In parishes across the Diocese of Lindchester this collect may be said:

> Risen Christ,
> for whom no door is locked, no entrance barred:
> open the doors of our hearts,
> that we may seek the good of others
> and walk the joyful road of sacrifice and peace,
> to the praise of God the Father.

It *may* be said; but it is not, of course, compulsory. Gone is the golden age of Book of Common Prayer uniformity, the days of 'Here's a digestive biscuit, take it or leave it.' Gone, too, are the late unlamented days of the *Alternative Service Book* ('Here's a choice: digestive, Lincoln, rich tea or Garibaldi.') We now inhabit the age of the biscuit assortment. ('Here, have a rummage.') Heck, we are pretty much in the age of the liturgical bake-off. Provided some of the right ingredients are used, frankly you can go ahead and make your own. Fresh biscuits, messy biscuits, biscuits to play with in a godly manner, old-fashioned traditional biscuits like granny used to bake. Anything, provided there are biscuits to feed the hungry people of the UK! For heaven's sake, tempt them in with the smell of baking!

Like the risen Christ himself, this narrative will find locked doors no obstacle. The hearts and homes of our characters stand ajar to us. We may slip in and snoop around. But let us always seek the good of others, the bishops, priests and people of our tale. As our earlier volume has already shown (alas!) they are quite capable of cocking things up without the mischievous intervention of your author. We set out now to walk the joyful road of sacrifice and peace in their company as far as Advent. Advent, the Church's New Year. New Year at the end of November? Yes, there it is again, that strange tension between the two realms we inhabit: the church and the world, with ever and anon the tug of homesickness for the home we have never seen.

Come, reader, and dust off the wings of your imagination. Fly with me once again to the green and pleasant Diocese of Lindchester. Ah, Lindfordshire, from you we have been absent in the spring! Even now, as the month draws to its close, proud-pied April is still dressed in all his trim. Look down now as we glide upon polite Anglican wings, and see how every road edge is blessed with silver and gold. Daisies and dandelions – no mower blade can keep them down. The spirit of youth is in everything! See where eddies of cherry blossom, pink, white, swirl in suburban gutters. Glide with me above parks and gardens, admire the fresh unfurlings of copper beech, the colour of old brick walls; gasp at the implausible lime of the limes! The horse chestnut candles are in bloom, and the may, here and there in the hedgerows, authorizes the casting of clouts. Sheep and cattle graze in old striped fields. Listen! The first cuckoo dimples the air, and for a heartbeat, everything stands still. The waters have receded, but signs of flooding are everywhere across the landscape. Even now, the distant cathedral seems perched like the ark on Ararat, as rainbows come and go behind the cooling towers of Cardingforth.

Let us head now to the cathedral. I'm pleased to inform you that the spire has not crashed through the nave roof in our absence. The historic glass of the Lady Chapel has not slipped from its crumbled tracery and smashed to smithereens. Fear not! Heritage Lottery funding is on its way to prevent so ruinous an end to the work of long-dead glaziers. Restoration work continues on the cathedral's south side, where a vast colony of masonry bees has been ruthlessly exterminated. Dean and chapter (how can they call themselves Christian?) were in receipt of letters from single-issue bee fanatics. A reply drafted by the canon chancellor, referring them to Our Lord's brusque treatment of swine, was never sent.

It is Saturday afternoon. Gavin, the deputy verger, is mowing the palace lawn before the rain starts. All downhill now till Advent, he thinks. The triumph of the Easter brazier still blazes in his mind. New paschal candle lit first go. Cut-off two-litre Coke bottle, that was the secret. Stopped it blowing out. Up and down goes Gavin. Keeping things under control lawn-wise during the interregnum. Tidy-up and big bonfire at the end of summer – there was that to look forward to. Then Advent, six hundred candles. Gavin smiles as he mows his nice straight lines.

Ah, but the garden misses Susanna's touch. Bleeding-heart plants nod in untended borders. Roses shoot unpruned since the Hendersons left. The laburnum walk is unforbidden, poised to rain its deadly Zeus-like showers on nobody at all. Everything waits for the new bishop, whoever he may be.

As you may have seen in the press, there was a brief outbreak of squawking in the ecclesiastical henhouse back in February, when it was (wrongly) rumoured that the Church Commissioners had decided to sell the palace and stick the next bishop of Lindchester in a poky little seven-bedroomed house in suburban Renfold. Indignant petitions were worded. SAVE LINDCHESTER PALACE! The bishops of Lindchester had always lived there, since . . .

It emerged that the bishop of Lindchester had, in fact, only lived in this particular house since 1863, when a vigorous and godly Evangelical bishop sold off the other two palaces. The Rt Revd William Emrys Brownlow used the money to clear the city's slums, provide clean water and good housing for the impoverished leather workers, build a hospital, schools and a theological college. Prior to that, no bishop of Lindchester had ever lived in the Close in such proximity to his clergy and people. It would have been tactless to do so, since they could not have afforded to ape his gracious lifestyle. No, far kinder to retreat to Bishop's Ingregham and eat quails in aspic with a clear conscience.

Shall we pause to lament the passing of those glorious historic buildings from the Church? Ingregham palace is particularly lovely, with its mellow sandstone walls, its acres of Capability Brown landscaping. Deer park, lake, obligatory historic oak tree that Robin Hood, Mary Queen of Scots and Charles the Second hid up, or where Shakespeare himself stubbed his fag out. I daresay petitions were got up in 1860. What was Bishop Brownlow thinking of, selling off the family silver like that? These treasures are not ours to dispose of – we are but custodians! Our duty is look after them and hand them on intact to the next generation! Yes, there are issues facing the Church, but selling off property is a short-term solution! It's just throwing money at the problem!

As is so often the case when the problem is 'lack of money', the throwing of money at it turns out to be the solution. A great many runty little leatherworkers' children failed to die of cholera. Many were educated. Scores of earnest young Evangelicals were trained and sent to work in places of great danger and deprivation across the Empire.

But the palace is very lovely. It's a shame the Church no longer owns it.

We will leave the bishop's garden in Gavin's care and glide gracefully to earth outside the deanery instead. Come with me, on tiptoe, to the old scullery, where the Very Revd Marion Randall (just back from a post-Easter break in Portugal) is standing amid open suitcases. She is discussing the identity of the next bishop with her husband. Or rather, *not* discussing it.

'There's nothing to tell. And even if there was, I wouldn't tell you. We take oaths, you know.'

'Oaths! How Shakespearian. Ods bodikins! By my lady's nether beard!' he declaimed. 'Like that?'

'Funnily enough, Gene, nothing like that.'

''Zounds, how dull. But can't you drop a tiny hint? In passing. I can infer. I'm an excellent infer-er.'

'Yes. And you're also an inveterate gossip. Which is why I'm not going to tell you anything.'

'Aha! So you admit you *do* know something!'

The dean sighed and continued to sort and toss dirty laundry into heaps. 'Of course I know *something*. Look, we're only at the consultation stage. People have been invited to submit suggestions, that's all. We'll get a long list from the Washhouse, which we'll sift, then decide who we want to mandate.'

'Ooh! Who's on the long list?'

'You're not actually listening.' She bent and began thrusting a light load into the machine. 'Nobody yet.'

'But who's *likely* to be on it?'

'Anyone whose name has come up.'

'Literally anyone? What if some bonkers old trout suggests her parish priest because he does a lovely mass?'

'Then I suppose he'll be on the list. Hence the sifting process. No.' The dean held up her hand. 'That's it. Shut up.'

'At least promise me it won't be another swivel-eyed Evangelical pederast with a muffin-making wife.'

Silence.

'Not funny?' he enquired.

'No.'

'But quite clever?'

'No.'

'Oh.' Another silence. 'Well, let me go and choose us a homecoming wine. I am confident I can get *that* right, at any rate.'

My readers will see from this that Gene's character has undergone no reformation in the last few months. He remains the same disgraceful reprobate. His mission is unchanged, too: to cherish, divert and pamper his beloved wife, and make the task of modern deaning more fun than it would prove were he not on hand (at all times and in all places) with the right wine and the wrong remark.

Marion sets the machine running, then gazes round her. The overhead airer, the Belfast sink, tiled floor. This was where staff of former deans toiled with their washboards and dollies and goffering irons. She thinks about the old servants' bells still there high up on the deanery kitchen wall in a glass case – BED RM 3, DRAWING RM,

TRADES. ENT – though they no longer work. Fell prey to health and safety regs when the deanery was rewired ten years ago. There is a button in Marion's and Gene's en suite bathroom (formerly DRESSING RM 1). She imagines her predecessors pressing it and summoning a valet to bring up a hip bath and pink gin. Gene, no doubt, would recreate this scenario with enthusiasm, were she to mention it.

Dear Gene. She smiles. But the brief holiday is already retreating from her mind. The thought bailiffs shoulder their way in to repossess the unpaid-for happiness. The spire. The stuff coming out about the school chaplain from the 1970s. The new bishop of Lindchester – would it be uncomplicated, someone she could work with and not be forever thinking, You are younger than me, less gifted, less experienced . . . ? How wearing it is, all the nuisance of being one of those tipped to be the first woman bishop. To know you're being talked about. Folk speculating: will she be suffragan somewhere, or is she holding out to be the first diocesan? Barchester, maybe? She shakes her head. Come on, you're still on holiday till Monday.

She casts her mind back to that basilica. Was it only this morning they were there? Muted palette of browns and terracottas. Easter lilies, a CD of plainsong alleluias playing. High above in the dome, blue sky glimpsed through glass. Peace, beauty. And then to emerge into the big bright spring world! Dazzled by full sunlight, buffeted by the wind, the whirl of life, the vast dome of the sky above. If the inside was the only thing you knew, how could you guess at all this? And yet it made perfect sense. Of course, *of course*! Would it be like this – resurrection?

She goes through to the kitchen and puts the kettle on.

Gene emerges through the cellar door. With a fey flourish, he presents the wine. '1996 Chateau Latour.'

'Lovely.'

He sees from her face that his magic words have conveyed nothing. 'Bless you, my darling, I know you love that vinho verde.' He gives a dainty shudder. 'But some of it was *so* young, drinking it was a safeguarding issue.'

And now it is Low Sunday. Where shall I take you today, dear reader? I know that you are eager for news of our various friends. How is Father Dominic faring in his new parish, for example? And what of our lovely bishop Bob, shouldering the weight of the whole diocese during the interregnum? To say nothing of our stout hero, the archdeacon, last seen haring off to New Zealand in pursuit of his lady!

You must be patient. I am going to introduce you to a new character, one I fear you may not find it in your heart to love, but Veronica plays an important part in our tale. There are times when we must stoically eat our plate of school liver (horrid tubes visible) before we are allowed out to play.

Come with me now to a church in Lindford. Not the parish church (where Fr Dominic now serves), but one nearby with a gothic revival building of the type that looks as though it might soon be cut loose by the evil archdeacon, Matt the Knife, and turned into a supermarket. No, more likely a nightclub called Holy Crap, or something similarly witty. It is in the clubbing district, such as it is, of Lindford. Beside the church is that narrow alley where last year – you may remember the incident – two men picked on the wrong faggot. A CCTV camera now keeps watch. Every Friday and Saturday night the church pitches its gazebo in the little yard behind the railings, and from here the street pastors operate, dispensing love, hot chocolate and flip-flops to the lost souls of Lindford.

We will pop in now and see what's going on in St James's church this Low Sunday morning. The first thing you will spot is the lack of pews. The Victorian Society took a tonking here, all right. There are cheerful banners. Someone plays thoughtful music on an electric piano. Can this be another Evangelical stronghold? By no means! This is an inclusive church, my friends, where God is mother and father of all, in the commonwealth not the kingdom of heaven. It is bishop Bob's kind of a place. Change from the bottom up not the top down. They do good work here in their rainbowy way.

Veronica wears a simple cassock alb and Peruvian stole in bright colours. Lent is now over, so she has laid aside her equal-marriage campaigning rainbow dog collar. She is not the incumbent, she's a university chaplain. Here comes Geoff the vicar now. It's a baptism, so he's wearing the stole with Noah's ark animals on. I believe somebody made it from upholstery fabric. It would cover a nursery chair very nicely. The baptism will move seamlessly into the Annual Parochial Church Meeting (getting in before the end of April) and be followed by a simple agape meal.

I don't suppose you want to stay for a church AGM, do you? No. Let us 'risk the hostile stare', and tiptoe back out as the congregation stand to sing 'Will you come and follow me if I but call your name?' (tune: Kelvingrove).

A glimpse of Veronica is all I vouchsafe you this week, dear reader. Instead, I will whisk you back to the Close and into the study of the Revd Giles Littlechild, the canon precentor. The Littlechilds have just returned from holiday in Heidelberg, visiting in-laws and older son (Gap Ya). Giles has read somewhere that you should do one thing each day that scares you. Opening his work email inbox surely qualifies.

He scrolls through, delicately, like a bomb disposal expert. Excellent. Nothing too dire. But then a new email pings in.

Oh God. A last-minute application for the post of tenor lay clerk. They can't *not* interview him, can they? And then they'll have to appoint him, because he'll be the best.

Lord have mercy! Frankly, Giles would rather have a tone-deaf moose on the back row of *dec* than Freddie May.